# HOME SWEET HOME

---

ROBERT M. KERNS

KNIGHTSFALL PRESS

Published by Knightsfall Press
PO Box 280
Mineral Wells, WV 26150

# ABOUT THIS BOOK

Earth. A world untouched by magic, or so its people believe.

Gavin Cross's return shatters that belief, throwing the world into panic.

And all Gavin wants is to return to Drakmoor.

Will he succeed?

Read now to find out!

# TYPOS

Typos and little slips in grammar are the bane of any author. Unfortunately, they are almost impossible to eradicate completely. I can show you many traditionally published books—twenty years old and more—that have a 'whoopsie' here and there.

That being said, if you find a typo or something that seems to be an error in grammar, please do not hesitate to contact me at typos@knightsfallpress.com.

I will periodically collate any emails and produce an updated PDF and eBook files, and I'll make an announcement in my monthly newsletter when the updates have been published.

# CHAPTER 1

Something hot and sticky warmed the front of his torso while the sun heated his back. His awareness returned at a crawling pace; he realized that someone lay against his side. A bone-deep throbbing ache consumed him, and he almost wished he could fall back into full unconsciousness. The non-existence of it was much more pleasant.

Awareness exploded at the forefront of his mind. He was Gavin Cross, Head of House Kirloth and Archmagister of Tel. His city was under attack and he'd been dueling the Necromancer of Skullkeep. The sounds of battle should have raged around him, but all was peaceful. In that singular moment, Gavin only heard birds. Instead of the foul stench of the undead assaulting his nose, he smelled only rotting garbage with undertones of rust.

Lifting his head and forcing his eyes open, Gavin saw a person at his side. From the hair length and the body shape, he assumed it was a woman, and she seemed to be unconscious. Her hair was a glossy black, and what skin he could see seemed to be olive-complected. She wore a gray t-shirt, blue jeans, and tennis shoes. He pulled his eyes away from the woman to take in more of his surroundings.

He and his companion occupied what appeared to be an alley.

Gavin would've laughed at waking up in another alley, except he hurt too much. He raised his eyes and froze. He recognized the aged store-front directly across the street. A large placard above the store's entrance held the business's well-maintained sign. It read: Cross General Store, Est. 1743.

It was then that Gavin knew... everything. He remembered his parents. He remembered his childhood, his wedding, and the birth of his daughter, Jennifer. He and his wife had named her Jennifer Anne. Jennifer was his wife's mother's middle name, and Anne was his mother's. His father's name was Richard. His family first settled in the region in the early 1700s, founding the town and protecting it during the War for Independence and all the turmoil that followed.

He was home. The home where he'd grown up. It hit him like a haymaker from a heavyweight pro boxer. Graham, Virginia. The United States of America. Earth. He was one of the most powerful arcanists to have ever lived... in a world that believed magic didn't exist.

Gavin put his head down on the alley's pavement, closed his eyes, and sighed. "Oh, boy..."

A car horn blared around the corner, and the person at his side flinched, pushing herself into a sitting position. Gavin recognized Kiri as he also shifted to sit with his legs crossed in front of him, and he couldn't keep from smiling as she scanned the area, her entire demeanor alert.

"Gavin, what was that sound? What kind of beast makes a sound like that?" Kiri patted her sides, waist, and thighs as if searching for something.

"That, Kiri, was a car horn, and it's not a beast. It's... well, it's a carriage that doesn't need horses."

"A carriage that doesn't need horses? What kind of carriage doesn't need horses?"

Gavin realized her t-shirt had writing on it and reflexively looked down before breaking into a huge grin.

# My Wizard

THE TEXT WAS WHITE, and the heart was the bright, candy apple red of a '67 Mustang.

Kiri looked down and pulled her shirt out to read it. She frowned, saying, "Well, that's totally undignified."

Gavin fought to keep from bursting into a laugh, barely converting it to a snort.

"What were you doing in Tel Mivar, anyway?" Gavin asked. "You could have died."

Kiri pulled her gaze away from her shirt to face Gavin. "And you nearly did. I saved your life, Gavin. People were flanking you." She patted herself down again. "I miss my blades."

"Yeah... those aren't really a thing, here. Most people don't carry blades anymore, aside from the occasional utility knife sized for pockets. In some parts of the country, you'd scandalize people just by having a single-blade pen knife that's smaller than my finger."

Gavin's voice trailed off as he turned his head to look at his family's store. It was the next stop. It was the only place that *could be* the next stop. And yet... a part of him was afraid of what he'd find. He remembered dying, now. It wasn't a pleasant process—at least, his hadn't been—but the dump truck that had slammed into the driver's side of the car probably had much to do with that. Gavin hoped so, anyway. No one should have to endure what he remembered as his last moments on Earth.

How long had he been dead? Bellos had told him when they spoke north of the ruins of Kalinor's estate that his daughter was older than he thought, but *how much* older? Something one of his high school buddies came back from the army saying flitted through Gavin's mind: *the only way out is through.*

"What do we do now?" Kiri asked. "Do you know the way home?"

Gavin pulled his focus away from the storefront across the street and gave a self-deprecating shrug. "I'd like to say I know the way home, but no... not really. If you'll ever see home again, I'll have to research cross-planar scrying and cross-planar portals. Not even Marcus did that."

"'If *I'll* ever see home?' That almost sounds like you're not coming back with me." Kiri worked her lower lip between her teeth, her expression a mask of worry.

Gavin chuckled. "Oh, I'm going back. It's just... I'm all tangled up inside right now. I have thirty years of memories and experiences saying *this world* is my home, but I have all those friends and relationships back in Tel and the surrounding lands. Not to mention being the Archmagister. I'm going back, Kiri, but as for calling it home? I just don't know."

"So, what now?"

Pointing across the street, Gavin said, "We go there."

Kiri turned her head, reading, "Cross General Store, e-s-t-dot one-seven-four-three?"

Gavin grinned again. "That's an abbreviation. It means 'established'. Those numbers after it are the year. When I died here, our family store had been in continuous operation for two hundred and seventy-three years. This town was started the same year, actually... and by my family, too." Gavin heaved a long sigh. "Putting this off will not make it any better. We might as well go."

Gavin pushed himself to his feet and held out his hand for Kiri. She accepted it, and the moment their hands touched, Gavin felt the spark he remembered from the early months of dating his wife. Aw crap... his wife. Was he still married? Had she remarried? He fought the urge to groan; sorting out that part of his old life would not be pleasant at all. Their vows had said 'till death do us part,' but death was usually rather final.

Come to think of it, he still didn't know why Valthon and Bellos had needed a true-born child of House Kirloth, either... but at least he now knew the circumstances surrounding why he'd been—what had Bellos said, ah yes—*available*.

Pushing all that aside in his mind for another day, Gavin led Kiri out of the alley, but her sudden stop pulled her hand out of his. He turned to find her staring off to their left, unblinking and jaw slack. In Kiri's line of sight, Gavin saw a maroon crossover SUV, one of Ford's models given the blue oval in the grill.

"Is that a... car... Gavin?" Kiri asked, stumbling across the unfamiliar word.

"Yes. Well, technically it's an SUV, but many people use 'car' for anything that's not a truck."

"A truck?" Kiri turned to Gavin, her expression scrunched into a frown.

Gavin scanned both sides of the street. He quickly spied a GMC dually across the street and a few storefronts down from his family's place. He pointed, saying, "Yeah... a truck. That one's what many people call a dually because it has dual wheels on each side of the back axle to haul or tow heavier loads. It's a lot like a cargo or freight wagon, now that I think of it. You can't really see it from here, but a truck has a large, open area in the back for easy access to whatever it's carrying."

Kiri walked around Gavin to look where he pointed, moving past the Ford, and motion in Gavin's peripheral vision was the only warning before the loud airhorn of a panel truck blared. Kiri spun to face the sound. The reflexes of his youth kicked in, and Gavin grabbed her by both shoulders, hauling her back to him. Without thinking, he held her against his chest.

In the frozen moment of holding Kiri against his chest, the panel truck trundling by them, Gavin realized how much he'd missed Kiri during the months between when he'd left Vushaar as the Archmagister and now. She felt *right* in his arms. She felt more right in his arms than his daughter's mother ever had. He wanted to hold Kiri in his arms, forget the world, kiss her... several times. In that moment, Gavin admitted to himself at last what a portion of his mind had known all along. He loved her.

Old memories rushed to the fore, and it felt almost like his two identities were warring for supremacy. Gavin Cross—son of Richard and Elizabeth Cross, father of Jennifer Ann Cross—loved Emily, his *wife* of thirteen years and mother of his daughter. Gavin Cross—Head of House Kirloth and Archmagister of Tel—was an orphan for all intents and purposes, with no awareness of any family beyond Marcus and his brothers; had fallen in love with Kiri. His love for Kiri felt stronger, more immediate, but Gavin couldn't help but wonder if maybe that was only because it was more recent and his life on Earth seemed so distant.

"What was *that*, Gavin?" Kiri's voice was almost a hiss, pulling Gavin out of his thoughts. "It didn't look like a car or a truck."

"It was a truck, what we call a panel or box truck. It's the next step up from that dually over there and designed to transport bulk goods strapped to pallets or inside boxes or crates."

Kiri shook her head. "And I thought it was bad back home. No wonder your words sometimes seemed so alien. Your world is nothing like ours."

No traffic was in sight from either direction. Gavin took Kiri's hand and led her as he hustled across the street, saying, "It was once... about a thousand years ago. But we never had magic. At least, nothing like the Art that arcanists wield."

Even as Gavin said it, though, his *skathos* flared to an even stronger tingling sensation than what he experienced in Tel Mi*var*. Earth didn't have magic, so his *skathos* should have been an absence, like sight for a blind person or hearing for the deaf. But it wasn't. If anything, his *skathos* felt more alive and active. Back in Tel or Vushaar, his *skathos* felt like he was wading chest-deep through a large pond or lake. But here? He was treading water in the ocean... with no land in sight.

Gavin focused on his surroundings more and frowned. "You know... something doesn't feel right. There should be at least *some* people out on the sidewalk."

He shook his head, filing those thoughts away for later examination. It was just one more thing he had to work through, and he had more pressing concerns at the moment. He was in arms' reach of the store where he'd grown up.

The Cross General Store was an institution in Graham, and had been since long before even Gavin's father was born. Graham didn't have any of the big chain stores, and as far as Gavin knew, there wasn't one within a two-hour drive in any direction. And so... the Cross General Store became a true *general* store. Hardware. Clothing. Groceries. The town's pharmacy. Feed for livestock. A person could find all that and more inside, including an impressive array of specialty items one wouldn't expect in a 'small town' store.

A large awning extended from the building, shading most of the sidewalk. It was a pleasant pastel blue, whereas the awning Gavin remembered was a vibrant green. Wooden beams and panels—finished in a natural tone and smoothed across many decades—made up the structure of the storefront, and solid plate glass filled the windows.

As far as Gavin knew, no one had ever replaced those sheets of plate glass, and standing less than five feet away from them, Gavin gaped, finally knowing *why*. The glass radiated Transmutation. It was faint to Gavin's *skathos*, like a whisper across a crowded reception hall... but it was there. If he hadn't been standing almost close enough to fog the glass with his breath, he never would've felt it. He reached his hand up and froze.

A memory from his youth slipped out of the recesses of his mind and clubbed him like a blackjack. He was maybe half as tall and mesmerized by his reflection. He reached out to touch, but his mother's voice stopped him: *No fingerprints on the glass, Gavin! I just cleaned it.*

He turned his hand and laid its back against the glass, closing his eyes to concentrate. As best Gavin could tell, the Transmutation fortified the glass's durability and resilience, and it was fading. It was gradual, like the sea eroding mountains across centuries, but perhaps in Jennifer's lifetime or a little longer, it would fade completely.

Gavin grinned, his eyes still closed. Well... the effect would've faded. Now that he was here and aware of it, he would need mere minutes to rebuild and re-anchor the effect for substantially greater longevity.

Squaring his shoulders, Gavin took a deep breath and stepped inside the home away from home of his youth.

Gavin's first impression was that nothing had changed. Nothing substantive, anyway. Each department of the store still occupied the same portions of the floor space. The counter still had a cash register on one end and a soda fountain and ice cream shop at the opposite end of its fifty-foot length.

The flat screen TV hanging over the counter was different, though. A flat screen TV existed in Gavin's memories, but it had been one of the early models, not this wafer-thin screen with amazing picture quality.

Gavin froze, his eyes locked on the TV. The chyron across the bottom of the screen said something about a hostage crisis at Graham University, but Gavin wasn't reading it. The camera faced a window in an upper floor of a building, and it zoomed in at the precise moment Gavin focused on the screen. A young woman—looking no older than mid-twenties—stood pressed against the glass, her expression a mask of terror. A woman stood behind her, lifting a pistol toward the back of her head. It seemed to happen in slow motion for Gavin. All of this, Gavin processed in mere heartbeats, but it wasn't really his focus. Gavin focused on the young woman's pendant, a silver angel-wing pendant with a ruby in the center... *exactly* like the one he'd given his daughter right before he died.

"Kiri," Gavin said, halfway between a whisper and his normal volume, "do you see the screen up there?"

"Yes. It's some kind of far-scrying artifact?"

"I'll explain it later, but we will arrive directly to that woman's right. I need you to immobilize the hand holding the gun. She's going to kill her. I'll explain guns later, but don't let her squeeze her fingers. I'll deal with the rest of the room."

"But Gavin, I don't have my blades..."

Gavin held out his hand and invoked a Word of Conjuration. "*Nythraex.*"

Two blades—longer than daggers but not long enough to be short swords—winked into existence. Kiri took the blades from

Gavin, tested their balance, and nodded. Gavin shifted his position to be on Kiri's left side instead of her right and invoked a Word of Transmutation. "*Paedryx*."

The world around them blinked.

Gavin and Kiri now stood in a presentation hall, and Kiri exploded into motion. Before the woman holding the pistol fully processed what was happening, Kiri buried half of a blade into her armpit while slicing through the inside tendons of her wrist with the other. Her now-inoperative hand released the pistol to fall to the floor. Fortunately, it didn't discharge.

Four other people—two men and two women—spun to face the disturbance. Gavin saw they carried variants of the ubiquitous Kalashnikov rifle, complete with banana magazines. Even as their expressions began registering a varying mix of surprise and anger, Gavin formed his intent.

"*Thymnos*." The explosion of power Gavin felt as his invocation took hold was unlike anything he'd ever experienced before. If his *skathos* felt like he was treading water in the ocean, he'd just unleashed a tsunami.

Two savage screams erupted—one behind Gavin and one from the group against the left wall. He both heard and felt a body collapsing against the floor behind him. The true targets of the invocation—the four armed people—collapsed as well; Gavin hoped they'd enjoy their five-hour nap.

No other immediate threats appeared, and Gavin turned to the women behind him. Kiri knelt by the woman she stopped from killing a hostage; the woman looked to be minutes—if not moments from dying of blood loss, and she begged for help. Gavin was unmoved. The young woman wearing the angelwing pendant lay unconscious on the carpet, some of her hair perilously close to the expanding pool of blood and her arms draped across her midriff.

Gavin moved to a better position and knelt at her side. He moved her hair away from her assailant's blood with the tender care of a father and searched her face for any remnant of the little girl he'd known so long ago. He thought he might've picked out some resemblance around her eyes and mouth, but he could just be projecting, too. He wanted to brush her cheek, like he used to do when he read to her, but he didn't in case this wasn't his daughter. The awakened core of power resonating against his *skathos* told him she was, but he figured certainty was best.

Turning from the young woman he thought to be his daughter, Gavin stood, his eyes roving across the room. Dozens of folding chairs occupied the center of the sizable room in chaotic disarray. A group of maybe fifteen to twenty people sat against the wall on Gavin's left, but several of them laid on the floor, their heads resting in others' laps. The group that lined the wall to Gavin's right easily numbered sixty to seventy, probably more. Every face Gavin focused on looked back at him with varying degrees of disbelief, anxiety, fear, and awe. There was a small stage at the far end of the room with a podium...

*Oh, shit.* The thought came unbidden to Gavin's mind as he focused on the podium. Right there on the front of the podium, in full view of the entire room, was the Seal of the President of the United States.

# CHAPTER 2

"Stay on your guard," Gavin said. "We don't know if there are more."

Kiri nodded without verbalizing a response as she flicked her blades around to point toward her elbows.

Gavin turned from her and went over to the smaller group of hostages. He saw several of them tense as he approached, and a woman with a pleasant cafe au lait complexion and hair streaked with gray turned from a younger woman who looked to be about Jennifer's age to regard him, her expression wary. He lifted his hands in a placating gesture.

"I don't intend harm," Gavin said, and several pairs of eyes flicked to the former hostage-takers now laying on the floor. "Okay... I don't mean anyone *else* any harm, but they're just sleeping anyway. Does anyone know if these five were the only ones?"

A man in a suit whose left shoulder was a mass of blood from his collarbone to his arm spoke, his voice weak but still loud enough. "There are at least two more. They were rigging bombs to the building's entrances and watching the stairs."

Gavin sighed. "I hate bombs. Right, then."

Scanning the room, Gavin's eyes landed on the four sets of double doors. This presentation hall wasn't very defensible; there were too many entrances. How was he supposed to protect all these people while he went off hunting for bombs? A thought popped to the forefront of his mind, and he couldn't keep from chuckling. He'd just ward the doors to keep anyone who would harm the space's occupants from entering. Hmmm... the walls looked like painted sheetrock, so he warded the entire room, walls and all. His eyes settled on the man in a suit; an earwig on a coiled cable hung near his ear.

"Okay," Gavin said. "My friend and I will find the other two and clear an entrance."

"The bomb squad usually just detonates the bombs if it's safe to do so," the man replied, grimacing as he shifted slightly. "Do you have EOD training?"

"Of a sort. We'll return soon. Don't worry, you'll be safe."

Without waiting for a response, Gavin went to the center of the presentation hall. He closed his eyes and focused on his intent. It wasn't nearly as difficult as it had been when he'd first tried it all those months ago. As soon as he was ready, he invoked a Word of Tutation, "*Sykhurhos.*"

Once again, the resonance of his invocation slammed into the ambient magic, each entrance taking on a vermillion aura. The same two people—the young woman the speaker had been kneeling beside and the woman Gavin believed to be his daughter—screamed.

"Stop that," the woman said, her voice full of accustomed authority. "You're hurting them."

Gavin turned to her. "I don't mean to, ma'am. The fact they respond that way means they're like me."

"Like you? What do you mean?"

"Now's not the time, but I'll be happy to explain later," Gavin replied as he glanced between the doors at the back of the presentation hall and the doors near the windows. "Well, one door's just as good as another, I suppose. We'll return as soon as we can."

Gavin turned and pointed to the doors he chose. Kiri nodded and met him there. She frowned as she looked at the door and nodded with new understanding when Gavin slapped the panic bar and pushed the door open.

They stepped into a cream-colored hallway, brightly lit by banks of florescent lights. Gavin's eyes immediately locked on a man standing in the alcove by the elevators and stairwell access. Like the others in the presentation hall, he too held a Kalashnikov.

"Hey! Who are you?"

Before the man could even fully turn, Gavin formed his intent and invoked a Word of Enchantment, "*Khraexar.*"

"What did you do?" the man said, frozen in mid-turn, his eyes frantically flickering all around. "I can't move!"

Gavin smiled as he approached the man. "You're paralyzed... well, most of your voluntary muscles, anyway. If I had included your involuntary muscles, your heart wouldn't be beating right now and your lungs and diaphragm wouldn't be working. Can we be civil about this? I will ask you questions, and I'd rather you just answer them without forcing me to get creative."

"C-c-creative? What do you mean by creative?"

"One of your associates planned to kill my daughter," Gavin replied. "I'm not exactly invested in your continued health and well-being. Just because I paralyzed you doesn't mean I did *anything* to your pain receptors."

"I... they've trained me to resist torture. By the time you get anything out of me, its value will be long past."

Gavin gave him a flat look. "Good thing I wasn't planning to torture you, then. *Zaenos.*"

The fear and hate that had been mingling in the man's expression faded, replaced by adoration. "What do you want to know? Please tell me how I can help you. I want to do whatever I can for you. Do you want someone killed? I'm very good at killing. I've killed over fifty people, some of them children, and even a few pregnant women."

Gavin clenched his left hand into a fist behind his back. It was all he could do to keep from ripping the life out of this man in the worst way possible. "No. What you *can* do for me, though, is tell me who else came here with you but wasn't in the hall, and which entrances have bombs."

"Oh, all the entrances have bombs," the man replied. "We've had the components in their drums stashed in Physical Plant's motor pool for quite some time now. Going active today wasn't the plan, but when the President came to visit the campus, it was too good an opportunity to pass up."

"So... you're terrorists, then?"

"Not at all, my dear friend. We're some of the only genuine patriots left. This country has lost its way and someone needs to step forward and show everyone where they've gone wrong. Can you believe they elected a Black woman to the White House? I mean, no one at the militia camp could believe it when the country elected that senator from Illinois, but now a *woman*, too? Just how far have we fallen?"

Gavin bit back a sigh. "But back to your associates who pulled this off?"

"Oh, yes. A full squad of us executed this operation, fourteen of us."

*Hmmm... that means there are still eight on the loose.*

"And do you know where they are?" Gavin asked.

"Four hold the security office. Two patrol the main floor, two on the roof, and there were five in the event room. But I'm guessing you handled them, since you came from there. Uhm... say... you're an amazing guy. Could you help me with my radio? It was time to check in when you came out of the event room."

Gavin focused his intent and made another invocation, "*Sykhurhos.*"

This time, Gavin bit back a wince and even felt a little winded. He was rather glad he wasn't in the presentation hall; that gracious lady he now suspected to be a rather important elected official would probably claw at his eyes. At least whoever these people were, they wouldn't be leaving. No one identifying themselves as militia members—any militia, even the National Guard—could pass through any doorway in the building now, and it was a rather sizable building, given how much power that invocation had required.

"*Thymnos.*"

The man's eyes closed, and the *crack!* as the man's head struck the tiled floor sounded rather ghastly.

"What are we going to do?" Kiri asked, wise enough not to use Gavin's name. "Even with our advantages, eight seems a bit much."

Gavin regarded the sleeping man on the floor with a slight grin. "I have an idea about that, but it won't be pleasant. Come on; I don't want to try this so close to the presentation hall. All these invocations must've had those two ladies in there screaming themselves hoarse."

GAVIN LED Kiri out of the stairwell on the main floor of the building. A sign on the wall opposite the stairwell door informed them they stood inside the Humphries Center, the newly built student union for Graham University. Glancing down the hall, Gavin didn't see anyone, so he squared his shoulders and focused on his intent, invoking a Word of Enchantment, "*Thymnos.*"

This invocation savaged Gavin, and he gasped, staggering and throwing his arms out to the wall to catch himself.

"Gavin, what did you do?" Kiri asked, rushing to his side.

"Everyone in the building who *isn't* in the presentation hall upstairs is asleep now. I figured an invocation that affected such an extensive area would be bad, but I never would've guessed it would be *that* bad. Come on. Let's go deal with the bomb on the closest entrance; then, we need to go back to the presentation hall."

It took Gavin about forty feet before he wasn't walking like a man three times his age, and his shoulders still sagged enough for Kiri to notice even by the time they came in sight of an entrance. Three fifty-five-gallon drums strapped together in a triangle touched the center post of the double doors. Wires ran from each drum to suction cups adhering to the glass and to magnets attached to the door frame. More wires ran to industrial suction grips on the floor, a solid five feet from the drums.

"Wow..." Gavin said, staring at the device. "That's impressive. It looks far too complex to try disabling the sensors. I'll disintegrate it."

"Whatever you think is best," Kiri replied. "This is your world, after all."

"*Zyrhaek.*"

Gavin swayed on his feet a little as his invocation took hold, and then, he and Kiri watched the complex explosive device become a pile of powder. However destructive it might have once been, it was safe now. He'd leave the other entrances for the authorities.

"Okay. Let's go back upstairs. Someone up there has to have a cell phone we can use."

* * *

GAVIN LED Kiri back into the presentation hall and found the woman he'd interacted with standing in the center of the room, pacing. She held a cell phone to her right ear and pivoted on her heel, her eyes locking on Gavin and Kiri.

"They just came back," she said. "No... well, I don't think so. If they meant us harm, they could've easily acted on it before now. Besides, you all saw the woman kill the one about to execute the hostage."

"Are you talking to the police out front?" Gavin asked as he approached the woman.

"Yes," the woman replied, a hint of steel in her voice. "Is that a problem?"

"Nope," Gavin replied. "Tell them that one entrance is missing its bomb. I don't know if the remaining bombs have timers, and all the hostiles *should* sleep for at least the next three hours. The four in here and the guy outside will sleep for a little under five hours, and I intended for everyone else in the building to sleep for five, too. But it's such a large building that the effect might not have been as strong as I wanted."

"Five hours?" the woman repeated, her control slipping enough that she gaped at Gavin. "You put an entire building to sleep for five hours? What about us? Why aren't we asleep?"

"Because I didn't want you to be asleep. I exempted my friend, here, and everyone in this room. Otherwise, anyone in this building went down for a nap." Gavin gestured to the woman over by the windows. "Now, if you'll excuse us, we'll take her and go."

The woman shook her head. "Your friend killed that man. I mean, only an idiot would rule it wasn't justified, but it's still a homicide. You need to give your statements to the police."

"I just made it back here," Gavin said, shaking his head. "I'm not about to spend my first afternoon and evening back home in an interrogation room. I hope your people recover quickly. If I could help them, I would, but they don't want the only healing I can do."

"Why not?"

"Because it's necromantic," Gavin answered. "I have to take life from something else to rebuild theirs, and from what I've seen, it hurts like you wouldn't believe. Now... I've let you stall us long enough."

Gavin focused his intent once more and invoked a Word of Transmutation, "*Paedryx*."

He, Kiri, and the unconscious young woman at the window blinked out of existence.

# CHAPTER 3

Gavin, Kiri, and the woman Gavin believed to be his daughter appeared in a room that was set up like a studio apartment. There was a kitchenette in one corner with an island and a dining table, a sitting area with several couches and chairs, and an area partitioned off for sleeping. As soon as he got his bearings, Gavin scooped the woman into his arms and carried her to the sofa. Kiri turned in place as she examined her surroundings.

"Where are we, Gavin?" Kiri asked.

"This is the back room of the family store. It's a combination break room and resting area for those times when the store is swamped and my parents can't leave to go home." Gavin pointed to a door over his shoulder with his thumb. "If you go out that door and turn left, you'll come out of a hallway right beside the cash register."

Just as Gavin finished, he heard the indicated door unlock and open, voices filtering in.

"No, Richard, I won't be reasonable," a tart, no-nonsense woman declared, her tone sufficient to soften metal. "Our little girl vanished from a building the authorities had cordoned off, right after some hoodlums nearly killed her on national television. I want our granddaughter back."

If Gavin had possessed any doubts that the woman he and Kiri had saved was his daughter, Jennifer, those doubts no longer existed. And, he recognized the woman's voice. How could he not recognize his own mother's voice, especially when he'd been the focus of that implacable will more than once during his life?

Gavin stood with his back to the door, so he couldn't see his mother's expression. He heard her surprise and confusion, though.

"Jenny? What... who are you people?" Then, surprise gave way to ire and steel. "What have you done to my granddaughter?"

This was so not the way he wanted to reunite with his family, but... there probably wasn't a *good* way, given his situation. Gavin turned to face the door and laid eyes on his parents for the first time since waking up in Tel Mivar.

"Hi, Mom," he said, not knowing what else to say. "Hi, Dad."

The color fled his mother's cheeks. Her jaw dropped. Her eyes rolled back in her head. For the first time Gavin could remember, Elizabeth Cross fainted.

Gavin's father gaped at his son, leaving Gavin to lunge across fifteen feet to catch his mother before she struck the ancient hardwood floor. Richard still hadn't recovered by the time Gavin moved his mom to one of the other sofas, laying her down and slipping a pillow under her head.

Turning away from his mom, it became Gavin's turn to stare. His father didn't possess the man's tall, wiry, powerful frame, but from the shoulders up, Richard Cross could've been Marcus's fraternal twin. The resemblance was beyond uncanny.

"So, that's why he was so familiar to me," Gavin said, his voice barely above a whisper.

Gavin's words jerked Richard out of his reverie, and a few quick strides brought him to his son. He reached out to his son and then froze. His hands inched closer to Gavin, then froze again.

"Gavin? Son?" Richard said, emotions flitting through his expression faster than Gavin could follow. "How... how can this be? We... your mother and I claimed your body from the morgue. We *buried* you!"

All at once—as if some barrier or restraint or reservation broke—Richard grasped Gavin's shoulders and pulled him close, his hands then exploring Gavin's shoulders, neck, and face. But his movements were cautious. Though the torrent of emotions still cascaded through Richard's expression, the predominant one was disbelief.

For what seemed like ages, Richard just stood there, his hands on Gavin's shoulders as his eyes took in everything about Gavin. Eventually, he angled his head toward Kiri. Gavin saw his eyes drop, and he guessed his father was looking at the blades Kiri still held.

"It was you?" Richard said at last, turning his head back and forth between Gavin and Kiri. "It was the both of you who saved Jenny and all those people?"

"Yeah," Gavin replied, adding a nod. "That was us."

"How?"

Gavin took a deep breath and released it as a heavy sigh. "That... isn't easy to explain, Dad. You'll probably think I'm crazy."

"Crazier than standing in the back room of the family store *thirteen years* after we buried you?"

"Thirteen years?" Gavin gaped at his father, then turned to look at the unconscious woman wearing his daughter's pendant. He knew he and she appeared to be the same physical age. "So, that's really Jennifer? That's my little girl?"

Richard nodded. "Yes. She's Jennifer. I'm still trying to process you standing here. My mind keeps screaming that this can't be real."

"Richard?" Elizabeth's voice was softer than it had been, without its steel and a little woozy.

Gavin's father moved to his son's left side and turned as Elizabeth lifted her hand to her forehead.

"What's wrong with me? We were talking about Jennifer, and then, I thought I saw—" Elizabeth stopped speaking mid-sentence. She gaped at the sight of her husband standing beside the son she'd thought long-dead. "Gavin? Richard, I'm seeing Gavin. He looks so real. He looks young, too, like he's just out of college."

Elizabeth closed her eyes and massaged her temples. While his mom had her eyes closed, Gavin moved to the sofa and knelt at her side. She slowly opened her eyes and flinched at seeing Gavin so close.

"It's really me, Mom," Gavin said. He reached out and took his mother's hand in his, moving it to his cheek. Elizabeth's expression was a mixture of disbelief and cautious joy as she brushed her son's cheek, then his forehead.

"How? How are you alive?"

"That will be a tough topic to discuss," Gavin replied. "And I'm not sure you'll believe me right away."

"What do you mean?" Elizabeth asked, sitting up. She saw Kiri and blinked. "Is she with you? And why is she... it was you? You two saved Jenny?"

Gavin nodded. "Yes, it was us. And yes, she's with me. Do you feel like you can stand?"

"Of course I do!"

Gavin moved back and held up his hands. "I'm not the one who almost bounced her head off the floor."

Elizabeth's eyes narrowed almost into a glare, and the tart steel returned. "You'd be unsteady, too, if you saw your only child after thinking he was dead for thirteen years."

Gavin smiled, realizing for the first time how much he'd missed bantering with his mom. He pushed himself to his feet and held out his hand. His mom gave him a mock glare and stood on her own, almost as if to prove a point.

Elizabeth moved to stand by Richard as Gavin gestured for Kiri to approach. "Mom, Dad... this is Kiri Muran. Kiri, these are my parents, Richard and Elizabeth Cross."

"It's very nice to meet you," Kiri said, the blades she held not detracting from her curtsy in the slightest.

"It's nice to meet you, dear," Elizabeth replied, Richard offering his own nod.

"I think we should visit the ER," Richard said. "Lizzy, you've never fainted before, and while I agree that it's understandable, I still want to get you checked out. Plus, there's Jenny and... well... Gavin."

"'ER?'" Kiri asked, frowning. "Forgive me, but I do not understand."

"Emergency room?" Richard asked.

Gavin turned to Kiri, saying, "It's like the trauma ward in the College's infirmary. People go to the ER needing all levels of urgent help, and the healers—who we call doctors and nurses—prioritize them based on what kind of care they need and how much. They most often see cases that need a fast response to save lives."

"But what about the clerics?"

"This world doesn't have magic, Kiri, or at least it didn't. The clerics here are simply scholars who have devoted their lives to a specific religion."

Kiri frowned. "You mean, no one here can heal others like Ovir healed us?"

Gavin shook his head.

"Then, it seems the wonders of your world come with a price."

"Healing?" Richard asked. "Are you part of a cult now?"

Gavin allowed a half-smile and shook his head. "No, Dad. The world where I spent the last two years is wildly different from Earth. One of those ways is magic, especially divine magic. The gods are much more active and responsive there. I've spoken with two; they seem like decent folks."

Richard and Elizabeth stared at Gavin. Their expressions slowly shifted into masks of confusion and disbelief while their jaws slackened without dropping. After several moments, Elizabeth shook herself, not unlike a wet dog removing excess water.

"A discussion for another time," she said. "Let's get you and Jennifer to the ER."

Letting the matter drop, Gavin moved to the sofa and gathered his unconscious daughter into his arms. Richard and Elizabeth led the way, Richard staying close to Elizabeth in case she wasn't as steady as she seemed. Instead of turning left to go into the store, Gavin's parents turned right, leading the procession down a short hallway to a door that opened up to the staff parking lot.

Gavin didn't see the Tahoe he remembered his parents having

and followed them instead to a GMC Yukon. It took a bit of wrangling to get Jennifer stretched out across the bench that made the third row seating, but once he had, Gavin turned to find Kiri not immediately in sight. He stepped out of the Yukon and looked around, spotting Kiri circling the vehicle in the midst of a detailed examination.

When he reached her side, Kiri looked up to meet his eyes. "There's so much about your world I don't understand. This carriage is a thing of wonder."

Richard and Elizabeth shared a look as Gavin guided Kiri into the Yukon.

Just as Gavin reached for the door handle, he stopped and turned back to Kiri. "Hang on. We need to do something about those blades. Besides, there's not too much time left on them anyway."

"How could something that looks so new have little time left?" Gavin's mom asked.

Gavin accepted the blades from Kiri and held them in his hand. Focusing on his intent, he invoked a Word of Evocation, "*Idluhn.*"

A small column of flame shot out of Gavin's palm, engulfing the blades, and Gavin kept the flame burning until the blades glowed. Then, once he was sure he'd burned off any blood that might have fallen when the conjured blades vanished, he invoked another Word, this time one of Tutation, "*Rhosed.*"

If Gavin's parents had been gaping at seeing a flame shooting out of their son's palm, they weren't prepared at all when the blades he held vanished as if they'd never existed.

"Well, at least that's handled," Gavin remarked and clapped his hands together as if dusting them off. "Shall we go?"

* * *

THE COUNTY HOSPITAL Gavin remembered was now a full-fledged regional medical center. Massive parking lots surrounded the structure, and four helipads sat right outside the entrance to the emergency room. Gavin was silently thankful that no med-evac helicopters were arriving at the same time they did. He didn't really feel up to explaining them to Kiri while he was trying to find something of the small, country hospital he'd grown up with in the gargantuan structure that took up an area equivalent to several football fields.

* * *

HOSPITAL EXAM ROOMS had changed little, from what Gavin could see. It just so happened, though, that the room Gavin, his family, and Kiri occupied was a double. Jennifer lay on one exam bed, still unconscious. Gavin and Kiri now sat in chairs across the room from his parents, waiting.

A quick double-tap on the door was the only warning before it opened to admit Scott Thompson, one of Gavin's classmates from high school. It shocked both Scott and Gavin to encounter each other. Gavin, because Scott was older than Gavin remembered, with receding hair, gray around the fringes, and the beginnings of lines around his mouth and eyes. Scott, because... well... he'd signed Gavin's death certificate.

Scott stared at Gavin as he closed the exam room's door before visibly shaking himself and regarding the clipboard in his hand. He moved over to the empty exam bed and hopped up to sit on it, completely disregarding any dignity or gravitas one should probably have when practicing medicine.

"Okay," Scott said, "I'll deal with the easiest part first. Elizabeth, you're fine. There's nothing in the blood work or the ultrasound that suggests it was anything other than shock—for obvious reasons—that caused your fainting spell. If it happens again, I'll worry.

"As for Jennifer, there's nothing in the test results to explain why she's unconscious. As far as we're able to determine, she's the picture of health. When was the last time she had one of the pain episodes?"

"Pain episodes?" Gavin asked. "Can you describe that?"

Elizabeth and Richard glanced to one another before Elizabeth spoke. "It started about two months ago. She randomly gets overcome by excruciating pain. It wasn't so bad the first time or two it happened, but now, it's debilitating. Whenever it hits, she just collapses and tries not to scream. It has made this semester of college very... challenging."

Gavin's mind went back to the screams that erupted anytime he'd invoked Words of Power in the presentation hall... and he knew. He had no idea how it had happened, or even what specific events had occurred, but his daughter had somehow invoked a Word of Power, just like he had all those months ago in the southwestern warrens of Tel Mivar.

"Scott, I'll be impressed if you can find anything specifically wrong with her," Gavin remarked. "Once she wakes up and gets semi-used to seeing me, I'll start training her."

"Training?" Scott repeated, his tone incredulous. "Gavin, this isn't something that training can do anything about. When she gets the pain episodes, every nerve in her body lights off; it's like the minuscule electrical charge our bodies need to work explodes by a factor of one million or more. I've seen nothing like it in all my years of medicine."

"She's like me, Scott," Gavin said. "She was born with the ability to reshape reality to her will, and somehow, she has used it. I can't prove any of this to you, right now, because we'd have to go a considerable distance away from the hospital just so I'm not technically torturing my daughter when I give you proof."

"Believe him, Scott," Elizabeth interjected. "His father and I saw him produce a flame from thin air and make two blades vanish like they never were."

Scott looked from Gavin to Elizabeth and back again, moving at a slow, steady pace that made Gavin think of a metronome. After several moments, he closed his eyes, shook his head, and shrugged. "Okay... uhm... well, I don't really know what to make of that, but okay. It's not like I can do anything for her anyway. If it weren't so intermittent, I'd say she has some kind of fibromyalgia that makes acute cases seem like stubbing a toe."

Jennifer blinked her eyes, starting to move into a sitting position. Her voice was weak and strained as she said, "Aw, geez... the hospital again? I'm sorry. It was the weirdest thing. I could've sworn I heard—

Daddy? Is that you?" Jennifer clamped her eyes shut and shook her head. "It can't be you. What's wrong with me? You're dead. You can't be here."

Elizabeth stood and walked over to Jennifer's bed. She sat beside her granddaughter and pulled Jennifer into her arms. "It's okay, Sweetheart. We're still figuring things out."

"Scott, do you mind?" Richard asked. "What did the tests say about Gavin?"

Scott flinched, Richard's words apparently calling his focus back to the present. "Huh? Oh, right... Gavin's tests. Well, that's where the wheels come off the wagon. The metabolic panel indicates you are very healthy; you do not have the bloodwork of a man in his mid-forties, not even someone in textbook-perfect health. The x-rays didn't show any of the mild arthritis you should have from forty-five years of wear and tear on your bones. Oh... remember when you broke your arm in junior high? Yeah, the x-ray didn't show that, either; I specifically looked for it. All the markers and medical indications that a man should have at your age... well, you don't have them. The DNA test won't come back until tomorrow, and neither will the dental comparison. We had to go to the off-site archives for those. For now, go home. Enjoy being alive. I'll call when I get those final results back."

* * *

NATHAN "NATE" Carruthers skimmed the news brief his producer handed him mere minutes before he went live. His eyes locked on one, specific piece of the brief, and he frowned.

"Kim, have you confirmed this?" he asked. "I don't want to make a fool of myself on live TV."

"Yes, Nate," Kim replied. "I vetted all the raw video, including the clips you'll introduce. A man and woman appeared out of nowhere, and the woman killed the person about to shoot a hostage. Law Enforcement still won't comment; all they say is, 'ongoing investigation,' but cell phone videos are going viral across the internet as we speak. It's not fake."

Nate shook his head. "It has to be some kind of hoax, Kim. I mean... people don't just appear out of thin air."

Kim threw up her hands and shrugged. "They do now, Nate. You're live in thirty seconds."

# CHAPTER 4

Alexis Hall returned her mother's smile as she entered her mom's side of the adjoining suites. It was tough being the daughter of the President of the United States, even tougher than being the daughter of the Governor of Michigan. It hadn't been so bad when her mom was in the Senate. She was sure some children would have resented their parents for pursuing such public careers that precluded any kind of 'normal' life for the child, but it had always been just the three of them... her twin brother, her, and their mom. There was no way Alexis would try to deny her mother the career it was apparent she loved so much.

Chelsea Hall wasn't just a record-breaker as the first African American woman to be elected President. She was also the youngest; when she took the Oath of Office, Chelsea Hall was only forty-one years and 108 days old, beating Theodore Roosevelt by a little over one year and John F. Kennedy by two.

"Hey, Sweetheart," her mom said, adding a smile. "How are you feeling?"

Alexis shrugged. "I'm okay. I feel a little weird, but it doesn't exactly feel bad. Not like the other times."

"Weird? What's different? What's weird?"

Alexis frowned. "It's difficult to explain, Mom. That guy, the one in the presentation hall... I can vaguely tell where he is. You know how different parts of you feel the heat when you walk around a campfire? It's like that, only kind of tingly or static-y."

Her mom frowned. "Where is he?"

Alexis closed her eyes and concentrated on the new feeling, something almost like a resonance. She lifted her arm and pointed with her index finger, saying, "That way. I don't know exactly *where*, but he's that way. The feeling is faint. Fainter even than when he first left the university."

Alexis opened her eyes to see her mom looking in the direction she indicated. The wall where she pointed had a window, but with just one bearing, there was no way to know.

"Do you think he might know what's wrong with me?" Alexis asked at last. "None of the doctors have ever found anything, and it hurt when he did whatever it was he did. It was the worst the pain has been."

Chelsea turned from staring out the window and pulled her daughter into a hug. "I don't know, Sweetheart, but we can find out."

A knock on the main door of the suite was followed shortly by Jenna Carmichael entering. Jenna was the President's executive assistant. She oversaw the President's schedule and guarded access to her like a jealous miser.

"Ma'am, Agent Timothy Gardner is here," Jenna said.

Chelsea released Alexis and stepped back, nodding. "Thank you, Jenna. Please send him in."

Jenna backed out of the suite, and the supervisor for both the President's and her daughter's protective detail entered, carrying a thick manila folder. His short stature combined with his stocky build and fiery red hair made Alexis think of a fire hydrant, and every time she saw him, she had to stop herself from chuckling at the mental image.

"What do you have for us, Tim?" Chelsea asked.

"Frankly? A mess, ma'am." Tim waved the folder. "Mind if we go to the table?"

Chelsea gestured for him to proceed, and Alexis followed her mom in Tim's wake.

Tim opened the folder and began laying out pictures and notes. "Okay. Everyone we apprehended in the building—most of whom haven't woken up yet—are members of a semi-radical militia group that has largely been under the radar. This group is so quiet that our background checks on the university's staff didn't flag any of these people. Most of them work in Physical Plant, which is the maintenance department and explains how they could stash and stockpile explosives across campus; they had access to all the places the average person never sees."

"I don't really care so much about them, Tim," Chelsea said. "What can you tell me about the man and woman who ended the standoff?"

"The building's security system caught good pictures of them both. The woman touched nothing for us to get her prints, that we found anyway, but the man did. The woman? We have no idea... no data, nothing. She doesn't pop up on any facial recognition. Records-wise, she doesn't exist. The man? Well, he's the biggest can of worms I've ever come across."

Alexis watched her mom frown and turn to Tim. "What do you mean, Tim?"

"Both his fingerprints and facial recognition flag the record of a man who's been dead for thirteen years."

"Are we talking dead or Black Ops dead?" Chelsea asked.

"Dead," Tim replied. "I have archived news footage of a dump truck running a red light and all but pancaking his car. He was on the way home after picking up his daughter at the mall. She walked away from the wreck with only a few scrapes and bruises. Here's the fun part. According to student records, the woman about to be executed on live TV was this guy's daughter. I'm still waiting on the files, but apparently, the daughter is also a person of interest to a task force the FBI and DEA have running." Tim's voice trailed off as he shuffled through the contents of the folder until he found the cover sheet for the FBI file of a man named Gavin Cross, holding it up. "Is this the guy?"

"Yes," Chelsea answered, nodding. "That's him. He looked younger, though."

"Okay. There's also a strange data code in the FBI file. I reached out to my guys over there, and they're tracking it down. From what I was told, it's an ancient cross-reference code... something about dating back to the 1930s or 40s."

"Okay. I have to stop you there, Tim. You just lost me. How could a guy who's only five years older than I am have a data code on his FBI file dating back to the eras of Prohibition and World War II?"

Tim lifted his hands in the classic surrender gesture. "I have no idea. Like I said, my contacts in the Bureau are still tracking it down. They'd never seen it before, either." The phone on Tim's belt buzzed, causing him to look down. "May I, ma'am?"

Chelsea nodded. Tim had the phone in his hand and unlocked before she completed the motion.

"Huh... this is really getting strange," Tim said before he lifted his head from the screen to face Alexis and her mom. "That was a text message from one of my contacts in the Bureau. Apparently, the cross-reference code connects to the National Archives. She already put in a call over there before texting me."

Chelsea stared at the cover sheet she held in her hands. After a few moments, she nodded. "I want to know everything there is to know about this guy, Tim. If the Bureau or DEA gives you any flack, tell me at once."

"Yes, ma'am," Tim replied. "May I ask why?"

Chelsea pulled her gaze away from the cover sheet, looking at Tim. "Because he may know what's going on with Alexis. He may be able to help her."

* * *

THEY SPENT the trip from the hospital to home in silence. There was so much to say—between every member of the family—that a car ride across the county wasn't the best place to start it. Besides, it was blindingly apparent that Jennifer wasn't handling seeing her father again all that well. Through the rear-view mirror, Richard saw his granddaughter keep casting nervous, almost fearful, looks at the back of Gavin's head. Gavin never saw them; he stared out the window, watching the countryside pass... lost in his own thoughts.

THE GRAVEL DRIVEWAY that had led to his parents' place was now black-topped. The wooded hills and fields surrounding the property hadn't changed, and Gavin leaned to the right to watch the gate approach. He couldn't believe his eyes when the archway over the gate was close enough to make out details.

"Dad, stop the car, please," Gavin said, breaking the silence that had existed since leaving the hospital.

"What is it, son?" Richard asked, but did as Gavin requested.

Gavin unbuckled his seatbelt, and the moment the Yukon stopped moving, he opened the door and stepped outside. The archway over the gates was a bronzed construction, the words 'Cross Estate' emblazoned across each side. At the apex of the arch—where the keystone would be in masonry—was the Cross family's crest, a coat of arms family historians had traced back to long before the Battle of Hastings in 1066.

What held Gavin's attention, though, was the very center of the crest. His eyes never left the crest as he walked alongside the Yukon until he stood right in front of the vehicle staring up at the crest. It wasn't long before his parents and Kiri were at his side.

"Do you see it, Kiri?" Gavin asked, pointing.

Kiri grinned, also looking up at the crest. "Yes, I do. That's your family's crest on this world?"

"Yep. It dates back over a thousand years... at least that we're able to prove with verifiable records."

"I don't understand," Gavin's mom said.

Richard nodded. "Me, either. What's going on, Son?"

Gavin pulled his silver medallion out from under his polo shirt and swept it off of his neck. He turned it around to face everyone and held it out for his parents to see. Both Richard and Elizabeth gasped. The symbol in the center of the crest—the symbol that family historians had puzzled over for generations because it matched nothing in any system of heraldry across the known world—was the Glyph of Kirloth.

"Gavin, what is that?" Richard asked.

"It's our true family crest, Dad. It's our House Glyph." Gavin hung the medallion around his neck once more but didn't bother hiding it under his shirt. "There's too much to explain here in the driveway, way too much. Besides, you need to get me caught up on quite a bit, too. My little girl's twenty-six now, right?"

"Next month, but yes," Elizabeth said.

His parents' house looked much like Gavin remembered. It was two-stories, white with green trim, but the metal slats Gavin had seen all over town now covered the roof, also green. The old rope swing he'd used as a boy still hung from the maple tree in the front yard, and his mother's flowerbeds were where he remembered them. Flagstone paths led from the garage to the side door and from the fence's gate and mailbox to the front door. It was home and somehow not... all at the same time.

Richard drove the Yukon into the garage where everyone filed out. Jennifer was passing the right-rear wheel when her face contorted in pain. She clutched her midriff and leaned against the Yukon, her legs trembling. She gritted her teeth, but an agonized groan escaped her control.

Gavin was at her side in an instant, placing his hands on Jennifer's shoulders and holding her at arms' length. "Jenny, listen to me. The pain... does it seem to come from the very pit of your soul, the very core of who you are?"

Jennifer nodded before crying out, unable to contain it any longer.

Gavin looked around and, seeing lawn furniture not too far away, helped Jennifer over to sit in a nearby chair. He pulled another to sit directly in front of her, and he took a heartbeat's time just to take in his daughter's countenance in its contortion of pain.

"Jenny, this will be the most difficult thing you've ever done, honey, but if you can do it, the pain will never bother you again. Are you up to it?"

Jennifer nodded, her eyes pinched shut against the agony.

"Okay. First, extend your right hand in front of you. Turn it palm-up and curve your fingers like you're holding an apple." Gavin waited until Jennifer did as he instructed. It took her a few moments, and her hand trembled, but she did it. "Good. Now, you need to take the core of pain inside you, pull it up out of the pit of your soul, and push it down your right arm to your hand. For me, I used to envision grabbing hold of it with my left hand and moving it that way, but use whatever method works for you. Now, when it reaches your hand, it will feel like it will fly away and join the world, but you need to hold it… right there above the palm of your hand."

A pin-prick of light appeared above Jennifer's palm. One last time, Jennifer grimaced and vocalized her pain, but that pin-prick of light swelled and grew. Within a minute, the pin-prick became a watermelon-sized kaleidoscope of incandescence. Every color of the rainbow swirled through the orb, as her torment eased.

"Now then, Jenny… reach out to the world around you through the power, and tell me what you feel. Tell me if you feel any resonance."

Jennifer was silent for several moments as she turned her head from side to side, as if listening for a whispered conversation. "This is so weird…" Her voice faded as she frowned, eyes still closed and her head angled toward her shoulder. "I'm not feeling any significant pain anymore, and there seems to be a pool of power like mine everywhere, like a blanket or maybe a fog bank. Uhm, Dad? I don't know how to say this, but you're sort of glowing. Like the sun. It's colored gold like the sun, anyway, and it hurts to concentrate on you. I can feel Grandpa, too. It's strange with him, though. It feels like an echo somehow. Am I getting this right?"

Gavin sat on the lawn furniture, staring at the orb of power above her palm that was now the size of a beach ball. He glanced over his shoulder to the three people standing behind him and grinned like the proud parent he was. Kiri grinned right along with him, but his parents had no expression beyond very wide eyes. In fact, on a closer examination, Gavin thought his mom looked a little pale.

"Jenny, I want you to open your eyes," Gavin said. "Be careful not to lose your concentration, but open your eyes."

Jennifer opened her eyes; Gavin was watching. In an instant, he saw in her expression what he remembered feeling that day so long ago in a sick room at the Temple of Valthon, and he grinned right along with his daughter.

"Dad, this is amazing! What's happening? What is this?"

"Jenny, how about we pull back and relax before I answer questions?"

"Okay, relaxing sounds good, but how do I do it? I mean, it feels like it's feeding itself."

Gavin smiled, saying, "It's not as hard as you might think. Concentrate on the orb. Somewhere in there, possibly near the center, you'll find the core you originally pulled out of yourself. Pull that core back to you."

Jennifer closed her eyes and concentrated. She broke into a sweat from the strain, but suddenly, the beach ball seemed to pop and then shrunk to an outsized basketball.

"Dad... this really doesn't feel good. The tingling is back so bad it hurts."

"Jenny, you've drawn in a lot of power. Do you feel you can release it bit by bit, like a dripping faucet?"

"Oh, Daddy, I'm not sure I can hold it for another two seconds, let alone long enough to do that."

Gavin looked around and found the object of his search, a rock slightly larger than his fist. He scooped it up in his right hand as he looked over his shoulder to his parents.

"Mind if I take this?" he asked.

His mother didn't react; her eyes remained locked on the orb of power hovering above her granddaughter's hand. His father, however, jerked his head in assent.

Gavin turned back to Jennifer, the rock in his right hand. "Jenny, you're about to feel me reach out for the power. Let me have it. Don't jerk away from it, but ease yourself back when you feel me reach for it. Okay?"

"I'll try, Dad," Jennifer said. The strain of holding the power was evident in her clothes, now soaked with sweat and clinging to her.

Gavin closed his eyes and reached out with his *skathos*. He felt the orb of power his daughter held, and what's more, he felt her control of it slipping. Gavin started drawing power into himself, pulling small bits from the ambient to start the process. Once the 'currents' established, he focused his draw on the orb Jennifer held and concentrated on it.

"Let go of it, Jenny," he said.

Jennifer didn't say a word but did as Gavin asked, and no one—not even Gavin—was prepared for what happened. The basketball-sized orb hopped from Jennifer's hand to his, and tendrils of gold curled up from Gavin's hand toward the orb. In a brilliant flash of light, the kaleidoscope of incandescence became an orb of golden power.

"My god!" Gavin's mother said. "What happened to it?"

Gavin heard his mother's exclamation, but he was too deep in his concentration to answer. He knew what he wanted to do, but he searched the recesses of his mind for the proper Word to use. After several seconds that seemed like epochs of time, Gavin found that Word, and he grimaced.

"This will really suck," Gavin said, his voice barely above a whisper.

Now sweating much like his daughter had been, Gavin cleared his mind of everything but his intent. In his mind, he saw the rock in his hand becoming a silver wizard's medallion, with all the protections embedded in it that his own possessed. Once the mental image of his intent was satisfactory, he spoke two Words, blending them together into one, "*Rhyskaal-Sykhurhos.*"

The first Word was a Transmutation. The second Word invoked a Tutation effect to create the protections he desired within the medallion.

Gavin felt the composite effect take hold, and he was grateful beyond words to be sitting. The pain felt like his body was being ripped apart at a rate similar to how stars age.

* * *

Jennifer wrapped her arms across her midriff and gritted her teeth to bite back a scream. She was unprepared for the true savagery the Art could wreak within a person, and she expended so much effort biting back the scream that she couldn't keep from wetting herself.

* * *

Meanwhile, Gavin treated Kiri and his parents to quite the show. A spire of golden power as thick as a bodybuilder's forearm arced out of the orb above Gavin's left hand to strike the rock in his right hand. Waves of power passed from the orb to the rock for several moments, during which even the sun seemed to dim. After a few heartbeats, the orb above Gavin's hand flashed so brightly everyone watching shut their eyes and turned away. When they looked again, Gavin held a silver medallion in his right hand.

Gavin started to sag back into the lawn chair and gasped for breath, but he surged to his feet and rushed in an uneasy stagger to the trash can beside the garage. He swept the lid off with his left hand and promptly, noisily, violently retched.

* * *

Gavin's creation of the medallion fulfilled the condition of an ancient contingency. For the first time in countless ages, a composite effect—true wizardry—was invoked on Earth. The ripples of the composite effect emanated outward from Gavin's location, much like the shockwave of an earthquake. All around the world, guardians felt those ripples in their millennia-long slumber, and they started to awaken.

* * *

"BY THE GODS, GAVIN!" Kiri said as she rushed to his side. "Are you okay?"

Gavin backed away from the trash can and nodded, but each motion radiated fatigue.

"It's not too bad, Kiri," Gavin said, moving toward the shop sink his father had in the garage, his movement more of a lumbering stagger than actual walking. Upon reaching his goal, Gavin turned on the cold-water faucet and rinsed off his hands and face before rinsing out his mouth a few times. "The slaver camp in Vushaar was much, much worse."

"Slaver camp?" Elizabeth asked from outside the garage. "What slaver camp? What happened there?"

Gavin made his way out of the garage, and as much of his strength returned, his gait and ambulation normalized. He regarded his parents for several moments, his eyes haunted, before he said, "Don't worry about the slaver camp right now, Mom. Let's just say the composite effect I invoked there made what I did just now seem like lights on a Christmas tree. What I don't understand is why it affected me so."

Gavin stopped in front of his daughter, who had moved to stand beside her grandfather, and he lifted the wizard's medallion to her. "Jennifer, you are my daughter by blood, deed, and right. Wear this medallion as a symbol of your birthright as a daughter of House Kirloth, and before these witnesses, I name you my heir."

# CHAPTER 5

Jennifer stepped into the shower and savored how the hot water relaxed every part of her body. She was too tense. She was too on edge. She knew that. But it wasn't like she didn't have a good reason, right? Just how often did a girl's dad come back from the dead?

What was she supposed to think about that anyway? Or feel? In the years since Grams and Grandpa found her, she'd made a lot of progress. On an average day, she didn't automatically feel like she'd killed her father anymore. But she still remembered what that felt like. Looking up at her mom, wanting to know what was wrong with Daddy.

*He's dead. You killed him. If you hadn't slipped out of the house, this would never have happened.*

Those words still sliced through her soul. It had taken years of professional therapy and uncounted dollars, but Jennifer *knew* she hadn't killed her father. But knowing she hadn't killed her father wasn't the same as feeling she hadn't killed her father.

In the dark of night, when she was so tired and the protections of her mind faded, it all came back to her. The fear. The self-loathing. And now, her dad was downstairs as if nothing had ever happened, and looking her age or younger. How was she supposed to process that? How was she supposed to feel about that?

The shower didn't have any answers for her. That much she knew.

Still, for the first time since the attack, she felt good. She didn't have that tingling pressure in her chest anymore, like it was only a matter of time until something burst out of her. In fact, she felt the best she had in ages... at least physically. It was a nice counterpoint to the turmoil in her soul.

* * *

Gavin listened to the sound of the shower running upstairs and fought the urge to smile. He was home. The furniture was different. The carpet was different. But none of that mattered. Sitting in the house where he'd grown up, Gavin knew without any doubt he was finally *home*. It felt... perfect, somehow.

They occupied the family room. The log-burning fireplace Gavin remembered was now a gas fireplace with fake logs. Kiri sat at his side on the sofa. His dad sat in his recliner. Elizabeth came out of the kitchen with a tea service, placing it on the coffee table between everyone before moving to the other recliner.

"I'm still having problems seeing you sitting there, son," Richard said as he put some honey in a teacup, then added tea. "I keep flashing back to seeing you in the morgue, then the funeral, then burying you. It doesn't quite seem real."

Gavin nodded. "I get that. It makes perfect sense. It's been thirteen years for you, but it feels like last week to me. And that's not even counting the couple of years or so of memories and experiences I accrued before I got my old memories back."

Elizabeth frowned. "Your old memories? What do you mean?"

"A little over two years ago, or what feels like two years to me, anyway, I woke up lying face down in an alley in a place called Tel Mivar. The only thing I knew about myself was my name. I would get flashes sometimes... words or images that only served to confuse anyone around me. My friends finally just accepted that I said weird things now and then, and they rolled with it."

"And what about you, Kiri? Have you known Gavin long?" Elizabeth asked.

Kiri smiled. "We've known each other since the day he appeared in Tel Mivar. It was... well... not a good time for me. Gavin kept me with him and safe until he could get me back to my family. I hadn't been home more than four months or so before we ended up here."

"I'm sorry," Elizabeth replied. "It must be hard being away from your family."

Kiri gave a half shrug, staring toward the floor at nothing. "This doesn't compare at all to when I met Gavin. I'd been away from home for two years, then; Father had sent me to Tel for my safety, but it didn't turn out like he wanted."

Elizabeth started to speak again, but Gavin made eye contact with his mom, a silent indication to not say anything. She apparently got the message, because she didn't ask for any further explanation.

Footfalls heralded Jennifer's arrival as she trooped down the stairs, still drying her hair with a towel. She wore a t-shirt, sweatpants, and socks, and Gavin smiled at seeing his little girl all grown up.

Jennifer snagged a handful of cookies from the tea service as she passed and curled up in the loveseat where she could easily see both her grandparents and her father. Two cookies disappeared before she spoke.

"So... what now? Am I healed? After the orb-melon-thingy, I feel better than I can remember feeling for weeks. Was that really all there was to it?"

Gavin smiled, fighting to keep from chuckling. "I wish. That was just a stopgap, something to give us time. You need training. The 'orb-melon-thingy,' as you put it, will stave off the cascade that will kill you... but only for a time. Six months. Maybe a year. But it won't take that long to train you. Once you're trained and have mastered your power, it cannot cascade. At that point, the only risk you face is using too much at one time."

Jennifer nodded and munched another cookie. "How much is too much?"

"There's no set guide. Early on, making a night light will feel like it's killing you, but as you practice and improve, it will take more and more to tire you, let alone harm you. A lot like exercising at the gym, really. So... do you feel like telling me what happened?"

Jennifer frowned. "What do you mean 'what happened?'"

"For you to be in the situation you were, you had to have invoked a Word of Power... probably around two—maybe three—months ago," Gavin explained. "From what I saw, you were right on the cusp of being too far along to save."

"What makes you think I did that?" Jennifer shot back, her voice taking on an edge. "You don't know me."

Gavin nodded, his expression showing his sorrow and regret. "You will never know how much I wish I did know you. How much I wish I'd watched you grow up, go to high school, have your first date. If I had any choice in the matter, I wouldn't have left you, Jennifer."

Jennifer's hand clenched into a fist, reducing her last cookie to crumbs. "You didn't 'leave,' Dad. That makes it sound like you moved somewhere. You *died*. How are you even sitting there right now? Is everyone else who ever died going to start coming back, too? Are we going to have to deal with Hitler or Attila or Stalin or... I don't know... someone else we thought long dead?"

Gavin took a breath. "No, I don't think so. I think I'm a unique case."

"So, you're the Second Coming, then? Is that what you're saying?"

"Jennifer Anne Cross!" Elizabeth gasped. "That is no way to talk to your father!"

"Is he, really?" Jennifer asked. "How can he be my father and not look older than me? Not *be* older than me?"

"No, Jennifer," Gavin said, his voice tired and seasoned with a dash of sorrow, "I'm not the Second Coming. Nowhere close. I've made too many... *choices*."

Now, all eyes were on him. And for the first time since being back home, it was a weight Gavin couldn't bear. He pushed himself to his feet and walked out of the house.

* * *

Kiri watched Gavin leave, and as much as she wanted to follow, she could tell he needed the time. She wasn't surprised to see his parents and daughter shift their focus to her. She sighed.

"You have no idea what he's faced... what he's had to choose," Kiri said. "He carries the fate of an entire world on his shoulders, and I would not wish that on an enemy, let alone Gavin."

"What would you know about it?" Jennifer asked, almost hissed. "You're probably some—"

"My name is Kiri Muran. I am the heir to a dynasty going back over seven thousand years. I only have one country looking to me, *relying* on me. That's a mere shadow of the weight he carries. Yes, he's grateful beyond measure that he's here now, with the opportunity to reconnect with all of you, but every moment he's here is one moment the world we came from tips closer toward ruin. You should keep this ever-present in your thoughts, because I assure you... *he* will."

Silence reigned for some time following Kiri's chilling statements.

Finally, Elizabeth spoke, shaking her head. "How can an entire world's survival depend on just one man? I mean... that's... it's too much. It's just too much. No one should have to shoulder that. Why does he?"

Kiri half-chuckled, scoffed really. But it held no derision. It held no mirth. The answer so clear to her would mean nothing to them. Still, she gave it.

"Because that's what it means to be Kirloth."

* * *

Gavin wandered aimlessly across the property he'd roamed as a child. A slight breeze whispered by his ears, carrying birdsong and a hint of rain. He now knew the price of coming home. He wasn't the

Gavin Cross they remembered. That man really was dead. Had he ever really been the Gavin Cross they knew, since waking up in Tel Mivar? Maybe... that first day or so.

No. He didn't even make it a full day. He might have been the Gavin Cross they knew, right up until he killed fifty-three slavers. Their Gavin Cross wouldn't have executed Iosen Sivas or snuffed out hundreds of lives in an instant when he destroyed the manor-turned-slaver-camp in Vushaar. Was Kirloth all he was now? Was 'Gavin Cross' nothing more than a remnant? All that was left of a life long since passed?

Gavin chuckled despite his dark mood. He realized he'd made himself sound like the tattered remains of cloth hanging on Othron's skeletal frame. Still... it was a valid question.

The next thing Gavin realized, he stood at the edge of the lake. It was where he'd learned to swim, and he'd spent many a day seeing how far he could skip rocks across the surface. Standing there, his focus drifted. He turned at the waist, looking behind and above him, and he smiled. The cracked and splintered nub was still all that remained of the branch that had dumped him in the lake and forced him to learn to swim. Turning away from both the tree and his reminiscing, Gavin's eyes fell on a concrete bench. It was so inviting, he couldn't refuse.


GAVIN HAD no idea how much time had passed when the snap of a twig jerked him out of his thoughts. For an instant, he wasn't home, wasn't safe on the shore of his family's lake. He rose to his feet and called to the vast sea of power he'd felt since waking up... and it answered. He felt the power saturate his entire being, and the air around him crackled with energy crying out to be tapped and re-make reality to his will.

"It's just me, Dad," Jennifer said, stepping around a tree into view. "Sorry, I didn't mean to startle you."

"It's okay," Gavin said, releasing the power he held. "I should've thought instead of reacting out of instinct."

Jennifer shrugged. "It happens with all of us. A guy I met right after Grams and Grandpa brought me home joined the Army, right in time for us to get caught up in some new mess somewhere in the world, and he wasn't quite the same when he came back. He never talked about what happened… but you reminded me of him, right at the end before you left the house. I'm sorry for pushing so hard back there; I hadn't put it together yet."

"Put what together, Jen?"

Jennifer walked right up to him and pulled him into a hug. "You're like me, now, Dad. The things you've seen, the things you've done… there's no going back for either of us, is there?"

His daughter's words might as well have torn open his chest and poured flaming acid inside. It would've hurt less. In a halting motion, Gavin lifted his arms and held his daughter, fighting to keep tears from flowing.

"I'm so sorry, Jen," Gavin said, little more than whispered. "Do you feel up to talking about it? I'd like to understand."

The only sound was the faint breeze rustling branches and leaves, some birdsong in the distance, the little critters sounding far too happy for Gavin's taste right now.

"I'm afraid, Dad," Jennifer said at last, her voice soft and vulnerable.

"Why are you afraid?"

A sob wracked Jennifer's torso, the first indication that she was crying. "I'm… I'm afraid you won't love me if you know. Do you even love me now?"

Gavin took a deep breath, fighting to maintain the control that felt so frayed. "Jennifer, I don't care how old I am. I don't care how old you are. I don't care how much distance there is between us or whether we're even talking. You're my daughter; nothing in the mortal world could keep me from loving you."

"Then let's sit on that bench," Jennifer said and took a shuddering breath. "There's a lot you need to know."

# CHAPTER 6

Jennifer pulled her father over to one of the concrete benches that sat around the lake's shore. She still couldn't believe this guy who looked so young was her dad. But he sounded like her dad, and he looked like her dad... and he felt like her dad. No matter what he said, she hoped he'd still be her dad at the end of what she had to say.

Even after they sat, she just stared at the water lapping gently at the shore. She knew where she needed to start, but it was hard. So hard.

"Okay," she said, more to get her voice working than anything else. "That night. After you... gave me this pendant. Mom showed up. She talked with the paramedics and turned to me. She said..."

Jennifer's breath caught in her throat. She hated going back to that moment, and there was no way to remember it without reliving it. She might as well have lost both parents that day.

"She said, 'He's dead. You killed him. If you hadn't slipped out of the house, this would never have happened'. I still remember it crystal clear after all these years. It doesn't hurt quite as bad anymore, but it's always been there, you know? Sitting in the back of my mind, just waiting to leap out of the shadows to ambush me."

Jennifer didn't visibly react when Gavin wrapped his arm around her and pulled her against him. She feared he'd try to speak, but if she stopped now, she didn't know if she'd start again.

"Before the year was out," Jennifer said, "Mom was with a guy named Jason White, and I had a shiny new half-sister. It was like they didn't even care, you know? Mom didn't care that you were gone, and most days, she acted like she hated me for existing. At least, that's how it felt. I started staying away from the house for longer and longer periods of time. They never challenged me, never asked why I was late or what I was doing. So, one day, I just left.

"Grandpa and Grams had bought me a big backpack for camping, and I stuffed it full of clothes and food that would keep... and I just left. I knew where Mom kept cash in the house, so I put some in my pocket and stuffed the rest in the pack. It was a few weeks before my fifteenth birthday when I walked out, and I haven't been back to that house since."

Jennifer paused long enough to take a couple deep breaths. This next part was the hardest. She was so ashamed of the next six years of her life. Those years were why she feared—why she *knew*—he wouldn't love her anymore.

"I... I bounced around a lot the first few years. I did the hobo thing on trains if I could. If you keep your eyes open, you'd be surprised what opportunities other people's laziness will give you. When the cash I swiped from Mom ran out, I did odd jobs for money. A lot of people wanted to take me to church or child services, but I wasn't having any of that. I just needed a job to earn money. Here..."

Jennifer held out her left arm, showing a nasty burn scar across about an eighth of her forearm on the inside.

"That was from an explosion of oil from a deep fryer in Memphis. I was washing dishes in a ratty old diner, and someone made some kind of mistake at the fryer behind me. There was a huge pop, and a big dollop of oil landed right on my arm. I hadn't hurt so bad in my whole life. I was almost seventeen, I think, when that happened."

Jennifer took another breath and let it out as a ragged sigh.

"I met a guy named Jerome Toussaint not too long after that. He was suave and classy and said all the right things... and he offered me a job. I started out carrying packages for him. Before long, he asked me if I knew any girls or young women about my age and if I thought they'd like jobs, too. And I did. The last two years I was with him, he called me his recruiter. That was how he referred to me. Anytime someone needed people, he'd always tell them, 'Talk to the Recruiter'."

Jennifer heaved a deep breath. She'd never told anyone the complete story. Oh, bits and pieces, sure... but never *all* of it.

"There was a girl, kind of like me. I met her in Memphis. I got her a job with Jerome, and one day, I ran into her. She told me she'd saved enough money and wanted to go home, visit her folks. I... I went to Jerome and told him Sally had saved money for a trip home to visit her family." The tears escaped at last, sobs wracking her body. "I watched him shoot her, Dad. Two of his guys dragged her into his office, dropped her on a plastic tarp, and *BANG!* She... she died because of me. Watching Jerome shoot her while she begged me to help her feels like the worst thing I've ever done... or maybe *not* done. All of it was wrong, but it's her face I see at night."

Gavin pulled his arm tighter around her. "Jennifer, you are not responsible for his actions. It wasn't your fault."

"Bullshit," Jennifer shot back amid her sobs. "I'm definitely responsible. I have no idea how many lives I've ruined. I'm sure it's well into the hundreds, if not thousands. People would contact Jerome with... well... might as well call it a shopping list. They'd want five brunettes, three redheads, and four blondes, or they'd list the ethnicities they wanted. Sometimes, they specified age ranges. You want to know something? People are always so focused on the creepers in the vans with no windows that they never suspect a teenage girl might have helped a runaway 'find a job'. In one year alone, we shipped out over five groups that were nothing but girls under seventeen. I've crossed the country hundreds of times collecting girls and young women. I knew *exactly* how to manipulate them into coming with me, because I'd been where they were."

Gavin didn't respond. He just rubbed her arm with his hand

while he held her with his arm. "How did your grandparents find you?"

"I had just turned twenty-one. We were operating out of Baltimore by then. Jerome asked me to take a package of drugs to one of his clubs, because he needed it there and didn't have anyone else on hand he could trust. It was the first time I'd muled a package in forever. Grandpa and Grams stopped me on the street, and I was so ashamed of what I'd become that I acted like I didn't know them. I kept telling them I wasn't this 'Jennifer' they were looking for, but they didn't listen. They kept walking with me, begging me to come with them to a diner. I reached the point where I couldn't take the hurt and pain in their voices anymore, so I agreed. I promised I'd meet them as soon as I took care of the job I had to do."

Jennifer paused again, another ragged shuddering sigh. The breeze picked up a tiny bit, and more birds settled into singing somewhere close by.

"I wanted to run to Jerome and tell him people from my past were in town and I needed him to hide me. I mean, I wasn't their granddaughter anymore. Their granddaughter would never have become what I was. But I didn't. After I dropped off the package at the club, I told Jerome's guy there I was getting some lunch before going back to Jerome, and I went to the diner where Grams and Grandpa waited. They didn't even say hi as I sat down in the booth. They just unfolded a packet big enough to cover the table and showed me... well... everything. Everything they'd done since I ran away was in that packet, and it started with them suing Mom and Jason for full custody of me shortly after I ran away... and winning. I still don't know how much money they spent to track me all over the country and find me."

Jennifer pulled away from Gavin and turned so she could face him straight on. A breeze swept a few locks of her hair down over her left eye, and she tucked them back behind her ear without conscious thought.

"The first year or so after they brought me home wasn't easy. In fact, it was pretty awful. I was so ashamed of what I'd become that I tried to kill myself, but I only tried that the one time. Grams and

Grandpa didn't lock me away in some kind of institution. I've lived right here with them. They paid psychologists and other therapists to come out here and work with me. Sometimes, we'd go to them, but it's only been lately—like the last couple years—that I felt even slightly safe being in public. I've always had this fear that Jerome would come for me or find me."

* * *

Gavin sat on the bench, looking into his daughter's eyes. She waited for him to respond, but he couldn't. He simply *could not* respond the way he wanted. Every fiber of his being cried out for *Kirloth* to respond, to wreak such havoc upon Jerome Toussaint that people spoke of his fate in terrified whispers for centuries. But this wasn't Kirloth's world. He didn't belong here, especially not the callous ruthlessness that typified him.

"I wish I knew what to say, Jennifer. You told me you feared I wouldn't love you anymore, and I stand by my statement. That won't ever happen. I have always loved you, and I always will. I just wish..." Gavin sighed. "I'm so sorry you experienced all that. Have you spoken with your mother?"

"No. Not since I left. I don't even know if she knows I'm back home. I mean, it's not that big a town; I can't see how she *wouldn't* know, but she certainly hasn't made any kind of effort to talk to me."

Gavin nodded. "Before... when you were little... I wanted to keep it away from you. I didn't want you affected by it until there was no other choice."

"You didn't want me affected by what?"

"Your mom had been seeing Jason White for about a year before my... uhm... wreck. I found out a couple months before that, and I was trying to figure out how to handle it. Basically, whether I wanted to try to fix the marriage or divorce her and fight for custody of you, tooth and nail. I'm sorry I hadn't figured that out. If I had, you probably would've gone to your grandparents instead of your mom and Jason."

Jennifer frowned, then shrugged. "If there's one thing all the therapy has taught me, it's that there's no point in dwelling on the past. Yes, we need to be mindful of it and learn from it… but not live there. I'm not always as good about that as I could be. I don't want you to feel guilty over everything that happened. *I* made those choices. I *chose* not to go to Grandpa and Grams and tell them what was going on with Mom and Jason. I didn't know it at the time, but if I would've testified that I wanted to live with Grandpa and Grams, given my age, there was every reason to believe they would've won custody of me right then. It was a kick to the gut when I learned that little detail."

Gavin nodded and pulled her into a one-arm hug.

"About the cascade," he said. "How did you come across a Word of Power? And how did you come to use it?"

Jennifer looked away, working her lower lip between her teeth. "It was an accident. Grams and Grandpa were at the store. It was just me here by myself. I found a room in the house I'd never seen before. There were all these ancient books that felt tingly when I touched them. The room had never been wired for electricity; I guess the lines run on the opposite side of the hallway from the hidden door. Anyway, I was trying to read one of those books and was sounding out a word when a ball of white light appeared over my head, and the worst pain I'd felt since the deep fryer burn put me on my knees. I never told Grams or Grandpa about it. I was afraid they wouldn't believe me or, maybe worse, would believe me and ask me to do it again. When I was able to move, I closed the book and crawled out of the room. I haven't been back since."

* * *

CHELSEA HALL LOOKED up at the knock, just as the door opened to reveal Jenna Carmichael.

"Ma'am," Jenna said, "Walter Parsons is here from the National Archives. He says you asked for information about a cross-reference code?"

For a brief moment, Chelsea had no idea what Jenna was talking about. Then it all came back. The odd code in the dead man's FBI file. "Yes, that's right, Jenna. Please show him in."

Jenna nodded and backed out of the room, leaving the door open. Moments later, a mousy man in a tan-colored tweed suit entered the room. Chelsea's eyes went straight to the case he carried. She'd seen cases like that before. They transported old documents that shouldn't be exposed to the open air.

"Good morning, Madam President. I'm Walter Parsons," the man said. Chelsea fought the urge to sigh; he even *sounded* mousy. "I left the Archives as soon as we verified you did indeed request this information. The FBI doesn't have clearance to know it, you see, so we couldn't very well tell *them* what the cross-reference code meant."

Chelsea blinked. The FBI didn't have clearance? What on Earth had she stumbled onto?

"And what is this information that's so secret?" she asked.

Walter didn't immediately answer. He walked across the suite to the table Tim had used a day or so before, withdrawing a thick piece of felt from a side pocket on the case and spread it out over the table. After working the combination tumblers of each latch around the case and using a key to unlock them, he hefted the case up to the table, opening it to lay like a book on a reading stand. He then turned and gestured for Chelsea to approach.

As the President, Chelsea wasn't accustomed to people not immediately answering her questions. But she did as he bade her, approaching the table. Her suspicion was confirmed; the case held a document, and it was so well-preserved she could read the flowing script as if it were new. Her eyes roved across it... and she gasped. Her attention darted back to Walter, her expression a question. He nodded.

"Yes, Madam President. This document has passed multiple methods of verification. It is genuine. The Cross family of the time was instrumental in the War for Independence. This document is the only mention of William Cross and his family in relation to the War, but it is an agreement between the United States of America, the

Commonwealth of Virginia under the signature of Governor Thomas Paine, and William Cross that an estate of sixteen square miles, centered on the Cross residence, shall be sovereign independent soil in perpetuity... so long as a blood descendant of William Cross holds title to the land. Like you read, this grant was apparently made out of gratitude for acts and achievements that should remain unspecified for the sake of posterity."

Chelsea Hall had experienced many moments throughout her presidency in which some facet of the federal government awed or surprised her. This was the first time she'd felt stunned.

"What did they do? I mean, this makes it sound like they weren't soldiers in the Continental Army."

Walter shrugged. "Madam President... we don't know. When I said there's no other mention of William Cross and his family in relation to the War, I meant exactly that. We've combed through Thomas Paine's papers, Washington's papers, Virginia's state archives... and the only thing we've been able to find is one line in the Virginia tax rolls that references this document. That's it. There may be records of what happened on the Cross Estate, but if there is, it's unlikely we'll ever see them. Even if we did, we couldn't add them to the public Archives. This document is under President's-Eyes-Only seal. If you look me up in the federal database, you'll see I have a clearance equal to the Director of National Intelligence, for the sole purpose of knowing this document exists.

"For that matter, ma'am, there probably isn't any way *to* know, not completely. I can't help but feel any records William kept were not a full and complete account, if you know what I mean. It's not like cameras or the internet existed back then. A few of us have tried piecing things together down through the years, looking for reports of British officials mysteriously dying during the War or sudden and extreme changes of policy toward the Colonies. But there isn't enough information to make even wild speculation. There is one other tidbit you might be interested in, though.

"The Cross family owns the town of Graham. They literally own it. It's not included in the four square-miles the document references, but we've been able to learn this much. Every person's rent goes into a fund. *All* of the property taxes come out of that fund each year, and anything left over gets fed into maintenance and upkeep. With the resurgence of shale oil, ma'am, this land is worth millions, and the Cross family owns all of it, even the mineral rights. You can go to the courthouse in Graham and trace the deeds for half the county from child to parent all the way back to William Cross. I've always thought part of the negotiations for this document involved Cross handing over western Virginia to the state. I've seen land grants by the Colonial Governor of Virginia where the King of England granted William Cross's ancestors enormous tracts of land out here. Frankly, I've never seen anything like this."

Chelsea nodded as she stared at the document inside the case. It was a puzzle wrapped up in a mystery and covered by an enigma. There was no doubt *something* had happened. But what?

"Oh, and ma'am?" Walter added. "There's one last thing. If you consider the conduct of our country in its first hundred years, you can't deny we didn't exactly respect our agreements. We broke treaty after treaty with the Native Americans, apparently without even a second thought.

"Now, with that in mind, think about this. Across all these years, this document has never been challenged, neither by the United States government nor the government of Virginia, and every time I ask myself why, I can only think of one or two reasons."

*That* was a chilling thought. Knowing all she knew as president, Chelsea could think of only one reason why past administrations would not have challenged the document or outright tore it up: they were afraid of what would happen if they did. Oh, sure... it may have been lost in history to some extent, but she was certain it wasn't forgotten.

# CHAPTER 7

Chelsea watched the Director of the FBI enter her suite. She knew a lot of people were raising flack over her being in Graham, but she wasn't about to leave until she had a better idea of whether Gavin Cross could help her daughter.

"Madam President," the FBI Director said.

"Hello, Jack," Chelsea replied, gesturing to the available seating. "Thanks for coming out. I know it's outside your usual haunts."

Jack Webster eased into an armchair and set his briefcase on the floor. "It's not as far as some places I've been, ma'am. How can I help you?"

"Jack, what can you tell me about the Cross family here in Graham, Virginia?"

"I'm very glad you gave me a heads-up before I left D.C., ma'am. I had to talk to quite a few people and make a few phone calls to get this information," Jack replied. "The youngest member of the family is Jennifer Anne Cross. She's twenty-six and now lives with her grandparents after several years spent mostly off the grid. The grandparents—Richard and Elizabeth Cross—are clean, three speeding tickets between them across their entire lives. Jennifer, though, is another story.

"I have summaries and photos here in my case, but the Special Agent in Charge tells me Jennifer Cross is a major person of interest to a task force shared between the Bureau and the DEA. The actual subject of the investigation is a Jerome Toussaint. He has dual citizenship with the US and France. Toussaint is someone we'd really like to get off the streets. He's involved in almost every type of crime with an international aspect... drugs, human trafficking specializing in young girls to young adults, illegal arms dealing, the gamut. If his organization isn't directly connected to it, he knows or has worked with someone who is. His organization has better security than some governments; there are a number of positions referenced in his file that we know nothing about the people behind them. The Recruiter —the person responsible for organizing all of Toussaint's drug mules, prostitutes, and such—is completely unknown to us; every mention we've been able to find has always just been 'the Recruiter'. Getting an arrest to stick to him would be as big a coup as getting the Silk Road people back in the day, especially if we could get him to talk."

"How does Jennifer Cross fit into all this?"

"For about three or four years, it appears she was highly placed within his organization. We have evidence that she moved money, drugs, and information between locations here in the States. Can we prove she *knew* what she was moving? Not yet, and to be honest, the task force only cares about her in as much as she could give us Toussaint. The US Attorney's office is willing to offer her immunity if she testifies, but the task force is planning to open negotiations with an arrest warrant. They have enough on her as it is that she could easily qualify for Medicare after prison if the judge says 'consecutive' instead of 'concurrent'. I don't know precisely when they're going to move, but the next six to eight weeks is not improbable."

Chelsea took a deep breath, feeling like she was about to cross a line she swore she'd never cross. "Jack, you have no idea how much it pains me to ask this, but there's... I don't even know how to say it. There's something between the Cross family, the United States, and Virginia. It dates back to the War for Independence, and it has never been challenged in all these years. Yes, you could argue that someone simply forgot about it in a corner of the National Archives, but I have a gut feeling that isn't the case. Jennifer's father stopped the hostage crisis at the university the other day. I'd like the task force to slow down on pursuing Ms. Cross. There must be other avenues of the investigation they can focus on. If they go after her right now... I just have the feeling that moving on her right now would be a very bad idea."

"Ma'am, that's not possible," Jack said. "Her father died in a car wreck thirteen years ago."

"I know, but I also know what I saw in the presentation hall that day. Tim showed me a DMV picture, and it was the same man, Jack. The *exact same* man, only he looked younger in person than the photo. Until we have a clear picture of what's going on, I think the wisest course of action for all concerned is to ease back and give us time to collect more information."

"Ma'am, just to be sure I understand... are you asking Justice to back off an investigation?"

Chelsea sighed. "No, Jack, I'm not. I think we can all agree that one President mucking about in the DOJ recently is beyond enough. I'm only asking the task force to slow down in regards to Jennifer Cross. If it helps, I'm prepared to say it's a matter of national security."

Jack sat in silence, staring at the floor for several moments before he lifted his head to meet the President's eyes. "Is it, ma'am? Is it really a matter of national security?"

Chelsea's mind went back to the then-unknown man putting an entire building of hostiles to sleep, plus what Tim had said about what he'd done to the bomb. If this Gavin Cross could disintegrate a bomb, what else could he disintegrate? The US Capitol?

"Unless we handle the situation precisely right, Jack, I think it could *easily* become a matter of national security."

"When will I get read in on it? I've heard some wild tales about how the hostage crisis resolved, but honestly, ma'am? They sound like something out of my son's favorite books."

Chelsea took a deep breath and slowly eased it out, shaking her head as she remembered the sheer unreality of what she'd witnessed

Gavin Cross doing. "I don't know what you've heard, but there's an excellent chance they weren't *tales*."

* * *

Gavin and Jennifer returned to the family room, drawing everyone's attention.

"You two were gone a while," Richard said.

"We talked, Grandpa," Jennifer said.

Richard's eyebrows shot up. "You did?"

"Yeah. I think it'll be okay."

Gavin and Jennifer returned to the seats they occupied prior to their talk. Richard and Elizabeth glanced at each other before turning back to Gavin.

"Son, we've seen you do some astonishing things," Richard remarked. "You might think we're holding it together rather well, but... I don't know about your mother, but I'm hanging on by a thread over here. Can we talk about it?"

"Sure, Dad," Gavin replied. "What do you want to know?"

Richard and Elizabeth shared another look.

"We don't really know where to start," Elizabeth said. "We watched you create a flame out of nothing and cause two daggers, or whatever they were, to vanish. I suppose you could've used some kind of flash powder for the flames, but doesn't that leave marks or residue or something?"

Gavin shook his head, trying not to grin. "No, Mom. It wasn't flash powder or any other kind of trickery. Here, watch." Gavin lifted his hand, cupping it as if holding an apple, and invoked his go-to Word of Evocation. "*Idluhn*."

A small ball of flame—about the size of a larger apple—faded into existence above his palm. The flames crackled and danced, just like they would in a campfire, but no sparks or ash or anything else appeared.

"This is only fire. It's not giving off heat or consuming any fuel. I created it using a Word of Power, specifically a Word of Evocation.

Evocation is the School of Magic that studies the manipulation of energy. I could produce almost the same ball of flame with a Word of Conjuration, which is how I gave Kiri blades for the hostage situation, but anything conjured isn't permanent. For that matter, the amount of power needed to create a conjured object goes up exponentially the longer you want the object to exist. It's almost impossible to conjure a permanent object... well, for us mortals anyway."

Elizabeth and Richard stared at the ball of flame dancing above Gavin's palm, their expressions flitting between shock and disbelief. Jennifer gazed at it in wonder.

"Can I do that, Dad?"

Gavin accessed his *skathos* and tugged at the thin strand of power he felt connecting him to the ball of flames. He couldn't resist a little showmanship and tried to time cutting the strand at the same time he snapped his fingers. The ball of flames vanished like a soap bubble popping, and his parents sat back in surprise.

"Right now?" Gavin replied. "Probably not. With training and practice? Absolutely. If he'd been trained for it when he was your age, your grandpa could do it, too."

Both Gavin's parents and Jennifer gaped at him now.

"What?" Richard asked. "Why can't I learn now?"

"Seriously? Grandpa could do that?"

Gavin lifted his hands. "Whoa, slow down. Let's not all talk at once. Yes, whatever makes us arcanists seems to travel along family lines. It jumps the occasional generation, but it's very uncommon for a child with power to be born to a family that has no history of wizards. But no, I'm sorry, Dad. I might be able to teach you a few things, but whatever you might be able to do would be a pale shadow of what you could've achieved. If a person with power doesn't use it and master it, the power will fade. That's why Jennifer said you seemed like an echo when she manifested the orb. I can just barely feel you through my *skathos*, which is the sense or awareness of magic our power gives us."

Elizabeth shifted her eyes to Gavin's left, and he guessed she focused on Kiri. She proved it when she said, "And how do you fit into all this? Do you have this power, too?"

Gavin shifted his attention to Kiri and tried not to show his surprise. She looked embarrassed. He wasn't sure he'd ever seen her show embarrassment before.

"No, I'm not an arcanist. I don't have that kind of power," Kiri answered. She turned, and making eye contact with Gavin, her embarrassment faded.

Gavin considered the two lives he'd lived, and in that moment, all of his indecision and doubt snapped into focus. Emily had told Jennifer that she'd killed her father. She'd doubled down on negligent disregard by effectively dropping Jennifer out of her life and treating Jennifer as if she didn't exist. He didn't know why she acted the way she had, couldn't fathom why, but those actions settled his mind far more than anything else might have. He died. Despite being alive again, his marriage with Emily was over and had been over for thirteen years. As he came out of his thoughts, Gavin realized Jennifer and his parents regarded him with soft smiles.

"What?" he asked.

"You never looked at Emily like that," Elizabeth said.

Gavin blinked. "I didn't? Not even when we first got married?"

"No, not even then," Richard answered.

"Who is this Emily?" Kiri asked.

Gavin turned back to her. "Jennifer's mom."

LONG INTO THE NIGHT, they talked, swapping stories and experiences. They only stopped long enough to eat and went right back to it. There was no way for Gavin to describe or communicate what the last two years had been like for him, but he tried. It was past midnight before everyone agreed it was time for sleep, but it was apparent no one wanted to stop catching up with each other.

# CHAPTER 8

The next morning, everyone gathered in the dining room for breakfast. No one really talked beyond superficial questions, like how well each person had slept. The morning came far too soon for any meaningful conversation to happen before food.

A breakfast of Elizabeth's fried eggs complete and the dishes cleared, everyone returned to the dining room table.

"So, what's on your agenda for today?" Richard asked.

"Well... I'm going to need a place to work on my research," Gavin said. "I need to find a way back to the world I came from."

Both of Gavin's parents blinked. His mom spoke. "But we thought... well, I thought... why do you have to leave?"

"I have responsibilities back there," Gavin said. "Like I said last night, I am the Archmagister of Tel and Head of House Kirloth. There's stuff that's probably not getting done because I'm here and not there. Besides, Kiri's important to her country, too."

"She... uhm... told us," Jennifer said. "Kind of."

Gavin looked to Kiri, his expression betraying surprise. "You did?"

Kiri shrugged. "It seemed the thing to do at the time."

"You said you needed a place for your research," Richard said, refocusing the conversation. "What did you have in mind?"

"I'd like to build back at the lake... on that rocky shelf if you don't mind. It's far enough away that any mishaps won't affect you, and besides, I'd forgotten how much I love it back there. I always wanted to build a cabin out there anyway."

"Do you know how long the research will take?" Elizabeth asked.

Gavin shook his head. "There's no way to tell. I could get a lucky break in two weeks, or it may take me two years. As far as starting, however, there's no time like the present. Would you like to watch me build?"

"Watch you?" Elizabeth asked.

Richard frowned. "Don't you want to hire a crew? It's an awful lot for just one man."

Gavin grinned. "What I want will be ready for furniture inside of two hours, I think."

Both Richard and Elizabeth shared a look before turning back to Gavin. Richard shared his son's grin. "Sure. Let's go!"

Once everyone was ready, Gavin opened the door and led the way outside. They reached the end of the short, paved walk as a black Suburban rolled to a stop in the driveway. Three people—two men and one woman—exited the vehicle. A raised eyebrow was the only indication of Gavin's surprise at seeing Jason White in the group, and Gavin allowed his father to lead, sliding in behind him.

Jason led his associates up to the white picket fence and produced a folded document.

"Jennifer Anne Cross, I have a warrant for your arrest."

Richard stepped forward, saying, "Let me see that." Jason handed him the document, and he read through it. "Hmmm... it seems legitimate."

"What are the charges?" Jennifer asked.

"I have a suspicion what they are," Gavin said, stepping into clear view.

Jason gaped. "G-G-Gavin? But... but..."

"You're starting to sound like a motorboat, Jason," Gavin

remarked, his expression cold. "I'm rather surprised to see you here serving this warrant."

Jason stiffened. "I'm the local Special Agent liaising with the task force."

"I can't believe you didn't recuse yourself. After all, you were Jennifer's stepfather for a time," Gavin enjoyed watching the other two agents stiffen, "and you were seeing my wife—Jennifer's mother—*before* she was a widow. Not to mention that my parents took you and Emily to court for custody of Jennifer... and won. That sounds like nine kinds of conflict of interest, but what do I know? I've been dead thirteen years."

Jason glared at Gavin. "You have no proof."

"The fact that there was a court case should be public record," Gavin replied, "and possibly even subject to subpoena. If you mean I have no proof that you and my wife were screwing, you're still wrong. Dad, do you still have that file folder I asked you to keep for me?"

"Yes, I do, Son. I could never bring myself to open it, so I don't know what's in it."

"It's all the evidence I collected that Emily was having an affair, including photos of her and Jason at the beach when she was supposed to be attending an academic conference on the other side of the country."

Jason's associates looked at him somewhat askance. Jason didn't notice; he still glared at Gavin and his father. "None of that changes the fact that this is a valid warrant. We're taking her in."

Gavin shook his head. "Dad, how's Graham Lake right now? Have you been getting a lot of rain?"

"You seriously think you're going to kill us with all these witnesses?" Jason hissed, his associates moving their hands toward their jackets while scanning everyone.

"Rain's been about average, I'd say," Richard replied. "Not too dry, but not too wet either. The lake is actually a little higher than normal for this time of year."

Gavin made eye contact with the two associates. "Can you two swim?"

The agents flinched, almost like they'd been slapped.

"Swim? What does that—" the man began.

"Yes," the woman replied, cutting off her associate. "We both swim."

"Good," Gavin remarked and shifted his attention to Jason. "Jason, you're not leaving here with my daughter. I don't care if you have a signed writ from God. I would prefer the lot of you leave of your own accord, but I promise you'll be leaving either way."

Jason outright *snarled*. "I don't have to stand here and listen to this. It sounds to me like you're interfering in a federal investigation. That's actionable right there."

"So be it," Gavin said. "Just remember. I gave you the choice."

His intent clear in his mind, Gavin invoked a Word of Transmutation, "*Paedryx*."

Jason White, his two associates, and their Suburban vanished.

His parents gaped, still not used to workings of the Art.

Kiri grasped Gavin's shoulder and forced him to face her. "Gavin, what did you do?"

He shrugged. "I told them they'd be leaving, Kiri. You know me. I keep my promises."

* * *

JED WALKER SAT in his bass boat on Graham Lake. He was easily a half-mile from shore. Since his retirement, he'd been coming to Graham Lake almost every day the weather was decent. He hardly caught anything, and what he did catch, he threw back. All he wanted was to sit in his boat on the water, fishing rod in one hand and thermos of coffee in the other.

A crackling pop off to his right drew Jed's attention, and he turned in time to see a black Suburban and three people in suits fall about five feet to land in the water. While most of his mind couldn't believe he'd seen a Suburban appear out of nowhere, another part of his mind noted that they were right over the deepest stretch of the lake – fifty feet deep, even during a drought.

*Well, damn... so much for fishing. The undertow from that SUV might drown 'em*, Jed thought as he tossed his rod down and moved to the outboard. He was just glad he'd put rope in the boat today in case he wanted to tie up anywhere. He normally floated with the currents of the lake.

It didn't take long for his outboard to putt-putt-putt its way over to the swirling water, and he shut off the motor to coast as he neared the site. A woman came up for air first.

"Here, Miss," Jed said, throwing the rope over the side. "Grab on."

It took some careful maneuvering, but she was soon in the boat.

"Thank you," she said, wrapping her arms around her torso as a slight breeze chilled her.

"I feel like I should ask how you came to fall into the middle of the lake out of a clear, blue sky," Jed remarked, at the same time a suited man broke the surface of the lake. As he tossed the rope back over the side, Jed saw his newest 'catch' had an arm around another man. Getting a better look at the second man, Jed couldn't keep from frowning at the sight of Jason White. That man had a reputation around town.

"It's a long story, sir," the woman said, shivering in the breeze again. "I'm not sure you'd believe me if I told you."

# CHAPTER 9

"Jack Webster for you, ma'am," Jenna said, leaning halfway into the suite.

Chelsea shifted her focus from the sheaf of papers in her hand, looking at Jenna over the top of her half-moon reading glasses. "Send him in, please."

Jenna nodded, backing out of the door. Jack Webster entered. Chelsea saw at once that something was wrong.

"What's wrong, Jack?" Chelsea asked. She gestured to the available seating as she put aside her papers.

"I wasn't fast enough," Jack said. "Or maybe the chain of command wasn't fast enough. Either way, a team of three agents from the local office attempted to serve an arrest warrant on Jennifer Cross while we talked or shortly after."

As much as she wanted to ask about the agents—because Jack said 'attempted'—Chelsea couldn't get her mind past the question of whether those idiots had cost her the life of her daughter. Would this Gavin Cross fellow even give her the time of day now? And if he could help Alexis, would he? If he did, what would his price be? Chelsea knew she'd pay it, whatever the cost... even if it were something a president probably shouldn't do. She'd been a mother long before she was President Hall or even Governor Hall; as much as she loved her job and country, she loved her daughter more.

Chelsea closed her eyes and took a deep breath. She fought the urge to sigh and wasn't wholly successful. "Okay, Jack... give me the short version."

"The lead agent—Jason White—turned out to be Jennifer Cross's former stepfather. I say former, because shortly after Jennifer ran away from home, Gavin Cross's parents took the girl's biological mother and her new husband, Jason White, to court for custody of Jennifer and won. The agent failed to disclose this and recuse himself from liaising with the task force and is now on suspension pending an inquiry. Your man from the hostage crisis was there and, after asking the agents to leave—which of course they refused, he somehow teleported them and their Suburban to the middle of Graham Lake. Well, about five feet above the middle, according to the local retiree who fished two of the agents out of the water and pulled Special Agent White ashore with the bass boat's tow rope.

"And come to find out, Special Agent White apparently has already made a name for himself, having had an affair with Gavin Cross's wife before she was his widow. Every local outfit with the equipment to get the Suburban out of the lake either refuses to talk to the FBI or won't 'be available' for at least four months, if even then. It seems the Cross family are something like local celebrities, and neither Special Agent White nor his wife and family are well-regarded. The Special Agent in Charge of the local office will probably have to call the Army Corps of Engineers if she's going to get her Suburban back before it's ruined past any hope of repair. She is *not happy*, ma'am."

"Is the Cross family putting pressure on these local businesses?" Chelsea asked.

Jack shook his head. "Not that we can tell. Did you know they own the whole town and considerable land around the town?"

"Yes."

"Well," Jack continued, "I found this out by chatting with the concierge downstairs. They do a nose-count of tenants every December, then divide the property taxes by the count, and that result is everyone's rent for the coming year. That's why there isn't a big chain store within two hours' drive. Nobody wants them messing up the local economy. He told me the family even pays—out of their own pocket—to maintain and upgrade all the telecommunication infrastructure in the area."

Chelsea shook her head. "Where do they get the money? Has anyone ever looked into them?"

Jack shrugged. "I don't know. Do you want me to put some people on it? Maybe reach out to the IRS?"

Chelsea turned the matter over in her mind. On one side, she didn't want to do *anything* that might anger Gavin Cross until she knew whether he could help Alexis. But... she also didn't want to be getting involved with a family that had skeletons in their closet. Oh, most families had one or two, but Chelsea needed to know whether the Cross family's skeletons were more 'average American' in nature or something approaching those of a cartel or mob family.

"Yes, please," Chelsea said at last, not quite hiding a sigh.

"If I'm crossing a line, ma'am, please tell me, but what is so important or special about this family?"

"You know about my daughter's medical condition, yes? The condition that the best doctors in the country have not been able to explain or cure?"

Jack nodded.

"I think Gavin Cross—the man from the hostage crisis—might be able to help Alexis."

Chelsea watched Jack's eyes widen a little before returning to normal, and he asked, "If he told you he could save your daughter and all it would cost was pardoning his own, would you do it?"

"Without a second thought. I know I shouldn't. I know he shouldn't even ask that, but if he asked it and it was within my power when he asked, I'd order that pardon and sign it without a second thought. Alexis is my little girl, Jack. Are you telling me you'd do any different if one of your children was at stake?"

Jack took a deep breath and released it as a sigh, running his hand down over his face. "No, ma'am, I probably wouldn't, and God help me for meaning it. If he was the *only* hope my child had versus an agonizing, cruel death and if he could guarantee me my child would be okay? I can't say I wouldn't sign that pardon. I know I shouldn't, just like you, but I can't say I wouldn't."

Silence settled in the room as Chelsea delved into her thoughts, and Jack let her. Finally, she returned her focus to him.

"This is wrong, but I'm going to do it," Chelsea said. "I'm taking Alexis, and we're going to visit him. Minimal protection, because a gun isn't going to stop someone who can teleport a Suburban to Graham Lake. How far is that from the Cross Estate, anyway?"

Jack shrugged. "Over land? Five—maybe ten—miles from the edge of their property, anyway. I imagine it's longer in driving miles, as there seem to be no straight roads around here."

Chelsea nodded and picked up her phone. She tapped out a quick message to Jenna and returned the device to the end table. Moments later, there were two knocks on the suite door, followed by Tim stepping inside.

"You asked for me, ma'am?"

"Yes, thank you, Tim. I want to visit Gavin Cross at his family's estate, and I want to take Alexis with me. I'm thinking minimal protection, because quite frankly, he teleported three FBI agents and their Suburban to the middle of Graham Lake earlier today. There isn't much Secret Service can do to protect me from him."

Tim closed his eyes for a moment. "If that's the case, ma'am, it's an excellent reason to keep you away from him. As far away as possible. But, I know why you want to visit him, and if we don't go, you'll find a way out there regardless, won't you?"

Chelsea beamed. "You know me so well, Tim."

* * *

GAVIN, his family, and Kiri stood at the shore of the lake on the Cross Estate. They looked across it to a rocky promontory jutting up out of the ground some thirty feet from the water's surface. The formation made a solid rock cliff that became a ridge line, extending for quite some distance away from the lake before it tapered to the point one could climb it.

"You're going to build there?" Richard asked.

Gavin answered by nodding. "You guys might want to grab a seat on one of these benches. I can't promise there won't be a disturbance. Jennifer... this will probably hurt, and unfortunately, it will only stop hurting after a certain amount of practice."

Jennifer nodded and moved to a bench of her own as Gavin's parents and Kiri each found a seat.

Clearing his mind and focusing on his intent was second nature to Gavin now, and it took little effort at all to prepare for the invocation he was about to make. "*Rhyskaal.*"

The resonance of Gavin's power slammed into Jennifer, and she fought with all her might to keep from screaming. At first, nothing seemed to happen, but the ripples that soon disturbed the lake's surface put the lie to that. The ground shook and rumbled, and the ridge extending away from the lake started to shrink, even as solid stone began rising out of the promontory.

It seemed to take ages, but once everything quieted, a plateau no more than one hundred yards on a side remained. The promontory's new construction resembled a square, stone keep with crenellated battlements. The keep had no windows or doors—yet—but the general structure was plain to see.

"*Rhyskaal.*"

Again, Gavin's power struck like a massive concussion, forcing reality to alter itself to meet Gavin's will. An arched doorway formed in the center of the keep's wall that faced the grassy plateau. Arched windows also appeared at set intervals all up and down the keep.

"*Sykhurhos-Gozdrahk-Zyrhaek.*"

Jennifer gave up all pretense of fighting the pain Gavin's invocations inflicted on her. With this composite effect, she rolled off the bench to her knees and violently retched. Kiri stood within arms' reach off her left shoulder and leaned forward to hold Jennifer's hair out of the way.

The keep seemed to take on a shimmering aura for a mere heartbeat, almost as if it winked at those watching. Then, flickering lights shone through the open windows of the keep.

"All right," Gavin said. "It should be ready to be made livable. Don't worry; I'm not going to conjure furniture or anything like that, but we will need money."

"Son, you know..."

"I appreciate that, Dad," Gavin replied, "but I'd rather not put any undue burden on you and Mom. You guys saw me all the way through college, and I figure that was enough. Besides, I'm not without options. Does the local bank still buy gold ingots?"

Richard scoffed. "The family is still the majority shareholder. They'll buy ingots from you."

Gavin turned toward his daughter. "Sorry, Jenny. One more."

Scooping up five stones that were each around one pound, Gavin held them in his hands. "*Rhyskaal.*"

Jennifer screamed. Richard, Elizabeth, and Kiri were able to watch the stones become gold ingots. It was gradual, but within a minute, Gavin held five pounds of gold.

"I'd say this ought to furnish the place rather nicely," Gavin remarked as his parents gaped.

"Don't let too many people know you can do that, Gavin," Richard said, his voice still carrying traces of awe. "You'll crash the market."

Gavin scoffed. "It's not like the Feds haven't been printing money for decades anyway, and I'm going to need funds."

"How pure is that?" Elizabeth asked.

"At least 24 karats, Mom."

"All the way through?"

Gavin nodded. "All the way through."

"Hmmm," Richard vocalized, frowning. "Gavin, you may want to have me sell the ingots, and I can give you the money. There have been a lot of changes to the banking laws, and I doubt the bank will allow you to open an account without identification and several other pieces of information that are no longer valid for you."

Gavin grimaced. "Ugh. I completely forgot about that. Yeah... if you don't mind doing that for me, Dad, I'd really appreciate it. I don't want to go through all the hassle of restoring all my identification and everything when I'm not going to be staying long-term."

"Will... will it always hurt this much?" Jennifer asked.

"No, Sweetheart," Gavin replied. He started to pull Jennifer into his arms, hold her like he remembered holding her when she was little, but he stopped. Those days were past. Should he even try to hug her? "After you've used the power a bit, your body builds up a tolerance to the pain. The more you do, the less debilitating the pain is. That's actually one of the dangers. You won't realize how close you are to burning yourself out or killing yourself."

# CHAPTER 10

"Stop the car!" Alexis shouted. The pain was intense, hitting her out of nowhere. Zero warning at all. She wrapped her arms across her midriff.

Everyone but the driver turned to her. Her mother spoke.

"Alexis, what's wrong?"

She couldn't hold it if she kept talking, but she had to get them to stop. "Stop the damn car!"

They still stared at her, so she grabbed the door handle and jerked it. Damned child safety locks. But the power window worked. Once it was down, she pushed the upper half of her torso outside before she stopped fighting. She even made sure to turn her head away from the front of the car. Thank goodness for really short hair. Throwing up was never fun, but it absolutely was not fun at sixty miles per hour cruising down a country highway. At least the vomit complimented the yellow lines well.

The car angled off the highway, and the rough berm bounced her between the upper and lower window frames like a ping-pong ball. *Oh,* now *they stop the car?*

Alexis pulled herself back inside, not really paying attention to what her mother and the agents were saying. The door locks popped, and she almost jumped outside. Not about to lean against the side of the car now sporting an aftermarket decoration, Alexis walked around to the passenger side. She'd just passed the passenger taillight when another concussion struck her. Her knees buckled, but she caught herself on the side of the car. She leaned against the passenger rear quarter panel, rested both hands on her knees and waited to see if she was going to hurl again.

"Are you okay, honey?" her mom asked, as she rubbed Alexis's back.

Alexis shrugged. "I don't know. I think so. How close are we to the Cross place?"

"Not even halfway yet... maybe fifteen miles just to reach the driveway," Tim said, arriving at her mother's side. "Why?"

"Holy smokes... he must be crazy powerful for me to feel *that* so far away."

"Alexis, I don't understand."

Alexis could hear the worry in her mother's voice, and she tried to smile, even though she still faced the dirt.

"That guy... the guy from the hostage crisis... he just did *something*. I don't know what, but it hit me worse than everything he did at the student union combined." Her body seemed to be settling down, so Alexis righted herself, standing beside her mom. She couldn't keep from making eye contact with Tim, almost glaring at him. "When I say stop the car, stop the damn car... or you'll be cleaning up the puke. There's already some down the left side you can get later."

* * *

Gavin, his family, and Kiri were just approaching the backyard when they heard tires crunching the gravel of the driveway. Gavin glared.

"I'm going to run out of patience with Jason eventually," he remarked. "He'd better get the message."

Gavin set the five one-pound gold ingots on the back deck and stretched his neck and shoulders. He led everyone else around the side of the house, already drawing power from the ambient. He wasn't sure where he'd drop Jason this time, but it definitely wasn't going to be Graham Lake.

But Jason White didn't step out of the Suburban. As a matter of fact, the only person in the group Gavin recognized was the woman who'd taken charge of the presentation hall after the hostage crisis. Hearing his parents gasp behind him, Gavin guessed the seal on the podium had been for her. He released the power he'd been drawing, thinking a President of the United States wouldn't come in person to start trouble, especially so light on Secret Service agents as she appeared to be. Not that an entire regiment of Secret Service would stop him if he were hostile. Bullets don't travel at the speed of thought.

"Good afternoon," she said, as a young woman stepped around the car to stand beside her. "I'm Chelsea Hall, and this is my daughter Alexis."

Gavin nodded. "I'm Gavin Cross. These are my parents, Richard and Elizabeth; my daughter, Jennifer; and Kiri. I'm guessing the seal on that podium the other day was for you."

Chelsea's mouth curled in a faint smile. "Yes, I'm a little over four months into my first term. I think your parents recognized me."

"Recognized you?" Richard said. "We voted for you."

A faint blush darkened Chelsea's cheeks. "Thank you for that." Chelsea focused on Gavin once more. "Mister Cross, I apologize for arriving unannounced, but do you have a few minutes to talk?"

Gavin could've played hardball. In fact, a part of him wanted to do just that... call her out on Jason White bringing a warrant to their doorstep. But he remembered the *two* screams in the presentation hall, and there was no denying his *skathos*. The President's daughter was a wizard. Yes, he could've played hardball, but Alexis was someone's daughter. No parent wanted to watch a child die. Especially the slow, agonizing death of a *skathos* cascade.

He eyed Alexis. "How long ago did the pain start?"

Alexis blinked. She glanced at her mother for a moment before bringing her eyes back to Gavin. "About two months ago now, maybe two and a half."

"Hmmm," Gavin vocalized. "We don't have much time. Come, sit with me."

He led Alexis over to the lawn furniture.

"Okay," Gavin said. "I want you to close your eyes and concentrate on your senses, specifically the new sense you developed over the past two months."

Alexis closed her eyes. For a few moments, she remained silent. Then, she spoke. "You're bright, like super-bright and yellow or gold like the sun. You make my nerves feel all fizzy. There are ripples still expanding out from behind me. I thought you did something a little while ago, because every nerve in my body went crazy and I threw up, but now that I'm here, I can feel the ripples of it. You made something? Changed something? I can't really tell."

Gavin smiled. "You're doing well, Alexis. Now... I want you to focus on yourself. Concentrate on the fizzing feeling and follow it to its source. Tell me what you feel."

After a few more moments of silence, Alexis said, "Oh, wow. There's a... it's like a peach pit of fizzy but bigger. It feels like it's at the core of me."

"Excellent, Alexis," Gavin replied. "You're doing just fine. I want you to concentrate on that peach pit. Try drawing it out of you and holding it in one of your hands."

Over the next few minutes, Alexis made her own seething orb of kaleidoscopic power. Her mother and everyone who had come with her gaped at the sight.

"That's good, Alexis," Gavin said, his voice calm and steady. "Try to pull the peach pit back into you now. Once it feels like it's almost 'home,' release it. It should snap back on its own."

The orb above Alexis's left palm gradually faded until it winked out of existence like it had never been. Sweat soaked Alexis from head to toe, but when she opened her eyes, she beamed.

"This is so amazing! This is the first time in two months I feel at peace. Thank you."

Gavin shrugged. "You're welcome, but that's just a stopgap. A Band-Aid, I guess you could say. If you want to ensure your power is no threat to you, you'll need at least rudimentary training."

"Couldn't she just do that every couple of months?" Chelsea asked, waving her hand toward Alexis. The gesture carried a nebulous, unspecific quality to it that struck Gavin as being at odds with her status as President of the United States.

"No," Gavin answered. "You might think that, but eventually, her power will cascade through it. And *that* cascade will be anywhere from ten to fifty times worse than it otherwise would've been. The only case where your daughter lives is if she learns to control and master her power. Make it as much a part of her as her sight or hearing."

Chelsea nodded. "And what is your fee for training her?"

Gavin chuckled. "That's not really how it works. If Alexis wants training, I will accept her as my apprentice. We'll need to determine her House and its associated glyph at some point, and I will pay her a living stipend while she's my apprentice."

"What of her Secret Service detail?" a man asked, stepping up to Chelsea's side. He had copper hair and a short, stocky build.

"And you are?"

"Timothy Gardner," the fireplug of a man answered. "I'm in charge of both the President's and her daughter's protection details."

Gavin considered the matter. "I have certain plans for our property here that will require—at most—five days to implement. Once that's complete, she'll be safer here than anywhere else in the world. Besides, I doubt any of your men will want to risk experiencing life as a frog if her concentration slips."

The Secret Service agents within earshot either paled or grinned.

"You're telling me that's really a thing?" Tim asked.

Gavin shrugged. "I've read authenticated accounts of an arcanist spending several months with his nose upside-down after a mishap, so being turned into a frog is certainly doable."

None of the other agents grinned now.

"Did you really teleport three FBI agents and their Suburban to the middle of Graham Lake?" Tim asked.

The right side of Gavin's mouth curled upward; the expression wasn't *quite* hostile. "Yes, I did, and if they didn't get the message, I won't be so nice next time."

Chelsea stepped between them, facing Gavin. "I've been informed that Jason White has been suspended, pending an inquiry, for not disclosing his relationship to Jennifer and recusing himself."

"Very well," Gavin replied, nodding once. "Alexis, the choice is yours. Do you wish to learn to wield the Art?"

"I'll die if I don't, right?" Alexis asked.

"Yes."

Alexis stood and squared her shoulders. "Then, I don't really see that I have much choice. I want to live."

Gavin's immediate reaction to Alexis's pragmatic response to his question was uncertainty. Part of him wanted her to be overjoyed at learning to master what she'd discovered, but then, a memory floated to the surface. A memory of just how much of a choice Marcus gave him, which is to say *none at all*. Besides, if he refused to train Alexis, how would her eventual death affect his goal of ending the federal government's harassment of Jennifer? He had an opportunity here to secure the President as a favorable party—if not an ally. Considering everything, there was only one option.

"By the authority granted in Article 23 of the Arcanists' Code and before these witnesses, I—Gavin Cross of House Kirloth—take Alexis Hall as my apprentice, as was in the old ways. I imagine you'll want to pack some clothes. You'll have a room at the keep here; the keep is what you felt me creating. We'll begin in one week."

"One week?" Chelsea asked. "To give you time to fortify this place?"

Gavin chuckled. "I wouldn't say 'fortify'. That creates images of weapons emplacements and roving sentries. No. What I have in mind will be far more subtle and far more effective." He shifted his focus to Alexis. "The first thing we'll do when you return is visit the local furniture store to outfit your room as you see fit; don't worry about bringing money. A furnished room, board, and the stipend are all part of the apprenticeship."

Chelsea looked at Gavin, almost stared at him. She finally asked, "You could've held my daughter over my head, used her as leverage to get me to intervene with you and the FBI. Why didn't you?"

"If someone threatened my daughter, I would burn this world to ash if that's what it took to make her safe... no regrets and no hesitation," Gavin replied. "Besides, children aren't leverage, even if they're legally adults. I would never use a child's life as a bargaining chip."

Chelsea nodded, saying, "Thank you. Some people would not feel the same, I fear."

Gavin shrugged. "Then they'd better be sure I never learn of them acting on their feelings."

The subtle changes in everyone's posture told Gavin they hadn't missed his statement for what it was.

"Well, thank you for your time today," Chelsea said as Alexis returned to her side. "May I drop Alexis off next week?"

"Of course," Gavin answered. "Just don't bring anyone who intends us harm. They won't make it past the gate."

Chelsea nodded as she led Alexis and the rest of her people back to the two vehicles. They loaded up, turned around and disappeared down the driveway.

"You really plan to get into a standoff with the FBI, son?" Richard asked.

"I don't trust Jason White, Dad. Beyond that, the only way my daughter will ever see the inside of a prison is over my dead body, and I guarantee you they won't have enough people left to bury *their* dead if it comes to that."

Richard and Elizabeth shared a look. Elizabeth asked, "You really have that kind of power?"

Gavin nodded. "Yes, I do, and now that I have my full memories—specifically high school and college chemistry and physics—I'm exponentially more dangerous than I ever was."

Kiri paled. "Seriously, Gavin? You're *more* dangerous here?"

"When we get back from town, remind me to explain strong and weak nuclear forces."

# CHAPTER 11

Silence reigned during the departure from the Cross Estate and for several miles thereafter. Eventually, though, Tim turned around in the passenger seat to look back at the other passengers.

"Was anyone else terrified by how casually he discussed burning the world to ash?" he asked. "I mean, did you look at his eyes? He wasn't bluffing, folks; he believes he can do it."

"I have a hard time believing any one person has that kind of power," Jack Webster said from his seat in the third-row. He'd masqueraded as a regular Secret Service agent during their visit to the Cross Estate. "Sure, he can do some impressive things, but burn a whole world to ash? Come on, Tim."

Tim shook his head. "No, Jack. You were standing over by the vehicles. You didn't see his eyes. Ma'am, can you break the tie here?"

Chelsea's expression quirked toward a smile. "I don't know, Tim. I just don't know. I did see his eyes, though, and I'll give you that much. If he was bluffing, we should set him loose in Vegas. He'd clean up."

"If you're right, ma'am," Jack said, "is it really safe to leave Alexis with him when she goes back for training?"

"I think so," Chelsea answered. "He wasn't bluffing about not using her for leverage, either. He'll train her in what she needs to know to keep from dying, and he won't use her as part of it. I'm just afraid Alexis will get caught in the crossfire between him and the task force."

Jack responded, "No, ma'am, I can't see that. If he truly won't use her as leverage and sees her as his charge or ward during the apprenticeship, he won't *let* her be caught in the crossfire. He'll do everything in his power to ensure her safety, while he's confronting the task force."

"Will you listen to us?" Tim scoffed. "You'd think this guy would remember that old saying about not fighting city hall, and the federal government has way more to bring to bear than any city hall."

"You're correct, Tim," Chelsea agreed. "My only concern is how much *he* has to bring to bear."

* * *

THE SHOPPING TRIP to town was a success. Richard sold the ingots at the bank and withdrew a tidy sum, which he handed to Gavin. There were a few odd looks as Gavin walked with his parents through the bank's lobby, but no one said anything... out in the open anyway. The trip to the furniture store was even easier. Gavin asked Kiri and Jennifer to help him furnish the keep, especially choosing furniture for their bedrooms. He arranged for a series of deliveries to bring everything out to the house that very day, and it was finally time to return home.

Gavin was a few steps behind his parents on the way out of the furniture store when a familiar voice accosted his father.

"Richard Cross, I thought I'd seen everything, but this is a new low... even for you."

Gavin froze mid-step, his expression betraying his shock.

"What is it, Gavin?" Kiri asked.

Jennifer didn't say a word; her expression just shifted into a glare.

"I know that voice," Gavin answered. "It's Emily, Jennifer's mom."

He took a deep breath and led the two ladies out of the furniture store, almost afraid at what he would see. What he found didn't really surprise him, not after hearing Emily's voice loud enough to carry through the open entry of the furniture store. Emily White stood maybe three feet away from his parents, Jason White behind her. She gestured with her arm in time with her tirade, her extended index finger jabbing her points home.

"Emily, sweetheart, don't do this... please? It won't end well," Jason said as he tried to get her to walk away, but Emily was having none of it.

"Frankly, I can't believe you had the nerve. I mean, sure... arrange for Jason and his team to get dunked in the lake; I can kind of see that. But make someone up to look like your dead son? That's not just low. It's sick."

Gavin stepped into view to stand beside his mother. "Hello, Emily."

"Really? You even..." Emily's voice trailed off as she truly looked at Gavin.

For perhaps a minute, the scene was a frozen tableau. Gavin knew it couldn't last, but he wasn't sure how Emily would react. She would either spike back into anger or... there she goes.

At the same time most of the color drained out of her complexion, Emily's eyes rolled back in her head, and her knees buckled. Jason didn't see it coming, and he was out of position to stop her from cracking her head against the concrete sidewalk. In two fast strides, Gavin moved close enough to catch her by her shoulders.

"Sorry," Gavin said as he handed her off to Jason. "I'm not one to touch another man's wife, but I didn't want her to hurt herself when she hit the sidewalk, either."

Jason accepted Gavin's jab for what it was; after all, he had done more than touch another man's wife. His and Emily's first child was born six months after Gavin's death.

After watching Jason carry Emily back to their car, Gavin scanned the surrounding storefronts. He smiled at the camera pointing toward them on the opposite side of the furniture store's entrance. It would've recorded everything. A quick word with the manager, and

Gavin returned to the others with three copies of the encounter on DVD.

* * *

THE STONE KEEP atop the rocky promontory was fifty feet on a side, giving each floor twenty-five-hundred square feet. Not all of that was usable; the staircase and internal walls took up some of it. Still, the place was rather roomy.

Jennifer watched her father walk through the arched door to enter the keep. Her grandparents followed. None of them reacted, so she wasn't prepared for the fizzing tendrils of static washing over her as she crossed the threshold. She shivered and shook herself.

"You okay?" Kiri asked, attracting the others' attention.

Jennifer nodded. "I'm good. It just felt weird walking through the door."

Gavin smiled. "That's what it feels like to step through a ward that you successfully pass."

"What does it feel like if you fail?"

His smile fell away. "My wards? The person will be shocked unconscious, much like a stun gun on steroids, but that's because I don't want to cause any lasting harm. I could've keyed the wards to kill all who fail the check or anything in between. First lesson: the effect is shaped by the invoker's intent. My mentor called it the one essential truth."

"So, if you can envision it happening, you can make it happen?" Jennifer asked.

"Within limits. The human body can only handle so much raw force of creation running through it. If the change you try to effect on reality is more than you can safely power, there will be consequences. Unconsciousness, perhaps burning yourself out to the point of no longer being a wizard, and possibly even death. I was unconscious for something like three to five days after my first invocation."

Jennifer felt herself gape, but she couldn't stop it. "What did you do?"

An expression she didn't fully recognize crossed her father's face. "I used a Word of Interation to save Kiri and myself, but because I didn't understand what I was doing, I killed fifty-three people across a small section of the city, instead of just those confronting us."

Jennifer's eyes shot wide. When she spoke, her voice was soft, little more than a whisper. "Oh."

THE REST of the day involved placing furniture throughout the keep. For each person's bedroom, Gavin created a scrying sphere over their furniture in the front lawn of the house and then teleported the pieces into the room first before using telekinesis to put them in the desired locations. They furnished the entire keep in a fraction of the time a professional moving or delivery service would have needed.

Richard and Gavin stood in the dining room while Elizabeth, Jennifer, and Kiri discussed curtains and other window treatments elsewhere in the keep. Richard stared at the dining set, shaking his head. "I don't know if I'll ever get used to the world you now live in, son. What you do simply boggles the mind."

Gavin grinned. "It is a bit unbelievable. I'll grant you that. To be honest, I was a bit surprised at how much I have to work with here."

"What do you mean?"

"Well," Gavin began, frowning, "back in Drakmoor, I can do some fairly impressive things, but after a certain point, I just know it will drain me. I have to pull so much from such a wide area to do the really impressive stuff that it's like dragging ten water-logged comforters. For instance, if I had tried raising this keep back there, it would've been maybe a third of my capacity. Here? Yeah, it hurt, but it wasn't really a thing. I feel like I could create fifteen or twenty of these keeps without really taxing myself. That's honestly one of the things I want to research, besides finding a way back. I want to know *why* the ambient magic here feels so much... more."

After a few heartbeats' silence, Richard asked, "So, you really weren't joking about turning this world to ash if that's what it took to save Jennifer?"

Gavin shook his head. "No, Dad, I wasn't. With as much ambient magic as I feel around here, plus what I know from a basic high school education, I could probably reduce someplace the size of Richmond or Cincinnati to ruins."

"I'm not sure I can even picture that. I'm not sure one person should have so much power."

"I'm not, either, Dad... but people do. That means someone has to stand watch against them using what they were born with for evil. All other things being equal, I'd be happy if I never knew half of what I know or done even a quarter of what I've done. But it needed to be done, and no one else was doing it."

Richard turned to face his son. "That's what it means to be Kirloth?"

Gavin flinched, then chuckled. "Kiri told you that, did she?"

"She didn't tell us everything... didn't tell us anything, really. She did tell us that."

Sorrow tinged Gavin's half-smile. "I didn't see it at first. Marcus—my mentor in the Art—tried to tell me, but I didn't listen. Good people fear evil. Evil people? They fear Kirloth."

"And you're Kirloth."

"When I have to be, Dad," Gavin replied. "Part of me wants to say Bellos may have messed up by naming me Archmagister. I mean, Marcus always worked behind the scenes, stepping into view usually at the right time to eradicate something or someone. I can't be behind the scenes if I'm at the top of the pyramid. Everyone's watching. I suppose I can do what Marcus did after a few years and step aside for someone else. I don't know. There's still so much left to do."

"Would you trust anyone else to do it?" Richard asked.

Gavin's expression became something between a grimace and a frown. "No... I probably wouldn't. The decisions that will have to be made over the next few years I wouldn't wish on an enemy, let alone one of my friends. It's better that I do it."

"Want to talk about it?"

Gavin shrugged. "We can, but I'm not sure you'd have any frame of reference. There's so much I'd have to explain for you to understand what's going on that we'd lose a lot of time just getting to the point where it became my responsibility."

"Try me. Pick one thing and tell me the crux of the issue in one sentence."

Gavin puffed out his cheeks as he exhaled, turning everything he knew about the state of Drakmoor around in his mind. "We have to re-take Skullkeep and eliminate the Necromancer. That's my first priority when I get back."

Richard nodded. "I imagine Skullkeep is a fortress of some type, and I want to assume the Necromancer controls it. But I could be assuming facts not in evidence."

"Oh, no. He controls it all right. A little over three hundred years ago, he marched a massive horde of undead into Hope's Pass and overwhelmed what few defenders remained."

"Are their years anything like our years?" Richard asked.

"I think they're shorter. Do you have your phone on you?"

Richard produced a smartphone inside a shock-resistant case. After unlocking it, he offered it to Gavin.

Gavin brought up the calculator app and started tapping. "Okay... so three hundred years over there is a little over two-hundred-forty-six years here. From your perspective, the Necromancer took Skullkeep sometime around 1783, but I don't know the precise year Skullkeep fell. Oh... remind me to have Jennifer show me the secret room she found in the house."

Richard blinked. "She found a hidden room in the house? Where?"

Gavin lifted his hands in an exaggerated shrug. "Don't ask me. I was in Drakmoor when she found it. In there, though, she stumbled across a Word of Power that she accidentally invoked... which is why I want to see it. I'm hoping there's something in there to help me in my research."

* * *

Nate Carruthers sighed as he leaned back against the passenger seat of the news van. It was a hot, muggy day. No clouds hung overhead that might have lessened the oppressive weight of the sun. Here he was—the most popular and highest-rated evening news anchor in the tri-state area—about to bake in the afternoon sun all because his producer wanted some 'action footage' of him on the scene interviewing the guy who'd pulled some FBI agents out of the lake.

He sighed again and shook his head, closing his eyes as he did so. The news report had to be a hoax this time. Three agents and their government-issued Suburban just do not appear out of nowhere to fall into a lake. That just doesn't happen.

"You okay over there, Nate?" the cameraman asked. Nate mentally winced. No, camera*person*. It was the twenty-first century, and he needed to get with the times. The person driving the van and operating the camera was Cara Weston, one of the most renowned people in her profession east of the Mississippi.

"Not really," Nate answered, almost a growl. "I didn't think evening news anchors did this 'on-the-scene' crap anymore. That's why I wanted the anchor slot so bad, so I'd have a nice comfy chair in an air-conditioned sound stage."

Cara chuckled. "And how's that working out for you?"

Nate grimaced, not even bothering to attempt hiding it. "It *was* working out rather well, until someone came along and started appearing places out of thin air. First, the hostage crisis at the university, and now, this. The way the internet is exploding, you'd almost think the world believes magic is real. What is the world coming to?"

Cara started to respond, but the breeze off the lake carried the sound of an outboard motor as it returned to shore. She opened the van's driver door, saying, "Come on. That has to be him."

Nate frowned as he hauled open the passenger door and felt the humidity settle around his shoulders like the storied albatross. "Fine, but let's do this in one take. Okay? I don't want to be out here any longer than necessary."

# CHAPTER 12

Gavin led Kiri and Jennifer into the lab that made up the top-most floor of the keep. It duplicated most of the contents of the lab Fallon had furnished for him in Vushaar, including the gold ring inset in the floor. The one item the keep's lab possessed that neither the Vushaar lab nor the Citadel's lab had were the massive, eight-feet-by-four-feet whiteboards. The dry erase markers and erasers already waited for him.

He picked up a black marker and smiled. "I didn't realize how much I missed these."

"Are we starting the training without Alexis?" Jennifer asked.

Gavin turned to face his daughter. "No… well, not really. Don't get me wrong; there are a few different things I will teach you that I have no intention of sharing with Alexis. Those lessons are for family alone. No, we're here today to work out the wards for the property. If you build them right, they are exponentially more effective than locks and cameras and various sensors. Why lock your doors or windows if people who mean you or the property harm cannot pass through the gate in the picket fence?"

Jennifer gaped. "You can really do that? I thought it was just… you know… story stuff."

"Oh, no. You can certainly do it, and I'll teach you how."

Gavin turned back to the whiteboard, but he hadn't raised the marker more than halfway when he turned back to Kiri, "Do you still have the ward stone Marcus made for you? Or the one I made for you while we were traveling to Vushaar?"

"Yes to both," Kiri answered, "but they're both back home. Besides, I didn't exactly come here with what was on my person."

"Fair point. We'll need to track down some of the weapon-smiths in this world to get you a proper set of blades. I can conjure whatever you need, but those are temporary at best."

Gavin moved to another section of the whiteboard. He drew a vertical line to separate it from the rest of the board and wrote 'To-Do' at the top. He then added the first item: Order Kiri blades. He went on to add the subitems: short swords, throwing knives, and daggers. He added a second item: Order Kiri high-quality leather armor.

"Okay, that's done, then," Gavin remarked, returning to the main section of the whiteboard.

Over the next couple of hours, he planned out the wards he wanted to craft for the property. The foundation was pretty basic... prevent entry to anyone who intended harm to the property's occupants or the property itself—including theft. He even designed the protection to be a rough rectangle, extending seventy-five feet into the ground and seventy-five feet into the air. In theory, someone who intended harm to the property could parachute out of a plane over the house and land on a 'surface' seventy-five feet above the ground. The nature of the ward wouldn't interfere with any trees that grew through it, either, essentially acting as if the trees didn't exist for the purposes of the protection.

From there, Gavin worked in a protection for the property occupants from weapons, poisons, fell magic, and magical diseases. It was a more complicated piece of warding than what most people did and, frankly, the protection from magic and magical diseases was laughable at the moment. Still, he'd rather have it and not need it, than need it and not have it.

Next, he designed the ability for the ward to summon elementals to defend the property. He'd never studied summoning to any great depth. Marcus's training focused almost exclusively on the one essential truth or illusions as a visualization exercise, and after that, there hadn't really been any purpose for Gavin to study summoning on his own. Those two points combined to make this section the only iffy aspect to the ward, especially since he included all four elements— air, earth, fire, and water.

Gavin stepped back from the whiteboard and rubbed his chin as he looked over the summoning part. It wouldn't be so bad if he had access to the College's library; if he could access the Citadel's library, it'd be a piece of cake. The more he considered the issue, he couldn't really bring himself to put an untested design into something intended to protect his family. The only thing to do was pull it from the design until he had the opportunity to study summoning. He retrieved an eraser from the tray and wiped away that section.

Only one thing remained: the anchor. He wasn't about to have the ward be like the dracons' original sky, so he took a page out of his mentor's book. Drawing in a Transmutation rune, Gavin made the note to anchor the ward to the family's bloodline. The ward would draw power from the ambient and 'work', as it were, only as long as a blood relative to House Kirloth held title to the property. Even someone who never developed their talent—like his father—would satisfy the condition.

Gavin put the cap back on the marker and returned it to the tray before stepping back to evaluate his work. It looked sound. Even more than sound, it looked viable. He wasn't going to just rush out and invoke the composite effect, though. He figured he'd given the FBI a sufficient black eye that he still had a day or two before they regrouped, which would allow him to sleep on the ward design for a night and be as sure as he could be that it had everything. It would be terrible to have to take down the ward and rebuild it if he missed something.

"All right, then," Gavin said, "I think that's it. I'm going to let it bake in the back of my mind for the night, and we'll work on setting the ward stones tomorrow. Hmmm... I need to ask Dad if he has any stone chisels." He turned to his daughter. "In the meantime, mind showing me the room you found?"

Jennifer shrugged. "Sure, I can do that, but you realize I don't understand any of that, right?" She pointed at the whiteboard behind her father.

"I know, Gavin said with a grin. "But you will."


A QUICK GATEWAY DELIVERED GAVIN, Jennifer, and Kiri to the walkway leading up to his parents' front door. Jennifer bounded up the steps and led them into the house. Kiri broke off from them to visit Gavin's parents. Gavin followed his daughter to the hallway connecting the front of the house to the back door and porch. The entire house had natural wood paneling, and Jennifer stopped at a section opposite the door to the basement, pressing two fingers against a knot in one of the panels. Gavin smiled as it slid into the wall until something audibly *clicked*. Then, a whole section of the wall swung inward on silent hinges.

"Oh, wait a second," Jennifer said, moving past her father toward the main areas of the house. "We'll need flashlights. It was never wired for electricity."

Gavin stepped into the hidden space, and the staircase illuminated. Gavin grinned at the Conjuration effect he now felt. Jennifer returned to the entrance and gaped.

"It's an embedded Conjuration effect," Gavin explained. "I'll bet it's keyed either to our family or a living person entering the space."

"Then, why didn't it do that with me?" Jennifer asked. "Am I not a member of the family?"

Gavin frowned. "Hmmm... I suppose they might have keyed it to wizard medallions, but that doesn't make any sense. I'd think whoever built this would want it lit for anyone."

Jennifer adopted her own frown. "So... who all has those medallions? Is it common for any members of the family to have them?"

"No, not really," Gavin said and broke off laughing. "Ah... now, it makes sense. If a person already knew of the existence of magic, as evidenced by the possession of a wizard's medallion, the place would light for them. If they didn't, it wouldn't. That's sneaky and rather creative. Let's see what's down here, shall we?"

Gavin proceeded down the steps that curved back under the house. At the foot of the stairs, he found a miniature library and reading room. One of the room's long walls had no bookshelves but a collection of carved bronze plaques about the size of modern business cards, spanning no more than a tenth of the wall. The Glyph of Kirloth in relief occupied a position at the top of the wall and centered along its length. Gavin moved straight to it and looked at the plaque in the top-left corner.

"What is it?" Jennifer asked. "I saw this when I was down here the first time, but I couldn't read over half of those."

Gavin pointed at the plaque, answering, "This is the common script in Drakmoor. This says, 'Gerrus', and gives the date of his birth and estimated date of his death. By the gods, Jennifer... this is our entire family line back to the Godswar."

Jennifer scanned the plaques and stopped at one, pointing to it. "This doesn't make any sense, Dad. This plaque says that Hiram Cross lived to be one-hundred-eighty-five. People don't live that long."

"Wizards do," Gavin countered. "We're not as long-lived as half-elves, but we live longer than base humans. I mean, does Grandpa look like he's in his... what... mid-sixties?"

Jennifer giggled. "No. He barely has any gray hair yet. If Grams didn't color her hair, people would swear she's his mom, instead of his wife. I always assumed he colored his, too."

Gavin turned and gave his daughter a disbelieving eyebrow. "*My* dad color his hair? Seriously? Describe that picture to me, please, because I'm just not seeing it."

"Yeah..." Jennifer said, giggling again. "That's not happening."

Gavin moved to the final plaque on the wall and smiled. "Did you see this?"

"What?" Jennifer asked as she moved over and crouched, then

gasped. "That's my name! How do I have a plaque on this wall? I thought Grandpa said he didn't know about this room."

Gavin lifted his hand to the wall and closed his eyes, concentrating on his *skathos*. Ah... there it was.

"This whole room has several low-level effects embedded throughout it. I'll bet this wall is tied to the direct family line, making a plaque each time a new heir is born. See? I have a plaque, too, and my original death date is scratched out."

Jennifer looked to the plaque above hers and shook her head. "That's just freaky. Wait a second... Jamison? Your middle name is Jamison?"

"Don't remind me. I've always hated it, but Mom loves the sound of 'Gavin Jamison Cross'. Never really understood why. I'm not even sure if your mom ever knew my middle name."

Jennifer stood and pointed to a book—thick as a person's hand from middle fingertip to wrist—sitting atop a lectern. "What do you suppose that book is? I mean, it has to be special, right? Otherwise, it would be on one of the shelves with the rest of the books."

Gavin walked over to it and smiled. The Glyph of Kirloth dominated the book's front cover, embossed in silver and sized to span its horizontal dimension. He opened the book and saw it recorded the names of Gerrus's family. As Gavin flipped pages, he realized the book chronicled *all* the descendants of Gerrus on Earth.

"It's the family genealogy," Gavin said. "I'm pretty sure every descendant of Gerrus is recorded in this book. That's why it's so thick."

Jennifer pointed over her shoulder to the bronze plaques. "But why are there more names in the book than on the wall?"

Gavin flipped back to the first page of the book and hefted it off the lectern. Carrying it over to the wall, he compared the listing for Gerrus's family to the plaque below Gerrus's. "It looks like the wall only chronicles the direct heirs, whereas the book has everyone."

Jennifer turned to regard the wall. From the way her eyes and lips moved, Gavin figured she was counting. "So, you're telling me there's only one hundred and twenty-four generations between me and this Gerrus fellow?"

"If that's how many plaques there are, then yes."

Gavin closed the genealogy and returned it to the lectern. He brushed his fingers across the Glyph of Kirloth on the cover as memories of Marcus came to the forefront of his mind. For the first time in a long while, the memories carried heightened sorrow and pain of loss.

"You're welcome to stay and explore," Gavin said, "but I need to go for a walk."

"Won't the lights go out when you leave?" Jennifer asked.

"You have your own medallion now," Gavin countered, starting up the stairs. "Aren't you wearing it?"

Jennifer pursed her lips. "Uhm... no? It feels all tingly and weird. Besides, it weighs like it's solid silver."

Gavin chuckled. "It probably is, but you should wear it all the time."

"Seriously? What about when I sleep?"

Gavin stopped on the stairs and turned to his daughter. "All the time... even in the shower."

He resumed his trek upstairs. The moment he stepped across the door's threshold, he heard his daughter shriek at the sudden darkness.

# CHAPTER 13

K iri found Gavin sitting on a bench at the shore of the lake. It wasn't the first time she'd seen him there or at one of the other benches, and since there didn't seem to be anyone else around, it was probably as good a time as any. He looked up at her approach, meeting her eyes with his, and she offered a tentative smile.

"May I join you?"

He nodded and scooted over on the bench, making room for her. "What's on your mind?"

"We haven't really talked about why I was in Tel Mivar. I think we should."

"Okay. Why—"

"Gavin, I love you," Kiri interrupted. "You have no concept of how much your refusal to discuss the betrothal hurt me, and I don't agree that I needed time to get acclimated back into being a princess again. But... it did remind me what life without you is like, and I don't like that, Gavin. I don't like that at all. When I told my father I was going to Tel Mivar, I told him I wasn't coming back until we settled this. I think you still see me as a slave in some ways, and if that's true, we need to change that. I know myself, Gavin. I know my mind, and I know my heart. Your own parents can see what we are to each other, and I don't want to lose you."

* * *

GAVIN LOOKED deep into Kiri's eyes, and he saw the truth of her words there. He felt uncomfortable, off balance. He knew they needed to discuss this, but he wasn't expecting it. Maybe that was just as well, and maybe it was good they were both here—on Earth—and away from all the trappings of Archmagister of Tel and Crown Princess of Vushaar.

"I don't see you as a slave, Kiri," he said. "I never did, really, and I'm sorry if I've done or said something to give you the impression I did."

"Then why did you refuse to discuss the betrothal?"

He leaned back, wanting to put his weight against the tree shading the bench but remembering it was a foot or so behind him. Instead, he stood and then sat back down straddling the bench so he could face Kiri full-on.

"You had just experienced a dramatic life shift, Kiri. Is it so wrong that I wanted to be sure you'd taken the time to think it through, to be sure it was really what you wanted? Do you have any idea what it would do to me to wake up one day and learn that we were married —maybe even had children—not because you wanted to be with me but because you thought you owed me over removing your slave mark? I can't read minds, so the only way I could think of to be sure was to put off the discussion until you'd had more time."

"Gavin, I understand everything you've said, and I can even see it from your point of view." Kiri took a breath, closed her eyes, and shook her head. After a moment, she opened her eyes and resumed eye contact with Gavin. "But Gavin, the proper thing to do would've been to discuss it. Sit down with me and explain your thoughts and reasoning. You made a choice for me, and to borrow something I've heard Jennifer say, that's just dirty pool."

Gavin grinned, then laughed. "I never thought I'd hear you say something like that, but I suppose you're right. I suppose I was making a choice for you."

He almost called her out on springing a betrothal on him in front of her father with zero warning whatsoever, but in the grand scheme of things, it didn't seem right to keep trying to score points off of each other.

"What, Gavin?"

"Huh?"

Kiri gave him an exasperated look. "Don't try that with me. We've known each other too long. What are you thinking right now? Because I can tell you're thinking something."

"Are you sure?"

"Yes."

Gavin flexed his fingers to crack his knuckles, both to alleviate some minor discomfort and to give himself a few seconds more. "Okay. I can understand you not appreciating me making that choice for you, but I didn't really appreciate having a betrothal dropped on me without any warning and in front of your father, no less. Sure, I probably screwed up, but that was edging a little toward dirty pool, also."

Kiri lowered her eyes and worked her lower lip between her teeth. After several moments, she brought her gaze back up to Gavin's and nodded. "I can see that. It wasn't fair to you, either. I'll do better."

Gavin smiled. "I'll do better, too."

Kiri scooted closer and leaned toward Gavin. "Kiss me?"

"Gladly."

# CHAPTER 14

The following day, Gavin returned to the lab to modify the ward's design. He included a Divination component that would inform any of the family if a vehicle turned onto the driveway from the highway, as their property line ran along the highway's right of way. That done, he looked back over the diagram for the ward, searching for anything that might lead to instability or improper function. When he couldn't find anything, Gavin shifted his attention to preparing the ward plinths.

The ward plinths were small stone obelisks, maybe fifty percent taller than the average headstone in a graveyard, and they would act as conduits for the ward's energies. Technically, the ward didn't need them, and if anyone ever managed to destroy one or even all of them, the ward would be just fine. What the plinths would do, though, was make creating the ward much, much easier. By this point in his life, Gavin was all about working smarter and not harder.

Looking over the design one last time, Gavin nodded and opened a gateway to the front lawn of his parents' house.

. . .

GAVIN FOUND his father sitting in the family room reading a newspaper. Neither his mother nor Kiri nor Jennifer, for that matter, were in the immediate area.

"Hi, Dad," Gavin said as he entered the family room.

"Hey, son," Richard said, looking over the newspaper at Gavin. "How's it going?"

"Not too bad. Do you have any stone chisels?"

Richard frowned and pursed his lips. "I have a couple chisels designed for wood, but they're probably too soft for what you're wanting. The store in town has some, though."

"All right. Thanks."

Just then, Elizabeth led Kiri and Jennifer into the family room. All three laughed at some shared joke. Gavin regarded them as Richard looked their way.

"Might want to leave that be, Son," Richard remarked as he lifted the paper once more. "I've found when multiple women are laughing it's generally best not to know why."

Gavin watched his mom stick her tongue out at the newspaper his dad hid behind as Kiri turned to him.

"I'm going into town for a stone chisel," Gavin said. "Would you like to go?"

"Sure. That's a local statement, right? It means 'yes'?" Kiri asked with a proud smile.

Gavin couldn't keep from grinning. "Yes, and yes."

"Are you taking the ca... I mean, the Yukon?"

"I suppose we could take the Yukon into town if Mom and Dad don't mind, but honestly, I was just going to use a gateway."

Kiri's expression shifted through consideration on its way to expressing her agreement, before she said, "That's much better."

"Mind if I tag along?" Jennifer asked.

Gavin shook his head. "Not at all. I'll take the opportunity to show you how to create a gateway, but I'll want you to practice it a lot before you try walking through one you make."

"You don't have to worry about that. I don't want my pieces scattered all over the world."

Gavin nodded and led the ladies outside. He pictured the back room at the store, the one where he'd brought Kiri and Jennifer after the hostage crisis, and invoked a Word, *"Paedryx."*

An arch of crackling sapphire energy rose out of the ground, and once it was a little taller than they were, it flashed into a doorway to another place. Gavin gestured for the ladies to step through first, following after them. The moment he crossed the gateway's threshold into the store's back room, the sapphire archway vanished.

"That is so much faster than the Yukon," Jennifer said as she strode over to the refrigerator and retrieved a soda. "Do either of you want something?"

Gavin shook his head as Kiri walked over to see what Jennifer meant, saying, "Keep an eye on each other, okay? I'll only be a minute."

He walked out into the store and headed straight for hardware. It took a couple minutes, but he found the stone chisels. With the local community college apparently having grown into a university, it seemed his parents had expanded the hardware section to carry specialty items that a student might not want to pay university book-store prices for. They now stocked an array of chisels and other sculpting supplies he never would've expected.

Gavin was still debating which chisel he wanted when Jennifer and Kiri arrived at his side.

"Dad, I'm going to introduce Kiri to the ice cream shop up the street. Do you want anything?"

"No, thanks. Do you need money?"

Jennifer grinned. "What girl would tell her father 'no' to that question?"

Gavin chuckled, saying, "Fair point," as he reached for his wallet.

Jennifer waved him off. "Don't worry about it, Dad. I have some twenties in my wallet."

"All right," Gavin replied. "Have fun. I'll catch up to you soon."

Kiri and Jennifer disappeared around the aisle's end, leaving Gavin to his consideration of the chisels.

. . .

A SHORT TIME LATER, Gavin left his family's store with two different chisels. The cashier hadn't wanted to sell them to him, being the owners' son and all... even if he was supposed to be dead, but Gavin wouldn't hear of just taking them. The poor girl looked mere seconds from a full psychological meltdown when Gavin walked around the corner and picked up the store's phone. A quick conversation with his mom cleared up the matter, leaving him free to find the ladies.

He was maybe halfway between the family's store and the ice cream shop when the roar of an engine drew his attention. Before Gavin could fully turn in the direction of the sound, a navy blue armored vehicle with 'FBI' emblazoned on the side and back flashed by and screeched to a halt right outside the ice cream shop.

*At the rate these idiots are moving, they'll meet 'Kirloth' far sooner than I'd like,* Gavin thought as he picked up his pace. *I do not want my body count to follow me home.*

Sure enough, the back doors of the armored vehicle exploded open, and a tactical team leaped outside to charge into the ice cream shop, rifles drawn as they left the vehicle. It was a nice sunny day; people go to ice cream shops on nice sunny days. Didn't the agents stop to think about any *bystanders* in the area?

Gavin's mood worsened the closer he moved to the ice cream shop. By the time he was close enough to see through the shop's plate-glass windows, he seethed. Everyone he could see in the ice cream shop lay on the floor, and two of the agents moved toward a person he assumed was his daughter.

"Fine," he said, his voice slipping into the cold ruthlessness many in Drakmoor had come to associate with 'Kirloth'. "Maybe they didn't get the message with a trip to the lake."

Knowing full-well over a dozen security cameras recorded him, Gavin lifted his arms in a 'behold' gesture as he invoked a Word of Transmutation, "*Pharhyk.*"

In a flash of gold light, the Archmagister of Tel and Head of House Kirloth—resplendent in the gold robe of his office—replaced the son of Richard and Elizabeth Cross wearing a polo shirt and khakis.

His purposeful stride brought him to the door of the ice cream shop in short order. As he passed the nose of the armored vehicle, a casual, "*Thymnos,*" paralyzed the driver's voluntary muscles. The rear guard of the SWAT team had already tracked his rifle toward Gavin, but it was far too late. "*Uhnrys.*"

Every FBI SWAT agent in the ice cream shop froze, even the two bending down to handcuff his daughter. Gavin scanned the area, looking for an appropriate location. He found one in the form of a raised, circular flower planter in the center of a roundabout at the end of the street. "*Paedryx.*"

The FBI SWAT officers in the ice cream vanished to appear in the center of the raised flower planter, positioned like performance sculpture art. By now, the people of the ice cream shop realized the loud guys with guns no longer shouted, and they started directing cautious glances to their surroundings.

"Yes, you're safe," Gavin said. "Feel free to go about your business."

One of his high school classmates ushered her children out of the ice cream shop and ran her eyes up and down Gavin's gold robe. She looked more than a little unsettled. "That's... a new look for you, right, Gavin? Sally didn't say anything about a gold robe when she saw you at the university."

Gavin couldn't keep from chuckling. "New for me here, Stacy, but I'm a few months into the office the gold color signifies."

"Oh... uhm, you wear it well."

"Thanks," Gavin replied, nodding his head with respectful deference. If Stacy had realized what the gold robe signified, she probably would've been more impressed that he chose to give her a deferential nod.

Jennifer and Kiri arrived at his side. Gavin nodded toward the ice cream shop, asking, "Is everyone all right in there?"

"I think so," his daughter answered. "The kids will either have nightmares or grow up wanting to be FBI SWAT, but nobody was hurt. What about them?"

Gavin's chuckle held no mirth whatsoever. It carried precious little warmth, either. "They'll spend the next three days like that. They're frozen outside of time. When the effect ends, it'll be like no time has passed for them. They won't have aged. Neither their hair nor fingernails will have grown. If you were to hook an EKG up to them and let it run for a whole day, it wouldn't record any heartbeats. They are literally frozen between one second and the next, and they'll remain that way for about three days. Maybe less. But I'm not finished yet."

"Gavin..." Kiri's tone sounded like a fierce gray-haired schoolteacher with a ruler winding up for a scolding.

He turned to face his friend, and Jennifer almost recoiled from what she saw in his expression. She'd never seen *anyone* personify such a cold, dispassionate danger before, and the chilling ruthlessness carried in his tone terrified her right down to her soul. "They haven't learned their lesson yet, Kiri. I'm trying to keep the body count back in Drakmoor, but these morons aren't helping."

Gavin turned and went to the driver's door of the vehicle. A casual Transmutation invocation reduced the door to iron filings on the street. He reached out to the paralysis he'd levied on the driver with his *skathos*, molding it to allow the man to move his head and speak.

"You've heard everything?" Gavin asked, his tone unchanged.

The driver turned to look at Gavin, his expression one of sheer terror about to slip the leash into full-blown panic. He nodded.

"Right now, the paralysis will fade in an hour or so. If you give me your word that you'll do nothing else but flee back to wherever you came from—no vehicles, only your own power—I'll release the paralysis now. But know this. If you agree and then draw your sidearm on me, you'll join your friends in the roundabout. Do you understand?"

The man gave a frantic nod.

"Do you agree?"

Another frantic nod.

"*Rhosed.*"

The man's relief was palpable. He scrambled out of the driver's seat and started back the way the truck had come.

"On second thought," Gavin said, and the man froze, though not of Gavin's doing. "Offload all your weapons into the back of the truck before you leave. I'm going to collect the arms carried by the performance art and seal everything in the truck. I don't want any accidental discharges when they finally rejoin the world."

The man moved to place his pistol in the back of the truck, and Gavin started to leave but remembered something else. He leaned into the truck's cab and found the key still in the switch. He retrieved it and whistled. The man glanced his way, and Gavin tossed him the key. The man seemed surprised for some reason, but Gavin didn't care. The armored truck was part of his lesson, and he didn't want anyone to take it for a joyride. The man was already jogging down the street, and Gavin asked Kiri to watch the truck before turning his attention to the SWAT team adorning the flower patch.

It took maybe twenty minutes to put the rifles on 'SAFE' and transport them back to the truck. Sure, Gavin probably could have used the Art for it, but he wanted to be visible to all the security cameras while he made his point. Once all the weapons were in the back of the truck, Gavin used a Word of Transmutation to turn the back doors into one solid piece of metal. Then, a quick invocation of Tutation created a ward keyed to the time effect; he didn't want anyone to tow the armored truck until the SWAT team returned to the world.

His final act was a composite effect, "*Thyphos-Klyphos-Uhnrys*," to conjure signs around every SWAT team member's neck that wouldn't vanish nor be removable for at least a month, because he wanted the signs to keep their mistake fresh in their minds for a while. The signs read:

Please do not molest these FBI SWAT agents while they are unable to defend themselves.

Photos posted to the internet—especially if the agents collect bird droppings—are highly encouraged.

# CHAPTER 15

It was the first time Chelsea had been in the West Wing of the White House in almost a month, but it was also the first time she could have honestly concentrated on being there. Despite the various demands of her office, she felt much closer to peace than she had since Alexis first started having sudden bouts of acute pain. She didn't know how long that feeling would last, but she planned to savor it as long as it did.

A knock drew Chelsea's attention moments before the door opened and permitted Jenna Carmichael's entrance. Chelsea tried not to frown as she worked to parse Jenna's expression. Unease, certainly. Maybe concern, as well?

"What is it, Jenna?"

"Ma'am," the assistant who'd been with Chelsea across years said, "you need to see the news."

Chelsea frowned. "Which station?"

"Any of them, really. Local affiliates are all on-scene."

*That* didn't help Chelsea's mood at all. She stood and followed Jenna to the reception office right in time for the TV station to come back from a commercial. Jenna's assistant turned the volume up as Chelsea stepped through the door.

"For those of you who may just be joining us," the newscaster said, "an unprecedented situation is unfolding in the town of Graham, Virginia. We're still piecing together the precise chain of events, but the narrative seems to be like this. Yesterday afternoon, an FBI SWAT team arrived in town and assaulted the local ice cream shop, which has been family owned and operated for over sixty years. It is unclear at this time their exact purpose for this action, as the local FBI office is refusing to comment, citing 'an ongoing investigation'. What is clear, however, is that the ultimate result of this action was the immobilization of all but one of the FBI SWAT agents."

The newscaster glanced to her right, the camera panning to show the flower planter. The image came into crisp focus, and Chelsea groaned as she read the sign. She knew *exactly* who was responsible.

"As you can see," the newscaster continued, "these agents associated with FBI SWAT currently face an unknown fate. Much like the vehicle they arrived in, however, there is an invisible barrier of some kind preventing anyone from stepping onto the planter with the agents. This leads me to conclude that the sign clearly shown is more for effect than any true warning. We are trying to obtain copies of surveillance footage of the events unfolding in real-time, but as yet, none of the local businesses are cooperating."

"Jenna," Chelsea said, "I'm going to need the phone number for the Cross residence just outside of Graham. You'd better get me the FBI director, too." Chelsea stopped at the doorframe into the Oval Office, resting her elbow on the frame as she rubbed her forehead. "When you get the FBI director, tell him I want whoever's in charge of the task force causing all this, too. We'd better include the Attorney General as well, but I want that call to the Cross residence first."

Chelsea stepped through the door and closed it like a mature, considerate adult... when she really wanted to slam the door and shriek curses in Gavin's general direction. Okay, yes... she understood the imperative to protect one's child, but he seemed to be taking things a little far. And he certainly wasn't making her days any easier, either.

She was arriving at her desk when the intercom beeped. Jenna said, "Ma'am, I have that call for you... Line One."

Chelsea sat at her desk, took a deep breath, released it slowly, and picked up the phone. She pressed the button for Line One. "Hello? This is Chelsea Hall."

"Richard Cross here, Madam President."

"Mr. Cross—"

"Please, call me Richard."

"Thank you. Richard, is Gavin there? I really need to speak with him."

There was a slight pause. "On the property, yes. In the house, no. He said something about setting the wards today; I don't know precisely where he is."

"Richard, are you aware of what transpired yesterday afternoon in town?"

"Yes, I am, ma'am. While I'm not fond of Gavin's response, I'm even less fond of the FBI considering my granddaughter a high-risk warrant and waving assault rifles around an ice cream shop full of children."

"Do you know what he did?"

Richard's sigh carried through the phone. "Not the precise details, ma'am. Gavin didn't discuss it at all, but Kiri later told us he'd trapped them in a moment of frozen time. Something about existing between one second and the next."

"That... that's impossible!"

Richard's voice sounded a little smug as he replied, "Apparently not, ma'am."

"Did Kiri say anything about how long it would last?"

"She did mention something about three days," Richard answered, "but I'm not sure. I may not have understood. She said it was Gavin's way of making his point without killing them."

Chelsea sighed. "Richard, would you please pass on to Gavin that I'd like to speak with him? I won't say it's imperative, but it is extremely important we discuss this as soon as possible. If this keeps escalating, the entire federal government is going to come crashing down on him, and I don't know that I'll be able to protect him from it."

Richard chuckled. "Ma'am, I know next to nothing about the world where Gavin spent the last two years or so, and I'm slowly getting to know my son for who he is now. I have no evidence on which to base this next statement, nothing I can hold up and show for you to truly believe what I'm saying. But the fact is, Madam President, you need to find a way to resolve this *before* the escalation you fear. Not for our sake or even your sake, but the government's. There is no doubt in my mind that none of you have ever encountered anyone like the man my son is now. The next time I see him, I'll tell him you called."

"Thank you, Richard," Chelsea said. "Goodbye."

As soon as she ended the call, Chelsea keyed the intercom. "Jenna, I need to speak to the White House counsel."

* * *

Gavin walked into his parents' house after warding the property. He didn't ward the *entire* property, only the four square miles or so centered on the house. It still unsettled him how much raw power was available in the world, just waiting to be used. Now that there was a true wizard on Earth, it almost felt like it *needed* to be used.

"Hey, Dad," Gavin said as he entered the family room.

Richard nodded. "Hello, Son. I was about to go help your mother with lunch. Care to join?"

Gavin considered the idea and shrugged. "Sure. Why not? Mind if we invite Kiri, too?"

"She and Jennifer are already in the kitchen with your mom."

Gavin followed Richard into the kitchen and saw straight away that there wasn't enough room for five people. "This is a train wreck waiting to happen. I'll stand right outside the kitchen and take whatever someone hands me to the table."

Richard looked over the kitchen and nodded. "That's not a bad idea, Son. I think I'll do the same."

Gavin enjoyed sitting down to lunch with his family. It was one of those simple pleasures he hadn't realized he missed until he regained all his memories. He especially enjoyed having Kiri with him at the same time.

As soon as the meal was over, Richard looked to Gavin, saying, "Son, the President called this morning... about two-and-a-half hours ago now. She wanted to speak with you. You're kicking a corked hornet's nest, the way you've been handling the FBI, and I'm afraid it's going to come back to bite us."

"Dad, I will not allow the Feds to bully Jennifer. I don't know for certain, but I suspect they're trying to arrest her so they can use it as leverage for her testimony. She can testify or not as she chooses, but as long as I'm alive, she will not be arrested over everything that happened after my death. I will go as far as I need to go to ensure that. I didn't want to bring my body count home with me, but if that's all they understand, then that's where I'll go."

"What of the SWAT team in the roundabout?"

Gavin shrugged. "They're fine. The effect will end three days from the moment I invoked it. I'd love to see the looks on their faces when they see any watches or smartphones they have will be three days behind. Well, the smartphones will eventually synchronize and fix the date, but they'll have to adjust any non-smart watches. You said Chelsea wanted to speak with me?"

Richard nodded.

"Well, I'd better go see to that, now that the ward is up. I'd like to get this settled so I can begin researching how to get back." Gavin pushed his chair back and stood. "If you'll excuse me..."

* * *

CHELSEA CONSIDERED the people assembled in the Oval Office. Two hours into the impromptu meeting that had shattered all their schedules, frayed nerves and confrontational attitudes came at her from all sides. She was the only person in the room who thought approaching the situation from a position of equality might be the best course.

"I mean, we're the United States of America, and this is one of our own people," the Defense Secretary growled. "Whatever was done is clearly criminal assault at the very least, maybe more. We ought to arrest him and be done with it. He's clearly interfering with a federal investigation."

The Attorney General started to speak, but an arch of crackling sapphire energy rising out of the floor by the doorway to the West Colonnade interrupted him. Once it took on the rough dimensions of a door, the arch flashed, and inside it, everyone could see what looked like someone's house. Chelsea fought the urge to groan out loud as Gavin entered the Oval Office through the archway, with it vanishing as soon as he passed through it.

Various exclamations erupted around the room, and three doors burst open to admit Secret Service. The Secret Service drew their sidearms and started shouting for Gavin to lie down on the floor. Gavin regarded them like house pets who'd just piddled on the carpet.

"Put those away before I take offense," Gavin remarked, his expression hardening almost into a glare. "If I intended anyone in this room harm, I wouldn't have needed to come here to deliver it."

The Secret Service agents looked to the President, who smiled and nodded. "Everyone's okay. We're just a little surprised he both chose to come instead of call and didn't use the front door."

Gavin shrugged. "You said you wanted to speak with me. I have too much to do to waste an afternoon being subjected to pointless posturing from the security staff or whatever minor functionary took over for them. What did you want?"

"I wanted to discuss the FBI SWAT agents in Graham," Chelsea said. "Are they harmed in any way?"

"No," Gavin answered. "When the effect ends in a little over two days, it will be as though only a second passed for them. Maybe less. I guess you could say they're taking a time out right now."

"Just who do you think you are, interfering in a federal arrest warrant?" an old warhorse on the sofa demanded, his voice a harsh growl.

Gavin shifted his attention to the older gentleman, and when he spoke, it seemed like the room's temperature dropped several degrees. "I think I am the man who refuses to allow you people to bully his daughter, and unlike most of the citizens in this so-called republic, *I* have the power to stop you. I have no interest in this confrontation escalating to the point where people die. I'm not an anarchist, terrorist, or some nutjob whose sole interest in life is to watch the world burn. I have very specific goals that do not involve the United States of America at all, and I would prefer we both agree not to interfere with each other so I can get on with my day. And to be clear, I define trying to bully my daughter as interfering with me."

"Would you be willing to sit down with some people from the Department of Justice to discuss this?" Chelsea asked. "Try to find some middle ground?"

Gavin saw everyone else's hackles rise at her words. He shrugged. "I'm willing to have a conversation, as long as everyone at the table approaches it as a negotiation in good faith. Don't expect me to react kindly if Justice comes in and tries to dictate terms. You know where to find me when you're ready to have that talk."

Without waiting for anyone else to speak, Gavin raised another sapphire gateway and stepped through it, vanishing from the Oval Office.

# CHAPTER 16

In the days that followed, the security videos of Gavin dealing with FBI SWAT leaked. Within minutes, those videos went viral. Within hours, epically viral, gaining views by the hundreds of thousands every minute. The proof that magic was not just sleight of hand and willing suspension of disbelief surged through Earth's population like wildfire through plains in drought. By the second day, it developed all the hallmarks of a global stop event. Stock markets plummeted, prompting suspension of trading. The rate of suicides spiked. And people mobbed news stations, all wanting information about the man in the gold robe; some asked out of fear, while others asked out of hope or awe or eagerness.

GAVIN FINALIZED his lab and tried to assemble some kind of overall map for his research into cross-planar travel. It was difficult to plan, though, when one didn't have some idea of where to start. It had been different with the slave marks; at least, there, Gavin had something visible to study. How was one supposed to study the fabric of reality itself?

His first step, at the very least, was to craft a form of the Speaking

Stones his mentor and apprentices had used during the Godswar. He didn't have a cell phone, and he wasn't going to get one. Since his keep was the better part of a mile from the house, it wasn't like his parents could pop over quickly if they needed to chat.

After a few hours' experimentation and crafting, Gavin sat back to consider the fruits of his labor. The two devices on the table looked like odd bastardizations of the old radio microphones in shock mounts. Except the mounts suspended crystals instead of microphones. A button on the front of the device's base actuated a rocker arm built into the housing; when the button was pressed, the rocker arm pressed against the crystal to activate it. The tip of the rocker arm near the crystal held a rune that Gavin had imbued with his power, and he hoped someone with no trace of magic would be able to use these devices. Leaving one in his lab, Gavin created a gateway to the front lawn of his parents' house. It was time to conduct a test.

* * *

KIRI LOOKED up at the sound of a twig snapping and smiled when she saw Jennifer a few dozen feet away. Kiri sat at the picnic table across the driveway from Richard and Elizabeth's house, so it wasn't any great effort for Jennifer to find her, especially since she was in view of the house's front porch.

"Hi, Jennifer," Kiri said. "Care to join me?"

Jennifer smiled. "Yes, please."

Gavin's daughter closed the distance in short order and sat across the picnic table from Kiri. She looked... uneasy, if Kiri had to choose a word.

"Is something wrong, Jennifer?"

"I... well, do you mind if we talk? About Dad, I mean?"

Kiri smiled. "I don't mind at all. What did you want to discuss?"

Jennifer sat in silence, staring at the tabletop for several moments. "Outside the ice cream shop the other day, when Dad was wearing the gold robe? He terrified me. I've never seen him like that."

"Ah, yes. You came very close to meeting Kirloth."

"Huh? I thought Dad was Kirloth."

Kiri rested her elbows on the picnic table and interlaced her fingers. "He is, and yet, he isn't. That was the first time I've seen him slip even close to Kirloth since we arrived here. Back home, it's usually much closer to the surface."

"Weird. That almost sounds like dissociative identity disorder."

Kiri frowned. "Huh?"

"Oh. Years ago, it was called multiple personality disorder. Basically, a person with it has constructed several identities or personalities to protect him or herself. It usually is associated with extreme prolonged abuse as a child. When he's Kirloth, does he remember what he says and does?"

"Yes," Kiri answered. "I've never had the feeling that he's actually someone else. It's just that 'Kirloth' is our shorthand for those times he needs to be... well... ruthless and uncaring. The last couple years have not always been kind to your father, and like I told you and your grandparents the other day, the person holding the title or position of Kirloth has traditionally been the one to make decisions no one should ever have to face. There was a period of time Lillian and I were afraid that we were losing Gavin to Kirloth. I think this unplanned visit home has equalized that a bit, even if your government isn't helping."

Jennifer chuckled. "I'm not sure you could find twenty people in the same place anywhere in the country who would agree on the last time the government actually did help. Who's Lillian?"

"Lillian is a friend of your father. She is Heir to House Mivar and one of his first apprentices."

After a few moments' silence, Jennifer lifted her gaze to Kiri. "So, you're a princess or something?"

"Yes," Kiri replied. "Back home, I am the Crown Princess of Vushaar; one day, I will be Queen. My family has ruled Vushaar for well over six thousand years. The confirmed records we have go back seven thousand, and the city already existed in those earliest records. It's unclear, though, how much of a kingdom it actually was."

"Wow. I'm not sure I can wrap my mind around that. Seven thousand years? We've only had writing here for..." Jennifer's voice trailed off, and she shook her head, chuckling. "I'm going to have to revise my view of our history. I started to say that we've only had writing here for around fifty-five hundred years, but I'm not sure when this Gerrus guy Dad says is our ultimate ancestor arrived here."

"Keep in mind that our year and your year may not be the same amount of time," Kiri remarked. "That's something to discuss with Gavin. He may know more."

Jennifer nodded, and silence ruled the table for several moments. Finally, Jennifer spoke again.

"What do you think of how Dad keeps pushing the government?"

"Honestly?"

"Sure."

"I think he's been remarkably restrained. These people have no concept of who they're dealing with, and Gavin will eventually lose patience if they won't see reason. I fear for your country if he does."

"Seriously? He's *that* powerful?"

"During the siege of Vushaar," Kiri replied, "he electrocuted over seven hundred people at once, using some kind of lightning effect. The resulting thunderclap shattered windows and crystal across the entire city and physically shook structures within one-hundred-fifty feet or so of where Gavin stood." Taking in Jennifer's incredulous expression, Kiri sighed and shook her head. "You people have no concept of the sheer devastation a true arcanist in full command of his power can produce. Gerrus's brother and four apprentices did what Gavin did with the keep, except they created four *cities*. Cities, Jennifer. If you include the College of the Arcane, Tel Mivar is easily twice the size of Graham, and your ancestor's brother literally *made* it with the Art."

"So you think Dad could really do it? Reduce this world to ash if things get that far?"

Kiri worked her lower lip between her teeth for several moments. "I think if he felt there was no other option he would certainly make the attempt. What I do not know is whether he'd *survive* it. I have no doubt he could devastate your world to the point it would never be the same again. Could he reduce the entire world to ash? I just don't know. I do know he doesn't *want* to do it. He doesn't want to have killed hundreds, if not thousands of people. If given the choice, I think he'd prefer to be a teacher. Helping those born with the power you both have, to understand it and come to terms with it. The Gavin Cross I first met possessed no shred of Kirloth in him."

Jennifer opened her mouth to speak, but her expression became a wince right before Kiri heard the telltale crackling of a gateway forming. She turned and saw a sapphire arch in the lawn across the driveway.

"I'm still not used to that feeling," Jennifer said, pushing herself to her feet.

Kiri likewise stood, and they approached the arch together. By the time they reached the decorative picket fence, Gavin stood on the grass, and the gateway was no more. Kiri saw Gavin carried something in the crook of his left arm, but Jennifer spoke before she could.

"Whatcha have there, Dad?"

Gavin turned toward them. "If I'm right, it's a way for anyone here at the house to speak with us out at the keep without being a full-fledged arcanist."

"Really?" Jennifer asked.

Gavin nodded. "If it works."

"That'll be neat."

That said, Gavin turned, and they made their way into the house where they found Richard in the family room, working his way through the paper's crossword puzzle. Elizabeth wasn't immediately in sight.

"Hey, Dad," Gavin said by way of greeting. "Is Mom around?"

"She's getting ready to go into town," Richard answered. "It's almost time for her weekly quilting get-together."

"Do you think she has enough time to help me with something?"

"Help you with what, Gavin?" Elizabeth asked as she entered the family room.

Gavin held up the device. "I'd like to put this on the dining room table and have you press the button on the base. If it works the way I expect, you'll be able to talk to anyone out at the keep."

Elizabeth shrugged. "I'm always horrendously early for these quilting meets anyway. Either that, or everyone else has no concept of punctuality. I don't see why not, but why do you want me specifically?"

"Dad, Jennifer, and I are all arcanists, even though Dad never developed it. I want to know if a person without magic abilities can use these. That's why I was going to ask Kiri to come out to the keep with me to push the button on that device out there."

"All right. Let's do this," Elizabeth said.

"Press the button whenever you're ready," Gavin said and handed off the device to Jennifer before he and Kiri made their way back out of the house. Outside, he raised another gateway directly to his lab at the top of the keep. They had just arrived and turned to face the other device when the crystal at its center lit up.

"Hello? Can you hear me?" Elizabeth's voice sounded as if she was standing right in the room with them.

Gavin grinned and nodded to Kiri. She approached the device and pressed the button, bringing the tip of the pivot arm into contact with the crystal.

"Hello, Elizabeth," Kiri said. "We heard you just fine. Can you hear me?"

"Oh, yes, dear; we certainly can. This is amazing. You sound like you're standing right beside me."

"How about me, Mom? How well can you hear me?" Gavin asked.

"You sound the same as Kiri, Gavin. Why?"

Gavin chuckled. "Because I'm standing about eight feet away from our device."

"Goodness! This is incredible. How far away will these work?"

"No idea," Gavin said, tapping his finger to his lips. "I'd assume anywhere in this dimension, but it may be restricted to the planet. It's not like we can travel to Mars..." Gavin's voice trailed off as his eyes widened. "Holy cow... I wonder if I actually *could* open a gateway to

Mars." He started laughing like a giddy child. "I'm going to have to try that."

Whether they were too stunned at Gavin's train of thought or simply didn't have anything to say, no response came from his parents or Jennifer.

"Thanks so much for your help, Mom. I don't want to make you late for your quilting," Gavin said at last.

"You're welcome, Gavin," Elizabeth said, and the crystal went dark.

Gavin nodded at the device where Kiri still held the button down. She released it, and he said, "My next project is a permanent portal so you and my parents can come and go from the keep whenever you want. I doubt they'll enjoy that part, though. Well, Mom won't. I'm going to ask her to prick her finger. And you, too, now that I think about it."

"Why not your dad?"

"By keying it to my bloodline, Dad and Jennifer are included by default. Honestly, Mom or her parents should be as well, since they're my ancestors, but I'm not going to take that chance. Besides, I'd rather be a little more selective in who can reach the keep."

Kiri nodded. "I can see that. You have accumulated a rather impressive collection of potential enemies in the short time we've been here."

Gavin shrugged. "I guess it's just my winning personality. I make friends and influence people wherever I go."

Kiri felt like rolling her eyes. "I guess that's one way to put it."

# CHAPTER 17

The knock on the Oval Office's door pulled Chelsea's focus away from the documents in front of her, and she sighed. She wasn't sure if she could take any more bad news right now. The report she held in her hands detailed how a religious cult in South Dakota had decided that the appearance of magic heralded God's surrender of Earth to Lucifer, and to avoid the coming Armageddon—where all the hosts of Hell would rise up and establish dominion over Earth—the leaders gathered their 'flock' and carried out the largest mass murder-suicide in the past fifty years, if not more. Over fifteen hundred people—many of them children... all dead. The local postal carrier found them.

When Chelsea didn't respond, the door edged open, and Jenna peeked inside, asking, "Ma'am?"

Chelsea snatched a tissue and dabbed at her eyes. The emotional turmoil threatened to overwhelm her. The authorities in South Dakota were still compiling the final count, but the information she had was horrific.

"What is it, Jenna?"

Jenna's expression held nothing but sympathy for her long-time friend. "Ma'am, Senators Campbell and Lawson and Representatives Bertram and Smith are here. They're not on the schedule."

"I need a minute, Jenna."

The executive assistant nodded and retreated. Chelsea closed the ghastly report inside a manila folder and pushed back from the Resolute desk. She stood and stepped outside to the Rose Garden. All her life, Chelsea had been blessed with the ability to cry without it destroying her appearance, and for a few moments, she gave herself to the raw heartache and horror.

She wept. It was almost cleansing, those tears carrying away the emotions that threatened to shatter her iron self-control. She didn't allow herself to weep for long, just long enough that she could face whatever batch of news the people from Congress carried. It wouldn't be good. It wouldn't be even a shadow of good.

At last, Chelsea took a deep, shuddering breath and returned to her office. She dried her eyes and her face, ensured she was presentable. Then, she keyed the intercom and said, "Send them in, please, Jenna."

* * *

"Son, do you have a minute?" Richard's voice filled the lab.

Gavin turned from the whiteboard that held his focus and walked to the table where the communication crystal sat. He pressed the tab to activate it.

"What do you need, Dad?"

"President Hall is on the phone. She would like to speak with you if you have time."

Gavin's eyes flitted across the notes he'd left on the whiteboard. He wasn't making much progress, so he might as well see what Chelsea wanted. He invoked a Word of Transmutation, "*Paedryx*," and the world blinked.

GAVIN WATCHED his father jerk in surprise as he appeared in the family room. Richard's right hand held the cordless phone, and his left hand pressed the activation button on the crystal housing. He glanced at the crystal and saw it was now dark and shook his head as he muttered, "I'm never going to get used to that."

He offered the phone.

Gavin accepted it and said, "Hello? This is Gavin."

"Gavin," Chelsea replied, "I need... no. The *world* needs your help. The security footage of your response to the FBI SWAT team has caused a global stop event. This is the fifth day stock exchanges around the world have suspended trading. We have people committing suicide."

"What do you want, Chelsea? We can't un-ring the bell. Personally, I would've preferred that this world never know that magic exists, but I've lost any shred of patience I had with the FBI. Those fools could've harmed *children*."

A heavy sigh carried across the phone. "Would you come to Washington and speak at a press conference with me? A number of people here think a press conference in which we show you're no threat to the people and you're not some harbinger of an apocalypse will go a long way in calming things."

"It's really bad out there?"

"Yes," Chelsea replied. "A religious cult in South Dakota did a mass murder-suicide just yesterday, Gavin. Fifteen hundred people died. That's not all, either. It's the highest shock value, but suicides have spiked something fierce. That doesn't even touch all the rioting and looting that's on the rise; some countries are making noises about martial law."

Now, Gavin sighed. He never considered that being home would cause all this, but he should have. He could have handled the SWAT situation much more low-key, not forced the awareness that he was different. But seeing as how he had a grave in the family cemetery and newspaper archives of the wreck that killed him, it was probably just a matter of time anyway.

"I'm not going to be some sacrifice to a room full of rabid journalists, Chelsea, but I will meet you halfway. If you'll organize an informal discussion involving you, me, and even a few members of Congress, if you like with no more than ten to fifteen hand-picked reporters, I'll do what I can to rein in this craziness. Oh... and I want international news services represented, too; this better not be an America-only affair. BBC and Reuters at the very least. It can be televised live, if you want, but I was serious about it being informal and conversational. If you can make that happen, I'll do my part."

"Thank you, Gavin. This means a lot to me."

* * *

CHELSEA and her travel team of Secret Service agents met Gavin in the Rose Garden. She looked tired, no. Weary. The world's reaction to his existence weighed on her. Her eyes didn't hold the same spark as they had less than a week ago. It seemed a colossal effort to square her shoulders and stand tall.

"I'm sorry, Chelsea," Gavin said as he approached her. "I never once considered how the world might react when I chose to make a spectacle of the FBI SWAT team. I didn't want this to happen. It doesn't change my conviction that the government won't bully my daughter, but I will help however I can to stave off this crisis. The confrontation between the government and me is just that... between us and us alone."

Some of the weight seemed to lift from Chelsea's shoulders. "Thank you, Gavin. I was... I was afraid you'd respond to this as you have the FBI, and I fear the world can't handle much more."

Chelsea turned and gestured for Gavin to walk with her. As they approached the White House, she continued, "I have the journalists like you wanted. I've explained that this is to be an informal, conversational meet-and-greet. I also have two members of the House, two members of the Senate, and selected ambassadors from our more trusted allies. Oh... I should probably warn you that one of the senators might try to create a problem."

Gavin stopped and turned to face Chelsea, asking, "Why is that?"

"He's... well... he won his election on a platform of bringing God back to our government, and he never misses an opportunity to preach to the godless heathens that surround him in his daily life."

"Is that so? My first thought is what happened to the concept of 'separation of church and state?' I didn't come here to be the whipping post for someone's personal agenda, or perhaps, vendetta might be a better phrasing. If he becomes too obnoxious, I'll just eject him from the discussion."

Chelsea gaped. "Gavin, you can't do that! This is going to be televised live; do you have any idea how many problems you'll create by doing that?"

Gavin forced himself to maintain a neutral expression and not glare like he wanted. "Chelsea, I was very serious when I said I didn't come here to be someone's venue for scoring cheap political points. If he forces the issue, I will respond. Now, where is this happening?"

"The Mural Room," Chelsea replied, her tone now just as weary as her expression.


NOT EVEN FIVE MINUTES LATER, Chelsea led Gavin into the Mural Room. He saw the journalists chatting among themselves in one corner of the room, while the government types occupied another corner. At Chelsea's entrance, everyone started ambling toward the center of the room.

A middle-aged man pushed himself forward and extended his hand. His voice carried a strong Southern drawl as he said, "I am Senator Clive Evans, young man. It was wise of you to answer our summons."

"Summons, is it?" Gavin asked, not moving toward the man's outstretched hand at all. "I don't remember any summons."

Senator Evans glanced at his right hand still extended for a handshake, replying, "Yes... well, one should never play their full hand. The velvet glove on the iron fist, as it were."

"If you need a good therapist for those delusions you have, Senator, I'm sure someone can recommend one," Gavin said and stepped past the man before he could fully process Gavin's words.

"You just made yourself an enemy," Chelsea whispered, leaning close to Gavin.

Gavin shrugged his response. "He can get in line and die of old age before he reaches the front. I understand that you're as much trapped within the system as you are a power player in it, so if you'd like for me to be the 'bad guy' and move this along, I need to know now."

Chelsea glanced over the assembled august personages and worked her lower lip between her teeth. After several moments, she replied in a whisper, "It might be best. I halfway expect our esteemed guests from Congress to attempt some showboating."

"Very well," Gavin replied. Then, he cleared his voice and spoke in a room-filling voice. "I don't have a lot of time, so let's get this started. Which seat is mine?"

"The one in the center," Chelsea replied.

A young woman came around the collected cameras and journalists. She pushed a small cart laden with all manner of items Gavin didn't recognize. When she reached Gavin, she gestured for him to sit as she picked up a thin paper towel like barbers use to cover a person's collar, saying, "If you'll just hold still a moment... we wouldn't want your forehead or cheeks to shine under the glare of the lights."

"*Rhyskaal*," Gavin said, invoking a Word of Transmutation. Faster than a finger-snap, his face lost all glare or shine. "How's that?"

The young woman gaped. "Uhm... yeah... that's pretty good."

As the makeup artist pushed her cart back out of the way, Gavin thought he heard someone behind him whisper, "That's just not fair."


Once everyone was seated, Jenna stepped forward, saying, "We have about ten minutes before all the networks are ready for us. They're already announcing that they'll be switching over to a live event."

"Thank you, Jenna," Chelsea replied.

Senator Evans leaned forward in his seat, saying, "Madam President, before we begin, I think we should address this man's breach of protocol and glaring insult to the great state of Mississippi. Never in all my years—"

Gavin slowly turned to face the senator. "You are here by my invitation, and you may consider this your one warning. No grandstanding, no showboating, no scoring political points. I'm not here for you. If you do not have a genuine question to ask, I suggest you be silent, unless you'd like to visit Fairbanks, Alaska."

Just then, the 'LIVE' indicator lit up, and Chelsea said, "Good evening, we're here to address the growing alarm and uncertainty facing our world, and to my right, we have our guest, Gavin Cross. Many may recognize him from a number of the videos taking over the internet. Gavin, thank you for coming, and before we get into questions, is there anything you'd like to say?"

"Thank you for hosting our conversation this evening, Madam President," Gavin replied. "After you called me, I perused several of the more popular sites that have sprung up to showcase the videos of me wielding the Art. A number of them are sites dedicated to debunking hoaxes. Some are New Age, sleight of hand claptrap. None of them are accurate. I am not a harbinger of any apocalypse. I am not an advance agent of any infernal powers." Gavin grinned and chuckled. "And yes, I realize that is *exactly* what an advance agent or harbinger would say. I did not intend to return to Earth, and frankly, I don't know why I did. My sole intent is to return to the world I came from, because I have many responsibilities there that only I can discharge. So, no matter what anyone else tells you, please do not regard me as some kind of messenger, harbinger, or advance agent. I have no designs for or on Earth beyond what I've stated." One of the journalists raised her hand, and Gavin smiled, adding, "Thank you, but as long as we're able to maintain the conversational atmosphere, I don't think raising hands is necessary. Please, proceed."

"Jill Townsend with the BBC," the journalist began. "Is it your assertation that what the videos show you doing is not a hoax or some other modern trickery?"

Gavin smiled. "Thank you for asking, Jill, and yes, it is absolutely my assertion that I am not a hoax or charlatan. Have we spoken before this moment?"

"No, sir. I just arrived in Washington, D. C., about two hours ago."

"Very good," Gavin replied. "May I ask what your favorite flower is?"

"Lilacs, sir," Jill answered, "but what does that have to do—"

Gavin invoked a Word of Conjuration, "*Khrypaex*," and a bouquet of lilacs appeared in his hand. No warning, no fading into view. The bouquet simply *appeared*. He extended the bouquet to Jill and said, "I hope those are the type of lilacs you like. I don't know much about flowers, so I couldn't guide the invocation as well as I otherwise might have. I'm afraid they'll only last for about five hours or so; making any conjured item permanent is often more trouble than it's worth."

Jill stared at the bouquet of flowers she held. After a couple heartbeats, she started glancing from the flowers to Gavin and back. After maybe fifteen seconds, she said, "They feel so real."

"They *are* real," Gavin replied, "at least for the next five hours or so."

A man sitting to Jill's right pulled his attention away from the flowers and said, "So, what is it you do, exactly? I mean, how did you create those flowers for example?"

"If you want a specific explanation of what happened, I'm afraid I don't have it for you. For what I do, I form a clear vision of my intent in my mind and invoke the proper Word of Power to implement my vision. The dominant thought in my mind when I conjured those flowers was 'conjure a bouquet of lilacs'. The Art did the rest. Everything I do is based around what my mentor called the one essential truth: the effect is shaped by the arcanist's intent. If I want a purple flame..." Gavin's voice trailed off as he lifted his left hand, cupped as if holding an apple. "*Khrypaex*." An orb of purple flame appeared, hovering over Gavin's left palm. He let it hover in the air for several seconds before he reached into his *skathos* and, focusing on the thin tendril of power feeding the flame, severed the tendril as he snapped his fingers. The orb vanished into nothingness.

"Can anyone learn how to do that?" Jill asked.

"That delves into the types of arcanists, and the honest answer is yes and no. Arcanists like me are often called wizards; we are born with a core of power within us, and it is that connection to the raw fabric of reality that allows us to use the Words of Power. So, to answer your question, only someone like me—who was born with the core of power—can learn to do what I do. The other type of arcanist is often called a mage; mages want to study and learn the Art so much that they spend years refining their mind and will to cast spells. Many wizards would argue that mages are our lesser cousins, but I disagree with that assessment. Because they rely on spells, mages do not possess the flexibility wizards do, and no mage ever born could hope to stand up to a trained wizard... but they are not 'lesser' for that distinction."

"And is the ability to be a wizard limited to the world you come from?" the man asked.

Gavin smiled. "Forgive me, sir, but I didn't catch your name."

The man's eyes shot wide for the briefest moment. "Ah, yes, sorry. Patrick Jameson from Reuters."

"Thank you, Patrick," Gavin replied, "and no. Both my father and daughter—neither of whom have ever traveled to the world I came from—have the potential to be trained wizards. My father never knew this, and as he didn't train the ability, it has since faded. If he retains any capacity to wield the Art, it isn't much. My daughter, however, is my apprentice. Wizardry does tend to follow familial lines, but it can skip generations, sometimes several."

"Does anyone here have the potential to be a wizard?" Patrick asked.

Gavin closed his eyes and focused on his *skathos*. The first resonance he noticed corresponded to Senator Evans, but it was just an echo now. Gavin wasn't about to 'out' him and give him additional ammunition to tout his supposed righteousness, but there was another resonance deeper into the White House.

"In this room, no," Gavin answered. "I can sense a faint resonance about fifty yards over my right shoulder, though."

Several journalists' eyes lit up. Patrick asked, "Can you tell who it is?"

Gavin laughed. "I can't even tell what the person's *gender* is. So, no... I have no idea who it is."

"But could you find out, though?" Patrick pressed.

"Hmmm," Gavin vocalized as he leaned back against his seat and scratched his chin. "I suppose I could invoke a Word of Divination to see the person and possibly use that as the basis for another divination to determine the person's name. The first is easy, but the latter is iffy at best. Normally, you need something with a direct connection if you want the best results in any divinations... something like hair or nail clippings. Even if I could reveal the person's identity, though, I wouldn't. One of my most fundamental beliefs is a person's free will for self-determination. If the person chose to be identified as a prospective wizard on international television, that's one thing, but frankly, it's none of your business who it is. The only reason you know about me is that I *chose* to be careless on the street in Graham during the FBI SWAT incident."

"You bring up an excellent point," Jill returned to the conversation. "What led to your disagreement with the FBI?"

Gavin sighed. "There was a period of about six years, plus or minus, during which my daughter found herself in a very bad place and made a number of very poor decisions. Those decisions haunt her to this day, and allowing the FBI to arrest and detain her is a death sentence until she masters her power. Beyond that, though, I don't like bullies, and the Department of Justice was bullying her to testify by threatening her with arrest and prosecution if she didn't accede to their wishes. There are also other factors at play that I am still researching, but suffice it to say that my daughter will never see the inside of a jail or prison as long as I'm alive."

"And you can guarantee that?" Jill asked.

Gavin nodded. The motion was slow, certain. "Yes, I can."

"Why should your daughter receive special treatment?" Jill

continued. "Doesn't the criminal justice system exist to act as a fair and impartial arbiter and keep us from devolving into vigilantism?"

Gavin laughed. "There is no such thing as a fair and impartial anything where humans are involved. That is a fallacy. I will grant you that the theory of criminal justice systems and bodies of law are to create implicit contracts within a society to which all members agree. But no human walking this planet is perfect, and anything created by imperfect beings is inherently imperfect. How many innocent people have gone to prison because the prosecutor was a better showman than the defense attorney? How many innocent people have been executed? I am sure I don't know, and I'm also sure I don't want to know. My daughter punishes herself for those six years far more completely than any so-called justice system ever could, and in my mind, she deserves the chance to spend the rest of her life trying to atone for them. But we've wandered a bit from this conversation's original purpose."

"Edgar Kensington, Reuters," a man spoke up behind Jill. "Is it true you can bring someone back to life?"

"No, Edgar," Gavin answered. "No arcanist has that ability. I *can* create various forms of undead, basically animating corpses and what not, but they're not alive like when souls still inhabited their bodies."

Edgar frowned, then asked, "Then, how do you explain sitting here with us when I have news articles showing you were killed in a car wreck thirteen years ago?"

"The short answer is that I was brought back to life in the world I was in prior to coming back to Earth. I didn't choose to come back, and what's more, I have no awareness of the time between when I died and when I woke up in the other world."

"So your grave here on Earth is empty?" Edgar pressed.

Gavin shrugged. "I have no idea. I'm kind of curious about that myself, but I'm sure it would be a huge kerfuffle to exhume the grave. I'm not sure that satisfying my curiosity is worth the hassle."

"What would you charge for training?" Patrick asked, rejoining the discussion.

"I don't charge for training," Gavin replied. "I do not have students; I have apprentices. Right now, I have two apprentices and no interest in having more. Further, I can't train mages; I know nothing of spells or the language of magic, merely that they exist. Beyond all of that, arcanists possess the ability to reshape reality to our will; that is incredible power, and I have no interest in unleashing a horde of people upon the world who only sought me out to learn how to literally make mountains out of molehills."

Silence reigned for several moments.

After what seemed like hours but was only a minute or two at most, Patrick asked, "You can do that? Raise mountains?"

"Raise them, collapse them... pretty much anything you can envision, an arcanist can attempt. I personally have melted a stone house."

"Now that you're back on Earth," Edgar asked, figuratively stepping into the ensuing silence, "what are your plans?"

Gavin grinned. "Devise a way to get back to the world I came from. I hold an office over there that doesn't really have much in the way of a line of succession, and I'm sure there are all kinds of things not getting done right now because I'm not there. I did not *choose* to come back, and while I'm glad to reconnect with my family, I still have my responsibilities."

"And what is that office?"

"Archmagister of Tel," Gavin answered. "The closest comparison to something here would be monarchs of the medieval era. In Tel, my word is law; I don't like that, but that's the way its constitution is written."

Jill frowned and asked, "But if your word is law, couldn't you change the constitution?"

Gavin nodded. "Yes, I can. But the circumstances surrounding the office of the Archmagister are a huge, snarled furball that date back over six thousand years. At the moment, the system is stable. If I tug on one tangle too much, the whole thing may come apart, and I don't have time right now to tear down the country's government and rebuild it. It's not like I can change anything over there from here anyway."

THE 'CONVERSATION' continued for another hour until all pertinent topics were addressed and, once or twice, addressed more than once. As Gavin left the White House to return to his research, he hoped the informal interview would help settle the immense chaos.

# CHAPTER 18

Gavin sat at a small table on the back deck of his parents' house working on the design of the composite effect he would use to create a permanent portal in the backyard. The sound of driveway gravel crunching drew Gavin's attention. He knew Kiri, both of his parents, and Jennifer were in the house. That begged the question of just who was visiting. A slight smile curled his lips. Whoever it was, they didn't mean the property or its occupants harm; otherwise, they wouldn't have made it past the main gate.

Gavin laid aside his pen and made his way to the front of the house. A black Chevy Suburban sat right outside the wooden gate of the decorative picket fence his mom liked so much. A suited woman he didn't recognize exited the passenger seat and scanned the area before moving to the rear passenger door, opening it. Alexis Hall stepped into the midday sun and, spotting Gavin almost at once, started his way.

"So, if I'm your apprentice," Alexis said, a playful smirk tugging at her expression, "does that mean I get to call you 'Master'?"

Gavin raised an eyebrow.

"No," he replied. "If you prefer being *that* formal, 'Mentor' or 'Kirloth' will do. 'Master', like 'owner', carries slavery connotations, and I imagine you'd be rather shocked to learn my preferred response to slavers or slavery in general. I much prefer 'Gavin'."

Alexis faltered, her eyes shooting wide as a deep blush darkened her complexion even further.

"Gather your luggage and stow it on the back deck for now. Then, go to the lakeshore and find me three stones sized for your palm. When you have those, I'll be on the back deck."

Alexis looked down, prompting Gavin to do so as well. It took all his willpower to sequester the laugh that so desperately wanted to break free. The President's daughter wore platform stiletto heels, and those skinny jeans probably carried a designer label somewhere.

"Uhm..." Alexis said, still looking at her feet. "These aren't exactly the shoes for walking in the woods."

"And that's my fault how?" Gavin asked. "You have your first assignment, Apprentice."

Gavin walked past her, approaching the Suburban and the Secret Service agents. He gestured for them to approach him, and the dark part of his soul enjoyed how one of the agents faced him with trepidation.

"I have given my apprentice two assignments," Gavin said, once they gathered. "Neither should present any threats to her life or well-being, and you may rest assured she is under my complete protection as my apprentice, no matter her actual location. I am not about to interfere with any of you doing your duty, and I expect that reciprocated. I am sure your reflexes as personal protectors to dignitaries have been honed to a razor edge. I advise you to temper that while you are here, and if you see something that triggers your reflexes, ask me before you act. You are welcome to walk with Alexis as she performs her first assignments, but I recommend assisting or interfering with them only if you wish to spend an afternoon barking like a dog or braying like a jackass. Hmmm... now that I consider it, forget the 'braying like a jackass'. I'll save *that* for Jason White. Do we have an understanding?"

"We'd like to discuss sleeping quarters and site security at some point, sir," the female agent said.

Gavin chuckled. "This site is far more secure than you can truly understand right now. I imagine you'll pick up on some of it as I train Alexis... assuming you don't get rotated out. There are no security cameras or the like; we don't need them. Sleeping quarters? Yes, we'll have to discuss that. I'm not sure I included sufficient space in the keep, but no matter. We'll either add floors or adjust walls as needed."

Gavin watched the Secret Service agents share looks with each other, all three a little wild around the eyes, and he almost felt sorry for them. If poor Thaddeus in the Vushaari Army couldn't handle being at his side with all the magic he was throwing around during the siege of Vushaar, these poor souls were in for a time of it.

Alexis chose that moment to trudge by them, pulling no less than five suitcases. The large rolling case she pulled with her right hand had two smaller cases stacked on it, and she held a case under her left arm as she pulled a second with that hand as well. She didn't look all that enthused about hauling her luggage, but arcanists had sufficient privileges just by being born an arcanist. Gavin wasn't about to encourage anyone to feel spoiled.

"Right, then," Gavin said. "I'll be on the back deck of my parents' house for the next little while."

Without waiting to see if the agents would follow him, Gavin went back to his notes.


As the minutes passed, Gavin realized he'd have to change the design of the protections he intended for the portal. The original plan was to key it to his bloodline and specific ward stones. If the Secret Service agents intended to stay on-site with Alexis, he wasn't about to give them stones that would allow them to pass through to the keep whenever they wanted. In theory, the wards would prevent them from entering the property if their intent changed to meet the exclusion criteria, but the wards were not set up to deal with someone already on the property whose intent changed. That was a glaring error to Gavin now, but it would be easy enough to fix. The change to both the wards and the portal negated the need for the stones he'd sent Alexis to retrieve. Setting aside his notes for the portal, Gavin picked up a fresh sheet and began working up the property's new wards.

* * *

"Okay. I have your stones." Alexis's voice pulled Gavin from his focus on the new design for the wards. He turned from the papers covering the tabletop and exerted quite a bit of willpower to keep from gaping.

Alexis stood on the second step leading up to the back deck of the house. Her shoes dangled from her right hand—one shoe sans heel —while she extended the stones Gavin no longer needed in her left. Drying mud caked most of her left side from ankle to ribcage.

Gavin couldn't keep his eyes from roving from her shoulder to her feet one more time, before he pulled his gaze back to her eyes. "I take it you faced some challenges?"

Alexis gave him a flat look, still holding her soggy, mud-caked arm out to him with the stones in her hand. "I told you these shoes didn't belong in the woods."

"Well, as it happens, the presence of your Secret Service detail both identified a key vulnerability to the property wards as well as changed my design for the portal. To allow passage through the portal to and from the keep, those stones were to become ward stones ... which I no longer need."

Alexis's expression—which hadn't been all that genial since she returned—now threatened hostility. Her eyes went to the three stones in her left hand, then her shoes, then her mud-coated self. When she returned her gaze to Gavin, her brown eyes looked hard as granite.

"You mean I ruined my clothes and shoes and almost fell into that damned lake for three measly stones *you don't even need*?"

"Well," Gavin replied, "I did need them at the time you left, and I suppose you could consider it a lesson in why you should always wear versatile clothing... and sensible shoes."

Alexis's left hand clenched into a fist around the stones as her nostrils flared. Gavin feared for his mother's kitchen windows if she suddenly chucked those stones at him, but as it happened, he feared for naught. Alexis gritted her teeth and closed her eyes for several moments, then dropped the stones on the ground beside the steps leading up to the deck.

"Is there at least running water in your damned keep?" she ground out through her clenched teeth.

"Yes," Gavin replied. "I finished it... yesterday, I think? Maybe a couple days ago."

"Would you please create a gateway so I can go shower and change clothes?"

"I think I can manage that."

Alexis turned to her designer-label luggage, still in a neat stack where she'd left it, and froze. She looked down at herself once more, and Gavin thought the sound she made resembled a distressed whimper. She closed her eyes for another moment, then squared her shoulders and trudged up to the stack. She collected the luggage, transferring some mud from her to a case or two, and turned to Gavin.

"*Paedryx.*"

An arch of crackling sapphire energy rose out of the ground a couple feet from the deck stairs, soon becoming a gateway to the keep. Alexis made her way down the steps once more and disappeared through the gateway, this time with her Secret Service detail in tow.

* * *

OVER THE NEXT FEW HOURS, Gavin replaced the wards on the property with the new version, which included provisions for anyone who changed intent while inside the wards. Against his first impulse, the wards would merely teleport that person outside the wards, leaving him or her on the grass beside the driveway just before where it passed through the main gate.

With the wards replaced, all that remained was to create the permanent portal from the house to the keep. It occurred to Gavin that it probably wasn't a good idea to place the portal in his parents' backyard. Anyone needing to use the portal would have to walk around the house to reach it, and with the portal being keyed like the property wards—open to anyone who didn't intend harm—his original intention just didn't seem to fit.

Gavin entered the house and found his parents in the family room with Kiri and Jennifer.

"So... Mom, Dad... I need your help," Gavin said. "I've modified the portal design. It will now be keyed like the wards; anyone who doesn't intend us or the property harm can use it. With that change, I don't think it's appropriate to put it in the backyard anymore. What do you think?"

"What's wrong with putting it in the backyard?" Richard asked.

Gavin shrugged. "Nothing really. It's just I was thinking that anyone who came here looking for me would have to use it to reach me, since I'm not going to bother you two with meetings in your dining room. I thought you might not want random people traipsing around the outside of the house."

"If it bothers you to put it behind the house," Elizabeth said, "you could always put it in the small grassy area across the driveway from the house if there's enough room for it there. It's not really doing anything other than providing a home for the picnic table. What do you think, Richard?"

Richard shrugged. "Works for me."

"Okay, then," Gavin said. "I'll put it there."

Gavin turned and left the house through the front door. He walked across the driveway, eyeing the Secret Service Suburban and thinking how that would have to be moved before too long. It blocked the driveway. He examined the grassy area his mother mentioned and decided it did indeed have sufficient space for the portal. He kind of felt sorry for doing this with Jennifer and Alexis both on the property, but it had to be done. A memory from his days playing pen-and-paper RPGs floated to the forefront of his mind, and he grinned. *Ah, well... they'd survive it.*

Gavin cleared his mind and focused on his intent. That image clear and firm in his mind, he invoked a composite effect, "*Rhyskaal-Zyrhaek-Paedryx.*"

The ground began rumbling, and within moments, two spires of bedrock pushed their way up through the topsoil. The spires were just far enough apart that a handcart or wheelbarrow could pass between them, and once the spires were a little over seven feet tall, they started curving inward, creating an arch whose apex was nine feet above the ground. Runes then etched themselves down the surface of the spires, and at the center of the arch—where the keystone would be in a man-made construct—the Glyph of Kirloth etched itself into existence. Mere moments later, the center of the arch flashed, becoming a gateway to its double outside the keep.

# CHAPTER 19

The next day, Gavin began training his apprentices in what it meant to be an arcanist. He took them outside the keep and wowed them—and the Secret Service agents—with the fireball and iceball invocations Marcus had used with him, driving home the one essential truth of a true arcanist wielding the Art: the effect is shaped by the invoker's intent.

Gavin enjoyed seeing how neither his daughter nor Alexis did any better than he did when it came to a static image of a horse using a Word of Illusion. Seeing the President's daughter create an image of a horse with a single monosyllabic word—no matter how out of proportion and frankly ugly the image was—seemed to unsettle the Secret Service agents. If he was being honest, he rather enjoyed seeing the Secret Service agents discomfited.

They quickly settled into a rhythm where Gavin would conduct a couple hours of class each morning, and Jennifer and Alexis would study and practice throughout the rest of the day while he started working through his research plan. Considering his goal was crossing planes—something no mortal had ever done on his or her own, as far as Gavin knew—he felt the first step should be a successful cross-planar scrying. Once he could scry Tel Mivar every time he attempted to do so, Gavin could apply what he learned to a cross-planar portal.

* * *

GAVIN SAT at the large worktable that dominated one section of his lab. Papers covered the tabletop in varying degrees of piles and arrangements, with the design for a Divination effect holding his current focus. It was only when someone shook his shoulder, coupled with Jennifer's exasperated "Dad!", that he processed someone wanted his attention. He looked up from the papers to see both of his apprentices at his side. Alexis held her cell phone.

"Yes?" Gavin asked.

"Mom's on the phone," Alexis explained. "She wants to speak with you."

Gavin accepted the phone and tapped the control to put the call on speaker. "Hello?"

"Hello, Gavin. This is Chelsea Hall. Did I catch you at a bad time?"

"No, not at all. What do you need?"

"I think I have all involved parties on our side of the DOJ dispute ready to sit down to a meeting. When—"

"With all due respect, Chelsea," Gavin interrupted, "I do not consider it a dispute. I told Jason White and his team that they were not going to arrest my daughter. It's up to her whether she testifies, but under no circumstances will I allow the federal government to bully her. They have insisted on progressive escalation ever since then, and it won't be long before I lose patience with the whole mess and escalate matters myself."

"I... see," Chelsea replied. "May I ask what *you* consider an escalation?"

"Quite frankly, I've had more important matters than the Department of Justice occupying my focus. I can say that one of the last times someone directly threatened someone under my protection, I eradicated a slaver base with something like two hundred to four hundred horses and all the appropriate tack and accoutrements for them. I don't know how many slavers were at the base at the time, and there really wasn't any way to find out... since the largest remains of people were rarely more than eyeballs and fingers."

Silence reigned on the call for several moments before Chelsea spoke again. "And you did that with just one word, like the presentation hall?"

"No, it was a composite effect," Gavin answered. "I don't remember the specific invocation right now. I tend to make them up on the fly; it's the intent that matters, you see. Alexis, please tell your mother the one essential truth."

Alexis squared her shoulders and recited, "The effect is shaped by the invoker's intent."

"And what does that mean?" Gavin asked.

"It means that invocations from two different arcanists could look or sound or appear totally different while still creating the same effect."

Gavin smiled, adding a nod of approval. "Excellent. Thank you."

Alexis beamed.

"But getting back to your original question, Chelsea," Gavin continued, "until I reach the point where I see no value in remaining diplomatic, I cannot predict what my escalation will be. I can tell you I tend toward finality. I much prefer to solve a problem once rather than have it pop up again and again, like some annoying rash. When would you like to have that discussion?"

Silence extended on the call to the point that Gavin felt like asking Chelsea if she was still there.

"How does tomorrow afternoon sound?" Chelsea eventually asked.

Gavin looked to his apprentices. "What do you two think? Want to visit the White House tomorrow?"

Alexis shrugged, and Gavin assumed the place was old hat to her by now.

Jennifer shrugged as well.

"Chelsea," Gavin said, "I'm getting indifferent shrugs over here, so I think we're on for tomorrow afternoon."

"And how many should we expect in your party?"

Gavin grinned. "Four."

"I think that covers everything we need for now," Chelsea said. "How does one o'clock sound?"

"That's fine. Where do you... never mind. Why don't you stand within a few feet of where you want us to arrive? I can open a gateway straight to you like I did the other day in the Oval Office."

"And if one of my meetings runs late and I'm sitting in the Situation Room at one o'clock?"

Gavin grinned again. "Then, you'll receive four unannounced visitors to the Situation Room."

A faint sound that made Gavin think of a choked off exclamation was the first suggestion there might be more people listening to the call on Chelsea's end than had spoken.

"Hey, Mom," Alexis said, "what about someone on my detail coming back to the White House? He could be standing in the Rose Garden or the Roosevelt Room or wherever, and Gavin could open the gateway to him."

"Would that work, Gavin?" Chelsea asked.

"That would be fine, and it would also save me from seeing a bunch of classified stuff I don't care about anyway."

"All right," Chelsea agreed. "That works. Alexis, flip a coin or however you want to decide who comes back. I'll send a helo from Andrews if you'll give me coordinates for your location."

"A helo from Andrews, Mom? Really? Won't the Congressional watch dogs go ape over you using a Blackhawk as a taxi?"

"Gavin, if we don't get this right, what are the odds that you'll turn Washington, D.C., into a parking lot?" Chelsea asked.

Gavin chuckled. "Honestly, Chelsea, none at all. There are too many innocents in the city, plus too many monuments I like. If it helps, I am technically a head of state."

"You are?"

"Yes. I am the Archmagister of Tel. All positions of authority within the Kingdom of Tel exist by direct grant from the Archmagister. I decide what laws exist. I set the tax policy. I name ambassadors to foreign lands, and I alone determine what treaties the Kingdom of Tel will establish."

Silence.

After a time, Chelsea asked, "What's your term of office?"

Gavin tried not to smirk. He failed. "It's a lifetime appointment, but I can resign or retire if I choose."

"Who appointed you?" Chelsea's tone communicated her curiosity.

Gavin chuckled. "Are you sure you want to know? Because I can tell you right now, you won't believe me. And whoever else is listening to this call will do their level best to convince you I'm insane."

"With that kind of lead-in, I have to know now," Chelsea remarked.

"Each Archmagister is chosen by Bellos, the God of Magic. I am the first person to fill the office in over six hundred years since the last Archmagister, Bellock Vanlon, was assassinated."

Gavin suspected one could hear a pin drop on the carpet of whatever room Chelsea occupied.

"I have to admit, Gavin, that is a new one for me," Chelsea said. "I'm looking at a few dubious expressions."

"I warned you," Gavin replied. "If there's nothing else, Chelsea, I need to get back to work. Don't worry about the coordinates. Tell the helo to fly to Graham and look for a beacon; we're about ten miles or so east of the town, so they should find the beacon before they reach the town... as long as the pilot can see lightning and hear thunder."

"What should I tell them to look for?"

Gavin chuckled again. "Trust me; they'll know it when they see it."

With that, Gavin thumbed the control to take the call off speaker and returned the phone to Alexis, making shooing gestures once she accepted it.

"Hi, Mom," Alexis said as she and Jennifer left the lab. "No, he handed the phone back to me."

Alexis's voice faded as the apprentices descended to the lower levels of the keep.

Gavin didn't know when Chelsea would order that helo into the air, and he wasn't sure how long it would take to arrive. He decided he should create the beacon now, and if the helo didn't arrive by nightfall... well, that would tell him Chelsea gave in to her skepticism. It wasn't difficult to decide on a beacon, either. Gavin grinned as he rolled his shoulders and focused on his intent.

"*Thyphos.*"

* * *

ALEXIS RAN out of the keep—Jennifer right on her heels and her phone still at her ear. They spun, both looking up in the sky, and Alexis was awed. A massive circle—easily fifty feet across—hovered a hundred feet or more in the air. She wasn't in the best position to get a good look at it, but she did recognize the symbol in the center. It matched the symbol in the center of Jennifer's and her father's medallions.

"Oh, yeah, Mom," Alexis said. "There's no way a Blackhawk pilot could miss this. If you're still serious about having that talk, you might want to get them on their way. As big as it is and as bright as it is, it might freak out some pilots if we're near commercial flight paths." She listened to her mom for a few moments. "Yes, Mom; I'll have whoever rides back take a picture from the helo before they leave. Now, I'm sorry, but I gotta go study. Love you! Bye!"

* * *

THE HELO ARRIVED SOONER than Gavin expected, if he were being truthful. He figured he should act the gracious host and at least see the man off. Besides, he'd made a teleport beacon for him to carry.

When Gavin stepped out of the keep, he found Alexis, Jennifer, and the Secret Service agents clustered a few feet away. The Secret Service agents and the helicopter crew stared at the square around the keep where the grass wasn't disturbed by the air from the rotor blades. Gavin chuckled and approached the agent who was going back, Chet apparently.

"Here," Gavin said, holding out his hand to the agent. In the palm of his hand, he held a small sandstone disc. Runes adorned the rim of the disc while the Glyph of Kirloth dominated the center. "Put that wherever you want us to arrive, and unless there's a torrential downpour or something, I highly recommend you drop it outside."

"Oh? Why?"

"Because it's a single-use teleport beacon," Gavin answered. "When I create the gateway centered on it, it will decay to plain old sand. I mean, sure... you could put it on the carpet somewhere, but I doubt the janitorial staff would appreciate the little cluster of sand that appeared out of nowhere."

"What kind of sand? Is it radioactive?"

Gavin shook his head and chuckled again. "No. Nothing I do involves radiation. I mean, I can create it or protect against it, but I don't need it to do what I do. Nor is it a byproduct of what I do. It'll be plain old sand, probably closely matching Virginia Beach since that's where I hopped this afternoon to get it."

Chet gaped. "You've been to Virginia Beach and back since the President called?"

Gavin nodded and lifted his left hand, snapping his fingers. "I can cross the country—or even the world—that fast, as long as I have some way to key in on the destination."

"How many people can you take with you?"

Gavin shrugged. "My personal record is something like three to five hundred. I didn't get an accurate nose count and never cared to go back and ask, but I've improved since then. I'm not sure what my upper limit is now. You'd better go. The helicopter crew is giving us dirty looks."

Chet looked a little pale as he nodded and turned toward the

Blackhawk. Gavin guessed the idea that he could drop at least half a battalion on the White House lawn unsettled the man.

"Hey, Chet," Alexis said before the agent could get too far, "don't forget to take a picture of the beacon for Mom once you're up in the air."

Chet gave her a thumbs up and hunkered down as he quasi-jogged to the Blackhawk. Moments later, the helicopter lifted off, going straight up and hovering for a second or three, before it angled back the way it came and soon vanished over the treetops.

# CHAPTER 20

The next day, at the appointed time, Gavin gathered his apprentices and Kiri. Alexis gaped at seeing Kiri decked out in leather armor and festooned with blades. The remaining Secret Service agents' expressions puckered like they sucked on lemons.

"Uhm, I'm not sure they'll like that," Alexis remarked, still staring at Kiri.

Gavin shrugged, utterly unconcerned for the Secret Service's discomfort. "There'll be how many Secret Service agents there for your mother? Their sidearms carry how many rounds per magazine?"

"Okay, I get that, but most times when someone visits the White House, their security team's weapons aren't so gratuitously visible. This... I'm not sure how everyone will handle this."

Again, Gavin shrugged. "All right, then. Let's see what we're walking into. *Klaepos.*"

A sphere of space in front of the group started shimmering and rippling much like the surface of a still pond into which a stone is thrown. Not even three seconds later, the shimmering flashed into a scrying sphere. At first, the scene seemed ordinary. Chet stood in the

Rose Garden; the teleport beacon Gavin had given him lay on a paving stone near him. Gavin adjusted the image to show more territory and chuckled.

"Well, well... what have we here? Is that another SWAT team? Oh, and nice sniper perch, too. Alexis, is all this normal?"

"Uhm... I don't think so. At least, I've never seen a SWAT team staged so close to the Rose Garden before. I know there are usually people on the roof of the White House, but I've never seen snipers like that."

Gavin's eyes narrowed as he considered the situation. "Kiri, we still have a few minutes. I think we're going to approach this a different way. Would you be so kind as to divest yourself of most of the blades? I'd say keep six throwing knives and two regular blades."

Kiri did as Gavin asked and rejoined them. Many of the sheaths built into the leather armor were now empty, and Gavin hoped that would serve as a statement. He knew his actions certainly would.

"Right, then. They're probably going to try some intimidation. I'm not too worried about it, but we're not going in there unprotected. *Sykhurhos.*"

The resonance of Gavin's power slammed into the ambient like the shockwave from a stick of dynamite under water. A shimmering effect surrounded Gavin, Jennifer, Alexis, and Kiri for a moment... then faded.

"What was that?" Gayle Wicks—the lead agent on Alexis's detail —asked.

"I gave us protection against normal weapons, poisons, harmful gases, and harmful sonics. Jennifer, is there anything I'm missing?"

"Do you consider tasers and stun guns to be normal weapons?" Jennifer asked.

At the same time, Gayle developed a slightly offended expression as she asked, "What about us?"

"Yes, to Jennifer," Gavin replied and turned to face Gayle. "I don't trust you. You're agents of the government I'm currently attempting to train, and while your primary task is ensuring Alexis's safety, I'm not at all confident you'd choose to remain neutral otherwise. Even though I'm fairly certain Alexis would side with her mother, simply because she's a loving daughter, that does not exempt her from the protection she enjoys as my apprentice. So, when your people betray us—like my scrying makes me think they're prepared to do, I suggest you get yourselves out of the line of fire. Alexis is safer than you could ever make her right now, and yes, I'm certain you'll report back on everything you've seen. I'm actually hoping for it. Jennifer, is it time?"

"We're still a couple minutes early."

"No matter," Gavin said, rolling his neck, "I'm tired of waiting. Let's go bring the unruly pups to heel. *Paedryx*."

A sapphire arch rose out of the floor and soon became a gateway to the Rose Garden at the White House. Gavin and Kiri led Jennifer and Alexis through, followed by the Secret Service agents. The moment the gateway closed, the SWAT team charged into view, all shouting for everyone to get down on the ground and put their hands over their heads.

Gavin effected a bored expression as he invoked a Word of Enchantment, "*Thymnos*."

Every SWAT agent and sniper on the White House property collapsed. The grass served to muffle the sound of that many bodies covered in so much equipment hitting the ground, so the shattering of the scope on someone's sniper rifle when it fell from the roof seemed inordinately loud.

"Ouch," Gavin remarked. "Someone's going to have fun re-zeroing that later."

Gavin shifted his attention to Chet. The Secret Service agent stood maybe twenty feet away, his eyes a little wild and his hand hovering near his jacket.

"If you're thinking of drawing your sidearm, Chet," Gavin remarked, "please feel free. Understand that you'll join the SWAT team if you do."

"Are they... did you kill them?" Chet asked.

Gavin shook his head. "No. They're just asleep... for the next two weeks. Now, is Chelsea truly going to have people meet with us, or was this nothing more than an elaborate ruse?"

"They have the President and the Vice President in the Situation Room," Chet answered. "I don't know if they're planning to speak with you or not."

"Fair enough," Gavin replied. He walked to the door that connected the Rose Garden to the Oval Office and stepped inside. Going straight to the Resolute Desk, Gavin picked up a pen and a piece of the President's stationary. He wrote a note on the stationary and then took it back outside with him. He folded the note in half and pointed his thumb at the camera over his shoulder.

"Chet, are they watching me right now through these cameras?"

Chet darted a glance at the camera Gavin indicated and shrugged. "I don't know. Maybe?"

Gavin chuckled. "Well, I hope they enjoyed the show." He lifted his hand and held it out flat as if feeding a horse, placing the folded note on it. Both his hand and the folded note were in plain view of the camera over his shoulder. "*Paedryx*."

The note vanished.

"Right, then," Gavin said as he returned to his apprentices and Kiri. "I think it's time to go home. Alexis, it is your choice whether you stay or go."

"Uhm... won't I die if I don't learn how to control this?"

"You've learned enough as it stands that you're out of danger," Gavin said. "Practice the illusions each day, and you should be fine. That, in itself, establishes the control you need. If you'd like to keep learning and understanding your full potential, you should come with us."

Alexis nodded. "If I want to visit Mom and think about it, can I come back?"

"Of course," Gavin answered, smiling. Then, his smile faded. "But do not allow yourself to get drawn into the disagreement between myself and the federal government. That would move you outside the protection of your status as my apprentice. Now, if you'll excuse us..." Gavin nodded to Gayle and her associate. "*Paedryx*."

Another sapphire arch rose out of the paving stones, and within seconds, Gavin, Jennifer, and Kiri stepped through the gateway and were gone.

Not even five seconds after the gateway vanished, Alexis's phone rang. She pulled it out of her pocket and looked at the screen.

"Hi, Mom," Alexis said after accepting the call.

"Alexis, honey, I need to speak to Gavin," her mom said over the phone. She sounded a little out of breath.

"They just left, Mom."

"Just left? What do you mean 'just left'?"

The door to the Oval Office burst open, and Chelsea Hall almost skidded to a stop. She still held her phone to her ear. Alexis smiled and went to meet her.

"Mom, are you okay? You're out of breath."

Chelsea pulled her daughter into a hug, then released her. "I ran from the Situation Room. I'm sure it'll be the talk of Washington before too long. When was the last time anyone ever heard of the President running through the White House, dodging mail carts?"

"What's going on, Mom? I thought we were here for a meeting?"

Chelsea sighed. "I... I let myself be convinced that we should establish a position of strength. A number of people decided that we would be able to dictate terms if we controlled the situation."

Alexis chuckled. "And how well did that work?"

Chelsea's eyes drifted over to the mound of SWAT agents. "Did he kill them?"

"Nope. They're just sleeping, except they'll be sleeping for two weeks. At least, that's what Gavin said. One of the snipers dropped a rifle off the roof, though. I'm pretty sure the scope shattered. Mom, what was in that note?"

Chelsea handed a piece of stationary to her daughter. Alexis unfolded it.


CHELSEA,

*Consider this a formal notice that I do not appreciate the United States government breaking faith with me. I will give the government one more chance. Do not expect a third.*

*—Gavin*

ALEXIS RETURNED the note to her mother. She thought it almost poetic that Gavin wrote the note on the President's personal stationery. "For what it's worth, Mom, he knew something was up before we arrived."

"What? How?"

"He scried the teleport beacon and surrounding area. We all saw the snipers and SWAT team, and we were standing in his keep at the time."

Chelsea sighed and walked over to a nearby bench and sat. "You have no stake in this, Lexi, but you're the closest I have to a subject matter expert. What do you think I should do?"

"Honestly, Mom?"

"Yes, please."

Alexis walked over and sat beside her. The bench was just large enough for two people if they didn't mind hugging while they sat.

"Stop listening to people who tell you Gavin should bend his knee to us. Gavin doesn't see it that way, and I'm not sure anyone can make him, either. The longer the government tries, the greater the chance he'll get fed up and decide the relationship can't be salvaged. *That* is what you want to keep from happening at all costs. At that point, he simply won't care anymore."

"He keeps talking about goals that are more important. Do you know what those are?"

"I think he's trying to find a way to go back to wherever he and Kiri came from."

Chelsea grimaced, combed her fingers through her hair. "The Secretary of Defense is already saying I should federalize the Virginia National Guard and blockade Graham until Gavin sees reason."

Alexis laughed. "Mom, Gavin froze a SWAT team outside of time for three days. If he can do that, do you really think blockading

Graham will accomplish anything besides convincing people to side with him? Half of the time he needs something from Graham, he opens a gateway directly to the store he needs; a blockade won't stop that."

Chelsea shook her head. "What's stopping him from teleporting a bomb to the Georgetown Mall... or even the capitol building? We can't defend against him, and that makes a lot of people afraid and prone to overreacting."

"Mom, he's not the bomber type. I really don't think he even cares all that much about the federal government beyond the DOJ task force that wants to coerce Jen's testimony. If they just approached her like a regular citizen and didn't try to hold potential crimes over her head, Gavin wouldn't care. Yeah... he might still have dunked Jason White in the lake, but that's personal."

"I know," Chelsea replied. "I saw the court records about the custody case Gavin's parents made against Emily and Jason White. I wouldn't object if he dunked Emily in the lake along with her husband."

"Mom!" Alexis said, her voice scandalized.

Chelsea laughed. "I'm glad you're here. I know Gavin said he'd never use you as a pawn, but a part of me still worried about you being out there with him. Are you risking your life by being here?"

Alexis shook her head. "No. Gavin said I know enough now to avoid a *skathos* cascade; I just have to keep up my daily practice. If I want to explore my full potential, I'll have to go back."

"Do you *want* to go back?"

"I don't know. I enjoyed being around Jen. It was nice to have someone I could talk to, who didn't care I was the President's daughter. I never got that at college. But I also missed you, too. I asked Gavin if I could think about it and maybe go back later."

Chelsea put her arm around her daughter, pulling her close. "And what did he say?"

"He said as long as I didn't allow myself to get drawn into taking sides, I was welcome anytime."

"Taking sides? That almost sounds like he's expecting a conflict."

Alexis sighed. "Mom, you turned loose a SWAT team and snipers when he was supposed to be coming to *talk*. I have to say, based on appearances alone, I'd be preparing for a conflict, too. What was it you always told me when I was little? 'Actions speak louder than words?'"

Chelsea wasn't in a position to disagree.

* * *

Gavin led Jennifer and Kiri into the lab at the top of the keep. He shrugged out of the gold robe and tossed it in the general direction of the coat rack. Either by magic or sheer accident, it found a hook.

"Not how you thought you'd be spending your afternoon, huh, Dad?" Jennifer said as she sat at the table beside her father.

"I'm largely indifferent as long as they leave you alone. But I doubt that's going to happen. Is all this about Jerome Toussaint?"

"I don't see what else it could be about, but I suppose they might be wigging out over you being alive and able to manipulate reality at will. I've lived here since I was twenty-one or so, ever since Grams and Grandpa found me and brought me home. My years with Toussaint were the only time I've ever been involved in anything sketchy."

Gavin nodded and invoked a Word of Transmutation. A pen and notepad levitated and made their way across the lab to the table. "Then, it's time we started hunting Jerome Toussaint. I need you to write down everything you know about his operation. What businesses he owns, where he spent his time... *everything*."

# CHAPTER 21

Tom Puller listened to the roar of the plane around him. He was a veteran of countless drops, both inside and outside of hostile territory. He never expected his CO to tell him that he should consider a section of Virginia as hostile territory.

Tom was the sergeant for his squad, all of whom were present. He didn't understand why a full squad of fourteen needed to HALO drop into some guy's backyard in Virginia, but the general himself delivered the orders and briefing. On paper, he and his squad were part of a training battalion for the Reserves, but in truth, they were assigned to Joint Special Operations Command (JSOC). This was his first mission on American soil. No one asked about Posse Comitatus during the briefing, and Tom wished he'd spoken up. He didn't have a good feeling about this drop.

Their objective was to secure one man—a Gavin Cross—for transport to a secure facility, but the briefing reported the target should be considered extremely dangerous. Any resistance at all, and they were cleared to use lethal force.

"Sergeant," the pilot's voice crackled over his headset, "we're approaching the drop zone. Expect drop in fifteen minutes."

Tom stood and clapped his hands. "All right, people! We're fifteen minutes out. Final gear check, then stack up and prepare for jump."

Seventeen minutes later, Tom fell through the atmosphere. It was a pitch black new moon. Perfect conditions for a parachute insertion at night. The mission orders specified a HALO drop, or High Altitude Low Opening. Tom didn't understand that; it wasn't like there were a lot of flak cannons in Virginia, but the brass wanted what the brass wanted. They'd open their chutes at three thousand feet. The general first insisted on the absolute minimum of two thousand, but Tom argued him up to three. On a pitch black night with no moon, he felt safer with the extra thousand feet.

Right on time, Tom pulled the ripcord for his parachute and winced when the chute caught air and arrested most of his velocity. Even with all his jumps, that was never a good feeling. Everything looked like it was going to plan, right up until five hundred feet above the landing zone when he hit something that felt like concrete. It felt like his legs shattered. The unfortunate part was that his entire squad lay incapacitated around him. The outright terrifying part was that he couldn't see what they hit.

* * *

"Dad?"

Gavin looked up at the sound of Jennifer's voice. He took in her running suit and her puzzled expression. "Yes?"

"Did you do anything to the wards recently?"

Now, it was Gavin's turn to frown. "No. Why do you ask?"

"I just went for a run, and when I took my earbuds out as I came back to the keep, I heard screaming and moaning... like painful moaning, not the fun kind. It kind of sounded like one of those 50s zombie movies."

"Screaming and moaning, huh? No, that's not anything I've added to the wards. Where did it sound like it was coming from?"

Jennifer closed her eyes and scrunched up her face, and Gavin fought the urge to smile. It was the 'thinking face' he remembered from her childhood, just all grown up. After a moment to two, she answered, "I think it was above me. I just barely heard it, though, so I could be wrong."

Gavin nodded. "Okay. I'll look into it. I could use a distraction right now. I think I've been working too long."

He pushed himself up from his seat at the table in his lab and followed Jennifer to the stairs, but unlike his daughter, he went up. Stepping out onto the roof, all Gavin heard was the rustling of the leaves overhead, but after he closed his eyes and concentrated for a moment, he did hear something like faint screams.

His first thought was to create a scrying sphere, but another idea occurred. Gavin formed a clear picture of his intent and invoked a Word of Transmutation, "*Rhyskaal.*"

The resonance of his power slammed into the ambient magic, and it answered his call. The overhead tree canopy became invisible and would be so for the next thirty minutes or until he canceled the effect, whichever came first. The source of the screaming soon became rather apparent: the cluster of people-shaped objects writhing on his wards.

Gavin invoked a Word of Conjuration so Jennifer would hear him and said, "Jennifer, come to the roof, please."

Moments later, Jennifer stepped out onto the roof. She wore a t-shirt and gym shorts, and she was drying her wet hair with a towel. "You called?"

Gavin pointed up. "Call Alexis, please. Ask her to have her mother get Uncle Sam's shit off my wards."

The mystery screaming explained, Gavin departed the roof without another word to return to his research.


WITHIN AN HOUR, news helicopters and drones of all sizes and sources hovered over the special operations squad as they awaited extraction and medical care.

# CHAPTER 22

Chelsea sat at her desk mere moments before the intercom chirped.

"I have that call for you, ma'am," Jenna said over the speaker. "It's on line three."

"Thank you, Jenna," Chelsea said, lifting the handset to her ear. "Governor Lawson, how are you?"

"I'm doing quite well, Madam President. How can the great state of Maryland help you today?"

Chelsea closed her eyes and sighed internally before speaking. "Governor, I would not normally ask this, but I need a favor. I'm asking this favor as President of the United States, knowing full well you could choose to use this as a political weapon against me at some point in the future. I would like for you to issue a pardon to Jennifer Ann Cross for any crimes she may have committed inside Maryland's borders. I have just signed a federal pardon for her."

"Is this Jennifer Cross in one of our prisons or arrested somewhere in Maryland? And why are you asking this?"

"Jennifer Cross is not incarcerated in Maryland; in fact, she's about three hours or so south of Bluefield, West Virginia... just outside Graham, Virginia, on her family's land. As for why I'm asking this of you, a DOJ task force keeps trying to use potential crimes to force Jennifer Cross to give testimony in a case they're building against someone who operated several criminal enterprises out of the Baltimore Harbor District. Her father does not appreciate this and has the wherewithal to harm a great many people if the federal government keeps pushing this. I have no intention of going soft on crime, but to be quite frank, sir, I am terrified of her father. I am asking for your help to resolve this situation in the hope that you might appreciate the President of the United States owing you a favor."

Governor Lawson was silent for several moments before he said, "Graham, Virginia. Isn't that where some JSOC troops broke their ankles and legs on thin air the other day?"

Chelsea fought the urge to sigh. Of course, he'd know about that. "Yes, Governor; it is."

"Dreadful business, that," Lawson remarked. "Has anyone made noises of Posse Comitatus yet?"

"Not yet," Chelsea replied, "but I'm sure it's only a matter of time. At least the general who ordered it did so on his own without authorization from his chain of command."

"It's always handy to have people available to fall on their sword. So, you're thinking that Justice might try to get a Maryland State's Attorney to pick up the torch, as it were, once you announce your pardon."

"I'm afraid that will be their next step, yes."

"What's so terrifying about Jennifer Cross's father, if you don't mind me asking?"

"If I told you everything," Chelsea said, "you'd swear I was drunk, crazy, or on drugs. Possibly all three. The simplest and easiest to verify is that her father—one Gavin Jamison Cross—died after a dump truck ran a red light and struck his car. This happened a little over thirteen years ago, and as of a week ago—maybe two, he's alive and well and walking around his childhood hometown. Oh, and he looks to be the same physical age as his daughter."

"Are you shitting me, Madam President? You seriously expect me to believe some guy came back from the dead? I wasn't aware the Second Coming had happened."

Chelsea sighed, this time loud enough for the Governor to hear. "See? That's the *easiest* part of all this to verify. If I told you the rest, you'd probably hang up on me. Please, Governor Lawson, at least consider it. That's all I ask."

"I can do that much," Lawson replied. "I'll let you know what I decide. Will there be anything else, Madam President?"

"No. Thank you."

"Thank you for the call, ma'am. Goodbye."

Chelsea returned the phone's handset to its cradle and hoped he'd help her. She didn't see how in the world she could ever ask Gavin to come back to the White House for another meeting, not after her disastrous conduct the day before. She'd been holding the pardon in deep, deep reserve, hoping she wouldn't need it... but she felt like her back was against a wall and she was all out of options.

* * *

GAVIN, Jennifer, and Kiri sat around an umbrella-covered table at Graham's most popular cafe. It was a free day for them... well, free from studies or research. Kiri wanted them to spend time together as father and daughter. The afternoon was perfect, going exactly as Kiri had hoped, with Gavin and Jennifer both sharing stories about their lives. The sun shifted, moving out from behind the umbrella, and caught Gavin full in the face. He sneezed. Just as his head dipped low in the sneeze, something struck the wall behind him, the sound of a gunshot echoing afterward through the air. The surrounding people panicked, running every which way.

Gavin invoked a Word, "*Sykhurhos.*"

The second shot wasn't any more effective than the first. Only this time, the bullet struck an invisible shield some three feet away from Gavin and disintegrated.

Gavin felt pretty sure he knew the location of the shooter. The visible contours of a rooftop several blocks down the street seemed wrong, but Gavin liked to be sure. He formed his intent in his mind and followed up with a Word of Divination, "*Klaepos.*"

A solid, bright red line as thick as a broom handle extended from the point where the bullet struck his protection all the way back to that odd shape on the distant rooftop. Gavin smiled and made another invocation, this time creating a scrying sphere. The scrying sphere showed a person decked out in black tactical gear laying prone on the roof and looking through a rifle scope. Gavin waved. The person jumped up and started gathering the kit scattered nearby. The person was far, far too late.

"*Thymnos.*"

Gavin watched the person—who he was pretty sure was a man—freeze right in the middle of breaking down the rifle. The person was still frozen a few minutes later when officers of the Graham Police Department stormed the rooftop.

"Right, then," Gavin said as he stood. "Let's go secure the would-be assassin from Graham's finest. I want to interrogate whoever it is myself."


In the end, it took a quiet word from Gavin's father to Graham's Chief of Police before the officers allowed Gavin to set up his own camera and interview the man who'd fired two shots into the crowded seating area of a popular cafe. Gavin's dad and Graham's police chief had been friends since Kindergarten.

As Gavin entered, the man looked up. His eyes went straight to the small camera and table-top tripod Gavin carried. Gavin didn't say a word as he went about positioning the camera and tripod where he wanted it and ensuring the power cord wouldn't come loose from the outlet or any nonsense like that. Then, he started the camera recording and sat in the chair across from the man who'd tried to kill him.

"Good afternoon," Gavin said. "I assume you already saw a rather interesting file on me, but I'll go ahead and introduce myself. My name is Gavin Cross. I am currently Head of House Kirloth and Archmagister of Tel. I realize that probably makes little sense and causes me to sound delusional, but to be honest, I'm past the point of giving a damn with you people. Over the next however long we talk, I'm going to ask you a series of questions, which you will answer. Once I have all the information I need, I'll decide whether to leave you with these fine officers or simply kill you. Incidentally, do you have a preference?"

"I hope you're prepared for a marathon," the man said. "I've been trained to resist interrogation, and my personal record is twenty days."

"Oh, my dear fellow," Gavin said with a laugh. "I have no intention of interrogating you. When I start asking questions, you'll probably volunteer information I never considered asking for. Here's the best part. I'm not going to lay a finger on you. You're going to *want* to tell me everything I ask... and more."

The man's entire demeanor dripped skepticism. "You are some kind of crazy. I'll give you that."

"*Thymnos.*"

The man's expression shifted from skepticism to adoration in an instant. "You said you want to ask me questions? Ask me; please, ask me! Whatever I can do... I just want to make you happy."

"That's good, and I know you do," Gavin replied. "First, who are you?"

"I'm Jackson Robards. I grew up outside of Springfield, Missouri. I was an orphan and joined the Marines right out of high school. I made my way to a Marine Force Recon unit assigned to JSOC, and from there, I was recruited by one of the direct action branches of our government's Black Ops establishment. They faked my death as a boating accident in the Chesapeake Bay."

"I see. Am I your first kill assignment?"

"Oh, no, sir! They've sent me all over country—and the world—to eliminate specific threats to national security."

"Really?" Gavin asked. "You've carried out orders to kill American citizens on American soil?"

"Yes, sir! I have fifty-one confirmed kills on American soil."

"Do you remember them?" Gavin asked.

"Yes, sir! Do you want me to tell you?"

Gavin shook his head. "Not right now. I'll probably ask you to write them all down later."

The man eagerly nodded his head.

"So, who gives you your orders?" Gavin asked.

"General Lester Samuels is in overall command of my branch, but my direct supervisor is Phillip Gardner."

Over the next three hours, Gavin sat with Jackson Robards asking him every question he could think of about the group he worked for. Then, he stepped outside for a notepad and pen, asking Jackson to write down the names and locations of every target he'd been assigned since joining the Black Ops group while reciting it for the camera.

When he was ready to leave, Gavin stopped the recording and gathered his equipment. He regarded the Black Ops agent gazing at him adoringly, almost like a puppy, and fought the urge to chuckle. Instead, he invoked a Word of Tutation, "*Rhosed.*"

The Enchantment effect on Jackson vanished, and Jackson's eyes went wide as he remembered everything he'd willingly told Gavin. He started to move, but handcuffs connected him to the table that was bolted into the concrete floor.

"I'm going to kill you," Jackson spat through clenched teeth.

"No. You won't. I would kill you myself right now, but I'll let your own people save me the trouble. Once CNN is showing clips of you telling me everything I want to know while you gaze at me lovingly like my new lapdog, I wouldn't give a wooden nickel for your life expectancy. But I do offer you my best wishes for whatever time you have left. Good day."

Gavin walked out of the interview room with his camera and tripod tucked under his arm.

* * *

CHELSEA RETURNED to her desk after stealing an hour to have dinner with her daughter. The first thing she saw was one of her private envelopes laying in the center of her desk, sealed. Gavin's handwriting displayed her name on the front. She knew she should alert someone that the Oval Office had been breached, but she also felt Gavin wouldn't directly harm her... no matter how much he terrified her.

She sliced open the envelope, finding a folded note—again, written on her official stationery—and a USB flash drive.

*CHELSEA,*

*A Jackson Robards took a shot at me today. Two shots, actually. I'm not as concerned about the attempts on my life; it happens in my line of work. However, I was sitting in a cafe surrounded by people... including innocent children. I cannot allow this to continue. The flash drive contains a copy of the raw footage of our conversation. I think you will find it educational.*

*Out of respect for both you and your daughter, I'll also mention that the major networks already have this. I don't know how long you have before it goes public, but I'd imagine shadowy Black Ops groups ordering the killing of American citizens on American soil—and paying the killers with taxpayer dollars, no less—is the kind of thing they'd consider breaking news.*

*I'm trying to keep from taking matters into my own hands, because it seems the only response most people understand is molten rock and charred earth, as my mentor would say. I do not want to do that; this is my home, the place I grew up. But this needs to stop, Chelsea. If you can't stop it—or won't—I will.*

*—Gavin*

CHELSEA ALMOST COLLAPSED into her seat. Her eyes went from the note in her left hand to the flash drive in her right. She felt a bottomless chasm yawning open beneath her, and she had no idea how to keep from falling into it.

# CHAPTER 23

Within hours, the internet and every major outlet exploded with Gavin's interview of Jackson Robards. It seemed the corroboration gleaned from the interview —plus what Gavin included—was sufficient for the story to grace headlines and chyrons around the country. More than one outlet made note of the would-be victim interviewing his would-be assassin. When brought to his attention, Gavin thought it was hilarious people had such difficulty believing he'd confront someone who tried to kill him. If they only knew...

GAVIN UNLOADED two handfuls of groceries from the back of his parents' Yukon and turned toward the portal. He was just exiting the portal for the next load when a van rolled to a stop in the driveway. For the first time in quite a while, Gavin knew true fear. It was a news van. A ginger-haired woman in a skirt suit leaped out of the passenger seat and advanced on Gavin like cavalry charging a gate.

"Excuse me, sir," she said. "Are you Gavin Cross?"

"I should probably be happy that you feel the need to ask," Gavin said with a wry smile. "Yes, I'm Gavin."

By now, the driver-turned-cameraman was at her side, hoisting an impressive piece of technology onto his shoulder. The light over the camera lens as well as the red recording indicator came on.

"I'm Angela Parker, Mr. Cross, and I'd like to ask you some questions about the information packet you recently sent to my news agency."

"I'm not surprised, though I am slightly offended you started recording without my permission. This is private property."

Angela replied, "Mr. Cross, as I'm sure you're aware, the Constitution grants Freedom of the Press in the First Amendment. Now, what is the nature of your dispute with the federal government?"

"I am by no means a constitutional scholar, Ms. Parker—at least not the United States Constitution—but I do not believe that the First Amendment gives you the right to invade my family's land as you will and thrust a microphone and camera lens into my face. Now, would you like to wipe the storage medium in that camera and try this again by asking my permission to interview me?"

"Why are you so opposed to speaking to the press, Mr. Cross? Is there something you have to hide?"

Gavin sighed. It seemed people never learned. "*Idluhn.*"

Cracks, pops, hissing, and smoke erupted from both the camera on the man's shoulder *and* the news van behind them. The horrendous smell of burnt electronics soon dominated the area. Both camera lights winked out as the man yelped and tossed the paperweight away from him.

Angela Parker gaped, her eyes flitting from the van to the camera on the ground to Gavin. "Do you have any idea how many thousands of dollars you just destroyed?"

"Please, take me to court. I look forward to watching your agency's legal team prove with a preponderance of evidence that I had anything to do with your technical difficulties," Gavin said, his smile carrying zero mirth. "Oh... and if you report this incident as anything other than you trespassing and not approaching me with the simplest respect by asking permission to interview me, you guarantee that I will make your public embarrassment and the ruination of your life my new hobby. Take a moment to think about what you saw in that video, and consider carefully what your next action will be. If you and your paperweights—both wheeled and otherwise—are not off the family land in an hour, I'll charge both of you with trespassing and sell the paperweights for scrap. Good day."


JUST BEFORE HE stepped through the portal with the load of groceries, Gavin grinned at hearing a forlorn shriek, "He got our phones, *too*?"

* * *


LATER THAT DAY, Jennifer entered her father's lab. "Dad, Grams and Grandpa said there's a government Suburban in the driveway to see us. Do you know anything about that?"

Gavin looked up from his current focus and frowned. "No. I can't say that I do. We might as well go see what they want."

He pushed himself to his feet and strode downstairs. At the last moment, he stopped and invoked a Tutation effect to protect himself and his daughter, then walked with her through the portal. The scene he found did little to help him make sense of the situation. Alexis Hall stood with her three-person Secret Service travel party, and she beamed from ear to ear.

As soon as Gavin and Jennifer neared the Suburban, Alexis stepped forward, holding two manila envelopes. "Jennifer Anne Cross, I—Alexis Hall—have been deputized by the President of the United States to deliver and present you with this Executive Pardon for any and all past federal crimes you may have committed."

Alexis extended one envelope to Jennifer, who accepted it amid frowns and blinking and shaking her head.

Alexis squared her shoulders once more and returned to a solemn, almost dignified expression and said, "Jennifer Anne Cross, I—Alexis Hall—have been deputized by the Governor of Maryland to deliver and present you with this Gubernatorial Pardon for any and all past crimes you may have committed within the borders of that state."

Jennifer wavered on her feet as Alexis thrust the second manila envelope at her. She accepted it and stared at both envelopes she held.

"I... I don't understand," she said, her voice distant. "What is this?"

Gavin broke into laughter. "It's Chelsea saving the government. That's what it is, Jen. By pardoning you, Chelsea has removed any leverage the Department of Justice might have over you, and what's more, they can't browbeat Maryland into trying anything, either. Alexis, have those pardons been recorded or officiated in both judicial systems, however that works?"

"Yes, sir," Alexis answered. "They're as good as carved in stone now."

Gavin replied, "Please, express my deepest gratitude to your mother for her resolution to the situation. I am especially grateful that I didn't have to solve it; it never ends well when I do that."

Alexis grinned. "For you or the other guy, sir?"

"No one involved wins with my usual solutions," Gavin replied, his voice heavy.

Alexis's grin vanished, and she nodded.

Jennifer shook herself and finally grinned. "It's over? The FBI hounding me is really over?"

Alexis and Gavin both laughed, Alexis saying, "Yes, Jen; it's over."

"So... are you coming back?" Jennifer asked. "It was nice having a study buddy."

"Am I still your apprentice?" Alexis asked, shifting her gaze to Gavin.

Gavin gave a single nod. "If you want to be."

"Well, I do have a bedroom in the keep that has a closet full of my clothes. I suppose it would be a waste just to pack them all up again." Alexis shoved her hand in a pocket and brought it back out, holding her phone. She tapped the screen a couple of times and held it up to her ear. Moments later, she said, "Hi, Mom! Gavin says, 'Thanks!' You should've seen Jen's face; she was so stunned."

Gavin gave Alexis a Look, and she rolled her eyes.

"Okay, okay... Gavin didn't say, 'Thanks'. He asked me to express his deepest gratitude to you for your resolution of the issue." Alexis fell silent for a few moments. "Yeah, I think it's best I stay here for a while, Mom... at least until Gavin says I've learned as much as I can. After thinking about it, this seems like the best course to me. Georgetown Law will still be there when I'm ready." Another silence. "I will, Mom; you, too. Love you!"

Alexis pulled the phone from her ear and tapped it once more, then stuffed it back in her pocket.

"So," the President's daughter asked, her voice bright and sunny, "do we start where we left off?"

* * *

ONCE GAVIN STARTED Jennifer and Alexis on their next practice session, he informed them he and Kiri would be stepping out for a quick errand and left the keep. Neither of his apprentices noticed that Kiri wore her leather armor with every blade sheath occupied. His ultimate destination was a Baltimore club named 'Undertow', but before he left, there was one other stop to make.

RICHARD AND ELIZABETH looked up when Gavin and Kiri entered the family room. Gavin fought the urge to smile at their reactions as their eyes locked on Kiri and her blades.

"Were all *those* in that crate that was delivered the other week?" Elizabeth asked.

"Yes," Gavin replied. "I embedded a few effects in them, too, but that's not why we're here. Mom, Dad... I'm going after Jerome Toussaint. I think the only reason the DOJ hounded Jennifer was to get her testimony against him, so I figured I might as well help them... given how Chelsea handled things on her end."

Richard and Elizabeth shared a look, Richard finally saying, "Are you certain that's wise, son? I mean, I want him off the streets as much as anyone, but I don't want you risking your life to see to it."

Gavin laughed over his father not yet comprehending the power his son wielded. "Dad, I guarantee you they don't have anything capable of harming me when I'm prepared. No one in this world understands the rules for killing wizards."

"There are rules for that?" Elizabeth gasped. "What are they?"

"Number one: never let the wizard *know* you're a threat. Number two: be within arms' reach."

Richard nodded. "Makes sense. Is there a third?"

"The good friend who taught them to me said something to the effect of, 'No. If you fail at the first and then fail at the second, having a third won't help you'."

"As Jackson Robards learned," Richard remarked. "Have you heard anything else about him, by the way?"

Gavin shook his head. "My concern or involvement with Mr. Robards ended with the conclusion of our chat; the why of it is largely irrelevant to me. We'll stop in and say hi when we get back. I don't imagine this will take long."

"Be careful," Elizabeth said as Gavin and Kiri left.

* * *

Given the line that stretched around the block and out of sight, *Undertow* must have been a popular club. Gavin had never understood why anyone paid for the privilege of gyrating in the midst of a mass of sweaty people they didn't know, but the nightclub industry showed no signs of slowing.

Gavin stepped off the sidewalk and crossed the street, approaching the mountain of flesh and muscle *Undertow* called a bouncer. Kiri followed in his wake, her eyes never resting on one spot for more than a few beats.

The bouncer glowered at Gavin and jerked a thumb toward the line as he said, "You're gonna have to—"

"*Thymnos*," Gavin invoked, smiling.

"—please tell me what I can do for you," the bouncer finished, gazing at Gavin in adoration.

"My friend and I need to speak with Johann Danzig about Jerome Toussaint," Gavin said.

The bouncer bobbed his head and reached for the door. "Oh, yes, sir! Mr. Danzig is in his office at the back of the club, third floor. There are stairs to your right just as you step inside; they'll take you right to him."

"Thank you," Gavin replied. He led Kiri through the door to the accompaniment of several groans and shouted protests from hopeful entrants.


The bass beats of the club music pummeled Gavin's skeleton as he walked the catwalks over the crowd. It wasn't pleasant. As he wound his way toward the offices, Gavin's eyes landed on a booth against the wall right below him, and he saw a guy slip a powder into the drink of the woman he sat with while she moved to the beat with her eyes closed.

He only needed a split-second to form his intent and invoked an Enchantment effect, "*Thymnos*."

The last Gavin saw, the man was showing the woman the small vial of powder, and she was drawing her hand back for what looked to be an epic slap.

"You can't help yourself, can you?" Kiri asked, Gavin barely hearing her over the brutal cacophony.

He shrugged. "I haven't lost any sleep over killing anyone who had ever used a slave brand. Do you think I'd let someone drug a woman if I could stop it?"

A slender hand grasped his shoulder, stopping him and turning him around. Kiri looked up at him, her entire expression radiating pride. "You wouldn't be who you are if you did."

She stepped close and pulled Gavin into a kiss. It only spanned the briefest of moments, but in that time, Kiri told Gavin without words how she felt about him.

"Wow," Gavin said when Kiri broke the kiss.

"I know," Kiri replied, smiling. "We need to do more of that, but we have something different to address first."

Gavin smiled and pivoted on his heel. A few short minutes later, he approached the sole office on what constituted the third floor of the club. A quick divination verified Johann Danzig's presence inside, along with five of his bouncers. A predatory smile curled Gavin's lips.

"*Idluhn.*"

At Gavin's evocation, the office door exploded inward in a shower of splinters and metal shavings. As every electronic device in the office *poofed* smoke, he stepped through the opening just as the cloud of debris settled.

"Johann Danzig," Gavin said, "my name is Gavin Cross, and I'm here to discuss Jerome Toussaint."

# CHAPTER 24

**D**uring the next few days, Gavin worked his way through Toussaint's entire organization until he identified a warehouse complex in the harbor district of Baltimore. His informants happily communicated that the warehouse complex was Toussaint's major transshipment hub in the United States. *Everything* Toussaint did passed through that warehouse eventually, and as such, the offices had data connections and complete inventories to all of his other sites... not only in the United States but around the world.

GAVIN AND KIRI stood across the street from the entrance to the warehouse complex. They both wore street clothes that matched modern America. Gavin held that day's issue of a major Baltimore newspaper under his left arm and carried a lawn chair whose seat and back were made of old-style nylon straps in a garish blend of orange and green.

"I don't like this," Kiri said, her expression *not quite* glaring. "I should be with you in there."

Gavin chuckled. "I've told you what I'm going to do, Kiri. Just how could you being there improve or add to it?"

"Just because I don't know doesn't mean it wouldn't."

"Look, I get it. You want to stick close to me and watch my back. I appreciate that, but this is only going to work if I walk in there alone. You remember Harold yesterday, right? The word is already out about us in Toussaint's organization. If you walked in there with me, they'd know *exactly* who I am, and that might change how they respond. I want them to think I'm not a threat. I want them over-confident."

Gavin released the lawn chair to lean against his thigh. He hooked his finger under Kiri's chin and raised her head to look at him. Then, he kissed her. He didn't think he did as good a job of it as she had in the club, but he certainly tried. When he broke the kiss, Kiri responded with a satisfied sigh.

"Okay," Kiri said, her tone edging back toward grumpy. "Send me back to the keep. I skipped my forms this morning anyway."

"*Paedryx*," Gavin invoked, and Kiri vanished.

Gavin turned and jaywalked across the street. As he approached the security booth, he considered that the two guards inside looked rather imposing. If he'd been the plain old Gavin who'd been born in this world, he would've been a fool to attempt what he was about to do... but he wasn't *that* Gavin anymore.

"Sir, this is a private facility. You need to—" the guard closest to Gavin said.

"*Thymnos.*"

The two men gazed at Gavin like they would've volunteered to have his child.

"Tell us how we can help you," the other guard said.

Gavin tried not to shake his head and grin. Having access to Words of Power made this almost too easy.

"I need you to open the gates," Gavin answered. "Then, you're going to keep them open and wait for further instructions."

The guard who'd spoken first hit a button without hesitation, and the gates on each side of the security booth began to roll open. Gavin crossed the perimeter of the fence and invoked a Word of Tutation, "*Sykhurhos*", warding the entire warehouse complex. Only those sworn officers of the law or sworn officers of the courts who upheld their oaths would be able to enter or leave the facility until midnight that night.

From his conversation with Harold the day before, Gavin knew Toussaint had a big drug and sex trafficking deal going down today. The site for the exchange was Warehouse Three in the complex. As he trudged along the pavement, looking for Warehouse Three, Gavin couldn't keep from whistling show tunes that he hadn't realized he missed until waking up back on Earth.

IT TOOK a few minutes to locate Warehouse Three. The structure was tucked back in the far corner of the complex, well out of direct view from the street. Of course, the rather impressive number of luxury SUVs outside the building was a good clue, as well.

A little transmutation unlocked the warehouse door without leaving any signs of tampering, and Gavin strode inside like he owned the place, whistling a jaunty tune while he carried his lawn chair and swung his newspaper. Every head turned his way as Gavin walked right up to within forty feet of the large group. He set up his lawn chair, sat, and lifted his right ankle to his left knee. A Word of Tutation created a ward that extended five feet from the center of the lawn chair in every direction; the ward protected everything inside it from simple weapons, projectiles, explosions, harmful gases, poisons, harmful sonic effects, and elemental effects. That done, Gavin leaned back against the lawn chair and unfolded the newspaper.

He looked up at the assembled criminals and smiled. "Don't mind me, guys; go on about your business."

Then, Gavin lifted the newspaper between him and thirty-odd criminals with automatic weapons to read about what was happening in Baltimore.

Not even a minute passed before Gavin heard a voice with a heavy Eastern European accent say, "Who the hell is this?"

A voice with a faint French accent replied, "Does it matter? One of you, kill him already."

A single shot rang out... followed shortly by the sound of the bullet landing on the concrete floor. It was flattened as if it had struck a six-inch steel plate.

"What the... ?" Frenchie said. "Go get the jacketed rounds." Heavy footfalls faded into the distance.

Gavin was several paragraphs into the front-page story about a city councilman embroiled in a corruption and prostitution scandal when the heavy footfalls returned. Soon, another shot rang out. Again, the sound of a bullet hitting the concrete followed almost at once.

"Uh... do you want me to shoot again, Mr. Toussaint?" a voice that reminded Gavin of a cartoon character from his childhood asked.

"Go get the depleted uranium rounds," Frenchie answered. Heavy footfalls again faded into the distance.

From what the article indicated, it seemed the city councilman had paid for an evening's entertainment with his city-provided purchase card, and it seemed the kind of Nevada brothel the councilman preferred was high-end and didn't come cheap. Or maybe he just liked big tips.

Gavin moved on from the corruption story to a headline about an upcoming replacement to several blocks of a city water main right about the time the heavy footfalls came back. Mere seconds later, another shot rang out, and like before, the sound of a bullet falling to the concrete followed it.

"You know, guys," Gavin said as he turned the page of the newspaper, "I read somewhere that Einstein once said the definition of insanity is doing the same thing over and over while expecting a different result."

Gavin heard a growl on the far side of the newspaper, followed shortly by a *ting!* that seemed far too loud in the otherwise silent warehouse.

"No, you idiot," Frenchie shouted. "Not the grenade!"

Something heavy *thunked* behind Gavin's chair at the same time Frenchie shouted again. "Get down!"

The explosion didn't even shake Gavin's newspaper. He looked over his shoulder and saw a black mark on the otherwise-pristine concrete just past the radius of the ward.

He clicked his tongue several times, sounding like a parent admonishing a child. "That's going to be a pain to clean, guys. You might never get that stain out."

"Stop pussy-footing around," the Eastern European accent growled.

Gavin heard what he thought was the action of a rifle chambering a round and smiled to himself behind the newspaper. Sure enough, the unmistakable sound of a Kalashnikov automatic rifle shattered the silence of the warehouse. More rifles soon joined in the symphony of futility. It was only when the shooters stopped to reload that Gavin heard the sirens... and they sounded *close*.

He casually folded his newspaper and collected his lawn chair once he was standing. "Well, time for me to leave. I do want to thank you for your hospitality, though. It's been a very pleasant visit. *Paedryx.*"

In the blink of an eye, Gavin vanished, newspaper and all.

* * *

THE INTERCOM FUNCTION of Chelsea's phone buzzed, and she pressed the speaker button. "Yes?"

"Ma'am," Jenna said. "Jack Webster is here to see you. He's not on the schedule."

"That's fine, Jenna. Please, show him in."

"Yes, ma'am." The intercom call ended with a click mere moments before two knocks heralded the entrance of the FBI Director.

"What do you have for me, Jack?" Chelsea asked as she stood and welcomed him, inviting him to sit.

Jack grinned. "I thought you might enjoy a report out of Baltimore that just crossed the blotter. My people passed it up to me because it indirectly related to a certain situation you recently resolved."

Chelsea couldn't keep from sighing. "What did Gavin do now?"

"That's a little unclear, to be honest. But the report that was passed up the chain involves Baltimore PD and their SWAT teams responding to reports of—and I quote—'World War III kicking off in the warehouse district near the docks'. Apparently, an anonymous caller reported at least one explosion along with all kinds of automatic gunfire. When SWAT rolled up to investigate the situation, they found upwards of sixty people beating their fists against some kind of invisible wall. Among the sixty people were Jerome Toussaint, a number of his lieutenants, and quite a few East European folks with rather unsavory reputations. It didn't help that a number of the people carried automatic weapons in plain view of the police, and when they searched the warehouse complex, they found an arsenal the Marines would be proud of, thousands of kilos of various illegal drugs, and over thirty young women who all have missing-persons reports on them. The young women were in cages, by the way."

"You can't be serious," Chelsea said. "You mean he pretty much wrapped them up and put a bow on top?"

"Well, the security footage was blank, so we have no proof or really any explanation of what happened. The techs are going over the security systems storage now, but they're not optimistic. Otherwise, the people on the task force who were harassing Jennifer Cross are ecstatic. I don't think it's possible to have gathered more damning evidence against Toussaint and his people."

Chelsea chuckled and stood, waving at Jack to keep his seat. She retrieved her cell phone from her desk and dialed her daughter, putting the call on speaker and returning to her seat.

"Hi, Mom!" Alexis soon answered the call.

"Hi, Honey," Chelsea replied. "I'm sorry to keep making you the go-between, but may I speak with Gavin please?"

"Gimme a sec, Mom. He's up in the lab." A short time later, Alexis spoke again. "Gavin, Mom's on the phone. Do you have time to speak with her?"

"Yes, Chelsea?" Gavin asked.

"By any chance, did you have anything to do with Jerome Toussaint revealing his criminal enterprise to the Baltimore Police yesterday?"

The sound of Gavin chuckling came across the call. "Now, why would you think I had anything to do with whatever happened?"

"Because there're all kinds of things that don't make sense and no one can explain. That seems to be an indication of your handiwork."

"Mysteries and enigmas beat bloodbaths and wholesale devastation, Chelsea."

"Well, yes... I'm not denying that. My main concern is whether there's enough wiggle room for defense lawyers to argue him out of charges."

All indications of mirth vanished from Gavin's voice. "If that is indeed what happens, I still have my usual options. I'd prefer not to use them, but their efficacy cannot be denied."

Chelsea exhaled a heavy sigh. "That's what I was afraid of. Thank you for your time, Gavin."

"You're welcome, Chelsea. Have a pleasant day."

The call ended, and Chelsea pulled her eyes from the phone to Jack Webster.

"So, do you want to place any bets on Toussaint's life expectancy if his lawyers get him acquitted?"

Jack snorted. "I may be crazy, but I'm not stupid. How do you want us to handle this?"

"On the one hand, the case could be made that Gavin's a foreign head of state... if his story is true. On the other, it's not like we can build a jail or prison that would hold him. Given the events surrounding Jackson Robards, what are we left with?"

"Not much," Jack replied. "Want me to keep you updated on how this develops?"

"Yes, please."

Jack nodded and stood. "Will there be anything else, Madam President?"

"No, Jack. Thanks for stopping by."

The FBI Director nodded once and left. She hoped Toussaint would remain safely behind bars... for everyone's sake.

# CHAPTER 25

In the days and weeks that followed, Gavin managed to devote his attention to training Alexis and Jennifer while starting his research into cross-planar scrying. On the surface, the concept of cross-planar scrying seemed simple enough... no different from regular scrying, really. And yet, Gavin's attempts to scry Tel Mivar continually met some form of resistance he could not get past. It frustrated him a little, especially those attempts that appeared to be successful only to fail at the last moment.

* * *

One sunny day, with a nice post-rain breeze, Gavin stood in front of a whiteboard in his lab, looking over his equations for cross-planar scrying when Jennifer arrived.

"Dad?"

"Yeah, Jen?"

"Grams is on the crystal," Jennifer answered. "She says Sheriff Dave is at the house and wants to speak with you."

Gavin pulled his focus away from the whiteboard. "Sheriff Dave?"

"Yeah. Dave Haskins ran for sheriff right around the time I came home, and he's won every election since."

"Dave Haskins? Really? Huh... I never would've expected him to go into law enforcement. He was always a bit of a rabble-rouser in school." Gavin returned his gaze to the whiteboard for another second or two, then shrugged. "Well, I'm not making much headway here. Let's go see what Dave wants. Say... what happened to Alexis?"

Jennifer fell into step beside Gavin as they left the lab. "Her mom called this morning. Alexis said she sounded kind of agitated and wouldn't say what was wrong, just asked her to come visit. So, she took her security and went back to D.C. in their Suburban. She said she'd call once she had a better idea of what was going on."

Gavin nodded. "I hope everything's okay. I also hope they're not afraid to tell me if I can help them."


A few moments later, Gavin and Jennifer stepped through the portal and found a Sheriff's Department SUV sitting in the driveway. No one was in it or around it, so Gavin shrugged as he and Jennifer went into the house. As they entered the family room, he couldn't keep from breaking into a huge grin at seeing Dave Haskins sitting on one of the couches in a Sheriff's uniform. Dave was chatting amicably with his parents and didn't immediately look toward the new arrivals, but when he did, he stopped speaking mid-sentence and simply gaped.

"Gavin? What the heck, man? You look like you ought to be back in college!"

Dave—unlike Gavin—did not look like he should be in college, except as a professor. Close-cropped salt-and-pepper hair wrapped around the back and sides of his head, leaving the center of his head bare and shiny. Lines already decorated the edges of his eyes.

"I'm still trying to get past seeing Dave Haskins, of all people, in a Sheriff's uniform," Gavin retorted as he strode across the room, holding out his hand.

Dave stood and shook Gavin's hand, his eyes roving from Gavin's head down to his feet and back up. "Seriously, how are you standing here? That wreck made the state papers."

Gavin sighed. "Dave, I highly doubt you'll believe me if I told you. I don't mind telling you, but I'm just saying you won't believe me."

Dave took a half-step back and gave him the Squint Eye. "Let's just see if you are who you say you are. What was the name of that girl I asked you to introduce me to during our Sophomore year?"

Gavin blinked and dug into his old memories. Then, he grinned, almost snorted. "Cara Kirby. Wow. I haven't thought of her in years. Whatever happened to her?"

Dave winced. "Yeah, that was her. She turned out to be something of a man-eater. She's on something like husband number four or five, and she stays with 'em just long enough to satisfy the community property laws and then shreds them in divorce court."

"Seriously? You'd think she'd have a reputation by now."

Dave chuckled. "Oh, yeah... she does, but she's still such a charmer that she's irresistible to guys who aren't from around here. She's been cutting a swath through the pipeline crews something fierce from what I hear. Okay... one more. Why did you toss the stink bomb into the girls' locker room before that big playoff game?"

Gavin searched through his memories again, and then, it was his turn to give Dave the Squint Eye. "That was not my idea, and I didn't toss it. You did, because you said Cara ripped out your soul or some such and she was captain of the cheerleaders. Somehow, you conned me into being look-out."

"All right," Dave said, a big smile slowly curling his lips. "You've satisfied me that you're the real deal. I don't think they ever figured out who did that. Probably just as well, too. They know enough of what I did as it is."

Gavin grinned. "I appreciate that, but somehow, I can't imagine you drove all the way out here for the sole purpose of seeing if I am who I say I am."

"Well... yeah, I kinda did. See, someone came in the office earlier today and wrote out a statement that there was a con artist out here pretending to be Richard and Elizabeth's dead son and that he was possibly holding them against their will. Sure, I could've rolled out with a couple truckloads of deputies and made it a big production, but I respect your folks too much for that. I didn't think a full response with all my deputies and the regional SWAT was necessary, but I thought I should drive out to be. sure."

"The person who wrote out that statement," Gavin said, "it wouldn't happen to have been someone who is a blood-relation to my daughter, would it?"

Dave pursed his lips and shook his head. "Now, Gavin... you know it's not right for me to comment on an ongoing investigation. But a person also has the right to face his accuser or accusers. If I tell you who wrote the statement, can I trust you not to plant the person in the roundabout for a few days to get a thorough coating of bird-shit? I saw one of those FBI boys the other day, and he still wears that sign, said something about not being able to take it off."

Gavin chuckled. "Those signs will disappear in a couple days. They were only supposed to last six weeks. And yes... I promise to be good, mostly."

Dave gave him another look. "That's not exactly filling me with a lot of hope, there, Gavin."

"What? I never *go looking* for trouble; it just seems to find me."

"Even I can smell that one, Dad," Jennifer opined.

Dave burst out laughing. "All right, all right. Yes, it was Emily who wrote out the statement. I'm going to write up my report as investigated without finding evidence to corroborate. You weren't even in the house when I arrived. Can't exactly hold two people against their will if you're not even in the house. My report and closing the case as 'unfounded' should put an end to it, but you might want to be watchful. She seemed to have an agenda."

"Yeah," Gavin said, drawing out the word like a sigh. "I'm not sure what her issue is." Another look from Dave. "Yes, I dropped her husband and his FBI Suburban in Graham Lake, but that didn't get him suspended. From what I heard, he was suspended for not disclosing his personal connection to Jennifer and then being insubordinate to the head of the local office."

"So, you're telling me you don't know?" Dave asked.

"Don't know what, Dave? Don't make me play twenty questions; that's not enough for a divination."

Dave blew out a breath and ran his hand down over his face. "The FBI guy with the sign still around his neck told me that word came down from On High that Jason White could resign or scrub floors for the rest of his career in the FBI."

"Seriously?"

Dave nodded.

Gavin turned to Jennifer. "Did Alexis let anything slip about Chelsea having a quiet word with the FBI Director about Jason?"

Jennifer shook her head. "Not that I know of, but would Alexis really know if she did?"

"Wait a minute," Dave interjected. "Who are 'Chelsea' and 'Alexis'?"

"Alexis Hall is my apprentice," Gavin answered. "She's an arcanist like me and Jennifer."

"Alexis Hall..." Dave said, his voice distant. Then, his eyes went wide. "Holy crap... you address the President by her first name?"

Gavin shrugged. "Why not? Neither the office nor the title impresses me all that much, and I have titles of my own that carry far more weight than 'President of the United States'."

Dave stood in silence for several moments, staring at Gavin. Then, he closed his eyes and slowly shook his head, his voice little more than a whisper, "Nope. Not gonna ask. Don't need to know."

After a couple moments, Dave shook himself like a wet dog and said, "Well, I've bothered you people enough. I'd better get back and write up my report. You know how to find me if you need me."

"Thanks for stopping by, Dave," Richard said as he started to stand. "Oh, say... has there been any news about that group of hoodlums robbing banks all over the south? The last I heard, they hit an armored truck somewhere in Tennessee."

Dave nodded. "Yeah, that's the last anyone has seen of them. They always steal ancient cars that don't have GPS or anything like that. If they happen to grab something with LoJack, they just tear it out and leave it where the car was. Listen, I probably shouldn't be saying this, but you should tell your people at the bank not to resist if they show up here. I'd prefer you not publicize this, because we're keeping the detail from the press, but they killed every single person working that armored truck. If they've killed once to get their money, they won't hesitate to kill again."

Richard grimaced. "That's tragic. Yes, I'll pass a word to the bank's management. Thank you for the heads-up."

"You're welcome, Mr. Cross, and I can see myself out."

Moments later, everyone heard the SUV's engine start up, followed shortly by the crunch of gravel as it left.

"If Emily is prepared to file a false report," Richard remarked, "she might be prepared to go further, especially since Jason is no longer in a position to maneuver into the D.C. social scene."

Gavin frowned. "Really? That's what she wants?"

"It didn't start coming out until after we won custody of Jennifer, but it seems Emily has had her eyes set on rubbing elbows with the Washington elite for a while now."

Kiri entered the family room from the back of the house and walked over to stand beside Gavin.

"You know, she said more than once how I ought to think about going into politics while we were married," Gavin said. "She probably thought to ride our local popularity into being a Senator's wife or some such. It might have been right around the time we had our last big fight over my total lack of interest in politics that she started seeing Jason. He was a hotshot up-and-comer at the Bureau back then."

"And just how do you know *that*?" Elizabeth asked, lifting one eyebrow.

Gavin grinned. "You wouldn't believe what's in that folder. The private investigator I hired gave me almost everything about Jason but his bank statements, and if I'd paid him more, he probably could've gotten me those, too."

Gavin felt a slender arm slide around his waist as Kiri maneuvered his arm around herself.

Elizabeth grinned. "I'd say you traded up. I just wish you could've gone the traditional route and divorced her."

"Oh, I don't know," Gavin said, smiling. "If I hadn't died, I would've never met Kiri or any of the other people in Drakmoor. There's a lot of good to be preserved over there."

"You think we'll ever be able to see it?" Richard asked.

Gavin nodded. "Oh, sure. I plan to create a permanent portal once I figure out cross-planar teleportation. The problem is that I'm kind of blazing my own trail here. No other arcanist I know of has ever researched this."

"What about all those books in the hidden room?" Richard asked. "Any chance they have something you need?"

"Who knows?" Gavin replied, shrugging. "But you're right. I probably should examine them. I've just been beating my head against a wall, otherwise."

"They'll be there whenever you're ready," Richard said. "I already had a look myself, and I couldn't read even a quarter of them."

Gavin shrugged again. "I might as well go have a look."

"Mind if I tag along?" Kiri asked, her arm still around Gavin's waist.

"Of course not."

Gavin and Kiri disappeared down the hall as Jennifer's eyes followed them and she shook her head.

"Something wrong, dear?" Elizabeth asked.

Jennifer chuckled. "It's so odd seeing my dad looking my age and with a woman who could make supermodels drool."

"Yes, well," Elizabeth replied, "none of us were born old, dear."

Richard chuckled. "No, we certainly weren't."

# CHAPTER 26

The next morning, a sleepy Jennifer joined Gavin in the keep's kitchen. She rubbed her eye with her left hand while she yawned and ambled toward the coffee machine. Unlike most people, she put her preferred additives in the cup first before pouring in the coffee. She turned to find Gavin watching her with amusement.

"What?" she asked, the word becoming a yawn.

Gavin shrugged. "Nothing. Sometimes, I catch myself wondering what happened to the little girl I used to read to every night before bed."

Jennifer moved around to sit beside him, putting her arm around him and laying her head on his shoulder. "I'm still here... just grown up. People might look at us weird if you still read to me before bed each night."

Gavin laughed. "Amid everything else I do? Nah... they'd never even notice. Did Alexis make it back last night?"

"No."

Gavin frowned. "Did she call?"

Jennifer shook her head.

"Can you call her, please?"

Jennifer nodded. "Be right back. My phone's in my room."

She came back a few moments later with the phone against her ear. She frowned and pulled it away to look at the screen. "That's odd. It went straight to voicemail. She never lets a call from me go to voicemail. What do you want to do?"

"About what?" Kiri asked as she sauntered into the kitchen. She wore her exercise clothes and carried two of her blades and a collection of throwing knives.

"Alexis didn't come back yesterday or call," Gavin answered. "And when Jennifer just tried to call her, it went to voicemail."

Kiri's eyes roamed over Gavin's expression. She nodded. "I'll go get ready."

Jennifer padded over to the kitchen's island that doubled as a bar and pulled herself back into her seat. The coffee was the perfect temperature now, and she smiled around it as she took a drink.

"*Klaepos.*" Gavin invoked a Word of Divination.

Soon, a scrying sphere hovered in the air in front of him but behind Jennifer. "Huh... something's wrong."

"What makes you say that, Dad?" Jennifer asked as she swiveled around. In the scrying sphere, Alexis and her mother snuggled on a couch in an unknown room. Sunlight streamed through the lace curtains, and both of their faces looked tear-streaked. "Yeah... something's wrong."

Gavin stood from the barstool and rolled his shoulders, invoking a Word of Transmutation. "*Pharhyk.*"

His house clothes faded into an upscale t-shirt, khakis, and comfortable but dressier shoes. The gold robe of the Archmagister of Tel then faded into view. Gavin reached inside his clothes and lifted his wizard's medallion from inside, letting it fall to rest against his sternum.

"If you're coming with us," Gavin said, "you might want to wear something other than pajamas... but that's entirely up to you."

Jennifer turned to go change clothes and froze for a heartbeat at seeing Kiri in her matte black leather armor, festooned with blades. She shook her head after a moment and resumed walking.

"What do you know?" Kiri asked as she joined Gavin at his side.

"Not much," Gavin replied, gesturing at the scrying sphere. "I know something's wrong, but they don't seem to be under duress or any direct threat to their persons. The Secret Service is one of the top agencies in the world in terms of dignitary protection. I can't imagine someone would get past them without making *a lot* of noise. We'll do this quietly. If it's something like a favorite great-aunt died, I don't want to add to their sorrow."

Not quite two minutes later, Jennifer returned. She wore what Gavin would consider 'business casual' and had her hair pulled back in a ponytail.

"I'd like to think whatever we're about to walk into is benign," Gavin said, "but there's always the chance that it isn't. Jennifer, I would not have you unable to defend yourself. *Othys.*"

A rune appeared in the air between Gavin and Jennifer.

"That is a Word of Interation; memorize it. Focus on the threat, and speak the Word. I suggest you keep your focus limited to the immediate threat, rather than a group."

Jennifer's eyes roved over the rune, and she nodded. "What does it do?"

"It kills the object of your focus outright."

Jennifer blanched. "Really?"

Gavin nodded. "The first time I used it, fifty-three slavers fell dead across a quarter of the city. I didn't know what I was doing and was a bit unfocused in my invocation. Please, do not repeat my mistake. Are we ready?"

"Yes," Kiri replied.

"I guess so," Jennifer said.

"*Paedryx.*"

The world blinked around them.

They stood in the lobby of the West Wing. Staffers gawked, even as they jumped away. Security reacted to them as a threat, but Secret Service Agent Chet was also in the lobby. He waved for the uniformed security to stand down.

"You certainly know how to make an entrance," Chet said,

approaching Gavin. "I thought you needed a teleport beacon or something."

Gavin smiled. "That's what I wanted you to think."

Chet's expression said, 'Oh, shit', even though his lips never moved.

"What are you doing here?" Chet asked at last.

"I have not seen or spoken to my apprentice since yesterday. I am here to ascertain her well-being."

Chet nodded. "She's fine. She's upstairs in the residence."

"I will personally verify her well-being before I leave," Gavin said.

Chet closed his eyes and sighed. "Right. Follow me, then."

Chet led Gavin and party through the White House to the section that served as the President's residence while in office. Gavin noticed Jennifer seemed horribly impressed, but after spending the better part of a Drakmoor year living in a floating castle with spectral staff, the President's Mansion with all its functionaries was a house like any another house.

They soon stopped outside a nondescript door. A couple people Gavin assumed were agents nodded to Chet as they approached. Chet nodded back and went to the door, knocking twice. Gavin thought he heard someone say something behind the door, and Chet opened it just enough to lean inside. Moments later, Alexis came out. As Jennifer had been not even fifteen minutes ago, she wore pajamas, and she rubbed her eyes as she sniffled.

"Sorry," Alexis said. "I should've called. I—" Tears overtook her, and her shoulders heaved as she sobbed.

Jennifer was at her side in an instant, throwing her arms around her. "Alexis, what's wrong?"

"It's my brother," Alexis managed between sobs. "He's in the Army, and his unit went out on patrol five days ago. No one's heard from his unit in three days. The Army finally told Mom yesterday. She's thinking of signing a letter to turn over her office to the VP until we know something."

"I can help if she'll let me," Gavin said.

Alexis nodded. "She's not really dressed to receive visitors." Then looked down at herself. "I'm not, either, honestly."

"I already scried you before we came," Gavin responded.

Alexis's eyes shot wide. "Oh… yeah, Mom probably won't like that, but since you've already seen her not looking Presidential, hang on a second."

She turned and disappeared back inside the room. A few minutes later, she came back out and motioned for Gavin and party to follow. The Secret Service agents twitched at the sight of Kiri and her blades, but Chet shook his head.

As Gavin entered what looked to be kind of a combination living room and bedroom, he heard Chet say, "She's safer with them in there than she would be surrounded by half the 82$^{nd}$ Airborne."

Inside the room, Gavin saw Chelsea step out of what he assumed to be a closet, wrapping a knitted robe around her. She walked back over to the couches and indicated for everyone to sit.

"So," Gavin said, "Alexis tells me your son is missing."

Chelsea jerked a choppy nod. "He and Alexis are twins. Frankly, I couldn't believe it when he said he wanted to join the Army. They'd always been so inseparable, and Alexis never showed any inclinations toward that. General Fitzcairn—the Chairman of the Joint Chiefs—came to the Oval Office yesterday and told me that no one had heard from my son's unit in three days. They were just supposed to be on a routine patrol."

"I can show him to you if you want," Gavin said, "but before you automatically agree, know that there's no way to know what we'll see until we see it. We could see him healthy and hale, or be looking down on his mutilated corpse. Give it some thought before you answer."

Chelsea regarded Gavin with steel in her expression. "Of course I want to see my son. Yes, I'd prefer to find him healthy and whole, but not knowing is killing me."

"Okay," Gavin replied. "*Klaepos.*"

The air between them started to shimmer and, soon, flashed into a scrying sphere. At first, the image was too dark to make out any details, but it seemed to shift and take on the appearance of a light-amplified view. Several people sat on what looked to be a dirt floor with earth-toned brick walls.

"That's him," Chelsea gasped. "He's alive. Can you tell where he is?"

"*Klaepos.*" The scrying sphere zoomed out, first showing a dusty desert town with a small sight of the President's son in the upper-right corner. The view kept zooming out, adding the view of the town to a lower corner and showing a red dot in a section of the Middle East.

"Wow… that's better than mapping websites," Alexis said, her eyes wide. "Will I be able to do that?"

Gavin nodded.

Chelsea walked to a nearby phone. She picked up the handset, and when she spoke, she was the President once more and no longer a grieving mother. "Jenna. Would you ask General Fitzcairn to come to the residence, please? Thank you."

She returned the phone's handset to its cradle and turned back to Gavin. "How long will that last?"

"As long as you need it to."

Thirty minutes later, both Alexis and Chelsea had returned to the room freshly showered and dressed. Not more than five minutes after that, there was a knock at the door.

"Yes?" Chelsea called out.

The door opened enough for Chet to lean inside. "Ma'am, General Fitzcairn and two of his people are here. They say you requested them."

"Yes, I did. Please, send them in."

The door soon opened to admit a Marine Corps General, followed closely by a Major and a Captain. As Gavin took in the new arrivals, he found the general reminded him of Ovir in that he was an older gentleman with close-cropped gray hair and a barrel chest. The man didn't look like he'd given into age.

"You sent for me, ma'am?" Fitzcairn said, not quite snapping to attention.

Chelsea gestured toward the scrying sphere. "It seems my son has encountered some trouble."

Fitzcairn turned and seemed to notice the scrying sphere for the first time. He started to gape but schooled himself back to a non-expression. He stepped closer, examining the sphere and what it showed.

"I don't believe I've ever seen something like this before," Fitzcairn remarked, his tone cautious.

Gavin chuckled. "I'd be amazed if you had. This is a scrying sphere."

"But this is real? It's not like a mock-up or something?"

"No. A scrying sphere is divination. A mock-up would be an illusion."

Fitzcairn's lack of understanding was writ large across his face.

Gavin grinned and gestured to the President's daughter, saying, "Alexis, care to elaborate?"

Alexis squared her shoulders and answered. "Divination can show you the present or the past with ease, and occasionally tidbits of a potential future. It cannot create false images or sounds or sensations. To do that, you have to use an illusion, the quality of which is dependent upon the caster or—in this case—invoker."

Now, the general did gape.

"Alexis is one of my apprentices," Gavin said with a proud smile. "And as you can see, she's taking to her studies rather well."

The general shook himself and returned his attention to the scrying sphere. He gestured to the red dot with his finger, sweeping around it in a circle.

"Madam President, this whole region through here is a hotbed of insurgency, as you well know. I've looked at the mission order for your son's squad, and I'd say they encountered a superior force and were captured. It was just a routine patrol, but there's nothing saying the *other* side couldn't have their own patrol out. Going in to get them will be dicey. They have Triple-A hidden all through the area."

Gavin chuckled. "Going to get them won't be dicey at all... if I do it."

General Fitzcairn and his two people turned to regard Gavin with open skepticism. "You expect us to wait for you to hop a plane and fly halfway around the world?" the general asked. "Those people could be tortured or worse in the meantime."

"Chelsea, how long have I been here?" Gavin asked.

"A little over an hour now."

"Ninety minutes ago, I was on my family's land in western Virginia, about three to four hours south of Bluefield, WV. I don't *need* a plane, car, or any other conveyance if I know where I'm going, and this scrying sphere is sufficient. To be absolutely sure of it, I'll use Alexis as a focus, since they're twins. Focusing on her brother will allow me to open a gateway right to that room."

Fitzcairn and his two officers shared looks before Fitzcairn spoke. "Is there any way we can see more of the town where they're held?"

"Sure," Gavin replied. He reached into the scrying sphere and 'pulled' the section showing the town to the center of the sphere. The regional view shrunk to occupy the top corner opposite the view of the President's son and his unit. "Treat it like a picture on your phone. Pull the image toward you to move in that direction. Push away to move back. You can turn the image, zoom, whatever you like."

The general stepped forward and started manipulating the scrying sphere. After several moments, he said, "I *know* this town. I was there, right out of the Academy during the War on Terror. I thought we bombed it off the map around '04 or so... after Al Qaeda insurgents took it back from us what must've been the fifth or sixth time. If they haven't changed much, the headquarters building used to be over here..."

The general now manipulated the scrying sphere so fast it partially blurred. Soon, he stopped, and the image settled on a large structure under heavy guard. He turned to Gavin for a moment as if to ask a question but turned back to the scrying sphere. He reached into the image and pulled it toward him. The image moved toward the structure and ultimately through its walls. After more manipulation, the general found a large room that looked like a planning or staff room. Large maps of the area hung on the walls, marked up with troop locations and movement vectors. Papers littered tabletops.

"Man," the general said, shaking his head, "I'd love to have the documents in this room. It looks like a regional headquarters. We've been over there again, the past couple years. It seems like every time we pull out, some idiot does something stupid that brings us to the brink of a world war and we have to dump more troops right back in there to keep the peace. Honestly, I'd say just wall the whole region off and let 'em fight it out, but I highly doubt any major conflict that erupted in the region would actually *stay* in the region."

"You seriously want what's in that room?" Gavin asked.

The general turned to Gavin. "That room represents the greatest intelligence windfall of this whole conflict. I ought to be taking pictures with my phone."

Gavin snorted. "Don't bother."

He moved to the scrying sphere, nudging the general out of the way, and slowly spun the sphere. The sphere revealed only one door into the room, and it was closed. Gavin focused on the door as he said, "*Sykhurhos-Paedryx.*"

In the scrying sphere, the door took on a vermilion aura as an arch of crackling sapphire energy rose out of the floor. It soon flashed into a gateway to the room shown in the sphere.

"Go on through and get whatever you want," Gavin said.

"Seriously? What about that door? We're not armed, and it could open any time," the general countered.

Gavin chuckled. "A nuclear blast wouldn't open that door. You'll be fine. If you really want what's in that room, now's your chance."

The general pivoted on his heel and almost leaped through the gateway, waving his arm for his officers to follow. It took them three trips to clear out everything of value, but in the end, they were grinning like children with free passes to a candy store.

"That's all well and good," Chelsea said, "but what about my son?"

Gavin turned to the general. "How likely is it there are civilians in this town?"

"There's no way to know," the general said with a shrug. "Sometimes, these people keep camp followers, and sometimes, they don't. For what it's worth, I've had soldiers under my command killed by camp followers, so the line between combatant and non-combatant is a bit gray over there."

"Fair enough," Gavin replied. "Alexis, I'll need you with me so your brother knows I'm for real."

"*Paedryx.*"

Another gateway soon appeared, and Gavin led Kiri and Alexis through it. It took a little convincing, even for Alexis, but soon, her brother and his unit started stumbling through the gateway. None of them were prepared to come out in a room in the White House, facing both the President *and* the Chairman of the Joint Chiefs, but they made it work, especially since they had been wounded.

"Okay," Gavin said to Kiri and Alexis, "the both of you get back through the gateway. I'll be right behind you."

Kiri's eyes narrowed. "Gavin, what are you doing?"

"An evolution of the slaver camp," Gavin answered.

Kiri's eyes went wide, and she pivoted on her heel, pushing Alexis back through the gateway.

Gavin fixed his intent in his mind, took a deep breath, and invoked a Word of Evocation, "*Idluhn.*"

He stepped back through the gateway and collapsed it, just as the brick wall took on a glow.


BY THE END of the day, the several-hundred-feet-tall mushroom cloud and the four-thousand-square-yard area of Middle Eastern desert that had been turned to glass made headlines around the world.

# CHAPTER 27

During the days and weeks that followed, Gavin stepped up his training for Jennifer and Alexis, introducing them to new concepts and considerations while he pursued his own research. He also introduced them to Words from the other Schools. Jennifer already knew 'Thraxys' from when they'd gone to make sure Alexis and her mother were okay, and Gavin expanded his apprentices' repertoire to include Words of Divination, Conjuration, Evocation, and Transmutation. He taught 'Thraxys' to Alexis as well and discussed its usage; when she finally processed exactly what that Word was capable of doing, she looked rather horrified. Gavin couldn't blame her.

As their training progressed, Gavin allowed them to start practicing the creation of gateways. For their earliest attempts, he asked that they restrict their efforts to the keep's plateau, while warning them to keep their concentration fixed on their desired destination until the gateway formed. He was not surprised *at all* when Alexis's concentration wandered during her invocation and she ended up treading water in the lake. Jennifer, being the good friend she was, ensured she had pictures to memorialize the event.

* * *

"DAD." The tone of Jennifer's voice—more than her words—pulled Gavin from his focus.

"Yes?"

"Grams is on the crystal. She says there's news on the TV you need to see. She sounded a little freaked out."

Gavin didn't bother leaving the lab. He pictured the front door of his parents' house and invoked, "*Paedryx*."

The world blinked.

Gavin, Jennifer, and a bewildered Kiri and Alexis stood on the front porch. Everyone turned to Gavin.

"What if one of us had been *bathing*, Gavin?" Kiri demanded.

"You'd be dripping soapy water on the porch, and I'd send you back," Gavin replied, deadpan, and stepped between the ladies to enter the house. They shared a look between each other and followed him.

Gavin spent mere seconds traversing the distance from the front door to the family room, and his eyes locked onto the TV as soon as he entered. The view showed a mountainside somewhere with the tail end of an avalanche. The camera did a slow pan to a nearby outcropping of rock, and even Gavin could barely believe his eyes. A massive four-legged creature with wings and scales perched on the rock, turning its head to and fro as if surveying the countryside.

"What the hell is *that*?" Alexis exclaimed behind him.

"That," Kiri said, her voice devoid of any emotion, "is a dragon."

The TV's speakers broadcast the newscaster's next comment, "As you can see, the supposed *dragon* is just settled there. Beyond saving the skiers from the avalanche its departure from inside the mountain created, it's made no attempt to communicate. Wait... wait... we're switching back to the newsroom for new developments."

"Thank you, Geoffrey," a woman's voice said, as the video feed of the dragon shrunk to the top-right corner of the screen. "We are now getting confirmed reports that an Air Defense Destroyer of the French navy has fired on another of these creatures flying through their airspace in the Mediterranean Sea. The dragon retaliated with a fire breath that reduced the destroyer to molten slag. Only five of the destroyer's crew made it to safety, and it is unclear at this time what damage—if any—the missile did to the dragon. We have also received confirmed reports from across Europe, Africa, and Asia that more of these apparent dragons have emerged from our world's oldest mountain ranges. We have no other reports of attacks at this time, and we will continue to update you as this situation unfolds."

Alexis's phone blared, pulling their attention away from the TV. She dug it out of her pocket and saw it was her mother calling.

"Hi, Mom," Alexis said. "You're on speaker."

"Is Gavin there?"

"Yes, Mom. He's right here and can hear you."

"Gavin," Chelsea said, "I realize you don't work for me and you haven't had the best experience with the government, but I would really appreciate it if you came to advise me on this situation. Our NATO allies are... well... concerned, to say the least, and I've already fielded calls from three European ambassadors asking what our response to these... *creatures* will be."

"They're dragons, Chelsea, and yes, I'll come. If you have any sway at all with the other governments of the world, please convince them not to attack anymore. At best, they'll only make the dragons mad, and at worst, they'll actually manage to kill one."

"Why would that be the worst case?" a voice Gavin didn't recognize asked.

"Because then, the dragons would have reason to retaliate on a grand scale. I refer you to the French destroyer that is now on its way to the bottom of the Mediterranean. I don't know how hot dragon fire is, but it reduced sizable portions of that destroyer to molten metal and converted the seawater it touched straight to steam. Take a minute and think about that. I'll be there shortly."

Gavin nodded to Alexis, who tapped the control to end the call.

"Okay," Gavin said. "Who's going with me?"

"Well, I know I'd *like* to go, and it wouldn't make any sense not to take Alexis," Jennifer answered.

Gavin shifted his eyes to Kiri. She shrugged, saying, "Do you see any reason you'll need me?"

"I have no idea," Gavin replied. "If you'd rather hang out here until I do need you, that's fine with me."

Kiri sighed. "I've been slacking on my forms. I was going to work on training today. I'm happy to come with you if you think you'll need me."

Gavin turned to Alexis and raised his eyebrow as a question.

"I'd say the government has learned its lesson," Alexis responded. "Well... probably not, but the pardons removed any leverage they had over Jennifer. Plus, with your little display in the Middle East, I doubt they'll be rushing to create conflict with you anymore."

"Fair enough," Gavin replied. "I'll grab one of the stones and tie it into the devices here and in the keep. That way, we'll be able to contact each other as needed. Kiri, enjoy your day; yours will probably be far more productive than mine at this point."

* * *

GAVIN FOLLOWED his apprentices through the gateway he opened to the Rose Garden... after scrying it to be sure there wasn't a pending press conference or anything. The last thing Gavin wanted was to appear out of an arch of sapphire energy on live, international television.

Alexis and Jennifer moved aside to permit Gavin to lead, and they headed straight for the door to the Oval Office. The Secret Service agent standing at the door held up his hand.

"The President asked me to inform you that they're waiting for you in the Roosevelt Room, sir," the agent said.

"Alexis?" Gavin asked.

"Through the Oval Office and across the hall. The middle door opens directly to the hallway, and the right door will take you through Jenna's domain."

Gavin turned to face her. "Who's Jenna?"

"Mom's executive assistant," Alexis answered. "She's been with her since the Michigan State Senate."

"With your permission, sir," the agent said, "I'll escort you to save on potential complications."

Gavin grinned. "Like some poor sod randomly falling asleep?"

"Something like that, yes, sir," the agent replied.

"Lay on, Macduff," Gavin said with a flourish.

The agent gave Gavin a flat look but opened the door to the Oval Office and conducted them through it to the hallway beyond. From there, it was a simple matter to reach the Roosevelt Room, where Gavin found a number of people he'd never seen before with the President.

Chelsea looked up at the agent's knock, and the moment her eyes found Gavin, an expression of complete and utter relief flashed across her face before she schooled herself back to a non-expression. She waved her hand, and the agent opened the door.

"Honored ambassadors, ladies, and gentlemen," the President said as she stood, prompting the entire group to stand as well, "allow me to introduce Gavin Cross. He is our expert on these dragons and will be able to advise us on the best response."

Taking the few steps necessary to do so, Chelsea extended her hand to Gavin, which he accepted and shook. She said, "Thank you for coming so quickly."

Gavin shrugged and smiled. "It's not like I was busy or anything, Chelsea... but in all seriousness, I'm glad I can help. I'm also glad you felt you could call."

Chelsea nodded and returned to stand beside her seat.

"These are my apprentices," Gavin said to the room at large. "Many of you already know the President's daughter, Alexis. Beside her is my daughter, Jennifer."

Gavin saw the four available seats at the opposite end of the table, and he noticed the seat directly opposite the President was available. He wondered if that was by intent or happenstance.

Chelsea gestured toward the open seats, and Gavin led his apprentices the length of the table. Despite his continued use of the

President's first name as his form of address, Gavin was *not* so crass that he sat before the President in her own seat of authority. As soon as they reached the open seats, Chelsea resumed her seat, and her guests followed suit.

"Gavin," Chelsea said, "during our call, you told me with complete certainty that these creatures are dragons. Care to explain the reasoning behind your assertion?"

Gavin chuckled. "Well, the simplest explanation is that old saying, 'if it walks like a duck and quacks like a duck, there is an excellent chance that it's a duck'." He saw several expressions around the table shift into varying emotional responses. A few people displayed anger or annoyance, a few contempt, and Chelsea was one of those who displayed amusement. "But the fact is that I have seen dragons before, and these creatures—as you call them—match those I've seen... for the most part."

"How are they different?" One of the men along the left side of the table from Gavin's perspective asked.

"Well, for one thing, coloring," Gavin replied. "You can even see that for yourselves in what video footage is available. Each dragon has subtly different coloring across his or her scales, and don't ask me how to determine gender. I don't know, and to be quite honest, I don't want to learn."

"I know in the games my sons play," a woman said, "different colored dragons denote different capabilities. Is that true?"

Gavin smiled. "You mean, are there Chromatic or Metallic Dragons that are tied to specific elemental types?" The woman looked a little embarrassed. "Honestly, not that I've seen. None of the dragons I've interacted with displayed breath weapons other than fire, but as scientists are wont to say: absence of evidence is not evidence of absence. I haven't encountered *every* dragon in existence, so I can't tell you for certain that's not the case. I do know that most of the coloring I've seen are gradients in the dragons' individual scales, kind of like rock strata, instead of the entire dragon being a specific color or hue."

"How do you suggest we deal with these dragons?" A man on

Gavin's right asked. Unlike everyone who'd spoken so far, he had a British accent.

"What's wrong with applying the Golden Rule, sir?" Gavin asked in reply. When the man looked a bit confused, Gavin continued. "'Do unto others as you would have others do unto you'. It's a pretty simple concept, and I'd argue extremely wise, considering the other party in this instance probably thinks you taste good with ketchup."

The man sputtered as several others around the table fought to hide their amusement.

"That is an excellent point," Chelsea said, drawing the focus to her. "What are the chances these dragons will start eating people? What do they normally eat?"

"Whatever they want, I'd imagine," Gavin answered. "In all seriousness, they might make a run on the elephant, sheep, cow, and other similar populations. For clarity's sake, we should just walk up to one and ask, but if these are the dragons I think they are, they're only a threat to the people of this world if you precipitate it."

"What dragons do you think these are, Gavin?" Chelsea asked.

"Are you sure you want me to answer that *here*, Chelsea? The information is rather high impact and might spark more than an argument or two."

Chelsea nodded. "Yes, please, Gavin. The people to your left are my closest advisors, as well as respected and trusted members of Congress. The people to your right are the ambassadors of our closest allies. Everyone here needs to know what you know."

Gavin laughed. "Chelsea, no one should know even *half* of what I know, but I see your point. If these dragons are the dragons I think they are, they came to this world as protectors for a sizable group of war refugees."

"Seriously, young man?" the British ambassador asked, his tone derisive. "I'd think we'd notice a group of war refugees appearing with these massive creatures."

Gavin shook his head. "No, you wouldn't, because the world's population—I'd guess ninety-eight-plus percent—are *descendants* of those refugees. They came to this world something like five thousand years ago... if my math is right. I myself can trace my genealogy back to the specific person who brought his family to this world."

Everyone gaped at Gavin, even the President.

"Are you saying these dragons are five thousand years old?" Chelsea asked, her voice quiet.

"Nope," Gavin answered. "They're older. They were adults when they came here with the refugees... assuming these are those dragons. I suppose there's always the chance that these are the dragon equivalent of children or grandchildren to those dragons, but we won't know unless we ask."

"How long do dragons live?" one of the President's people asked.

Gavin shrugged. "No idea, but one of my closest friends is a dragon, and he's over six thousand years old."

A rapid knocking on the door drew everyone's attention. Chelsea motioned for the person to come in. It turned out to be Jenna carrying a laptop.

"Madam President, please forgive the interruption, but you need to see this," Jenna said. "One of the dragons is talking to the press."

Chelsea nodded, and Jenna walked to the flat screen TV mounted to one wall. She hurried through the connections and turned on the TV. Once it was on, she shifted the display of her laptop to it, then hit 'play'.

The TV immediately lit up, and the image of a dragon filled the screen. A chyron appeared as the video started.

"Hello," a woman's voice said, sounding vaguely British, "I'm Mikayla Brennan with the International News Network. May I ask you some questions?"

The camera zoomed back to show a dark-haired woman from the waist up. She faced away from the camera. Next to the dragon, she looked like an ant.

"You're not afraid of me, young one?" the dragon asked, the resonance of its deep voice causing the camera to vibrate.

"Well, honestly, yes. I am afraid, but if I don't take the chance of asking if we can talk, I'll never know."

The dragon threw back its head and laughed, before returning its focus to the reporter. "I have no knowledge of how long it has been since we came to this world, but it is apparent that humans haven't changed much in that time. Ask your questions."

"Well, first, how should I address you?"

"You would harm yourself trying to speak my name, young one," the dragon replied. "You may call me Firestreak."

"Thank you, Firestreak. What makes you think time has passed since you came to this world, as you say?"

"None of these structures or black roads existed when I began my slumber," Firestreak replied. "The conveyance you arrived in certainly did not. I must commend your stable master, by the way. Horses normally flee our presence, but I have yet to see any escape from the conveyance."

Mikayla looked over her shoulder, frowning. It was clear she wasn't looking at the camera. Suddenly, her eyebrows shot up, and she turned back to Firestreak.

"Oh! You mean our news van? It doesn't have any horses in it. It's totally mechanical. You said you went to sleep. Do you know why you finally woke up after all this time?"

The dragon returned its focus to Mikayla, who seemed to fight the urge to flinch away. "Yes. For the first time since the refugees pacified this world, an arcanist has wielded the true Art. That means it is time for us to seek out this arcanist and return home." The dragon looked up, and the camera panned up to show an airplane flying high overhead before returning to the dragon. "You clearly do not need our protection any longer."

"If I may ask, how are you speaking my language if you've been asleep for so long? The English language in its current form is less than a thousand years old."

"I am not speaking your language, young one," Firestreak replied. "I'm speaking mine. I currently have an effect active that allows any listener present to hear my speech in his or her native tongue."

"That's rather impressive, but you said you seek an *arcanist*? I'm not familiar with that word," Mikayla said. "What is an arcanist?"

"Hmmm... how odd. The term enjoyed near-universal use when I began my slumber. An arcanist is one who possesses the capability of reshaping reality to his or her desire by manipulating the very essence of existence. In truth, there is very little they cannot do, and they pass on their knowledge through a mentor/apprentice agreement."

In the Roosevelt Room, every person at the table turned to look at Gavin.

# CHAPTER 28

"If you will excuse me," Gavin said as he stood, "I think I'm going to go speak with Firestreak."

"And if we won't excuse you?" a man wearing the uniform of a US Army general asked.

Gavin shrugged. "In all truth, I was being polite. I don't really care whether you excuse me or not. Alexis, I'm leaving you here with your mom; I'll reconnect with you once I've discussed matters with the dragon... or dragons. Jennifer, I'm sending you home."

Before Jennifer could get wound up to protest, Gavin invoked a Word, "*Paedryx*."

Jennifer vanished.

"*Klaepos*." A sphere of space in front of Gavin started shimmering and flashed, becoming a scrying sphere. Gavin studied the terrain, the news crew, and the dragon for several moments before he invoked another Word, "*Paedryx*."

An arch of crackling sapphire energy rose up out of the floor. When it reached sufficient size, it flashed, becoming a gateway to another place. Chill winter air blew into the Roosevelt Room through the gateway, along with more than a few snowflakes. Gavin stepped through it, and the gateway vanished.

The entire room sat in silence for several moments before the British ambassador looked down the table to Alexis. "May I ask you some questions, young miss?"

Alexis shrugged. "Sure. I can't promise I'll be able to answer them, but you're welcome to ask me anything you want."

"Those strange words he used... what were they?"

"Those were two of the Words of Power," Alexis answered. "I'm not sure how many there are; I've only worked with a few."

The British ambassador nodded. "So, they're like spells?"

"No. I don't think so. Gavin has never used the word 'spell' or 'spells' to describe anything he taught me."

"He used the same word to teleport Miss Cross and to create that archway," the British ambassador continued. "I would have thought that would be two different words."

Alexis smiled. "Ah, no. Maybe it would be two different spells, but I don't know anything about that. You see, there's a concept that Gavin calls the one essential truth: the effect is shaped by the arcanist's intent. Jennifer and I could both create a fireball. Jen could make hers look like a regular campfire flame, and I could have mine be a bright pretty pink. But that wouldn't change the fact we imposed our will to alter reality in creating those fireballs. Likewise, Gavin teleported his daughter home and, then, created a gateway to wherever the dragon is. The effect was shaped by his intent. One time, he wanted to teleport Jennifer, and the other he wanted to create a gateway."

"That sphere he created to view the site of the interview," another ambassador said, "what's stopping him from viewing the Situation Room here or one of our countries' most secure facilities?"

"I honestly don't know enough about scrying to answer that question," Alexis replied. "I'd imagine there's a way to ward a location against scrying using something in the School of Tutation, but we haven't reached that point in our studies. But if you mean what's stopping Gavin specifically from doing it? Well, with all due respect, he doesn't really care all that much about your country... any of your countries, really. It would be time spent for which he received no valuable return."

"Do you know how he froze the FBI SWAT team outside of time?" the Attorney General asked from her seat beside the FBI Director.

Alexis shrugged. "I *think* I know the Word he used, but I'm not about to attempt it to find out... not for a long, long time. If ever."

"May I ask why?" the Attorney General continued, her tone curious but not pressing or interrogative.

"Well... Gavin is scary powerful. He does things with the Art sometimes that you can just tell are casual, off-the-cuff invocations—maybe like you using a newspaper to brush off a park bench before you sit—that have almost knocked me off my feet. I... I'm not saying this right. Let me start over. People like us—I mean, Gavin, Jennifer, and me... arcanists, I guess—have an additional sense regular people don't seem to have. Gavin calls it *skathos*, and he says it is a manifestation of our connection to the ambient magic. Through our *skathos*, we can sense magic. Before I started working with my power, it physically hurt to be anywhere close to Gavin when he was working the Art. Think of the absolute worst pain you've ever experienced and then multiply that by at least five, if not ten. When I first met Gavin, what he did in this room would've had me on the floor crying like a baby. It's gotten a lot better since I've started developing my control and making my power part of me.

"What I'm trying to say is, different workings of the Art require different amounts of control and/or power. Some Words of Power require more control to use them. I'm not about to experiment with manipulating time until I *know* I'm not going to break something that has wider implications than just me. I mean, think about it. What if I was practicing in my room upstairs and accidentally broke time for the White House or even Washington, D.C.? Is that really something a complete novice should mess around with?"

"How would you rate Jennifer in comparison to her father, regarding raw power?" Chelsea asked, surprising Alexis.

Alexis took a deep breath, making an 'O' with her lips and slowly exhaling as she shook her head. "That's a tough question. I've never been around Jennifer practicing when Gavin wasn't within a hundred yards or so. When it comes to raw power, he overshadows the neighborhood. If I really had to guess, though, I'd say she feels less powerful than Gavin, but I don't know *how much* less. And I also don't know how much a person can change that through practice and... well, exercise, for lack of a better term. Without knowing what Gavin felt like through my *skathos* when he was first learning the Art, I have nothing to compare his current power against... which in turn means I have no way to gauge where Jennifer is on the power spectrum."

Heads nodded around the table.

* * *

GAVIN STEPPED THROUGH THE GATEWAY, arriving beside the INN news van. The wind carried more than a little chill, so Gavin invoked a Word of Tutation to give himself protection from the cold, "*Nysphaes.*"

"Ah, here is the arcanist now," Firestreak's voice boomed.

The reporter and cameraman both pivoted, and the reporter almost slipped as she hurried over to Gavin.

"Hello, sir," she said, "I'm Mikayla Brennan, INN. Are you the arcanist Firestreak seeks?"

Gavin regarded the microphone shoved into his face and the camera on the man's shoulder. It took all his willpower to keep from frying every piece of technology in a hundred-yard radius.

"I believe so," he said.

"What is your name, sir?"

Gavin lowered his eyes from Mikayla's face to the microphone maybe three inches from his nose for a few moments before lifting his gaze back to her eyes.

"Kirloth," he said.

"Oh, ho," Firestreak boomed. "*Kirloth*, is it? I daresay this will be an interesting conversation."

"Kirloth?" Mikayla repeated. "What kind of name is that, sir?"

"The only one you're getting," Gavin replied. "Now, step aside."

"Is that a title?" Mikayla pressed, showing no intention of moving.

"Young human," Firestreak boomed, "when Kirloth speaks, you'd be well advised to listen."

Mikayla pivoted and walked back to Firestreak. "So, you know him, then?"

"Him, specifically? No. But I know of the family. That's what Kirloth is, you see. An arcanist House, one of the most powerful and respected, in fact."

Gavin crossed the intervening space to approach Firestreak, saying, "I'm not sure this is the best place for a conversation. If I craft a beacon for you, do you feel up to a bit of travel?"

"I'm always up for a good flight," Firestreak replied. "May I bring others?"

"Of course," Gavin answered. "If you bring more than five or so, I'd ask you assume a less massive form, or available space will be a problem."

Firestreak chuckled, sounding like a human's booming laugh. "This is not the first time we've encountered that. I think we'll manage."

Gavin nodded. "I'll create the beacon for you to find me. Bring whomever you like."

"Thank you, Kirloth. I look forward to our conversation."

Firestreak and Gavin nodded to each other. Then, to keep the reporter from seeing where he lived, Gavin teleported himself directly home instead of using a gateway.

* * *

ONCE BACK AT THE KEEP, Gavin set about designing the beacon for the dragons. He wanted it to be both effective and low-key. It was going to have to be a composite effect; there wasn't really any other way to accomplish it. He'd use Enchantment to create a subtle call and Transmutation to filter it to dragons only *and* ensure it reached throughout the entire world. He also worked a specification of just Earth into what world or worlds it affected, because he didn't need all the dragons back in Drakmoor sensing the call and ripping apart the planar boundaries to find a way to Earth. He had enough problems as it was.

It took perhaps three hours to work through the design and look over it one more time to see if he'd missed anything. As with all wizardry, it wasn't so much a matter of crafting the design like one would a spell; it was more about developing a clear picture of his intent. Without that, there was no way of knowing what his invocation would do.

When Gavin was as ready as he'd ever be, he stepped outside the keep and considered where to center the beacon. Wherever it was centered, that was the point the dragons would try to reach. The keep's plateau wasn't large enough, and Gavin didn't really feel like enlarging it. Even if they all adopted human forms, Gavin didn't want to try fitting who knew how many dragons into it. So, he teleported to the opposite side of the lake. The lake created its own quasi-clearing, and Gavin could clear some trees if he received more draconic guests than there was room along the shore.

Location chosen, Gavin cleared his mind of everything but his intent. As soon as he felt he had the clearest image of his intent possible, he invoked the composite effect, "*Zaenos-Rhyskaal-Zyrhaek.*"

As with every other working of the Art he'd done on Earth, the ambient magic seemed to swell to him—much like high tide on the ocean shore. He felt it whirl around him as it swelled, and the moment his power executed his intent, the ambient magic exploded outward. Massive waves of power greater than any tsunami that would travel the globe to fulfill its design.

Gavin closed his eyes and examined the result of his invocation through his *skathos*. It was exactly what he wanted. He could detect no flaw or imperfection.

Now, all that remained was to await the dragons.

## CHAPTER 29

Connor Matthews sat behind his desk in the Commonwealth's Attorney's office. He was new to his job, having passed the bar a short four years earlier. He had a good conviction rate, but he was still looking for that one big case that would catapult him to headlines across Virginia in furtherance of his career goals. As he looked over his desk to Emily White and considered what she had just told him, he thought he'd found it. That didn't mean he was going to make it easy on her, though; he needed to be sure of her commitment to the case.

"Mrs. White," Connor said, "it would be unheard of for a Commonwealth's Attorney to file charges against someone without an underlying criminal complaint from either the Graham City Police, the county sheriff's office, or the Virginia State Police. I'm not sure there are sufficient grounds to do so in this instance."

"Mr. Matthews," Emily replied, "I was hoping you'd see the situation for what it really is. Dave Haskins went to school with my late husband, and somehow, this charlatan has convinced him that he is indeed Gavin Cross. I had hoped that Sheriff Haskins would've been able to see him for what he really is—a predator with no morals or ethics—but that apparently did not happen. I know deep down in my soul that he is preying on the memory of my late husband with my former in-laws, and I'm afraid of just how far he'll go if he's not stopped."

Even though Connor wasn't a local, he knew the Cross family was big in Virginia... at least the western half of Virginia. If he saved them from a nasty situation, perhaps they'd be grateful enough to contribute to his election fund when it came time to run for Attorney General.

Conner nodded. "Mrs. White, without a formal criminal complaint, we have to proceed carefully. I will take your written statement and consult with Judge Thomas for advice on how best to move forward."

"Thank you, Mr. Matthews. I appreciate your time."

* * *

GAVIN STOOD about ten feet from his newest creation, and he had to admit, he was rather pleased with his work. It was a massive sign about fifty feet before the stone plinths that served as the gate to the Cross family homestead. The sign advised anyone coming down the gravel road to the property that reporters and anyone who intended to harm the property or its occupants would not pass the gate, advising them to turn around lest they damage their vehicles. His parents suggested the sign after Gavin told them he was considering adding reporters to the 'block list' in the ward. One of his motivations for getting back to Drakmoor was the lack of cut-throat journalism there. He could walk through the markets of Tel Mivar anytime he wanted without concern of being accosted. Though, perhaps his reputation and that of his House factored into that.

Thoughts of Tel Mivar carried feelings of homesickness, and that surprised him. He didn't realize he had come to think of Tel Mivar as home. He resisted the urge to heave a sigh. He remembered hearing a song from decades ago that was about not being able to go home any more. At the time, the song hadn't made sense to him, because you could always go home, right? No matter what else happened in your life, home was always there waiting on you, right?

Not so much.

Graham was no longer his home. Now his family's land was just where he had grown up. He had so little in common with any of these people that a part of him wished he'd never ended up back here. Then, he thought of Jennifer. If he hadn't come back, she would've died. The *skathos* cascade had already been approaching that point. Was *that* why he was here? But what could the old man have possibly wanted with Jennifer? A piece of the puzzle clicked in his mind. No... not with Jennifer. With *his daughter*.

Gavin pivoted and walked to a nearby tree stump. The stump had been there as long as Gavin could remember, and it looked like the perfect place to sit and think this through.

Once perched on the stump, Gavin closed his eyes and sent his mind back to the roadside conversation with Bellos, all those months ago. He had just visited the site of Kalinor's manor that his mentor had laid waste, and Bellos had appeared to him as a black-robed wizard. Ah... there it was. He and the old man had needed a wizard of House Kirloth, and Gavin had been available.

At the time, Gavin thought that it had something to do with the Conclave of the Great Houses. As a matter of fact, Bellos may have implied that, but there were several questions Gavin had asked that Bellos refused to answer, saying Gavin wasn't ready yet to know those answers.

Then, there was his mentor's slip-up when he made Kiri's pendant to access the suite. Without Kiri's blood, the pendant would've acted like a skeleton key, able to open any door secured by the Kirloth bloodline... because that's what Marcus's medallion signified even if he hid it. House Kirloth.

*Holy cow.* That's it. Marcus and his apprentices had apparently loved using bloodlines as anchors for all kinds of persistent effects. Like the protections built into the manors and manor walls at Mivar Estate. Probably the other ducal estates, too. There was something— maybe even something *extremely* important—anchored to the Kirloth bloodline. The more he thought about the matter, sitting there on the tree stump, the more Gavin thought that maybe he was better off not knowing what it was.

* * *

Not knowing how long it would take the dragons to arrive, Gavin returned to the keep. It was a simple matter to locate his daughter.

"Hey, Dad," Jennifer said, looking up from where she stretched out on one of the couches in the family room area. "What's on your mind?"

"Feel like contacting Alexis and asking if she's ready to resume training?" Gavin asked. "I've done as much as I can do on the dragon situation for now. We should be receiving guests, but I don't know for sure when that will be. Therefore, there's no reason for us to sit around and waste the time."

Jennifer scooped up her phone off the coffee table beside her and tapped at it for a few moments with her thumbs. A few seconds later, her phone pinged.

"She's ready now, Dad."

Gavin grinned. "Okay, then. Go get her."

Jennifer gaped. "Uhm... do what now?"

"You heard me, Jen. Go get Alexis."

"But... I'm not ready! I've never used that Word before. What if I goof?"

Gavin smiled. "That's why I want you to use a gateway and not a direct teleport. If you goof, it's no big deal... as long as you don't open a gateway to the bottom of the Atlantic or the surface of the sun. *That* would be a bad day. Just concentrate on the Rose Garden; you've been there enough times now that you should have a decent feel for it. Oh... and when you two are ready to come back, have Alexis create the gateway."

With that, Gavin turned and started up the stairs to his lab, effectively ending the discussion.

* * *

CREATING her first gateway freaked Jennifer out a little, but it was so worth it to see the look on Alexis's face when *she* stepped through and not her father. The President and Alexis's travel party looked a little surprised as well.

"Seriously?" Alexis almost wailed. "He taught you to make a gateway *first*?"

"Chill, girl," Jennifer replied. "It's not like we both haven't seen my dad do it dozens of times. Besides, he said you're supposed to create the gateway to take us back."

"Really?" Alexis asked, her eyebrows perking up.

Jennifer nodded, and Alexis cheered. Jennifer chose not to mention the expression of pleased maternal pride she saw coming from the President as Alexis prepared herself.

"You'd think she's about to create her first fireball," Chet remarked as he, Gayle, and the other Secret Service agent followed Alexis.

Alexis pivoted on her heel. "Oh, please. Fireballs are easy. Anyone can make a fireball."

"You know what?" the President said, walking over. "I've never seen you make a fireball or anything else. I suppose it's just something I'll have to get used to now. I'm not the cool mom I was when you came running in the door each day after school all fired up to show me what you'd learned."

Alexis turned to Jennifer, asking, "Think it would be okay?"

Jennifer shrugged. "Ask forgiveness, not permission. But don't use the Word my dad always uses; you're just starting out, and it will kick your butt."

"Which Word should I use?"

Jennifer pursed her lips and pulled her phone. She tapped on it for a moment and turned it so Alexis could see. "That one."

Alexis nodded and took a deep breath. She held out her hand as if holding an apple and invoked a Word of Evocation, "*Kaephys.*"

Jennifer felt the resonance of her friend's power as reality reshaped itself to her will. Not even three heartbeats later, a small orb of fire the color of a campfire hovered over Alexis's palm. Jennifer looked to her mom and saw the President smiling the smile of a proud parent. When Jennifer saw the President's expression turn to a frown, she turned back to Alexis. Her friend now scrunched up her face, and the dominant emotion seemed to be pain... or at least discomfort.

"What's wrong, Alexis?"

"Hot... so hot." Alexis started moving her hand around, trying to get the fireball away from her, but the orb persisted in hovering just a short distance above Alexis's palm. "Burning hot... what do I do, Jen? I think my hand's on fire."

Jennifer scanned the area, her eyes landing on a small fishpond. She didn't know if there were actually fish in the pond, but it looked deep enough. "There, Alexis! Picture the fireball flying over to that fishpond, and then, release it from your control. That's the important part; once it's at the pond, release your control of it."

Alexis turned and faced the pond. The fireball seemed to leap from her hand, whooshing between everyone and leaving a small trail of smoke in its wake. It struck the calm, peaceful surface of the pond and vanished as an impressive amount of water flashed to steam.

"Okay," Jennifer said. "Let me see your hand."

Jennifer accepted Alexis's hand in hers, and she looked it over, first with her eyes and then her *skathos*. Alexis's hand looked a little redder than normal, but to her *skathos*, all seemed well enough.

"It may feel uncomfortable for a bit," Jennifer said, "but I think you'll be fine. We can always put some Vitamin E lotion on it if you want, but I don't think it warrants burn cream or anything like that."

Gayle appeared at their side and gave Alexis's hand a once-over of her own. She nodded. "I agree with her assessment. If you'd held onto it longer, though, you might have had a problem."

"It already feels better," Alexis said, "but I do like the idea of Vitamin E lotion, just to be sure."

She stepped around Jennifer and Gayle, walking to her mother.

She pulled her into a tight hug and whispered, "I love you, Mom," before she released her and stepped back.

"Take care of yourself, sweetheart," the President said. "And don't forget to call me once in a while. I like to know how you're doing."

Alexis nodded. "I will, Mom. Take care of yourself, too."

Then, Alexis turned and focused on her memories of the keep. Once she felt she had a clear picture of the keep's grassy lawn in her mind, she invoked a Word of Transmutation, "*Paedryx*."

An arch of crackling energy—colored hot pink—rose out of the ground behind Jennifer. When it reached the necessary height, it flashed into a gateway to another place. Jennifer and the Secret Service agents stepped through. Alexis waved to her mom one more time, then vanished through the crackling portal.

# CHAPTER 30

Gavin leaned back against his chair. Others might have lifted their feet to the table, but he didn't. He swiveled the chair around to face his whiteboards, and this time, he did prop one foot up on an adjacent chair. Every single attempt to scry Tel Mivar failed. The closest he'd ever come was a wispy sphere that looked as if it would form a scrying sphere but *poof*ed into nothingness before it had the chance. The frustrating part was that he was clearly missing something, but he didn't even have a hint of what it might be.

The books in the hidden room of his parents' house hadn't helped at all, either, and he had wasted an afternoon skimming them to prove it. Well... from a purely educational perspective, the afternoon hadn't been a waste, but in terms of finding the answer to his problems in one of those books, it had been. The first shelf or so was nothing but Gerrus's journals. Apparently, Gerrus routinely scried his home, specifically his brother—the man Gavin had known as Marcus... but he never cared to write *how*. He either took the method for granted, or he'd promised never to disclose it. Considering the man was a wizard of House Kirloth, Gavin didn't feel like laying any odds as to which was the case. Not that it would matter five thousand years later, anyway.

"Hey, Dad," Jennifer said, poking her head into the lab, "where's the notebook you wrote all the furniture measurements in?"

Gavin frowned. "Uhm... I think I stashed it in the study on the same floor as the library. Why?"

"I wanted to see if you wrote the dimensions of that second wardrobe I liked in it, the one we ended up not buying. I'm thinking of redecorating my room, and if it will fit, I'm going to go buy it."

"Have fun, sweetheart," Gavin replied, a faint smile curling his lips. He turned back to his whiteboards just as a thought clicked in his mind. "Dimensions. What if the planar boundary I have to cross is actually a *dimensional* boundary? If it is, I'd need to modify the scrying to account for that. Huh... I wonder if it would work."

Gavin stood and cleared his mind of everything except his intent, focusing his entire consciousness on one goal: scry Tel Mivar. Then, he invoked a composite effect, *"Klaepos-Uhnrys."*

Unlike every other working of the Art he'd performed on Earth, this composite effect savaged him. It almost felt like the power fought to rip the very life from his bones. He collapsed to his knees and coughed, feeling a faint wet warmth on his lips as flecks of blood settled on the floor. When he forced himself to look up, though, he whooped with joy.

A scrying sphere hovered about two feet above the table's surface, and it looked down on Tel Mivar.

Gavin's strength returned in a rush, and he leapt to his feet, throwing his arms in the air. "Yes! Ha, ha, ha! Yes!"

Right about then, Jennifer and Alexis entered the lab. They looked like they were dragging themselves to move, and they caught him jumping up and down as he thrust his arms in the air. Alexis made it about three feet inside the door and collapsed to her knees, gasping. Jennifer pushed through the pain and remained standing, but her entire demeanor silently screamed she was enduring immense pain.

"What the hell did you do, Dad?" Jennifer groaned out as she fought to stand without the wall to support her. Then, she noticed the scrying sphere. "What is that?"

"That, my dear daughter, is a cross-planar scrying sphere," Gavin said, his voice still cheering. "You're seeing my capital, Tel Mivar, from a bird's-eye view."

"What's all the shouting?" Kiri asked from the door, then saw Alexis. "Alexis, what's wrong? Do you need help?"

Kiri moved to help Alexis stand and then helped her to the closest chair. In doing so, she saw the scrying sphere and what it depicted. She almost let Alexis fall back to the floor as she gaped. "Gavin! That's Tel Mivar!"

"Yes, Kiri, it is," Gavin replied. "I finally figured out why all my attempts to scry the city before failed."

"Why?" Kiri asked.

Gavin grinned. "Because the planar boundaries are *dimensional* boundaries, and you have to account for that. Jennifer gave me the solution, honestly. Well, I don't think she realized she was giving it to me, but either way, she did."

"Dad," Jennifer said, her voice cautious, "is that blood on your lips?"

"Huh? Oh, sorry, Jen. Yeah, the cross-planar scrying hurt like a... well, let's just say it *hurt*. If I had tried that any earlier in my experience with the Art, it probably would've killed me. It certainly felt like it was going to."

"So, I guess this means you'll be leaving soon?" Jennifer asked, her voice still cautious.

"Hmmm?" Gavin responded, pulling his eyes away from the scrying sphere. "Oh, no, sweetheart. This was just the first step. There's still a long way to go before we contemplate attempting a cross-planar gateway. Besides, I'm not ready to leave just yet. After all, I can't abandon my apprentices."

Jennifer broke into a smile and moved to Gavin, pulling him into a hug. "Thank you, Dad. I'm not ready to lose you again quite yet."

"Lose me?" Gavin asked. "Who said anything about you losing me? The final thing I will do before I return to Drakmoor full-time will be building a permanent portal between here and there, keyed to our bloodline. You'll be able to visit me any time you want, and I'll be able to visit you and your grandparents, too."

Jennifer beamed and buried her face in his shoulder.

While Alexis recovered from the resonance of Gavin's scrying, Gavin pointed out places to them. First, the College of the Arcane. The Temple of Valthon. He shifted the scrying and showed them the rough area where he woke up in the city.

As he was going to shift the scrying to show Kiri her home, the communication crystal in the device Gavin built lit up. It broadcast Elizabeth's voice. "Hello? Is anyone there?"

Jennifer pulled herself away from Gavin and went to the crystal, pressing the button to activate their side. "Hi, Grams! You won't believe what Dad just did. He created a cross-planar scrying sphere to see Tel Mivar! He was just showing some places in the city to me and Alexis."

"That's wondrous news, dear, but would you mind asking your father to come to the house? There's an officer of the court here to speak with him."

"An officer of the court?" Gavin asked, arriving at Jennifer's side. "What court? What's this about?"

"I'm sorry, sir," an unknown woman said. "I cannot discuss this without first verifying you are the intended recipient of these documents."

Gavin's eyes narrowed at the crystal. She had documents, did she? That sounded like she was serving him with something, probably a subpoena. But why? It didn't make any sense.

"I'll be right there," Gavin replied.

Pivoting on his heel, Gavin sunk into his *skathos*. There was still a wispy tendril of power connecting him to the scrying sphere, and he wasn't ready to dispel it yet. "*Rhyskaal.*"

Alexis screamed.

Through his *skathos*, Gavin watched reality bend to his will. The wispy tendril connecting him to the scrying sphere disconnected from him and became a series of wispy tendrils reaching out from the sphere. It no longer drew power from him. It now drew power from the ambient magic, and it would persist until that power no longer existed... or he chose to dispel the scrying sphere, whichever came first.

Then, Gavin moved to Alexis. "Alexis, I'd like for you to move over to the anti-magic ring for a bit, until you feel better. It won't block your or your power's recovery, but it will insulate you from me."

Alexis's jerked a choppy nod and moved to stand.

"Here, let me help you," Kiri said.

Between Gavin and Kiri, Alexis made it to her destination. Gavin set down her chair, and Kiri eased her into it, before they walked the short distance back to Jennifer.

"Do you want to go?" Gavin asked, looking at his daughter.

"Yes, but shouldn't someone stay here with Alexis?"

"It's okay, Jen. You go with Gavin," Alexis said. "I'm texting Gayle and asking her to come sit with me for a bit."

Gavin nodded and turned toward the table. He focused on the family room of his parents' house, specifically the door leading into it from the dining room. His intent clear in his mind, he invoked a Word of Transmutation, "*Paedryx.*"

His crackling arch of sapphire energy rose from the floor and soon became a gateway. Just as it formed, a feminine scream carried through from the house, and it wasn't his mother.

Jennifer and Kiri stepped through, and Gavin followed. The moment he stepped into his parents' house, the gateway vanished.

Gavin immediately focused on a brunette with curly hair sitting on one of the sofas. Her eyes were wide, her lips still parted from the scream. She wore the uniform of a court process server.

"Hello," Gavin said, stepping between Jennifer and Kiri. "You wanted to see me?"

"Wha... what... was that?" the woman asked, still hyperventilating. "What are *you*?"

Gavin tried not to smile or laugh. "That was an arcane gateway, a door between two physically separate places, and I am Gavin Cross. I am Head of House Kirloth and Archmagister of Tel."

"What did that fool sign me up for?" the woman hissed. She lifted her eyes to Gavin and jabbed her left index finger first at him and then in the direction of where the gateway had been. "I'd say you're some kind of drugged-out crackpot, but after dragons, I suppose anything is believable."

"I assure you, ma'am, I am no crackpot. Nor do I use drugs... well, beyond caffeine. I like tea."

The woman jerked a manila envelope out of her messenger bag and threw it at Gavin. She jumped to her feet and made for the door. "There! You're served; now, let me the hell out of here!"

Gavin caught the manila envelope in his hands before it smacked him in the face and turned toward the woman's retreating form. "I thought I was supposed to sign something?"

"Don't care," the woman shouted back as she opened the front door. "Those creeps in the clerk's office can deal with it."

She sprinted off the porch and almost leaped into her car. After starting the engine, she turned the car with considerable haste and gunned it, rocketing down the driveway like a shot.

Gavin considered the open front door and the fading sound of the roaring engine. He shrugged. "I guess some people can't handle the Art."

"What is it, Gavin?" Elizabeth asked.

He opened the manila envelope and withdrew folded documents. Unfolding them, he skimmed the first page.

"Huh," he said. It was almost a grunt. "It seems I've been subpoenaed to appear before Judge Thomas for a hearing to determine if I am faking my identity and holding you against your will."

"What?" Richard gasped. "That makes no sense. I just played a round of golf with Mike last week. Let me see that."

Gavin handed the subpoena to his father and watched him skim through it. His skimming slowed to reading, and it wasn't long before he glared at the document.

"That—" His eyes darted to Elizabeth. "—Emily; this is her fault. I'll guarantee you that."

"Well, should I retain an attorney?" Gavin asked. "I mean, I can prove nine ways from Sunday that I'm Gavin Cross. I know all kinds of things only I'd know, and what's more, there's always a paternity test with Jennifer... or you for that matter, Dad."

Richard still glared at the subpoena. "I *knew* I should've run her out of town after that custody fight."

"Richard," Elizabeth countered, her voice reproving, "we discussed that and decided it wouldn't be right. Plus, her husband was an FBI Special Agent at the time."

"Don't care," Richard growled. "If she wasn't still in town, she would never have known Gavin was back in the first place. I don't suppose you could... *you know*."

Gavin raised his eyebrows. "You don't suppose I could what, Dad?"

"No, you're right," Richard remarked. "Killing her isn't a good idea."

Gavin gaped. "No, Dad... I'm not killing Emily. Especially not after she's convinced your golf buddy to bring this hearing. Somehow, I don't think that would go over well at all. Plus, doesn't she have kids, too? I'm not doing that to them. Besides, nothing she's done so far warrants killing her."

"I said you're right already," Richard groused. "Fine. I'll call Kurt. He's done both criminal and civil work; he'll have an idea how to approach this."

"Kurt who?" Gavin asked.

"Kurt Sellers. He's a lawyer out of Richmond."

Gavin shrugged. "Well, we have three weeks until the hearing, so it's not like we don't have some time. If he's willing to consult on this, let me know where I need to be and when I need to be there."

Richard nodded as he reached for the phone.

Gavin turned and opened a gateway back to the keep.

# CHAPTER 31

Two days had passed by the time Kurt Sellers arrived at the Cross Estate. Gavin went to his parents' house and conducted Kurt back to the keep. The portal unsettled him. The scrying sphere in Gavin's lab blew his mind.

"So, according to the subpoena, the hearing is to determine whether there are grounds for charges of a false identity and unlawful detainment," Kurt said as he sat with Gavin at the table in the lab. He kept casting wary glances toward the scrying sphere hovering over the table. "Personally, I don't see how anyone could visit this place and say that you're unlawfully detaining your parents; it's absurd. The false identity, though... that's a little different. It all hinges around the claim that you're Gavin Cross, Richard and Elizabeth's son who died. Returning from the dead isn't really a thing, except in very specific circumstances involving medical professionals within moments of the actual time of death. So, it's possible we'll have an uphill slog, there, but I won't know without more information. Now, ask me questions."

Gavin leaned back against his chair and directing an appraising look to Kurt. "Why would an attorney who drives a high-end luxury sports car and wears Armani suits travel all the way out here to consult with me about this case? I'm missing something."

Kurt nodded. "My father served in the Gulf War with your father, the same unit in fact. My father didn't make it home, and your father sponsored me in law school."

"That explains it, all right," Gavin replied. "So, what do I need to do to convince you that I am indeed Gavin Cross?"

"Honestly?" Kurt asked and pointed at the scrying sphere with his thumb. "That is an excellent start. I have no idea what that is or what it's showing. I've also done a little research. I saw that clip of you on INN. Has the dragon shown up yet?"

Gavin shook his head. "Nope, but the beacon is subtle. And there's no way to know what they're doing. They may be discussing the matter between themselves. *That* is a scrying sphere, and it is currently showing Tel Mivar, the capital of the Kingdom of Tel. This may complicate matters for you, but that is where I belong. I'm making excellent progress toward getting back there, and I'd be a lot closer if all these inconsequential issues stopped popping up. My widow, ex-wife, former wife—whatever you want to call her—is behind this hearing. I have no proof of it, but I know for sure and certain she is. She filed an almost identical complaint with the sheriff. He came out, and we talked. I convinced him I am who I say I am, and he filed his report that the claim was unfounded."

"That's good," Kurt said, making a note on his notepad. "I'll subpoena a copy of his report. What else?"

"The family doctor took blood and tissue samples when my parents insisted on me going to the ER to get checked out. I think that was more of a shock reaction than anything else. There wasn't anything wrong with me, but the doctor did the complete work-up... full-body x-rays and everything."

"What about your... uhm... grave?" Kurt asked. "Has anyone exhumed it?"

"Not that I know of," Gavin replied, "and now that you mention it, I'd kind of like to see what's in there, if anything."

Kurt nodded. "That's something we can discuss with Judge

Thomas. Well, I have a good start on some notes here. Let me get started on this, and I'll follow-up with you as I have more questions."

"Before you go, let's talk fee."

"With all due respect, I'm not sure you could afford me."

Gavin grinned. "Try me."

Kurt replied with a number that held a rather impressive amount of zeros."

"Fair enough," Gavin replied. "Call my parents and tell them where you're staying once you've secured lodging. I'll deliver a cashier check to retain your expertise for eighty hours. Keep records and receipts. I'll cover all reasonable expenses, like fuel and lodging and meals, while you work this case. When you run out of retainer, tell me. Any questions?"

Kurt shook his head. "No, I think that about covers it for now."

Gavin snapped his fingers. "There's one last thing. *Nythraex-Uhnrys-Sykhurhos.*"

A stone small enough to fit in the palm of Kiri's hand faded into existence in Gavin's hand. It bore the Glyph of Kirloth. He extended it to Kurt.

"That is a key to the portal and keep for you," Gavin explained. "It will exist for one month or until I dispel it, whichever comes first. If this case extends beyond a month, I'll make you more as needed. It is tied to you and you alone. It will dispel itself if anyone else tries to use it."

Kurt nodded. "Thank you."

Gavin shrugged. "It'll save you from bothering my parents every time you want to speak with me. If there's nothing else, I have a couple of apprentices who are overdue for their daily lesson."

Kurt shook Gavin's hand once more, and Gavin walked him out of the keep.

* * *

THE DATE of the hearing quickly approached, and the dragons still hadn't shown up at the site of the beacon. In fact, they'd disappeared from the world once more, which led Gavin to wonder if maybe they were involved in extended discussions and deliberations. When you had thousands of years to look forward to, there wasn't really much of a rush to make decisions.

GAVIN, his family, Kiri, Alexis, and Alexis's travel party entered the courtroom. Kurt arrived just as the portal door closed from their entrance. Gavin and Kurt went to their table, while Gavin's parents, Jennifer, Kiri, and Alexis sat in the first row of the gallery.

"I'm not sure your choice of attire is the wisest," Kurt remarked, looking over Gavin's gold robe and silver wizard's medallion.

"This is my official dress," Gavin replied. "The Archmagister of Tel wears gold robes, especially in formal situations that would rate a suit or dress uniform for anyone else."

Kurt pursed his lips. "The judge may not appreciate it."

"If he turns out to be an ass, I'll take steps. I didn't *have* to do all this; I don't want to make waves, so I'm playing along."

"I'm almost afraid to ask what your other options are," Kurt remarked as the courtroom doors opened once more.

Gavin chuckled. "Don't ask, especially not here."

The Commonwealth's Attorney, Connor Matthews, stepped through the swivel gate separating the court from the gallery and placed his briefcase on his table. He approached their table and extended his hand.

"Connor Matthews, Commonwealth's Attorney," he said.

Kurt stood and shook his hand. "Kurt Sellers, representing Gavin Cross."

Connor's expression faltered. His handshake went limp.

"It's a pleasure to make your acquaintance, sir," Connor remarked. "I never expected to face such *prestigious* counsel."

Kurt smiled. It was almost predatory. "Oh, I'm certain there's quite a lot about this case you'll find unexpected."

Connor retreated to his table.

At the appointed time, Judge Thomas entered, and the bailiff called out, "All rise. This court is now in session, the Honorable J. Michael Thomas presiding."

"All right, people, it's a busy day," the judge said after sitting. "Let's get to it. For the record, we're here today to conduct a hearing into the matter of possible identity theft and unlawful detainment. Counselors, introduce yourselves, please."

"Connor Matthews, Your Honor. I'm the Commonwealth's Attorney."

"Kurt Sellers, Your Honor, representing Gavin Cross."

The judge looked at Gavin and raised an eyebrow. "Mr. Cross, are you wearing a robe in my courtroom?"

"Yes, Your Honor, I am," Gavin answered. "As I explained to my counsel, this gold robe is my badge of office, for lack of a better term. It is as much a part of who I am as your own robe is for you, sir."

"And just what office do you hold?"

"I am the Archmagister of Tel; I hold the power of high, middle, and low justice within the Kingdom of Tel, along with complete authority over it."

Judge Thomas nodded. "Very well. What proof do you have of this?"

"Unassailable proof is difficult to come by in my present circumstances, Your Honor. I am conducting research into cross-planar travel with the ultimate goal of returning to Tel Mivar, the capital of Tel. I can show you Tel Mivar, if you wish."

Judge Thomas remained silent for a few moments, finally saying, "Yes. I do believe I'd like to see this Tel Mivar."

Alexis schooled her face into a non-expression as she fought to contain a whimper.

Judge Thomas didn't miss Alexis's reaction. "Young lady, what's your name, and why are you afraid of this man showing me Tel Mivar?"

Alexis took a deep breath and stood. "Your Honor, I am Alexis Hall, Gavin's apprentice. Your request to see Tel Mivar caused me fear, because this particular effect causes me great pain. All wizards have a resonance, Your Honor, and the more powerful wizards can indirectly cause less-experienced wizards to feel pain in varying degrees. This will be the second time Gavin has performed this effect, and if it's anything like the first, I'm not sure I'll be able to stop myself from screaming."

"I see. Are you the same Alexis Hall that is the daughter of our current president, and would you swear to your assessment under oath?"

"Yes, Your Honor, I am, and I would."

The judge shifted his eyes to Gavin. "Is there anything you can do to help her and still show me Tel Mivar?"

"Yes, Your Honor," Gavin replied. "I can partition the courtroom so that any workings of the Art in this space won't affect anyone in the gallery."

Judge Thomas nodded. "Please do so."

"*Sykhurhos.*"

A faint shimmer moving across the courtroom along the wooden gallery partition from the left wall to the right was the only visible indication of Gavin's invocation.

"And the gallery is protected now?" Judge Thomas asked.

Gavin nodded. "Yes, Your Honor."

"Very well. Show me this place."

"*Klaepos-Uhnrys.*"

Just as before, the invocation savaged Gavin, and he staggered, catching himself on the table where he sat. A sphere with a diameter of a hula-hoop began shimmering like the surface of a still lake into which a stone has been thrown. The shimmering increased until, in a flash, the sphere became a window to another world.

Connor Matthews came out of his seat, giving voice to his shock.

"Impressive," Judge Thomas remarked, then looked at Gavin. "Young man, are you well?"

Gavin nodded. "Yes, Your Honor. That particular effect takes a lot out of me for a few moments, but I'm fine. If you'll look to the scrying sphere, you'll see a keep in the center of four obelisks; that is the College of the Arcane. The city's harbor is toward the bottom, and in the top right, you can see the Temple of Valthon. The river that runs along the city's western edge is the Vischaene."

"Very well," Judge Thomas remarked. "As I've never seen anything like this in the natural world, I'm willing to grant that you appear to be the Archmagister of Tel for the purposes of this hearing. Are you good to proceed, Mr. Cross, or would you like a brief recess?"

Gavin rolled his shoulders and returned to stand in front of his seat. "Please, proceed, Your Honor. Everyone's time is valuable, so I'd rather make haste than tarry."

"Your Honor," Connor Matthews said, standing, "I object to the summary decision that this man is the 'Archmagister of Tel' – whatever, or *whoever* that is. This is nothing more than Hollywood theatrics."

Judge Thomas chuckled. "It is, is it? Show me the projectors. Show me the wires. Pull back the curtain, Mr. Matthews, and show me how the magician performed his trick."

"Ah... well," Connor stammered.

"We're all waiting, Mr. Matthews. You assert that this scrying sphere—I believe he called it—is nothing more than Hollywood special effects? Prove it. Unless I'm mistaken, this country still operates on the assumption of innocence, with burden of proof being upon you and your colleagues that a person is guilty. I do not appreciate society's gradual decline toward automatically assuming someone is guilty merely because a court case has been filed. If the accused or defendant pleads guilty, that's one thing, but this is an exploratory hearing. Present your evidence to me, Mr. Matthews. Lay out the information that leads you to believe criminal proceedings are warranted."

Connor Matthews looked away and said, "Objection withdrawn."

Judge Thomas nodded. He turned to look at Gavin, waving his hand in the general direction of the scrying sphere. "How long can we expect to enjoy the extra scenery, Mr. Cross?"

"If you'd like it removed, it can vanish right now, Your Honor," Gavin replied.

"I think it has served its purpose."

Gavin dipped into his *skathos* and severed the thread of power linking him to the cross-planar scrying sphere. It vanished faster than the blink of an eye.

"Mr. Sellers," Judge Thomas said, "present your case, if you please."

"Your Honor, I would call Sheriff David Haskins to the stand," Kurt replied.

Over the next hours, Kurt Sellers called witness after witness of people who had interacted with Gavin since his return, and all of them supported the assertion that the concerns of the Common-wealth's Attorney were baseless. The man in question *was* Gavin Cross.

After calling a recess for lunch, Judge Thomas turned to Connor Matthews. "Gavin Cross and his counsel have had their say, Mr. Matthews. Now, it's your turn. Let's hear your case."

"Your Honor, Emily White brought this case to me, and I now call her to..." Connor's voice faded as he scanned the gallery behind him. Emily White was nowhere to be found. "Uhm, Your Honor, it seems my primary witness is no longer present."

"Did you subpoena her testimony?"

"I... I did not, Your Honor," Connor answered. "Since she brought me the case, I didn't think it was needed."

Judge Thomas nodded. "Very well. It is the judgment of this court, Mr. Matthews, that you have been had. There is no evidence anywhere to support the assertion that this man is faking the identity of Gavin Cross. Mr. Sellers has presented witness after witness, all of whom believe without any doubt that this man is indeed Gavin Cross. Neither is there any evidence to support your assertion that Richard, Elizabeth, and/or Jennifer Cross are in any way being held against their will. Further, I will be forwarding the transcripts of this hearing to the Virginia Bar's ethics committee for review. This hearing is now dismissed."

# CHAPTER 32

In the days that followed the hearing before Judge Thomas, Gavin continued the easy rhythm he'd established over the preceding weeks. From around eight in the morning until noon, he taught Jennifer and Alexis. He took the noon hour off for lunch and to shift his mindset from teaching to research, and while Jennifer and Alexis practiced the day's lesson during the afternoon, Gavin worked on his research into cross-planar teleportation. He'd relegated the question of when—or even if—the dragons would arrive to the back of his mind, as there was no point obsessing over something that would—or wouldn't—happen.

* * *

ONE AFTERNOON about two weeks after the hearing, Jennifer and Alexis took a break from their practice to go for a walk outside the keep. Gayle and the other members of Alexis's travel team accompanied them, more out of an interest to maintain their professionalism than any true concern for Alexis's safety. Stepping outside the keep, they encountered a sight that stopped the Secret Service agents cold.

Kiri worked through her forms—both armed and unarmed—in

her exercise yard a short distance from the keep. The space given over to Kiri's practice held a number of cloth-covered straw dummies at various angles and positions from the primary sparring area, even though Kiri had no one to spar with.

The five people stood stock still, entranced by the smooth fluid grace Kiri exhibited as she moved from one stance to the next. Kiri wore street clothes appropriate for walking around Graham—or anywhere, really—and flowed from form to form with the practiced ease of muscle memory. The Secret Service agents gaped when a throwing knife appeared in Kiri's hand seemingly out of nowhere before she sent it on its way with a powerful throw. When the knife buried over half its blade in the right eye of one of the dummies, all three agents checked their sidearms out of reflex.

Jennifer walked over to the tasteful wooden fence that partitioned off Kiri's practice area and leaned on the top-most crossbeam. Kiri completed her form sequence, sending four more knives that the agents hadn't realized she carried into more dummies' eyes or throats, before she turned and walked over to Jennifer.

"Exercise clothes would be easier to move in," Jennifer remarked.

Kiri nodded. "No doubt, but then, I might not be prepared if I ever have to fight when wearing normal attire. Most days I wear exercise clothes, but today was my scheduled day for street clothes."

The others joined Jennifer at the fence-line. Gayle nodded toward the dummies, saying, "You're impressive."

"Thank you, but I'm not," Kiri replied. "I've only been practicing for a little over a couple of years now. The one who trained me, though, is death walking when he needs to be."

Gayle pursed her lips while Chet and his associate glanced at each other. Gayle said, "Would you be open to sparring with us? Maybe teaching us some of what you know?"

Kiri offered a slight smile tinged with regret. "Sorry, no. The secrets imparted to me are not mine to share. My trainer only trained me on the order of Gavin's mentor. Otherwise, I would never have known he possessed the skills and knowledge he used to train me."

"Really? How's that?"

Kiri sighed. "The full information is not mine to share, either, but suffice it to say, he is a member of an order dating back thousands of years that swears unwavering loyalty to Kirloth."

"And Gavin is Kirloth?" Chet asked.

"Right now, yes," Kiri replied. "In time, Jennifer will be, or her child. Given their relative similarity in physical age now, it's difficult to predict how or if Jennifer will outlive her father."

Jennifer frowned. "I don't have any children."

Kiri smiled. "All things in time. If you will excuse me, I must complete my practice for today."

She turned and walked back to the practice area to retrieve two short swords from a nearby weapon rack. She took a couple deep breaths, adopted a ready stance, and began a fluid dance with those blades that shredded her imaginary opponents.

"Thank goodness we have guns," Chet muttered.

"She doesn't need them," Jennifer remarked.

Chet scoffed. "Sure, she does. She can't reach us from fifty feet away with those swords or throwing knives."

"Of course not," Jennifer agreed, "but Dad can."

* * *

Jayce Timmons sat his board for his shift, as he had since transferring into the unit. The screens before him showed radar scans of the western Atlantic along the eastern US coast. He looked away to get a drink, and a blip appeared. By the time he finished getting a drink and turned his full attention back, dozens more blips followed the first. He pressed the key that called for his supervisor's attention. By the time the supervisor arrived, the dozens of blips had become hundreds. The blips moved east in a multi-layered triangle formation, almost a pyramid laid on its side.

"What do you have, Timmons?" Sergeant Ames asked as she arrived at Timmons's shoulder.

Timmons pointed to his screens. "We have incoming, Sergeant. About the size of Cessna's, but they're moving too fast."

"Very well. Give me coordinates and a vector, and I'll kick it up the chain for satellite imaging."

* * *

THE INTERCOM FUNCTION of Chelsea's phone buzzed. Without even pulling her full focus from the document she perused, she tapped the button, saying, "Yes?"

"General Fitzcairn is here to see you, ma'am," Jenna reported.

Chelsea frowned, turning to look at the intercom. "I didn't see his name on my agenda today."

"No, ma'am. He says there's been a development."

Chelsea closed her eyes and took a slow, deep breath. 'Developments' were rarely good, and lately, it seemed they were almost catastrophic.

"Very well. Send him in, please."

The intercom clicked off, followed almost immediately by the door from Jenna's office opening to admit General Fitzcairn, the Chairman of the Joint Chiefs. Chelsea smiled her greeting and led him to the sitting area she used for important discussions.

"What do you have for me, General?"

Fitzcairn opened the folder, laying it on the coffee table in front of her. "We have incoming, ma'am. A little over five hundred dragons are flying across the Atlantic as we speak. If they maintain their speed, they'll make landfall in a little over three hours. They'll fly right over the southern third of our metropolitan area. How do you want us to handle this?"

Chelsea chuckled. "Well, we're certainly not going to ask for their passports or a customs inspection. Besides, we already know where they're going."

"We do?" Fitzcairn asked, blinking. Then, Chelsea saw it click. "Ah... they're going to the Cross Estate to converse with Alexis's mentor."

Chelsea nodded. "We need to put the word out to every federal, state, or local authority. Do not take any aggressive or hostile action toward the dragons. They will respond if provoked, and we don't need them destroying a town because someone took a shot at them. They are not hostile. You handle the military side of the notifications, and I'll get with Justice for the civilian side."

"Do we know they're not hostile for certain, ma'am?"

"Their conduct to date supports that conclusion. They have never attacked anyone or anything without provocation, so let's not provoke them."

"Very well, ma'am," Fitzcairn replied. "Will there be anything else, Madam President?"

"No, thank you, General. I appreciate you making the drive to bring this to me."

"Of course, ma'am; it's my job. Take care."

As the general left the Oval Office, Chelsea returned to her desk. She called Jenna and said she'd need the Attorney General on the phone as soon as she made a quick call to her daughter.

* * *

THE SUN SHONE through a cloudless sky, and Gavin estimated it was mid- to late-afternoon as he stepped outside the keep. Jennifer had tried to get him to carry a smartphone, and while the smartphone did have a certain amount of utility on Earth, it would be worse than useless when he returned to Drakmoor.

Putting aside the thoughts of timepieces and Drakmoor, Gavin walked to the edge of the keep's plateau that overlooked the area he'd prepared for the dragons. There were more than he expected. Many more. Fortunately, all of them assumed a humanoid form and size; the grove Gavin prepared wouldn't have had enough space if they hadn't.

Jennifer and Alexis arrived at his side. They stared at the mass of robed humanoids.

"Are they all dragons?" Alexis asked, her voice shaky.

Gavin nodded. "Yes. They are all dragons. So... who wants to meet them?"

He thought he heard a whimper from Alexis's direction, but he noticed Jennifer grinned.

"Right, then. Let's not keep them waiting. *Paedryx.*"

The world blinked, and they stood about five yards inland from the edge of the lake. Five of the dragons walked toward them, and Gavin moved to meet them.

"Greetings, Kirloth," the center dragon said. "I am Firestreak. We met on the snowy mountainside. You may address my associates as Cindar, Smoke, Dawnflame, and Flameweave. We have been chosen to represent our host."

"Well met, Firestreak," Gavin replied. "This is my daughter and apprentice, Jennifer."

The five dragons nodded in greeting. Firestreak said, "Young Kirloth."

"And this is Alexis Hall, my other apprentice," Gavin finished.

"And what is her House, Kirloth?" Firestreak asked. "I see no medallion."

Gavin pursed his lips. "You know... I don't think we've established that."

"I'm guessing 'House' is something like family or clan?" Alexis asked.

Gavin, Jennifer, and Firestreak nodded.

"How do we find out?" Alexis asked.

Gavin smiled. "If our guests will forgive me, we might as well make this a lesson. The important piece of information is that your blood knows its House, whether or not you are consciously aware of it. Given this, how would *you* discern your House?"

Alexis frowned and lowered her head to stare at the ground. She worked her lower lip between her teeth for several moments before lifting her gaze to Gavin once again. She said, "Couldn't I use an Illusion effect to create a static image of my House Glyph?"

Gavin smiled. "Excellent, Alexis! That is *precisely* how you should do it. Why don't you take a couple steps back and try it?"

Alexis's eyes flitted to the dragons for a moment before returning to Gavin. She nodded and took a couple deep breaths as she backed away from the cluster of people. Once she had about fifteen feet between her and everyone else, she closed her eyes as she cleared her mind and established her intent, then invoked the Word, "*Othys.*"

A House Glyph winked into existence in front of Alexis, and for the briefest moment, Gavin felt the claws of panic reach for his heart. He stamped down on that reaction and shook his head.

"What is it, Dad?" Jennifer asked.

Gavin chuckled. "Out of all the Houses Alexis could possibly be, I was not expecting *that one* at all."

"Why?" Jennifer asked, her eyes flitting between her father and Alexis's House Glyph. "What House is it?"

"I bid thee welcome among us, Young Sivas," Firestreak said, "and well done on this next step of your journey."

"No," Gavin said, almost sighing out the word. "She isn't 'Young Sivas'."

The dragons turned to regard him, and Jennifer asked, "Why isn't she 'Young Sivas', Dad?"

"In the culture the dragons are from, 'Young' is typically used to denote a House's heir. Hence, you are Young Kirloth. She can't be her House's heir, because I am as close to certain as I can be that she is the only wizard of House Sivas left alive. She's the Head of her House."

# CHAPTER 33

Gavin led Jennifer and Alexis into the keep, after a brief conversation with Firestreak and his associates about handling accommodations and food. He started to take them up to the lab, but as he considered it further, the sitting room would probably be a better place. He gestured to the room's other furniture as he sat in a handy armchair. Then he looked at Alexis.

"So, do you have questions?" he asked.

Alexis nodded. "Why am I the Head of my House and not Mom?"

"The Houses are based on proficiency with the Art. Your mother is not an arcanist. While she is technically a member of your House, she cannot lead it."

"Mmm," Alexis vocalized, as she gave the far wall a thousand-yard stare. "In that case, why am I the last of my House? Why did you seem so certain of that?"

Gavin shrugged. "So, I can't be one-hundred-percent certain you're the last of your House. It's completely possible that you have a distant cousin somewhere who would technically be a member. That being said, I am certain you're the only trained arcanist of your House... because I wiped out your very distant relatives over a year ago in the world I'm trying to go back to."

Both Alexis and Jennifer gaped at him.

"What?" Alexis almost shrieked.

"Dad?" Jennifer added her voice to the matter.

Gavin sighed. "Before you swear a blood feud or something, let me explain. The crux of the matter is that House Sivas was not a credit to the Art in Drakmoor. I caught the heir, a Rolf Sivas, attempting to rape a young woman on whom he had used a paralysis scroll to restrain. When the appropriate authority chose to do nothing, I challenged him to a duel and killed him with a tomato."

"A tomato, Dad? Seriously?" Jennifer asked. "Isn't that a little... I don't know... anti-climactic?"

"I wanted to humiliate him," Gavin replied. "The Council of Magisters should've executed him for his crimes, but they chose not to act at all. I used the rules of the wizard's duel against Rolf. By hitting him with a tomato, I knocked him off-balance, and he fell outside the dueling ring. He forfeited the duel and his life.

"His father took exception to his son's death, especially since he encouraged the boy to approach life from the viewpoint of 'no consequences', and arranged for a couple meatheads to take me off the streets of Tel Mivar. He wanted to torture me to death, but my friends found me before he could. There was a lot going on, and frankly, I'd just as soon not rehash all of it. Both Iosen and Rolf were abhorrent human beings, and the world is better off without them."

Alexis turned to look Gavin in the eye. "And what if I follow in their footsteps? What you've taught me would enable me to ensure Mom remains President after her second term, and it might even give me the wherewithal to establish American primacy across the world."

Gavin closed his eyes and leaned back against the armchair. "Don't do that, Alexis. Please don't do that. That path has only two possible outcomes." He paused long enough to meet Alexis's eyes once more. "If Jennifer didn't end you, I would. And if I had to do it, I'd take out as many people around you as necessary to ensure the matter settled."

Alexis took a deep breath and nodded. "That's what it means to be Kirloth?"

"Yes." Gavin leaned forward, resting his elbows on his knees. "I would prefer that Jennifer never has to assume such duties, but all that would mean is that it would fall to her child... whenever she decides to have one or four."

"Four?" Jennifer gasped.

Gavin chuckled, then his expression sobered. "I would much rather see you stand with her, Alexis, than against her."

Alexis looked at Jennifer and smiled. "I'd much rather stand with her, too. Jennifer is the first person to treat me as a person and not the President's daughter... or the Senator's daughter... or the Governor's daughter. It's nice."

"Very well," Gavin remarked. "Since we know your House, you need a medallion. Well, I suppose you technically don't, since the Society has no presence in this world, but it would be wiser to have one. Come. For this, we should go to the lab."

* * *

CHELSEA LOOKED AT THE CLOCK. 12:42. Goodness... was that all the further into the day it was? She leaned back against her chair, closed her eyes, and pinched the bridge of her nose. She couldn't possibly think of a job that could prepare someone to be President. Governor could... to a certain extent... but even being governor of a state failed to capture the sheer mass of responsibility facing whomever sat at the Resolute desk. The chirp of the intercom drew her from her moment of peace.

"Yes?" She asked.

"The Attorney General and Director of the FBI are here, ma'am," Jenna answered. "They're not on the schedule, but like everyone else, they insist it's important."

Chelsea fought the urge to chuckle and won. As much as she would like to say she didn't have time—for she truly did not—

Chelsea knew these two wouldn't arrive unannounced without reason. Odds favored the reason wouldn't make her smile.

"Might as well send them in, Jenna."

"Thank you, ma'am."

Chelsea stood to greet and receive her impromptu guests before inviting them to sit with her around the coffee table on the interior side of the office. Pleasantries concluded, she speared both of them in turn with her concerned expression.

"What do you have for me?"

The two guests looked to one another for a heartbeat before the Attorney General spoke.

"Jerome Toussaint appeared in court today. The judge granted him bail, and he went straight to the Port of Baltimore and boarded a container ship registered to one of his shell companies. We didn't learn of this until it was too late to interdict the container ship. It's now in international waters."

Chelsea closed her eyes and fought the urge to sigh in frustration. "Do we know where the ship's headed?"

"The paperwork they filed with the harbormaster indicated their next port of call is Marseille."

"And France doesn't extradite its citizens." Chelsea chuckled.

"Ma'am?" the attorney general asked.

"Honestly, the fact that France won't extradite him to us isn't the worst part of this."

Both the attorney general and the FBI director frowned. Jack said, "It isn't, ma'am? How so?"

"The worst part of all this is deciding whether to tell Gavin," Chelsea replied.

She watched Jack connect the dots ahead of her AG. She thought Jack might have paled a little.

"That... I'm not sure there's a good way out of that decision, ma'am," Jack said. "Tell him, and a container ship disappears at the very least... maybe a piece of France if he waits for Toussaint to go to ground. Don't tell, and then he comes to us asking why we didn't."

The attorney general looked to each of them in turn before

saying, "Does the United States even have a responsibility to inform him? What business is it of his, beyond his daughter being a former victim?"

Chelsea sighed. "His daughter is the powder keg in all of this, at least in terms of Gavin's response. Beyond that, Gavin is a sovereign ruler back wherever he came from, like the kings and queens and emperors of old."

"Come on, ma'am," the Attorney General interrupted. "You don't really believe that, do you?"

"It doesn't matter what we believe. Gavin believes it. For that matter, so do the dragons. My read on Gavin is that he ties international diplomacy to the people, not the offices, which honestly also has historical precedent here on Earth. Right now, he considers me a friend, so the question isn't what *the United States* should do but what *I—Chelsea Hall and Gavin's friend—*should do." Chelsea sighed. "When viewed through that lens, the answer seems clear."

Chelsea stood, and her guests stood as well. She returned to her desk and activated the intercom.

"Yes, ma'am?" Jenna asked.

"Jenna, would you please call my daughter's cell?"

"Alexis's cell, ma'am?"

Chelsea sighed again. "Yes, Jenna. It's an official matter, so I should probably make the call from the office instead of my personal cell."

"Yes, ma'am. One moment..." Silence dominated the intercom for a few moments, as Jenna saw one of the lines light up. Soon, Jenna returned to the intercom. "Ma'am, your daughter is holding for you on line two."

"Thank you, Jenna," Chelsea replied and closed the intercom call, then switched to line two. "Alexis?"

"Are you okay, Mom?" Alexis asked. "You've never called me from an office line before."

"I know, sweetheart. I'm sorry, but I'm afraid I need a word with Gavin."

Chelsea heard her daughter exhale. "He's up in the lab with three or four dragons. I think they're working on the design for the permanent portal back to wherever he came from."

Chelsea forced herself not to wince. She knew he wouldn't look kindly on any interruptions of that task, but in a way, she felt she had no choice. "Would you please ask him if he can spare a few minutes? There have been developments in a matter that affects him and Jennifer, and I'd rather he hears from me before anyone else and certainly not some news broadcast."

"Okay," Alexis replied, drawing out the word. "Give me a minute. I have to go back to the keep. *Paedryx.*"

Chelsea heard several clicks, and the call went silent. After a couple heartbeats, she had to ask, "Alexis, are you there?"

"Yeah, Mom," Alexis answered. "Something wrong?"

"No. I just heard some clicks on my end and no background noise. I was afraid the call dropped."

"Oh! Sorry. Totally should've thought about that," Alexis said. "Jennifer, Kiri, and I were at the ice cream shop in town, and I never considered that the call would change cell towers. We're probably lucky it didn't drop."

Chelsea heard Alexis knock three times on a door before saying, "Gavin, my mom called using the office line. She says she needs a couple minutes to discuss something."

The phone didn't pick up whatever Gavin said in reply, but Alexis soon added, "Okay. Are you sure you want the call on speaker?" The call's ambient noise changed, and Alexis said, "Mom, you're on speaker. It was Gavin's choice."

"Hello, Gavin," Chelsea said.

"Hello, Chelsea. What do you need?"

"I wanted you to hear this from me first," Chelsea said. "A judge granted Jerome Toussaint bail this morning. He was already aboard one of his container ships in international waters by the time we learned of it."

"I... see." Silence dominated the call for several moments before Gavin continued. "So be it. As long as he leaves Jennifer alone, I see no point in engaging him further. I imagine he's going to use his French citizenship to avoid extradition?"

"That's what we think, yes," Chelsea answered.

More silence.

"Gavin," Chelsea began, "what are you thinking?"

"I am debating the wisdom of my first response. I do not like leaving enemies behind me, Chelsea, and he constitutes a potential, grave threat to my daughter as long as he's alive. The more I consider the matter, I am questioning the wisdom of allowing him to live."

Chelsea worked her lower lip between her teeth. She had to thread this needle *very carefully*. "Gavin, adopting a 'wait and see' attitude right now costs you nothing. Beyond that, federal authorities are dismantling his organization here in the US. He's no threat to Jennifer anymore."

Silence... extended into seconds.

"Very well," Gavin replied, and Chelsea's shoulders released the tension they'd been holding. "Between not having the time right this moment to deal with that waste of life and my thought that I should respect your judgment, I will take no action at this time."

"Thank you, Gavin. You have no idea how much better that makes me feel."

"I do appreciate the call, Chelsea, and you're right. I wouldn't have wanted to learn of this via the news or some such, but if you will forgive me, I must return to my work."

"Of course, Gavin," Chelsea replied. "Thank you again, and goodbye."

"Goodbye."

Chelsea pressed the button to end the call and turned to face her guests. From Jack's expression, she figured her relief was apparent.

"Ma'am," the attorney general said, "may I ask why you treat that man as someone to be feared? He's only one man."

Jack erupted in full-bodied laughter. The attorney general gave him the Squint Eye.

"Forgive Jack," Chelsea replied. "The fact of the matter is that

Gavin, his daughter, and Alexis are nuclear powers. You should read the classified after-action report for how my son and his unit were rescued. Gavin turned a ten-mile-wide circle of the Middle East to glass. They were being held in the ruins of a village that the insurgents were using as a logistical base, and his parting shot at the end of rescue was to wipe that village off the face of the world. And he did it with *just one word*. So, yes, I treat him as someone to be... not so much feared as respected. He is an incredible friend, right now, but could just as easily be an incredible enemy. I know which I prefer. How about you?"

Chelsea watched the attorney general purse her lips and nod. Gavin's treatment of the Black Ops soldier someone had sent to kill him wasn't so old that it had faded from institutional memory, and she hoped the after-action report—complete with satellite photos of the aftermath—would convince all elements of her government to avoid provoking him.

"Will there be anything else, ma'am?" Jack asked, since the attorney general seemed to have lost her voice.

"No, thank you, Jack. I appreciate both of you bringing this to my attention, but I have a stack of work to do."

"Thank you, ma'am," Jack replied and led his boss out of the Oval Office.

# CHAPTER 34

Chelsea leaned back against her seat and fought the feelings of despair that clawed at her. In the wake of Gavin's press conference, things started rebounding. Suicides dropped. Stock exchanges opened and didn't collapse. Fewer nutjobs—she couldn't think of them as anything else—touted the end of the world.

But then, the dragons emerged. Even worse, from her perspective, a dragon destroyed a naval ship. Yes, the ship fired on it first; no one denied that, not even France, but the fact remained that a dragon—a creature existing only in myth and legend until just a few weeks ago—*sunk* a modern warship... in less than twenty minutes.

The only thing she knew to do was try another press conference, now that the dragons had re-emerged and congregated on the Cross Estate. She leaned forward just far enough to press the intercom button on her phone.

"Yes, ma'am?" Jenna answered.

"Jenna, please call my daughter's cell on an office line."

"Yes, ma'am, and also, the German ambassador called. She would like a word in person when you have time."

Chelsea fought the urge to sigh. "Do I have time, Jenna?"

"Honestly, no, ma'am, not for at least a week. But I can juggle a couple things to give you at most thirty minutes if you like."

Chelsea combed her hands through her hair. After a couple deep breaths, she replied, "One to ten, Jenna... how urgent did the ambassador sound?"

"Uhm... six to seven-ish? She didn't sound like she was delivering Germany's declaration of war, but there was an underlying tone of needing to speak with you."

"Very well," Chelsea said. "Do what you can with the schedule and let me know when I'll be speaking with her once she accepts, please."

"Of course, ma'am. I'll get that call for you right now."

MOMENTS LATER, Jenna came on the intercom that Alexis was waiting, and Chelsea picked up the phone.

"Hi, honey," she said without preamble. "I feel terrible doing this to you again, but I need to speak to Gavin."

Alexis's chuckles carried across the phone. "It's okay, Mom. It's not like Gavin carries a cell phone. I'm going to put you on speaker."

"Yes, Chelsea?" Gavin asked.

"Gavin, would you and one of the dragons be willing to do a press conference? That's the only thing I can think of that might calm down the worldwide panic happening right now."

Gavin didn't answer at once, and the silence extended to the point that it almost became awkward.

"Firestreak is agreeable to the idea," Gavin said. "When do you want us?"

"Uhm, tomorrow? I think we can have everything ready by tomorrow."

"Very well, but I recommend scheduling it for afternoon. You'll want to be able to see Firestreak in natural lighting; he's rather impressive up close."

Chelsea felt the tension in her shoulders ease. "Thank you, Gavin. I really appreciate this."

"You're welcome, Chelsea."

Alexis then said, "You're off speaker, and I'm out of the lab now. How are you doing?"

"I'm okay, honey. How about you?"

"Mom, don't brush it off. How are you doing?"

Chelsea sighed. "It's rough, Lexi. People are panicking and dying, and nothing the government leaders have done has affected it at all. As far as I know, we haven't had another happening of something like the massive murder-suicide, but the world is panicking right now. Panicked people never respond well to anything."

"I'll come with Gavin tomorrow and stay a couple days," Alexis replied.

Chelsea shook her head out of reflex. "No, Lexi, I'll be fine. You're welcome to come tomorrow with Gavin and Firestreak, but I want you to focus on your studies."

"Okay, Mom. I'll see you tomorrow."

* * *

THAT EVENING, Jenna knocked on the door to the Oval Office and leaned inside to say, "Ma'am, the German ambassador is here."

"Thank you, Jenna. Please, show her in."

Jenna led the German ambassador—Elsa Schneider—inside, and Chelsea greeted her near the door before offering the sitting area in front of the Resolute desk.

"Thank you for making time to see me on such short notice, Madam President," the ambassador said.

"Of course, Elsa. What did you need?"

"I have been directed by my government to advise you that a number of countries around the world are not pleased with how America is monopolizing the dragons. This is a singular opportunity for study and relations, and many feel they belong to the world."

Chelsea fought the urge to clench her teeth. "Elsa, they're sentient beings. They don't *belong* to anyone but themselves."

"There are those, Madam President, who disagree with that view."

"Well, they're welcome to disagree all they want, but I have it on very good authority that it won't be too long before the dragons are gone entirely."

Elsa nodded. "Yes, Madam President, and that is why it is imperative we retain a few—perhaps two breeding pairs—for our global interests."

Chelsea leaned back in her seat and considered what Elsa proposed. She saw it leading to one outcome and only one: conflict with Gavin and the dragons. Conflict with Gavin alone was terrifying, but adding in the dragons made it incomprehensible.

"Elsa, I've invited Gavin Cross and one of the dragons to the White House tomorrow to hold a press conference, much like we did with him not too long ago. Why don't you attend and meet Firestreak face-to-face? After that, if you still feel like it's in our best interests to try capturing four of them, I'll consider the proposal."

Elsa sat silent and unmoving for several moments before she nodded once. "Very well, Madam President. I accept your invitation."

* * *

It was a beautiful, cloudless day. The temperature was in the low 70s, with little humidity. The Rose Garden was ready for another informal chat, only this time a dragon would attend with Gavin. At the appointed time, a gateway formed where Gavin usually arrived, and he stepped through with a red-robed figure. The gateway vanished, and Gavin and the figure made a show of looking around. Finally, Gavin turned to his associate.

"What do you think? Is there enough room?"

"It should be sufficient as long as I don't need to stretch," the robed figure replied.

"Just a second, then," Gavin remarked and turned toward the crowd. "Ladies and gentlemen, if you would please turn this way and adjust your cameras for the widest possible angle." He waited until it was done. "It is my honor and pleasure to introduce to you Firestreak."

The robed figure lifted his hands and pulled back the hood of the robe. The figure seemed to swell in size as wings and a spiked tail grew out of the robe. In less than ninety seconds, the White House Rose Garden hosted its first dragon.

"Good afternoon," Firestreak said, his deep voice resonating against their bones like the heavy bass of a rock concert. "I understand you have some questions for me."

Most of the assembled people—reporters and politicians alike—stared at Firestreak in his true form. Senator Evans fainted, flattening a few rose bushes in his unnoticed collapse.

"Firestreak," a woman said, stepping closer, "I'm Jill Townsend with the BBC. A number of governments have advanced the position that dragons belong to the world and should not be completely clustered here in America. What is your response to that?"

"I find it rather rude that you would decide you own us in some way, after we agreed to sacrifice our participation in the Godswar to come here with your ancestors and act as guardians and protectors until they could get themselves established. No. Soon, our work with Kirloth will be complete, providing a way to return home. And return home we will."

"Mister Cross," Jill said, "are you the 'Kirloth' Firestreak mentioned?"

Gavin nodded. "I am, and please, call me Gavin."

"What is your response to this?"

"The dragons are sentient beings who have a right to self-determination," Gavin answered. "If they want me to help them return home, then I shall do so. Besides, their home happens to be the same world I'm trying to get back to, so there's a confluence of desire. Besides, I thought most of the governments in the world were civilized enough to outlaw slavery. Are they saying that's not the case?"

"Will Carrington," another man said, stepping forward. "Gavin, a number of people are calling out for you to train them or determine if they have the same capability you do. Are you aware of any of this, and what is your response?"

Gavin sighed and fought the urge to shake his head. "I didn't come here to train people. I have the two apprentices I do, because they somehow managed to invoke a Word of Power and were slowly dying from *skathos* cascade. Beyond that, I don't see the value in spreading my knowledge throughout the world. That may change with time, but for the foreseeable future, it's unlikely."

THE DISCUSSION RAN FOR HOURS, and as the sun dipped below the horizon at last, Gavin and Firestreak decided it was time to end. As everyone bid their goodbyes, Chelsea hoped this would be enough to re-focus people on Gavin's refusal to train others and stabilize the world's panic.

# CHAPTER 35

Kiri, Jennifer, and Alexis (and Alexis's travel team) walked down Main Street in Graham. Even when there wasn't a hostage situation happening at the university, the place still carried the sleepy, small town vibe. The ladies chatted as they walked, no part of their conversation touched training or wizardry or anything like that. They were simply three young ladies enjoying a warm, sunny day.

"Oh, hey," Jennifer said, cutting off her previous sentence. "Mind if we run by the bank real fast? Grams asked me to make a deposit for them, since I was going out."

Alexis and Kiri shrugged, so they turned into the ancient stone building that was only a few years younger than the town itself. Entering the bank, they found a lobby moderately full of people, and Kiri thought she heard a muttered groan from Jennifer.

Jennifer looked at her wrist watch. "I should've looked at the time. Several of these people are from local businesses doing their daily deposits. This... might be a while. Sorry."

Alexis waved it off. "Don't worry about it."

They continued to chat for several minutes as the lines creeped closer and closer to the teller windows. Movement caught Kiri's attention out of the corner of her eye, and she looked toward the entrance just in time to see three people enter the lobby. They wore long, black trench coats; ski masks; and dark sunglasses. Almost as one, they opened their trench coats and lifted shotguns into view.

"Good afternoon, ladies and gentlemen," one of the people said, the muffled voice sounding male. "We are here to relieve you of your money and the gold in your vault. We're not interested in harming anyone, but if you resist, we will kill you."

Before the speaker fully finished his introduction, Kiri moved. A full sprint brought her to the speaker right as he finished, and she threw one of her knives at the next-closest person with her right hand as she raked the blade in her left across the speaker's throat, triggering arterial spray. A glance showed her the second person collapsing as blood leaked around the knife in the person's throat, and Kiri was already charging the third robber.

"No, wait, please," the robber said.

Kiri didn't wait. She leaped into the air, put her knees into the person's shoulders, and rode the robber to the floor as she jammed her remaining knife through the robber's throat and into the spine. Everyone in the lobby stared at the grisly scene, and the only sound was the second robber gagging and drowning in his own blood.

"Not even three minutes," Chet—one of Alexis's travel team—muttered as he held his sidearm at low guard.

"And she says she's *not* Death walking?" Mike—the third member of the travel team—replied. "Kinda makes you worried to meet her trainer, doesn't it?"

"Cut the chatter," Gayle said, her voice low as well as she watched Kiri walk back to Alexis and Jennifer. "Let's secure this scene until local law enforcement arrives."

Kiri stopped about six feet away from Jennifer and Alexis, who looked like they were trying very hard not to gape at what Kiri had done.

"This is what you truly need to learn," Kiri said. "The power you wield should be second nature to you, like scratching your nose or taking a drink. Those three should've been dead before I crossed half the distance. I will speak with Gavin about augmenting your training, as the one who trained me augmented his."

* * *

SEVERAL HOURS after the attempted robbery, Gavin entered the sole precinct of the Graham Police Department and approached the receiving desk; as this was an official occasion, he wore the gold robe of his office with his medallion resting in full view atop his sternum. Betty Flanaghan—one of Gavin's classmates from high school—sat at the desk, her uniform sleeve bearing sergeant's stripes; she didn't look up from her current task when he stopped a short distance from her desk.

"Hi, Betts," Gavin said after a few moments.

"That's Sergeant—" Betty stopped speaking when she saw who addressed her, and Gavin saw a little color drain out of her face and neck. "Gavin? Seriously, is that you? I've heard the rumors around town, but wow... you look *young*."

Gavin nodded. "It's me, Betts, or should that be Sergeant Flanaghan?"

Now, Betty smiled. "It's Thompson, actually. Jimmy and I finally got married about six months after your... uhm... wreck."

"I hope congratulations are in order," Gavin replied.

"Oh, they are. The kids have him wrapped around their fingers, but I love the big goof. So, what brings you to our fine precinct today?"

"I'm here for Kiri Muran. She'll be leaving with me."

Now, Betty paled across her entire complexion, and Gavin thought he saw fear in her eyes. "Uhm, Gavin, I'm sorry, but she's been arrested for those murders, and I'm pretty sure I heard someone say something about calling INS, because she doesn't have an entry visa or passport or anything like that."

"Betts, I'm not here to start a war, okay? You don't need to be afraid of me."

"That's a little difficult, given how you've been going head to head with Uncle Sam. People are scared of you, Gavin."

Gavin sighed. "I never wanted anyone to be afraid of me, but the fact remains that Kiri Muran is a foreign head of state, just like I am now. She *will* be leaving with me, Betts, so you should probably get whoever's in charge here."

Betty nodded and reached for her phone. The handset had just touched her ear when a woman arrived at Gavin's side. She wore a tasteful suit and carried a burgundy briefcase.

"Hello, Sergeant," the woman said. "I'm Gloria Reyes from the State Department. I am here to speak with your Chief of Police, regarding the foreign national you currently have in custody. A woman answering to Kiri Muran, I believe."

Betty flicked her eyes to Gavin for a moment before she dialed the chief's extension. After a few moments, she said, "Sir, this is Sergeant Thompson at the front desk. I have Gloria Reyes from the State Department and Gavin Cross . They arrived independently, but both are here to discuss Kiri Muran." She listened for a few moments. "Yes, sir. Thank you."

After hanging up the phone, Betty stood and gestured to both Gavin and Gloria Reyes, saying, "Please, follow me."

Betty led them to the bank of elevators, pressing the call button, and one elevator dinged and opened. She said, "Take this the fourth floor. When you step outside, turn right, and the chief's office will be straight ahead."

"Thank you., Gavin said, smiling at his former classmate.

"Yes, Sergeant, thank you," Gloria said as she led Gavin into the elevator.

The fourth floor seemed to be all administrative offices, and they arrived at the chief's outer office in short order. After about five minutes of the chief attempting to prove how much power he had by playing the 'make them wait' game, Gavin made eye contact with Reyes.

"So, what brings someone from the State Department to Graham?"

"You do," Reyes replied. "When the president learned of the bank incident, she wrote and signed her first executive order, affording you and Ms. Muran the status of foreign heads of state and full diplomatic immunity. Secretary Irving dispatched me to advise Graham Police of the change in status and arrange for Ms. Muran's immediate release."

"Well, it seems like my presence here is no longer necessary. I'm going to find Kiri." As Gavin stood to leave, the receptionist lifted her eyes and spoke just loud enough for Gavin to hear, "Second floor, Interview Room 5."

"Thank you," Gavin replied as he left the office to return to the elevators.

As Gavin approached the interview room, an officer held out his hand.

"This area is off limits."

"Officer, I've come to see Kiri Muran. She and I have full diplomatic immunity as foreign heads of state, and there's a representative from the State Department up with the chief right now."

Before the officer could wind up for a response, a woman in a suit with a badge on her belt arrived at Gavin's side. She held a gray tote with 'Property Office' stenciled on several sides. "Officer, " she said standing inches from the uniformed man, "Ms. Muran is being released at once. Open the door, so I can return her property and she can get dressed."

"Her blades included?" Gavin asked.

The plain-clothes officer's eye twitched for a moment, but she nodded. "Yes, this is all of her property."

Gavin turned back and found the officer hadn't moved yet. "Here, Officer, allow me. You seem to have forgotten how to use keys. *Rhyskaal.*"

The doorknob fell to the floor in a pile of metallic dust.

"Was that really necessary?" the plain-clothes officer asked.

"I don't like people dragging their feet," Gavin replied, as he scooped the tote containing Kiri's property out of the woman's hands. "We'll return all the department's property once she's home."

Gavin entered the interview room to find Kiri sitting at a table with her hands cuffed to it. He stopped and turned back to the officers outside. "You have thirty seconds to unlock those handcuffs or I'll disintegrate the whole table."

The uniformed officer made no reaction, still gaping at the pile of metallic dust that used to be the interview room's doorknob. The plain-clothes officer frowned at him and dashed inside to unlock the handcuffs.

When the officer stepped back, Gavin placed the tote on the table. "Kiri, please take a moment to go through this and be sure you're not missing anything."

Kiri stood and opened the tote. Moments later, she smiled and lifted her eyes to Gavin, nodding. "It's all here, Gavin."

"Very well," Gavin replied. "Officer, I'll leave the tote and those sweats Kiri's wearing at the front desk. *Paedryx.*"

Gavin, Kiri, and the tote vanished from the interview room.

* * *

STANDING in the foyer of the keep, Kiri took the tote from Gavin. She looked up at him and smiled. "So, who was there first, you or the person Chelsea sent?"

"I was," Gavin answered. "Although, full disclosure, the person Chelsea sent arrived not too long after I did."

"Do they have any concept of what Chelsea averted for them?"

"No way to know, really. I hadn't reached the point where I announced my intentions."

"This isn't the first time you've come for me," Kiri remarked, a playful smile curling her lips. "If you persist, people will think I'm special to you."

Gavin leaned in and delivered a quick kiss to Kiri's lips, then shifted to whisper in her ear. "You are more than special, Kiri."

# CHAPTER 36

The days passed and became weeks. Aside from his morning classes with Alexis and Jennifer, Gavin spent most of his time cloistered with one or more dragons in his lab. Complex runes and diagrams festooned every whiteboard in the lab, and Gavin had even added additional whiteboards when they ran out of space and felt they couldn't erase anything to make room.

JENNIFER AND ALEXIS found Gavin in the lab, surrounded by dragons. They all stood at a new whiteboard and, from what Jennifer could tell, debated the best method to anchor the permanent portal to a local ley line.

"Dad?" Jennifer asked.

With zero hesitation at all, Gavin pivoted to her. "Yes, Jenny?"

"Grams just called on the crystal. There are some people at the house wanting to speak with you, and they're making Grandpa and Grams nervous."

Jennifer watched her dad's eyes narrow as his expression hardened. "That is... monumentally unwise of them." Gavin turned to the dragons. "Would you please excuse me long enough to investigate this and respond as needed?"

The dragons nodded, almost in unison.

"Mind if we come along?" Jennifer asked.

Gavin shrugged. "Why not?" Then, invoked the Word, "*Paedryx*."

The world blinked.

* * *

THE TELEPORTATION EFFECT delivered Gavin and his apprentices to the living room of his parents' house. Within a heartbeat of his arrival, a golden orb of roiling, seething power hovered over his right hand as he regarded the two people—one man and one woman—sitting on the sofa. They both wore suits, and the woman held a briefcase between her feet. The man looked to be early middle age—not more than a few years above Gavin's chronological age—and his salt-and-pepper hair wrapped around the sides and back of his head. The woman looked maybe a decade younger—or perhaps she just took better care of herself—and her auburn hair reminded Gavin of Lillian Mivar.

"You have sixty seconds to convince me not to burn the both of you down to ash for threatening my parents," Gavin said. "*Gozdrahk*."

The moment Gavin invoked the Word of Conjuration, a timer appeared in the air, flashing '0:60,' and started counting down.

The man shot to his feet, his jaws clenched and his neck as red creeped up his neck toward his cheeks. "How dare you!"

The woman had more sense. "We need to speak to you regarding a sensitive matter relating to national security. We'd like your help."

Gavin's eyes flicked to the conjured numbers that hovered in the air. The timer passed forty-five seconds, and he took a deep breath before releasing it as a sigh. He pointed at the man, saying, "You. Return to your vehicle and leave. If you show up here again, I won't be as understanding." Turning to the woman, "You can come with us to the keep and present your case. I will provide you transportation to whatever location you desire, regardless of my response."

"Now, see here," the man growled, "she works for me. If anyone delivers your mission briefing, it will be me."

"Excuse me?" Gavin asked, a flicker of anger piercing his eyes.

"We are here to discuss your assignment on a matter of national security," the man replied. "As I am the case officer in charge, *I* will deliver your mission briefing."

It was impossible to miss the woman closing her eyes and forcing herself not to wince.

"Miss, how are you with heights?" Gavin asked.

The woman's eyes shot wide. "Heights? What do you... I mean, I'm okay. I guess. I don't get vertigo when I look down from a ledge or anything."

"Excellent," Gavin replied with a slight smile. The tone of his voice was almost a purr. "*Paedryx-Gozdrahk-Sykhurhos.*"

The resonance of Gavin's power fueling his composite effect slammed into the ambient magic like a blacksmith's hammer striking an anvil. Not even a heartbeat later, the world blinked.

* * *

JENNIFER BLINKED her eyes against the sudden sunlight to the accompaniment of an oddly-pitched, almost girlish scream. Puffy, white clouds extended as far as she could see in any direction, and they moved as if carried by a fierce wind. But she felt none of it. The five of them stood on solid nothingness directly above the clouds. They seemed so close, Jennifer wanted to reach out and touch them.

Alexis and the woman—with her briefcase between her feet once more—seemed similarly awed. The man, however, stood as if petrified. His eyes pinched shut as his jaw clenched, small whimpers escaping his lips every other moment or so as a dark spot spread outward from the crotch of his trousers.

"Now," Gavin said, his tone slipping into the cold, unyielding ruthlessness Jennifer had heard Kiri call 'Kirloth', "you will explain to me just what gives you the right to assume I in any way work for you. I suggest you impress me—and do so quickly."

The man didn't respond. In fact, he seemed little more than a whimpering collection of locked joints and tensed muscles.

"Sir," the woman asked, "are we really standing in the air above the clouds?"

"You tell me," Gavin replied, pointing over his shoulder with this thumb.

All three women turned just in time to see an airliner appear out of the clouds as it climbed to its cruising altitude. They were so close, they could see the pilot's gaping expression at the sight of five people standing on air. Jennifer couldn't resist; she smiled and waved. The pilot returned her wave, though hesitantly so.

"This is so cool!" Alexis gushed. "I can read the tail numbers!"

"Hey, Dad, shouldn't the jet's engines be louder? It's maybe seventy feet away from us."

"Part of the Tutation aspect of the composite effect protects us from all sound outside it. If you walked to the edge and leaned out, your eardrums would probably burst."

The man's whimpering intensified. His pallor took on a pasty white sheen as sweat beaded his forehead.

The woman turned and gasped at the sight of her associate. "Sir... Mister Cross... please, take us back. He needs an emergency room. He has a heart condition. I'll tell you whatever you want to know, but please, get him help."

Jennifer shifted her attention in time to see her dad turn his head just enough to regard the woman. He maintained his silence for several moments before he invoked another composite effect, "*Paedryx-Rhosed.*"

The world blinked again.

* * *

GAVIN WATCHED the women blink and scan their new surroundings. He knew Jennifer and Alexis would recognize the dining room of the keep, but their guest seemed bewildered.

"Where are we?" the woman asked. "What did you do with my associate?"

"He's outside the ER at the local hospital," Gavin answered. "You're welcome to take your vehicle and check on him once you've explained why you interrupted my work."

"Uhm... he has the keys," she said, still looking around the room.

Gavin bit back a chuckle, instead saying, "Well, that's unfortunate for you. It's twenty miles to town from where the driveway meets the road."

The woman sighed. "I tried to tell him laying down the law with you wouldn't work. I'm sorry about all this. We really do need your help."

Gavin lifted his left eyebrow. "Explain."

The woman retrieved her briefcase from the floor and gestured toward the dining table. "May I?"

With his arms crossed, Gavin gave a single nod.

From the briefcase, the woman withdrew a thick folder with the words 'TOP SECRET' stenciled on it in bold, red letters. She unwound the string from its fastener and opened the folder.

"I'm sorry. My name is Sandra Barstow. I'm a junior case officer with the CIA. One of our colleagues went to South America—the Triple Frontier, specifically—to assist an asset in extracting to the United States and has since disappeared. The information the asset possesses is vital to our national security interests, and right now, we have no way of knowing if the asset or our officer are even alive. Given your extraction of the President's son, we were hoping you could locate and extract both the asset and our officer."

Gavin regarded Sandra in silence for several seconds, never once looking at the folder or its contents. "And what about me looks like a hyper Labrador eager for a game of fetch?"

The agent's jaw went slack, and she blinked a slow blink. "But... but you located and extracted the president's son and his unit."

"The situation with the president's son impacted my apprentice's ability to pursue her studies. I will be shocked and amazed, frankly, if the president even knows the name of the officer you'd like me to retrieve." Gavin shook his head. "I see no reason to waste my time supporting your geopolitical machinations. When you leave the dining room, hang a left. You'll see the keep's door straight ahead. The portal to my parents' driveway will be to the right once you step outside. Now, whether you will excuse me or not, I have important work to do."

Gavin pivoted on his heel and left, intent on resuming his work with the dragons.

* * *

JENNIFER WATCHED Sandra stare in silence after her dad. In truth, she almost gaped. After a few seconds, she shook herself and turned back to the folder on the table.

"He didn't even read the file to see why we need the asset's intel," she said, little more than a whisper.

In a manner that kept Sandra from being able to, Alexis waved to get Jennifer's attention. Then, Alexis pointed first to herself and then to Jennifer. Jennifer hoped her friend was meaning that they should do it, and she raised her eyebrows in a silent question. Alexis nodded with emphasis. Jennifer shrugged the shoulder outside Sandra's peripheral vision and flicked her eyes toward the stairs that led to the upper levels of the keep. Alexis rolled her eyes.

"Sandra," Alexis said, "we may not be Gavin, but we could retrieve your officer and asset. Well, we could locate the officer easily enough and hope he or she can direct us to the asset."

Sandra stepped back half a step so that she could easily see both apprentices. "Seriously? You can do this? I thought you were students."

"Technically, we are," Jennifer replied. "But we've been practicing all the skills and Words of Power we'd need to do this. Plus, we're more than capable of defending ourselves."

Sandra closed her eyes and sighed. "Do you have any idea the level of career suicide I'd be committing if I used the president's daughter for this? And if I'm going to be honest, I don't like the idea of touching you—Ms. Cross—with a ten-foot pole after everything that happened to people from Justice. I *do not* want to be the cause of your father nuking D.C. or Langley. I'd be lucky if they just executed me."

Jennifer chuckled. "Yeah... My dad's a little protective."

"A little?" Sandra asked, not quite snorting her amusement. "I'd pay money to see what he does to whatever poor sod asks you out on a date. Every other father on Earth would hang his head in shame that he couldn't top it."

"Oh, my dad wouldn't..." Jennifer's voice trailed off as she considered everything her dad had done when the DOJ was hounding her. "Maybe it's just as well I'm not seeing anyone right now."

"Sandra, neither of us are disputing what you're saying," Alexis interjected. "but would anyone ever have to *know* you used us to retrieve your officer and asset? If we get what we need, we could be there and back before anyone knows we're gone."

It was Jennifer who snorted this time. "That's not true at all, Alexis. My dad will know we went *somewhere*, but I think he would trust us with something like this."

Sandra closed her eyes and bowed her head, shaking it side to side for a couple moments. "I can't believe I'm going to do this. Is there somewhere we can go so he won't see I didn't leave? After he had us standing in the clouds, I really don't want to piss him off."

"I know just the place," Jennifer said with a grin of satisfaction.

# CHAPTER 37

Their destination was a small, cozy cabin on the fringe of the nearby national forest. Inside, the cabin was appointed with two bedrooms, a combined kitchen/dinette, and a small living area furnished with a long sofa, a loveseat, and a couple armchairs. A range of summer flowers lined flowerbeds in front of the deck and in circular beds in the yard.

"Oh, my," Alexis said, her words almost a sigh. "This... this is beautiful."

Jennifer's face lit up as she beamed. "Thank you. I'm glad you like it. Come on inside, and be sure to make yourself at home. The fridge has cold cuts, cheese, salad fixings, and a few different drinks. There's Dr. Pepper, Pepsi, and Coke for sure, but you may find a few others in there, too." Sandra and Alexis seemed to hover at Jennifer's shoulder, and she smiled. "Go on; it's perfectly safe, and the cabin's unlocked. I just need to check the wards to make sure they're still good. Say... five minutes?"

Alexis still stood where the teleportation effect deposited her. "This is just such a beautiful place, Jen. Are we anywhere close to your parents' place?"

Jennifer pointed across the one-lane, gravel road. "You see that fence line over there?"

"Yeah."

"That's the northern edge of what my dad and grandparents consider to be the Cross Estate," Jennifer explained. "A few years back, I realized I needed a place of my own every now and then to sort out my feelings and goals and stuff like that, so I used a little bit of my inheritance to purchase this plot. I designed the cabin and everything. I really like it better now that I know how to teleport."

"Your inheritance?" Alexis asked with a frown of confusion.

Jennifer grinned. "Yeah, from when Dad died."

Sandra spun, her eyes wide as she stood maybe three feet from the cabin's door. "But... but... he's not dead. He's back at the keep right now."

"Yep. Don't ask me how *that* works, and I figure it's safe to assume my dad's a special case. I wouldn't start looking for your Great Aunt Matilda or whoever to pop back into your life anytime soon."

Sandra closed her eyes and shuddered. "Wow. Yeah. Okay. I'll leave that one alone. Wrapping my head around dragons and how you people manipulate reality is enough for me."

FIVE MINUTES LATER, or thereabouts, Jennifer entered her cabin to find Sandra and Alexis sitting at the small dining table. The contents of Sandra's folder could have served as an Avant Garde tablecloth; Jennifer could only see the sides of the tabletop.

"Okay," Jennifer said, dropping into one of the two open chairs. "What do we have?"

Sandra held up a picture of an attractive Hispanic woman. The picture appeared to have been taken on a busy street somewhere with the sun straight overhead. A sheen of sweat glistened on her forehead, and she wore her glossy black hair in a ponytail. Mirrored aviators hid her eyes, and the set of her lips seemed to suggest a frown as she looked beyond the frame of the photo.

"This is Fiorella Castillo. She's a veteran officer who has

worked various South American stations over her nearly twenty years with us. She grew up in southwest Texas, and we recruited her straight out of college. As I tried to explain to your mentor, she disappeared in the Triple Frontier a few weeks ago while attempting to locate and extract a valuable asset who possesses information critical to our national security interests in the region."

Sandra set aside the photo and lifted a second which depicted a young man; honestly, he looked little more than an older adolescent. He bore the same complexion and dark hair as Fiorella, but he was barely more than skin and bones.

"This is Mateo Garcia," Sandra continued. "He's the asset who Fiorella swears possesses critical intelligence. Whatever it is, he won't give it to us unless we extract him and his little sister to the United States. Fiorella obtained permission to do just that and disappeared when she went down there to handle it."

Jennifer leaned forward to inspect the photos. "Where does Fiorella live? Is she local? Does she live somewhere in South America?"

"She maintains an apartment in McLean, Virginia," Sandra answered, "and when she's lucky, she actually manages to spend a whole month there. Come to think of it, she spent the last couple months there doing casework out of an office at Langley."

Alexis turned to Jennifer with a frown. "Get some hair or something from a brush and scry her for a portal?"

Jennifer nodded. "That's exactly what I'm thinking. Sure, we could create illusions for ourselves, so we looked and sounded like locals down there. But in the long run, I don't really think that's necessary. Let's just find out if she's still alive, and if she is, bring her and her asset back."


FROM JENNIFER'S COTTAGE, they went to the hospital and retrieved the Suburban's keys from Sandra's associate. Then, Jennifer, Alexis, and Sandra climbed inside while Jennifer teleported them and the vehicle to the vicinity of McLean, Virginia. From there, it was a simple drive to the apartment Fiorella kept.

The apartment turned out to be a small house, styled like a bungalow. Trees lined the property, and from the various flower beds dotting the yard, Fiorella appeared to like flowers as well... or at least paid a landscaping company for them. Sandra led them around to the back and retrieved a key from under a clay vase amid a collection on the back porch. Inside, Fiorella had decorated with a tasteful combination of film noir and pictures of the various locations around the world she'd visited... including Casablanca.

They wasted no time in locating the bathroom Fiorella used, and Jennifer felt a swell of relief when she saw a hairbrush that still had hairs in it. Alexis plucked a couple of them from the brush, and they retreated to the main room of the house.

Alexis's eyes shot wide for a moment before her shoulders slumped. When she spoke, her tone sounded like nothing more than a heavy, resigned sigh, "Aw, crap."

Jennifer frowned. "What?"

"We left my nannies at the keep."

"Your nan—" Understanding erupted in Jennifer's mind. Alexis often referred to her Secret Service detail as 'her nannies'. "Aw, crap... do you think they know we're gone yet?"

Alexis frowned. "Not sure. If they do, they haven't told my mom yet. Otherwise, my phone would be ringing endlessly. If we hurry up and get this done, maybe they won't even know we were gone."

"In that case," Jennifer replied, "would you like to do the honors?"

"I'll handle the scrying, but I don't think I'm ready to open a portal to a place halfway around the world from us. That's all you." Without further ado, Alexis lifted the hand that held the hairs from the brush. Moments later, she invoked a Word, "*Phezdys.*"

A two-foot diameter of open air began shimmering. Not even a heartbeat later, it flashed and became a window to another place. The scrying sphere—though smaller and hazier on the fringe than Gavin's were—depicted a room lit by sunlight. Bare dirt served as the floor, and three people lay bound and gagged on what appeared to be grimy straw-tick mattresses. Bruises dominated one side of both Fiorella's and Mateo's faces.

Jennifer nodded and took a deep breath. Then, concentrating on the room shown in Alexis's scrying sphere, she formed her intent and invoked a Word of Transmutation, "*Paedryx*."

An arch of crackling ruby energy rose up from the room's floor. Once it reached the height and rough shape of a door, it flashed, becoming a gateway to another place.

"We have to hurry," Sandra said. "They need medical attention."

Alexis led the way, her scrying sphere winking out as she crossed through the gateway. Jennifer followed Alexis, and Sandra brought up the rear. At the moment Jennifer started to turn to ask Sandra to help Alexis, pain exploded across the back of her head. The last thing she saw was a fading image of the dirt floor rushing toward her face.

* * *

WHEN JENNIFER CRUMPLED to the floor beside her, Alexis spun on her heel. Sandra held a heavy, leather-enclosed sap in her right hand and a small subcompact pistol in her left. The woman's expression looked hard as granite.

"Sandra?" Alexis asked. "What... ?"

"Do you have any idea how much of a bounty certain people are willing to pay for someone who can do what you can? Sure, I came to Gavin wanting Fiorella back, but that many zeros in the number became too much to ignore," Sandra said. "Neither of you are anywhere close to Gavin, but I'm hoping I'll get at least partial credit for his daughter and you."

Alexis waved her left hand at the other three people in the tiny space. "And what of them? Are they part of this, too?"

"Oh, no," Sandra replied. "Mateo, here, saw me meeting with the head of the local crime family about a few other matters. He recognized me from my brief stint at the local station and hustled to inform his handler, Miss Castillo over there. Of course, I didn't learn about any of this until my employer notified me that Mateo was making trouble. I never wanted Fiorella caught up in this, but I guess we're too far along now for that to matter. You can turn around and accept your new status, or I can shoot you and still tie and gag you."

Not knowing what else to do, Alexis turned and put her hands behind her. As rough hemp rope bit into her wrists, she couldn't help but think about Kiri and her practice. She wished she had sought Gavin's permission for Kiri to train her.

* * *

Gavin entered the keep's kitchen to the accompaniment of his growling stomach. As was often the case, he'd been so focused on his work in the lab that he'd worked through both lunch and dinner. He wasn't quite certain of the hour, but he saw twilight through the windows, so it had to be late. He opened the refrigerator and started the process of setting out the components of what would be his meal. As hungry as he was, he saw no reason not to put together one of his 'tower' sandwiches; they were both very, very good and very, very fast.

"Where's Alexis?" he heard someone ask behind him.

Gavin backed away from the refrigerator and turned. Gayle stood in the arched doorway to the kitchen, her expression overflowing with concern.

"Alexis?" Gavin asked. Gayle jerked several wide eyed nods, and Gavin shrugged. "I haven't seen her since I told that CIA officer I wasn't interested. Why?"

"She's not in her room, and she's not answering her phone. We can't find Jennifer, either. Kiri hasn't seen either of them all day."

Gavin frowned, his eyes roving across the assembled ingredients on the prep table before him. Being gone all day without at least checking in was very unlike them. Sure, he knew they skipped off from time to time and left Alexis's minders at the keep, but he'd always trusted them to use their skills and knowledge to be safe. Part of him wanted to say there was nothing wrong and that they'd probably turn up tomorrow acting suitably chagrined. But he couldn't... not quite.

"*Klaepos.*"

Had any wizards stood within a mile of the Cross Estate, the resonance of the power Gavin put into that invocation would've driven them to their knees at best. A scrying sphere winked into existence in the center of the kitchen. No shimmering. No gradual fade in. One heartbeat, it wasn't there, and the next, it was. And Gavin didn't like what it showed him.

His apprentices lay on a dirt floor somewhere, bound and gagged. Three other people lay around them, and two of them showed signs of having been beaten.

Gayle let out a strangled cry and whipped her phone out of its holster at her side.

"Don't bother with that now," Gavin said. "Get your associates. We're going to get them."

Gayle gaped. "What? How? We have no idea where they are, how they ended up there, or who else is there! For all we know, they're bait to lure *you.*"

Gavin's response was a dark—almost malevolent—laugh as he replied, "If the people responsible for this want to meet me so badly, then I promise you... they shall."

Clearing his mind of all but his intent, Gavin invoked a Word, "*Sykhurhos.*"

A faint shimmer washed over Gavin and Gayle from head to toe.

"What was that?" Gayle asked.

"Protection against conventional weapons, explosions, harmful gases, paralysis, poisons, and the various elements. For the next twelve hours, we cannot be burned, electrocuted, frozen, dissolved in acid, suffocated, or drowned... plus the other protections I cited. *Paedryx.*"

An arched gateway winked into existence, connecting the kitchen in the keep to whatever room held Alexis and Jennifer. Without hesitation, Gavin stepped through and held the gateway open through sheer force of will, allowing Gayle and the other agents to follow. Alexis's eyes shot wide above the gag just as something passed through Gavin's form. Once it passed out of him, Gavin saw that it was a heavy, leather sap. He turned to his left and saw the CIA woman lurch forward to catch her balance when her strike didn't connect with anything solid.

"Well, well," Gavin remarked, his tone still deep into the cold and uncaring ruthlessness of Kirloth. "It seems you have some explaining to do. If you survive our... conversation, shall we say... I'm sure one or more facets of the federal government will want what's left. *Uhnrys.*"

Sandra Barstow froze mid-lurch.

Gavin turned to survey the other occupants of the room, his eyes finally settling on his apprentices. Jennifer looked back at him, her almost-defiant expression marred by one pupil being larger than the other, but Alexis's shoulders slumped as she bowed her head. Once more, he cleared his mind of all but his intent and his will that the gateway remain open and invoked another Word, *"Rhyskaal."*

Everyone's bindings and gags dissolved into piles of what looked like dust, just as Gayle and the two men of her team charged through the gateway. Gayle's expression suggested she was ready to tear a strip off Alexis, but Gavin placed his right hand on her left shoulder.

When Gayle turned his way, he said, "Not here. Get them—all of them—back to the keep. I'll settle matters here before I return. If Alexis is otherwise unharmed, let her open a gateway to the local ER for these people, my daughter included."

Gavin thought Gayle might argue, but she didn't. Simply jerked a choppy nod and gestured for her teammates to see to the others in the room. Alexis helped Jennifer stand and didn't let her walk on her own as they stepped through the gateway.

A Hispanic woman Gavin didn't know stopped at his side, staring at Sandra Barstow where she was frozen between one second and the next.

"I want to be here when you interrogate her," she said.

Gavin didn't bother to look at her as he replied, "Who are you that I should care what you want?"

"Fiorella Castillo. I..." Her voice trailed off as she heaved a sigh. "I was a case officer for the region with the CIA."

"Was?"

She shrugged. "After this, I may consider another line of work... but not until I know *why* someone who was supposed to have my back had me beaten and waterboarded."

"Fiorella Castillo," Gavin said, "I assure you she faces a fate worse than anything you can possibly imagine, and it will come to pass over the next hour or so. Are you certain you want to witness that?"

The woman stood in silence as she stared at the frozen form of the former colleague who betrayed her. After several moments, she heaved another sigh and shook her head. "On further thought, you're probably right. I don't think I should watch whatever you have in store for her."

As the woman stepped through the gateway, Gavin said, "Very wise of you."

* * *

OVER THE FOLLOWING DAYS, a number of individuals—including an entire South American cartel—died through various grisly means. One of the ghastlier accounts described a man found with most of his respiratory system pulled inside out through his mouth and lit aflame. The only people to come through the quiet devastation unharmed were infants—now orphans for the most part.

* * *

THE DAY after the hospital released Jennifer, Gayle informed Gavin, Jennifer, and Alexis that the president would like to speak with them in the residence of the White House. Gavin thought that Chelsea had read a complete report of what had occurred by now, and he suspected she would either lump him in with his apprentices as recipients for her motherly ire or hope to use him as an ally. Gavin reached a decision that very morning about his response to what his apprentices had done, and he felt very confident that neither Chelsea nor his apprentices were prepared for what he would say.

.  .  .

THE ROSE GARDEN didn't look much different from the last time he'd seen it, and he led the procession of his apprentices and Alexis's Secret Service detail beside the agent escorting them to where the president waited. Gavin supposed he should've taken the time to appreciate the federal mansion for the museum of presidential history that it was, but in truth, he couldn't quite work up the effort to care. Not with an entire world depending on him.

Their Secret Service escort and guide delivered them to a second-floor set of double doors, where he knocked once and leaned inside before leaving them to their fate. Gavin led his apprentices into the room and noticed Gayle and her team chose to remain outside in the hall. Well, at least they didn't feel Alexis's life would be in danger inside this room; that was always a plus. The room was sitting room of sorts. Paintings depicting momentous events in the country's history adorned the walls, along with a portrait or two of famous presidents.

The door hadn't even completely latched when Chelsea Hall pivoted on her heel and almost shouted, "I would just like to know what in all of creation you thought you were doing, Alexis Leigh Hall! Did the thought that you could be kidnapped or killed ever once enter your mind? Did you even consider the ramifications of your actions on others? Do you realize that it is only because Gavin stood up for Gayle and her people that they still have their jobs, let alone positions on your detail? I thought you knew better than this." Chelsea tapered off to silence as she combed her fingers through her hair. "Thank goodness I didn't find out about any of it until after you delivered Jennifer and the others to that ER in Graham. I would've been a nervous wreck, let alone the potential implications for national security what with the president's daughter being abducted and all." She looked to Gavin. "Would you like to add anything while I recover my breath?"

"Thank you; I believe I shall," Gavin said in a voice that indicated he was all business.

Jennifer winced hearing a tone from her dad that she hadn't heard since she snuck out of the house in middle school.

Gavin turned to his apprentices and regarded them with a non-expression, taking in a deep breath. "Your actions have shown me that I cannot in good conscience consider you apprentices any longer. While I would argue you could've taken greater precautions to ensure your safety, I cannot deny the mastery you displayed. Personally, I would prefer that Alexis had created the gateway to the location where Fiorella and her asset were being held, but given the distance involved and inherent power required, it's a minor quibble overall. By the authority vested in me as your mentor and within the Arcanists' Code, I hereby confer upon you the rank of *Magus* and membership in good standing within the Society of the Arcane."

"What?" Chelsea shrieked. "They go against your wishes to help a woman who ultimately betrayed them, get captured—even injured Jennifer's case—and you *reward* them for it? Are you out of your mind?"

Gavin turned to face Chelsea, and his expression deflated her faster than a balloon pierced with a needle. "I will allow that outburst because you are Alexis's mother and exist under the constraints and pressure of your office. Do not presume to question me again. In point of fact, I spoke with Alexis and Jennifer at length while my daughter enjoyed the hospitality of the Graham Regional Medical Center. Their mastery of what they have learned cannot be denied, and our discussions educated me on the reasons for their actions and the thought processes that led to them. I feel very safe in concluding this is one lesson neither will *ever* forget, like several situations *I* have survived. I have evaluated there is precious little left to teach them. As such, and as neither of them did anything especially egregious during their apprenticeships, they passed."

Chelsea glared at Gavin, both Jennifer and her daughter forgotten. Her nostrils flared to the accompaniment of her jaw clenching and unclenching. Finally, she closed her eyes; clenched her fists; and released a deep breath as a long, slow sigh.

"Damn you," she said, little more than a whisper. "I was trying to keep her safe."

"'Safe' is a pipe dream, Chelsea. It doesn't exist. There are merely many levels of threat or risk. A strung-out junkie jonesing for his next hit could storm into the ice cream shop in Graham with no warning at all and kill children in his quest for money to secure his next fix. Is that possible? Of course. Is it likely? Who can say? Your daughter was born with the ability to re-shape reality to her will. If you deny her the opportunity to learn and practice that trait, you are forever limiting her development."

"I know," Chelsea replied. "It's just…"

"You're her mother. You love her. You want her safe and happy."

Chelsea nodded.

Gavin turned to face his former apprentices. "There's one last thing to do. A ritual or ceremony, if you will. Alexis, when you're ready, return to the keep. You and Jennifer should perform it together."

That said, Gavin turned and led Jennifer out of the room. They returned to the Rose Garden, and Gavin opened a gateway to return to the keep.

# CHAPTER 38

Two days passed before Alexis returned to the keep, and when she did, she was not alone. Beyond her own travel party of Secret Service agents, a much more extensive travel party accompanied her mother. Half the president's travel party stepped through the gateway first and fanned out across the plateau surrounding the keep. Faint traces of unease—if not fear—lurked around the edges of the president's expression as Alexis gestured for her to step through the gateway.

"Come on, Mom," Alexis said. "You have to go ahead of me. I'm not practiced enough yet to step through the gateway and hold it open like Gavin does."

Chelsea squared her shoulders and stepped through. The rest of her travel party followed, then Alexis's team. Alexis stepped through last, and the gateway vanished as if it never was.

"So this is the keep I've heard so much about?" Chelsea asked.

Alexis nodded as she approached her mom's side. "Yep. That fenced-off section is where Kiri practices with her blades, and if the Secret Service watched her, they wouldn't let you within five miles of her."

"We already made a full report," Gayle said. "Shortly after you began your studies. Kiri's demonstrated skill and proficiency is one of the reasons you could be here with just the three of us."

"Was Gavin the other reason?" Alexis asked with a knowing grin.

Gayle replied with a non-committal shrug.

Movement at the front of the keep drew everyone's attention to Gavin stepping through the arched doorway. He smiled in welcome.

"Good day. I must confess I wasn't expecting to host the president, but please, come inside and make yourselves at home." He turned to the Secret Service agents he didn't know and smiled. "I want you to feel welcome as well. I realize each and every one of you are constitutionally incapable of accepting this, but your charge is exponentially safer here than anywhere else on Earth. A nuclear blast could go off above our heads, and she wouldn't even develop a tan."

"We understand all that and appreciate your welcome," Robyn Marsted, the head of Chelsea's person detail, said. "But we simply cannot relax while we're on duty. We're just not wired that way."

"I understand," Gavin replied. "Can you at least relax as much as you would if she were still at the White House?"

Robyn sighed. "I'd like to, but no. We've all seen the reports of your protections and how they work, but the fact remains, she's outside what the agency defines as a safe perimeter."

"Very well. We'll try to make this as fast as possible, so you can get back to the White House."

"Thank you for your welcome," Chelsea said as she approached Gavin, "especially your welcome and regard for my minders. Robyn and her people do their jobs very well, and I'm sure they appreciate those who take my safety just as seriously as they do. Now, I'm guessing this ritual you mentioned is some kind of graduation?"

"That's a close analogue, I suppose," Gavin concluded. "And it won't take all that long. Alexis texted Jennifer and gave us a heads-up you were coming. We have everything ready. Please, follow me." Gavin turned and led them into the keep. "If any of the agents who have never been here would like to walk the halls and open doors, please feel free to do so. You can even say hello to the dragons in the lab upstairs, if you like."

A group of agents did indeed break off from the main group, fanning out to walk through the keep.

Gavin led everyone else to the dining room, where Jennifer waited beside one of two chairs pulled away from the table. Another chair sat about six feet away from those two, facing them. Alexis frowned at seeing her friend wrapped in a brown robe and frowned all the more when Jen offered her one just like it.

"What's this?" Alexis asked.

"If we had conducted your apprenticeships in Drakmoor, you would've worn a brown student's robe as your outer garment to signify your status as a student or apprentice," Gavin explained. "The ritual we are about to conduct will reveal your philosophy toward the Art and change the color of your robe to signify it. Based on what I've observed in the past, you may want to sit before we recite the ritual."

"Will it hurt?" Alexis asked.

"Not that I'm aware. Given how my friends described the experience, I would say it is more akin to running a marathon with your mind."

Alexis nodded, pulling on her robe and joining Jennifer before she said, "Let's do this."

"Take your seats, then," Gavin replied. As the young ladies did so, Gavin lifted his left hand and snapped his fingers. In a flash of gold-colored light, a gold robe with black runes on the cuffs of its sleeves appeared, with Gavin already wearing it. He reached inside his clothes and withdrew his wizard's medallion, prompting Jennifer and Alexis to do likewise as they sat. Then, he assumed his own seat.

"It is my conclusion that there is nothing left for me teach you," Gavin said. "Only one task remains before you can take your rightful places within the Society of the Arcane. Do you wish to complete this task?"

"Yes," the ladies answered, almost in unison.

Gavin nodded. "Very well. Pick up the sheets of paper beneath your seats and recite along with me."

He waited until the young ladies held the papers in front of them and began reading the ritual. It took them no time at all to recite it, and just as with Lillian and the others, nothing happened right away. Gavin heard more than one gasp, though, when small motes of light about the size of a wooden pencil's eraser appeared wreathing the ladies' heads. Those beads of light spun around each person so fast that they became halos. Soon, a shower of small motes of light cascaded down over the ladies, and in their wake, the brown robes were no more.

Gavin couldn't restrain a smile of fatherly pride at seeing his daughter in a black robe with white rank runes on the sleeves of her cuffs. And in all truth, Alexis's white robe with black runes didn't shock him, either. Given what he knew of her, it seemed fitting.

When the lights faded, the ladies sagged against their seats. Their chests heaved as they recovered their breath, and they looked exhausted.

"You were not joking at all," Alexis said. "I feel like my mind and soul have just been through a wringer."

"That will pass with some rest," Gavin remarked.

Chelsea took a cautious step forward. "What do the colors mean?"

"The color of an arcanist's robe signifies that arcanist's philosophy toward the Art," Gavin explained. The black robe represents a philosophy of the Art above all else. The white robe proclaims that, in the core of her soul, Alexis would use the Art to protect and defend others. The rune color signifies the arcanist's specialization, if any. Alexis's black runes and Jennifer's white mean they are generalists."

"You told me once that your robe was your badge of office," Chelsea said. "How is that, if their robes mean their respective philosophies?"

Gavin met Chelsea's eyes. "There is only one instance in which a robe's color *does not* indicate the arcanist's philosophy, and that is the gold robe. Only the Archmagister of Tel wears that."

"And if you were not the Archmagister of Tel, what color would your robe be?"

Gavin allowed himself a smug grin. "Do you really need to ask?"

A moment of unspoken communication passed between Gavin

and Chelsea before she turned back toward her daughter. "What's next for them now?"

"Whatever they want," Gavin replied, adding a shrug. "I would like to see them continue their studies and expand their mastery, but the path they walk is up to them."

Alexis's eyes lit up with excitement as she asked. "Can we work with you on the portal?"

"If you wish."

"I know I'd like to," Alexis said. "What about you, Jen?"

Jennifer picked at her finger for a moment before answering. "I do, and I don't."

"Huh? Why?" Alexis replied.

Jennifer shook her head without replying, but Gavin knew what she otherwise might've said if the place didn't have so many ears. She was afraid she'd lose him all over again once the portal work was finished. He had no intention of leaving and not ever coming back, but that wasn't something he could just tell her and have her believe. It was something he'd have to *show* her, a project for another time.

"Would anyone like some refreshments?" Gavin asked as he stood.

Alexis and Jennifer stood as well, as Chelsea offered a weak smile.

"I would gladly accept, but I shudder to think of the work that has piled up in my absence," Chelsea replied. "I don't know if anyone has ever termed my job a sacrifice or not, but someone should have. Almost every day feels like my life isn't my own."

Gavin understood her sentiments, commiserating with her in silence. After a moment or three, he swept his hand inside his robe and withdrew an item from his pants pocket. He extended his hand toward Chelsea and opened it to reveal what appeared to be a sandstone disc bearing all manner of runes and glyphs.

"Keep this on your person at all times, Chelsea," Gavin said. "If you ever have urgent or dire need of my help, break it. I don't mean the President of the United States needing my help, Chelsea. I mean you personally, Chelsea Hall."

Chelsea retrieved the disc and held it in her hand as she stared at it. "Do I need to worry about breaking it by accident? Like if I lean it against the wall in my pocket?"

"No. It can only be broken through conscious will."

"Will it still work once you finish your portal and return to Tel?"

"Yes, but we can test it once I finish the portal if you like. They're ridiculously simple to make."

"What happens if I break it?"

"Two things. One, it will layer you in multiple protections that will last for twenty-four hours. Two, I will know you broke it, and I'll send someone I trust to you immediately if I myself can't respond. There are times—much like you—when I simply can't drop what I'm doing."

Chelsea nodded and slipped it into the pocket of her trousers. She lifted her eyes to meet Gavin's. "Thank you."

"You're welcome, Chelsea. I try to protect my friends. So far, I've succeeded."

"Well," Chelsea said, "I should probably be getting back."

Gavin smiled. "Alexis, that's your cue."

"I'll be outside as soon as you've gathered up everyone," Alexis replied as she left the keep.

Gavin and Jennifer watched them go in silence. When only father and daughter remained in the dining room, Jennifer asked, "Do you think you'll ever regret giving her that disc?"

"I doubt it. Chelsea is a good, decent person... regardless of the job she holds at the moment. If she ever faces a circumstance that my help means the difference between life and death, I want her to have that disc."

The next thing Gavin knew, Jennifer wrapped her arms around him and rested her head on his shoulder. "Don't worry, Dad; the secret that you're a big, ole softie is safe with me."

# CHAPTER 39

One week after completing Jennifer's and Alexis's apprenticeships, Gavin finalized the design for the portal that would return him and Kiri to Drakmoor. For the first step, Gavin and the dragons would invoke the composite effect to verify the efficacy of the design. The second step would involve crafting the forms for the permanent portals... both on Earth and Drakmoor. The final step would see the creation of a permanent portal between the Cross Estate outside Graham, Virginia, and a location in Tel of Gavin's choosing.

GAVIN SAT at one of the cement benches that lined the lake's shore. A breeze kissed his left cheek, and leaves rustled in the tree overhead as he stared across the tranquil waters. Hints of wild mint and other woodland scents wafted along on the breeze, enhancing the peace he felt. He became aware of a presence just over his left shoulder and, turning to look, saw his father standing six feet away. Gavin smiled his welcome.

"Hey, Dad. Care to join me?"

"Don't mind if I do." Richard walked around and sat on the opposite end of the bench from Gavin. "So, Kiri was telling us the big day has arrived. You're planning to test the composite effect for the portal today?"

Gavin nodded. "Yeah. I have no reason to doubt it will work, but it's always better to trust based on test, instead of just trust. After all, I'd rather not open an interdimensional portal to someplace like the elemental plane of fire in your front lawn. That might have a detrimental effect on your property value."

"That could happen?"

"Possible?" Gavin asked. "Absolutely. Likely? Not really. I've been doing composite effects a little while now and have them pretty well in hand. I'm just glad the dragons are here. Trying to do this by myself—or with only Jennifer's and Alexis's help—would not be fun. It wouldn't even be a vague impression of fun."

Richard leaned forward and frowned. "Oh? Why is that?"

"The power requirements are obscene," Gavin replied. "Cross-dimensional scrying is almost beyond *me*. Attempting a cross-dimensional portal might very well kill Alexis or Jennifer right now. At the very least, it would knock them on their butts for several days. Fortunately, our ancestors picked an almost-perfect location for the estate. A number of ley lines pass through the property, and I'm hoping I'll be able to use them to maintain the permanent portal, once we're ready for that."

Richard nodded. After several moments of silence, he waved his hand toward the keep overlooking the lake. "Once you go back, what becomes of all this?"

"I figure I'll leave it for Jennifer. I'd like to see her continue her studies and explorations of the Art, and to do that, she'll need a place that is both reinforced and protected. The keep is that. Besides, it's not like I won't come back and visit from time to time. This can be my vacation home for those times when I really, *really* need to get away from being Archmagister. To paraphrase a frog, it ain't easy wearing gold."

"No... I don't suppose it is," Richard replied. "I feel you deserve fair warning, by the way."

"How so?"

"Your mother refused to teach Kiri how to cook and share recipes until they discussed the status of your relationship... and potential grandchildren."

Gavin fought back a wince. "Seriously? There is Jennifer, you know."

"There's no such thing as too many grandchildren," Richard replied, slapping Gavin's back." You'll understand when it's your turn; trust me."

Gavin gave his father a sidelong glance. "That almost sounds like Mom wasn't the only one having a quiet word with Kiri."

Richard lifted his hands in a gesture of surrender. "I learned a long time ago not to meddle in the affairs of women... but I wouldn't be opposed to more grandchildren, either. I've always felt we failed Jennifer, to a certain extent."

"Nope. I don't agree with that at all. When she truly needed you the most—whether she wanted to admit it or not—you two were there for her. I wish I had the words for how grateful I am that you were."

Richard sighed. "I just wish we hadn't let it get as bad as it did. I wish we had sued for custody right out of the gate, when we learned what Emily had said to Jennifer at the scene."

"Seriously, Dad... don't let yourself fall into that trap. It's over and done, all in the past. And while hindsight is always 20/20, it can also be *very* misleading. Who are we to say that what Jennifer survived wasn't the proper path for her? We'll never know how she might've turned out if I hadn't died. Who knows... if she had still discovered that Word of Power without me living in Drakmoor, there's a good chance we would have already buried her because of the *skathos* cascade. So, don't let yourself fall into the 'I wish I had' game. It's not productive at all, in my experience."

"You're right," Richard replied. "Damn... I never thought I'd be taking life advice from my son. How did you get to be so wise?"

Gavin heaved a sigh, laden with everything he didn't want to say. "Dad... if you have to ask, you don't want to know the answer."

* * *

A SHORT TIME LATER, Gavin, his former apprentices, and several dragons gathered at the grassy area across the driveway from the house and beside the portal to the keep. Kiri and Gavin's parents watched from the porch of their house. A second group of dragons—those brave souls who would first step through the test portal and help with the construction of Drakmoor-side of the permanent structure—stood off to one side, awaiting the time to play their part.

Gavin ran through his intent one more time in his mind. He wanted—no—*needed*—his focus to be perfect. The dragons making up the "Earth team" all stood in silence, their eyes on him. This composite effect would be just a little bit different than those Gavin often invoked. Instead of pulling the power for the effect through himself or a group of others, he intended for the bulk of the power to come from the ley lines running deep below his family's homestead. If he was correct and if they were successful, the portal would open without knocking any of the arcanists involved unconscious—especially Gavin. In Drakmoor, he would never have attempted it; there simply was not sufficient ambient power to make it work. But here? On Earth? He wasn't sure he could sense the full depth of Earth's ambient power through his *skathos*; it was that deep and pervasive.

With one last sigh, Gavin admitted to himself that he was as ready as he'd ever be. It was time. He lifted his gaze to meet each pair of fiery red eyes regarding him in silence, asking, "Is everyone ready?"

Silent nods were the replies.

"Right, then. Let's get this party started. Recite with me—in three—two—one—*Paedryx-Uhnrys-Rhyskaal.*"

When Gavin invoked a regular gateway, he always envisioned an archway of sapphire energy rising out of the floor, ground, or whatever he stood on—unless he chose an instantaneous teleportation. This time, Gavin gave no thought whatsoever to the physical manifestation of the portal; he just wanted it to work.

At first, nothing seemed to happen, even though Gavin *felt* the effect take hold. After several heartbeats, though, a pin-prick of purplish-crimson light appeared in the air in front of Gavin. It hovered at about the level of Gavin's heart, and it swelled with a certain rapidity as time passed. First, it was about the size of a pin-head. Then, a peanut. An apple. A beach ball.

By the time it reached the size of a beach ball, crackling tendrils —much like one might see inside a Van de Graaff generator— covered the orb's surface like whiskers. The tendrils roiled and seethed across the orb, never staying in one place for even a fragment of a second. By the time it grew to the size of a commercial tractor tire, the energy crackling in and around the effect echoed throughout the area.

The orb continued to grow in size until it reached the diameter of a Great Sequoia. Then, with zero warning, it flashed bright, and a thunderclap loud enough to reduce an 80's Heavy Metal concert to stunned silence shattered the otherwise-peaceful moment. The concussion put anyone standing on the ground and shook every structure for fifteen miles in any direction.

Gavin couldn't keep from smiling as he positioned himself to stand. A window to another world hovered about ten feet in front of him, and through that window, he saw the courtyard of the College of the Arcane. But nothing could have prepared him for what happened next.

Not even a full five seconds after the cross-dimensional portal solidified, an unintended consequence of the refugees' flight to Earth corrected itself. If the ambient power was a pool Gavin and his former apprentices had been bathing in, the portal became an opened drain. In a great rush that drove Gavin back to his knees mid-rise, the vast sea of power Gavin had felt since waking in the alley across from his family's store surged through the portal like the tide withdrawing before a tsunami. As he struggled to remain on his knees and not outright collapse, Gavin couldn't help but wonder what arcanists in Drakmoor experienced.

It seemed like the vast sea of power spent countless ages flowing through the portal from Earth to Drakmoor, and the sensation of being sucked out to sea with a tide overwhelmed Gavin's other senses. He possessed no concept for how much time passed while he gave the grass in front of him a thousand-yard stare. Soon enough, though the rush lessened. Then faded. Then ceased altogether.

Gavin still stared at nothing when he felt a touch on his left shoulder. He turned to look, and the simple movement of turning almost robbed him of what balance he still held. The world didn't *quite* spin around him as he looked drunkenly up at Kiri from his knees... but it was a near thing.

"Gavin?" Kiri asked. "Are you okay?"

Gavin reached out his left hand to steady himself, not even aware that what he found was—in truth—Kiri's right thigh. His head wobbled, and his eyes rolled of their own accord.

"I... I don't know." His speech slurred. His torso swayed, despite Kiri's hand on his shoulder. "I've never felt anything like that."

"Whatever it was, Gavin," Kiri replied, "you seem to be the only one affected. Neither Jennifer, Alexis, nor the dragons reacted like you have."

"I cannot speak for his former apprentices," Firestreak said, arriving at Gavin's right side, "but we dragons do not have the same connection to the ambient magic that true arcanists do, despite our strength in the Art. Think of us like mundanes, in a way. Yes, we wield power, but it is just part of what we are. We are not dragon wizards, just dragons."

Gavin drew breath to speak, to explain what he felt. But he didn't have time. A wave of power—smaller and far less forceful—washed through the portal from Drakmoor. In his compromised state, Gavin could muster no resistance; the wave struck him through his *skathos* and swept him to the ground as gently and implacably as the returning tide.

* * *

HE BLINKED OPEN his eyes and felt grass tickling his left ear. What was he doing on the ground? What happened with the portal? He blinked again, forcing the world around him to come into focus. Robed people—their faces shrouded in shadow—clustered near him, and the most beautiful woman he could imagine knelt at his side. And... relief. There, in the background, the portal hovered, a window in reality.

Gavin Cross. He was Gavin Cross, and that meant she was Kiri Muran. And they were both on Earth, his home; they'd been there a while. He smiled up at her, and Kiri beamed.

"Hi, there. I feel weird. Okay... but weird. I think I know why Marcus was always saying the Art is not as it was."

Kiri's eyebrows shot up, revealing her surprise. "Really? Why?"

Gavin forced himself to sit up, then stand. "I think Nesta's act of forging a path between these two worlds created a one-way path that somehow slowly siphoned the ambient power in Drakmoor to here, adding to whatever was already permeating this dimension. I don't think she meant for that to happen, but I suppose we'll never know. And I think creating this portal served as a stabilizing valve to equalize 'the pressure,' as it were. I'll bet Lillian and the others are sitting over there somewhere wondering what in the world just happened."

"Do we still proceed with the plan?" Firestreak asked. "Should the team for the Drakmoor portal step through and await you?"

Gavin turned to look over his right shoulder at the portal. He still hadn't sorted out just where he wanted to put the Drakmoor side of the permanent gateway, because he didn't have an estate to call his own... not like House Mivar, House Cothos, or the others. A memory rose to the forefront of his mind, and he couldn't help an uneasy laugh. He did have an estate; he just never thought about it. The former Sivas Estate that he'd claimed in the wake of Iosen Sivas's death. He could put the portal there, but a part of him felt like he should turn that estate over to Alexis as the rightful Head of House Sivas.

There was nothing for it. His conscience would never let him rest if he didn't give her the option, at least.

"Everyone hold here a moment. I just remembered something

that needs clearing up." Gavin turned and walked the short distance to approach those waiting on the porch.

"Is that it?" Elizabeth asked as he neared. "Is that Tel Mivar?"

Gavin nodded. "A piece of it. You're looking at the courtyard of the College of the Arcane. I have no idea how long I was laying on the grass, but I'm starting to get a little worried that the portal hasn't developed a crowd over there."

"It wasn't even a full minute, Dad," Jennifer replied, "and I haven't seen anyone walking around the courtyard to notice the portal yet."

Gavin nodded. "Alexis, there's something we need to discuss. When I killed Iosen Sivas, I claimed the Sivas Estate, but it is by all rights yours. Do you want to claim it?"

"Uhm... I don't know. Do I?"

"I can't answer that for you. Personally, I would like to see you and my daughter be active members in the Society of the Arcane. You can get away with choosing not to, but I'm afraid Jennifer doesn't have that luxury."

"Because I'm heir to House Kirloth?"

Gavin nodded.

Alexis took a deep breath and shook her head. "No, I don't think I want it. I'm sure it's a good world, but my place is here. If nothing else, I can buttress Jennifer against all the world-hopping she'll have to do."

"Fair enough," Gavin replied, chuckling. "I need a little bit of time to finalize the permanent portal, and then, I'll take anyone who wants on the nickel tour."

He turned and walked back to those waiting for him. The dragons that would help him establish the Drakmoor side of the permanent portal stepped through first, then Gavin. In the blink of an eye, the portal popped into nothingness, almost like a soap bubble.

* * *

KIRI STOOD WITH JENNIFER, Alexis, and Gavin's parents. She stared at the space the temporary portal had filled mere moments before. As the seconds dragged into minutes, she couldn't help but feel something was wrong. He should've created the permanent portal already, right? Was the Lornithrasa waiting for him? Had the Necromancer actually managed to capture Tel Mivar?

She cursed herself a fool for not insisting on going with him as she worked her lower lip between her teeth. This was taking too long. Gavin was in danger. He needed her.

Kiri put one foot off the porch to return to Firestreak and demand they open another temporary portal when all around them the ground rumbled. It wasn't quite on the order of an earthquake, but it felt like the rolling thunder of a major storm took place not even ten feet below the ground's surface.

Then, about twenty feet to the right of the portal to the keep, a massive stone rectangle—ten feet wide if it was an inch—forced itself out of the earth. Bits of sod and grass and even some worms fell away as it rose almost to fifteen feet in height. It stopped rising when the bottom of the rectangle extended far enough out of the ground for a comfortable step up, and the rumbling ceased as abruptly as it had begun.

The ensuing silence felt oppressive, unnatural, eerie.

Another massive thunderclap knocked everyone off their feet once more, and in its wake, the center of the rectangle was now a doorway to another world. And through that doorway, Kiri saw Gavin, resplendent in the gold robe of the Archmagister.

# CHAPTER 40

In the year-and-a-quarter (plus or minus) since that fateful day in the Temple Plaza, the Dukes and Duchesses of Tel had made a gradual withdrawal from their positions within Tel, easing their heirs into positions of authority and shifting themselves into advisory roles. Of course, there were 'growing pains' from time to time, and not all of the heirs approved of the idea when they realized what was happening. But, by and large, the process went well.

It was not a good day. Of course, none of the days since Gavin and Kiri vanished had been especially *good* days, but today was about as far from being good as possible without being outright horrible. Tensions within the Society of the Arcane and certain segments of Tel's general population approached what seemed to be a tipping point. Just what that tipping point would set in motion was anyone's guess.

Lillian stood at the head of the table, scanning the faces looking back at her. Her friends, her grandfather and his counterparts, Nathrac, and even Ovir attended this meeting. As had been the case for quite some time now, they met in a conference room in the

Citadel. Lillian still felt presumptuous about doing so, but no one could deny Nathrac's point that no one could eavesdrop or otherwise spy on their meetings there.

"We have to do something," Lillian said. "Even without Tauron's poisonous presence, the Council seems on the edge of breaking ranks with us. Outside of Valera and Kantar, they seem to have bought into the belief that Gavin is gone for good, despite the sconces and braziers still burning. I fear we now stand in the calm before the storm, and I further fear that storm will be a general, armed uprising."

"Well, that wouldn't be good..." Lillian's thoughts and fears so dominated her focus that she didn't process the voice came from *behind* her. "... nor would it end well for them. I like to think of myself as patient and understanding, but I do have limits."

By the end of the statement, Lillian's senses pushed through her focus. She realized that everyone looked behind her and—with the exception of Nathrac—grinned like fools. The silent despair she'd carried all these long months flared into hope, and she pivoted on her heel. Then, she grinned like a fool herself.

Gavin stood in the room's arched doorway, his gold robe gleaming. Kiri stood at his side, and four people clustered behind them that she didn't know. Her eyes landed on the older man, and she fought the urge to gape. He looked so much like Marcus it was uncanny. Giving not even a whit of a thought to decorum or respect for their persons, Lillian crossed the intervening distance in a finger-snap and threw her left arm around Kiri and her right around Gavin, pulling them to her in a tight embrace.

"Thank the gods," Lillian gasped, her face buried between them. "I wanted to hope, but I despaired they were right."

"Right about what?" Kiri asked, her voice a little strained.

"That neither of you were ever coming back."

Gavin broke free of her arm and stepped back. He placed his hands on her shoulders and gave her a rakish grin. "To paraphrase a character from my youth, you can't keep a good wizard down."

Lillian grinned, hope swelling within her once more. "Does that mean you have your memories back?"

Gavin nodded. "I do, and introductions are in order."

Lillian stepped back from Kiri as everyone else moved to join them.

* * *

"Okay," Gavin said, almost sighing the word, "to keep this from being cumbersome, let's form two lines. Everyone who was in this room before my arrival forms one line, and everyone who came with me and Kiri forms the other. Both lines face each other... and... go."

Both groups of people complied with Gavin's request, though not without some chuckles on each side. As soon as both lines arranged themselves, Gavin nodded.

"Right, then. On the Drakmoor side, starting farthest away from me and moving down the line, we have Nathrac, Ovir Thatcherson, Carth Roshan, Wynn Roshan, Braden Wygoth, Sypara Wygoth, Mariana Cothos, Lyssa Cothos, Torval Mivar, and Lillian Mivar. On the Earth side, we have Elizabeth Cross, my mother; Richard Cross, my father; Jennifer Cross, my daughter; and Alexis Hall, Head of House Sivas."

At Gavin's final words, the eyes of everyone in the Drakmoor line locked on Alexis. Precious few of their expressions were welcoming. Lillian and Mariana looked one step below outright hostility.

"I guess their reactions have to do with why I defaulted into Head of my House?" Alexis asked.

Gavin could tell from her posture and faint expression changes that she fought the urge to be intimidated.

"Probably," Gavin replied. "Folks, up until about a week ago, Alexis was one of my two apprentices on Earth. I realize the fact that she's House Sivas is a bit unsettling, and I would argue I have far, far more reason to be unsettled by that than any of you; after all, Iosen Sivas did try torturing me to death, and I kept the scars. I would like to think that we can all move past Iosen and Rolf, granting Alexis a clean slate, for two very specific reasons. One, she had no idea what her House was until she invoked the divination to identify it. Two, and probably the most important, aside from a brief visit here and now, she has no intention of ever setting foot in Drakmoor again. If I can get past my memories of House Sivas here and treat Alexis no differently than I did before I knew her House, the lot of you had damned well better do the same, or we'll have words. Any problems so far?"

Gavin watched his former apprentices—especially Lillian and Mariana—shake themselves. After a few heartbeats, Lillian stepped forward.

"Alexis Hall," Lillian began, "it was unfair of me in the extreme to paint you with the brush colored by Iosen and Rolf Sivas. I apologize and hope you can find it in your heart to forgive me."

Alexis smiled. "Of course, I forgive you, and please, don't think anything of it. Gavin never explained in great detail why Sivas doesn't have the best reputation, but only an idiot would fail to notice the emotions that swirl just beneath his demeanor when he mentioned my House's name."

The others added their apologies in short order, and Alexis was quick to accept and forgive them as well.

"So," Gavin said, once the tension faded, "I take it there is some unrest?"

Braden chuckled, sounding not unlike a minor rockslide rumbling down a slope. "There has been, yes, but it'll vanish soon enough once everyone sees you're back. Nothing takes the fight out of someone quite like being face-to-face with Kirloth."

Gavin closed his eyes for a moment and fought an urge to groan. "I really hope I don't need Kirloth in this. There's always an unfortunate tendency for bodies to drop when he's around. But before we get too far into getting me updated on everything I missed, I would like to invite you all to accompany us in returning Kiri home. I have some unfinished business with Terris."

Kiri's eyes shot wide, and unless Gavin was mistaken, they glistened with extra moisture as well. "Are you sure, Gavin?"

"Yes."

With exception of Nathrac, everyone accepted the invitation.

Gavin was just about to open a portal to the palace courtyard when Lillian held up her hand, saying, "Wait... we need to find Declan. He'd never forgive us if he missed what's about to happen."

"Oh, I don't think we need to wait," Gavin replied. "I've already made sure he's waiting for us at the Vushaari palace."

* * *

THE BREEZE COMING through the windows carried hints of the vanilla blossoms in the courtyard outside. No clouds marred the sky, and the temperature was on the warm side of perfect. Varne, the Royal Herald of Vushaar, looked up from his desk outside the throne room at the sound of several footfalls heading his way. He blinked at the sight. No... it couldn't be.

"Hello, Varne," Kiri said, standing beside Gavin in her formal court attire and looking all the more beautiful for it.

Varne shot to his feet as he began his response, but his mind locked. Who should he address first? As Archmagister of Tel, one could argue Gavin stood equal with the King of Vushaar, but that post existing as the last of the Divine Emissaries probably tipped the balance in favor of superseding the king. Therefore, one could argue that the Archmagister of Tel superseded the Crown Princess as well. And yet...

Gavin smiled. "She comes first, Varne, no matter the circumstance."

Varne felt certain his relief was writ large across his expression.

"Welcome home, Your Highness," he said. "This past year has been... well... difficult for us all, but especially your father."

"Court is already in session?" Kiri asked.

"Yes, Your Highness," he replied, "but I feel safe in thinking His Majesty would welcome this particular interruption. May I announce you?"

A sparkle lit Kiri's eyes as she smiled. "Of course, Varne."

Varne nodded and pivoted on his heel, scurrying to the throne room doors and slipping inside.

* * *

It wasn't very long before Gavin heard Varne announce in his hall-filling voice, "Your Majesty, my lords and ladies, and good people of Vushaar… it is my honor and privilege to present Her Royal Highness, Kiri Muran. She is escorted by the Archmagister of Tel, Gavin Cross; Lady Lillian Mivar; Lady Mariana Cothos; Lord Wynn Roshan; Lord Braden Wygoth; and sundry others."

As Gavin fell into step with Kiri, he thought he heard his daughter say, "Are you 'sundry' or 'other?'"

"I don't know," Alexis whispered back. "I think I'll pick 'other'."

The procession made its way through the throne room and came to stand in front of the royal dais where Terris Muran sat in the Throne of Vushaar. He outright beamed at his daughter, not even bothering to fight the tears that traced wet tracks down his cheeks.

"Your Majesty," Gavin began, "I wasn't aware your daughter intended to visit Tel Mivar so soon after I brought her home, and I deeply apologize it has taken me this long to return her to you. I'm afraid we took an unintended side trip."

"Is that so, Milord?" Terris asked, his fight to remain stoic obvious to anyone with eyes or ears. "And just where did this trip take you?"

Gavin smiled. "It took me home, and I'm afraid your Crown Princess went along for the ride. The individuals among our party that you don't recognize are my parents, my daughter, and my former apprentice, who is getting something of a whirlwind tour before she returns home. If I may Your Majesty, I ask your permission to present a petition."

Now, a smile did escape Terris's otherwise-ironclad non-expression. "It seems this is the *second* time you have interrupted a session of our court, but it would be the height of disrespect to your office to deny you. Please, speak your petition."

"I thank you, Your Majesty, and apologize to all the petitioners before me for jumping the line. I come before you today to petition you for your daughter's hand in marriage."

The ensuing silence highlighted the waves of hushed gasps that preceded it throughout the crowd.

"Regardless of what I may think of your petition, Milord," Terris replied, "I would never presume to proceed without consulting my daughter on the matter. What say you, my dear?"

Without missing a beat, Kiri replied, "Across countless centuries, the Throne of Vushaar has known no greater ally than Kirloth, and while Gavin Cross has maintained that alliance, he has also shown himself to be a man of uncompromising integrity. When I first met him, I was a slave, having washed ashore after the *Sprite* sank, but Gavin never treated me as such. Further, he promised to bring me home, and he did. I could keep listing reason after reason that you should accept his petition, but the simple fact is that I have come to love Gavin with all my heart and cannot imagine marrying anyone else. Does that answer your question, Father?"

"Ermm... yes. I rather think it does," Terris replied. "So be it. Gavin Cross, Archmagister of Tel and Head of House Kirloth, I accept your petition. Before the souls gathered here and the very gods themselves, I declare the two of you betrothed."

* * *

LATER THAT DAY, after Kiri had insisted on showing Gavin's family and Alexis around the palace and capital city, everyone gathered in one of the larger sitting rooms in the royal residence. Terris chatted with Gavin's parents while Kiri and Lillian renewed their friendship. Jennifer and Alexis drifted between Gavin's friends and their families, and Gavin stood off to one side, enjoying the sight before him.

"So, Dad," Jennifer said as she arrived at Gavin's side, "when do you think the wedding will happen?"

"No idea, really. There's a lot going on. I don't know the first thing about putting on a royal wedding, and I can't see how it will be a simple endeavor. Realistically, I don't see it happening until after we deal with the Necromancer of Skullkeep."

From her position not too far away, Kiri paused her conversation with Lillian and pivoted on her heel, interjecting, "Absolutely not! Don't you dare think I'll let you lead a military expedition to Skullkeep without being my husband. I've waited too long, and I'm not about to risk that you won't return from that. I'm sure it will be a major scandal among the nobility, here in Vushaar, but I have every intention of seeing to our wedding in no more than half a year."

By now, every other conversation in the room faded in the wake of Kiri's insistence, and the room's focus shifted to Gavin, awaiting his response.

A slight smile curled Gavin's lips as he took in the sight of his fiancée, and he nodded. "If that's what you want, it's fine with me."

"Very good," Kiri replied and turned back to Lillian.

Jennifer leaned close and whispered, "Good save, Dad."

"One displays true wisdom in choosing one's battles well," Gavin whispered back. "Besides, I wasn't wild about waiting, either."

Before long, Alexis approached the cluster of Terris and Gavin's parents. When they turned to greet her, she said, "Your Majesty, I ask your leave to depart. I've been away longer than I fear I should have been, and my protection detail will be... unsettled."

"Protection detail?" Terris asked.

"Yes, Your Majesty. My mother is the head of state where Gavin's family and I live, and as such, I'm a target. I probably should've brought them, but I wasn't sure how well they'd handle traveling to another world."

Terris chuckled heartily. "Yes, all of us here have become accustomed to Gavin's... ahem, unique... approach to things. I have enjoyed making your acquaintance, and I ask that you consider yourself welcome to visit Vushaar whenever you like."

"Thank you, Your Majesty," Alexis replied. "I shall."

"I think I'm going to head back with her," Jennifer said, whispering to Gavin. "Should I ask his leave, too?"

Gavin nodded. "It's the respectful thing to do, if you follow protocol. Usually, I just say bye, but then again, I'm Kirloth."

Jennifer faked a shudder as she made her way to Alexis's side. "Your Majesty, forgive the interruption, please; I ask your leave to depart as well."

"Of course, Young Kirloth," Terris replied, "and like your friend, know that you are welcome here whenever you choose to visit."

By now, Kiri stood at Jennifer's side. "Oh, she'll be visiting all right. Jennifer, would you agree to stand as one of my ladies at the wedding? I warn you now that I'll have to invite a few of the nobility's daughters, but I don't want our wedding to be any more political than it has to be."

"Of course, I'll stand with you, Ki—I mean, Your Highness," Jennifer said, her expression lighting up with happiness.

Both Terris and Kiri chuckled, Terris saying, "Young lady, you are the heir to House Kirloth. No one of that House ever needs to stand on ceremony with us. Please, call me Terris."

"And call me Kiri."

"Thank you, and thank you for your welcome," Jennifer replied.

Terris and Kiri both nodded, and Gavin watched his daughter and Alexis slip away. Moments after the doors closed, he felt the tell-tale resonance of his daughter invoking a Word of Transmutation and walked over to join his parents and Terris.

# CHAPTER 41

Jennifer saw Alexis safely back to the Secret Service travel team, and as Alexis surmised, they were a bit miffed that she'd once again gone gallivanting off without them. With the permanent portal completed, at least, Gayle and her associates hoped things could get back to what passed for normal.

"What are your plans?" Jennifer asked as they lounged in the keep's primary living room.

Alexis tucked her feet under her and shrugged. "I figure Mom will want to hear about Drakmoor. I think I'll probably skip their initial reactions to me, though. I doubt Mom would appreciate that. Otherwise, I don't know, really. I mean, I'm only alive right now because of Gavin, and as much as I hate to say this, I had kind of resigned myself to dying young. When I graduated high school, I thought I'd follow Mom into practicing law, but now? I don't know." Alexis lifted her left hand and manifested an orb of power. "How could I possibly spend my days in a stuffy law firm when I can do this?"

"You do have a point. The world will never be the same for us again. We could always work together on something. I mean, it's not like either one of us would ever truly fit in at a conventional office."

"What do you have in mind?"

"I'm not quite sure yet," Jennifer admitted. "The idea is refusing to gel."

Alexis shrugged and stood. "Well, while you're trying to gel, how about some goodbye ice cream at the shop in town? I'd say we should do it proper and find a bar, but I'm not sure we should really mix booze and arcane power. That probably wouldn't end well."

Jennifer laughed and joined Alexis. "Why not? I can think just as easily at the ice cream place as I can here."

THE DAY WAS NOT GOING WELL for Pierre Martin and his crew. No. The *week* wasn't going well. He and his associates had a simple task, one they had accomplished countless times across their careers. All they had to do was locate, collect, and deliver one Jennifer Elizabeth Cross. What's more, she wasn't even trying to hide. Everyone around the smallish town of Graham knew her and said they'd seen her multiple times over the past few weeks. But now, it was as if she somehow knew they sought her, for she hadn't been seen anywhere for a few days.

He didn't even want to consider their disastrous attempt to case the family home. The car rental agency had not been happy they'd managed to total a vehicle on a gravel road during a cloudless, sunshiny day... hitting air. He still didn't understand why the air felt solid to his touch as he stood at the gate onto the property.

A nudge against his arm drew Pierre out of his musings.

"Isn't that her?" Anton whispered, making a miniscule gesture toward two women walking across the street.

Pierre risked focusing his eyes on the group and fought to restrain a smile. It *was* her, and he wasn't about to let the presence of three obvious bodyguards ruin his satisfaction at finally seeing his mark.

"Don't stare," Pierre whispered as he returned to his newspaper, "and walk around to sit across from me so you're looking away from them."

Anton did as Pierre said, and Pierre busied himself looking over the classified ads for livestock. He didn't care a whit about cattle or sheep, but he was too professional to risk drawing the bodyguards' attention.

"Send a text to the crew," Pierre said, tapping his finger on the newspaper as if choosing an ad. "They need to prepare."

Anton withdrew his burner phone from a pocket and tapped out a message. It chirped after a successful send.

Pierre circled a couple of ads as he tried to watch the reflection of the group across the street in the café's glass window. It was difficult. For one thing, his own reflection got in the way. The far more insurmountable problem was that they were moving 'behind' him, and he couldn't turn far enough to watch without being so obvious a child would notice.

"The team acknowledged," Anton said.

"Can you tell if they've made us?" Pierre asked. "I can't see them anymore."

"Not sure, but I don't think so. They've gone into that ice cream store we visited the other day."

"Okay," Pierre replied. "Send them the 'go' code. Tell them the target is the ice cream store, and we're heading in now."

* * *

JENNIFER SMILED as she watched Sally Kirkman's twins debate their choice of ice cream with all the sober deliberation of Supreme Court justices, and it hit her just how much she'd changed. She realized in that moment that she was no longer afraid of the idea of having children of her own. The thought of her dad's reaction when she finally brought someone 'home' widened her smile quite a bit, and she silently apologized to whatever future soul subjected himself to that.

The chime of the doorbell heralded the entrance of a couple guys debating a soccer match. They laughed through their disagreement over the best player in the game, and as she turned away from seeing who had entered, Jennifer couldn't figure out why Gayle and her team tensed up all of a sudden. There weren't any obvious threats she could see.

Tires screeched outside, and Jennifer turned just in time to see a white panel van with no windows rock as its movement ceased. Both the side and the back doors opened, and eight guys leaped out. They wore ski masks and carried submachine guns.

Gayle and her team exploded into action... or at least they *started* to explode into action. One of the two men pulled a military-grade taser in each hand, firing them at the two men on Gayle's team.

*That's enough of that*, Jennifer thought as she recalled the one Word her father hoped she'd never have to use, the Word of Interation. She focused on the man with the tasers and the eight men charging inside and took a breath to speak, just as the *other* man who'd been debating soccer jammed a stun gun into her side and flicked the power switch.

* * *

SOMETHING JABBED PAINFULLY into the small of her back, and Alexis tried to move to see what it was.

"Dammit, stay down," Gayle growled. "I think we're safe, but Chet and Greg are still out."

Alexis looked around as much as she could, and she focused on one glaring absence. "Where's Jennifer?"

No response came forth.

"Gayle, where's Jennifer?"

She heard something that sounded like a growl and sigh mixed. After several more moments, Gayle said, "They took her. I don't think you were ever the target."

"Then, what are you doing holding me down? I can find her! I can get her back!"

"The hell you can," Gayle shot back as sirens wailed ever closer. "You might be some all-powerful wizard, but you're my principal. As long as I'm alive, the only thing on my mind is keeping you safe.

Besides, all that power didn't do Jennifer a whole lot of good, not against a prepared team of ten men."

"Ten? You think ten are a problem? Gayle, *let me up!*"

"I will handcuff and hog-tie you if I have to, Alexis," Gayle shot back. "I'm not letting you go after them."

Alexis hit the floor with her fist. "Fine! If you won't let me save my friend, can we at least go tell her father? I'd like to see you bully him into not finding Jennifer."

"We're not going anywhere until a team arrives from Washington, and even then, we're going straight to the White House. It's protocol, Alexis; you know this. I finished calling this in right before you came to your senses. Sorry about that, by the way. I didn't control my tackle like I should have."

"By the time you get to the part of the protocol that lets you relax, Jennifer will be long gone, Gayle. Damn it all, she's my *friend!*"

"And you're my principal. I have zero latitude here."

Alexis beat her fists against the floor again, her anger and frustration seething throughout her mind like a caged animal. She *knew* she could rescue Jennifer. She knew it without a doubt, but Gayle was right. There were ten of them, and she wasn't sure she could perform well enough to keep from getting harmed in the process or needing a rescue herself. But... there was no reason—aside from the fact her mom was President—that she couldn't go back to Drakmoor and tell Gavin what had happened. If she acted quickly enough, he could find her before they took her too far away. She knew what she had to do, and she knew she would put Gayle and her people in an impossible position. She couldn't take Gayle with her, because she'd fight every step of the way. Alexis didn't have the skills or the stamina to fight her that long, but she also knew that what she contemplated would quite possibly cost her someone she considered a friend. Was doing the wrong thing for the right reason the right thing? There was no right answer to her dilemma; each option facing her was a double-edged sword. The one thing she couldn't do was not act.

"I'm sorry, Gayle," Alexis said.

"Sorry? Why are you sorry?"

Alexis took a deep breath and invoked a Word of Transmutation, "*Paedryx.*"

The world blinked.

* * *

ALEXIS PUSHED herself to her feet and did a quick scan for grass stains. Not that she was especially worried about grass stains, but she felt she should be aware of them. But... she didn't see any. She turned and stepped through the portal to Drakmoor, crossing worlds with no more difficulty than changing rooms.

The moment she stood at the estate that could've been hers, she focused on her memory of Gavin and made another invocation.

* * *

GAVIN LEANED against the palace wall as he watched Kiri and Terris personally give his parents a tour of their private gardens. From what he could see, his mother couldn't be happier, but he thought his dad appreciated his wife's happiness more than the gardens. Declan lounged on a bench under a nearby tree, his pen scratching furiously on parchment; he'd turned up not too long after Jennifer and Alexis left. Lillian and the rest were long since back in Tel.

Gavin felt the teleportation through his *skathos* before any visual effect occurred, but the Cavaliers stationed throughout the gardens had no warning whatsoever when someone appeared not six feet away from Gavin. He recognized Alexis at once and lifted his hand, gesturing for the Cavaliers to hold.

"Alexis?" Gavin asked. "I thought you and Jennifer went back to Earth."

By now, the Cavaliers relaxed somewhat, everyone else moved to gather around Gavin.

"We did, Gavin, and we went to the ice cream shop in town as kind of a goodbye thing before I went back to Washington. I... they...

a team assaulted the ice cream shop not too long after we entered. They took her, Gavin. They took Jennifer."

The ambient temperature in the gardens seemed to drop several degrees.

"Is there any chance they wanted you and took Jennifer as a target of opportunity?" Gavin asked.

Alexis shook her head. "I don't think so. As good as they were, I think they would've taken me if they'd wanted me."

"So be it," Gavin replied. "It seems Earth gets its own object lesson after all. Forgive me, Terris, but my parents and I need to leave at once."

"I just need five minutes," Kiri said, halfway turning toward the palace door.

"Not this time, Kiri. You're staying here."

Kiri spun back, fire in her eyes. "We're betrothed, Gavin. I'm going to be your *wife*. You don't *leave me* when you go off to war. That's not how our marriage will be."

"One... we're not married yet. Two... forgive me, but for what I have in mind, your presence will make no difference. You should stay here with your father."

Kiri stepped close, her jaw clenched and her eyes promising murder. "She may not be my daughter, but she is my friend. Would you stand aside if a friend was in danger?"

Everyone there knew he wouldn't; he'd laid waste to an entire slaver camp over a 'friend'. Gavin looked over Kiri's shoulder to make eye contact with Terris, who shrugged and nodded.

"Fine," Gavin said. "Don't dawdle. For something like this, every second counts. As for you," turning back to Alexis, "you've done your part. Do us all a favor and return to your Secret Service detail before your mother wants to hang me from the Washington Monument."

Alexis had the grace to wince. "Gayle will probably resign, just so she can kick my butt all over your parents' lawn."

"She'll have to take you outside the wards if she wants to do that," Gavin remarked. "But seriously, thank you. Bringing this to me so quickly means all the difference."

Alexis gnawed at her lip. "Do you mind creating a gateway back to the portal for me? I'm not really sure where it is. Jennifer did it when we left here, and I have no idea how. It's not like she paid any more attention to the place than I did."

Gavin chuckled and said, "*Paedryx*."

An archway of crackling sapphire energy rose out of the ground nearby and soon flashed into being a doorway to another place. Alexis stepped through it, and the gateway vanished.

"What's the plan?" Declan asked, arriving at Gavin's side.

"Kiri was right; I'm going to war. I just need to make a quick visit to Tel Mivar to find an old friend."

# CHAPTER 42

Gavin led Kiri, his parents, and Ovir through the portal to the grassy section across from his parents' house.

"This is the Refugee World, is it?" Ovir asked, turning in place to look all around him.

"It's a small piece of it," Gavin replied. "I can show you a map of the entire world inside the house later, if you like."

"That would be nice."

"Would you like some tea or coffee or something while we wait for Gavin to do his thing?" Elizabeth asked.

"That might not be a bad idea, milady," Ovir answered.

"Oh, please call me Elizabeth. I don't know about that 'milady' stuff everyone bandied about."

Ovir chuckled as he allowed Gavin's parents to lead him toward their home. "Elizabeth, let me assure you of one thing. No one—and I mean *no one*—will ever consider offering you even the most minor slight back home."

"Well, that's very nice of them," Elizabeth said, then stopped. "Wait... that isn't a comment on my age, is it?"

"Not at all," Ovir said shaking his head for emphasis. "It was a comment on how most people are utterly terrified of your son."

The last thing Gavin heard as they stepped out of earshot was his dad's reply, "That would do it."

Instead of trying to overhear any more of the conversation between Ovir and his parents, Gavin cleared his mind of everything but his focus and invoked a Word, "*Klaepos.*"

A scrying sphere winked into existence before them. Jennifer lay on what looked like the floor of a van or some other similar vehicle. Eight people sat on crude benches anchored both to the floor and their respective sides. Gavin pulled back the scrying sphere to show the van's surroundings. The van traveled along a four-lane, divided highway. Given the angle of shadows Gavin could see, they were going east. The traffic wasn't bumper-to-bumper, but it was by no means a lonely stretch of road.

"Can you tell where they are, Gavin?" Kiri asked.

Gavin shook his head. "Not precisely. The highway isn't that familiar to me, but then again, it's been several years since I traveled this world's roads. But in the long run, that isn't a major impediment. *Rhyskaal.*"

The van started leaving a trail of what looked like multi-colored dirt as it lost a noticeable portion of its forward momentum. Gavin watched it ease into the slow lane, then drift to the shoulder. The van coasted to a stop no more than five hundred feet from where the trail of 'dirt' began.

"What did you do?" Kiri asked.

Gavin gave a smile that held no mirth. "I disintegrated everything in the van's engine compartment."

The driver's door of the van swung open, but before the person inside could exit, Gavin invoked, "*Thymnos.*" Then, "*Paedryx.*"

The van—with its open driver's door and all its passengers unconscious—appeared in the grassy lot of his parents' home, about ten feet beyond the picnic table... so about thirty feet overall from where Gavin and Kiri stood.

"How long will they be unconscious?" Kiri asked as they approached the van.

"Not sure, really. I wasn't too specific on the duration when I formed my intent, but that's a minor matter. When I'm ready to proceed, I'll just dispel the enchantment. For now, though, I'm going to carry Jennifer inside. Do you mind getting the doors for me?"

IT TOOK VERY little time to deliver Jennifer to her room, what had once been Gavin's room in fact. Ovir and Gavin's parents followed them inside, bringing the room a body or two past its maximum comfortable occupancy.

"Should I call the hospital?" Elizabeth asked.

"No, Mom," Gavin countered. "Ovir can see to whatever ails her; I promise you that. Kiri and I are going to search the van."

Elizabeth directed a worried look toward her unconscious granddaughter, but in the end, she jerked an uneasy nod.

"What's to be done with the men in the van?" Richard asked as he followed Kiri and Gavin back downstairs.

Gavin stopped at the foot of the stairs and turned to his father. "I don't want you or Mom involved in that, Dad."

"You don't have to go it alone, son," Richard responded.

Gavin held eye contact with his father in silence for several moments, finally saying, "Yes, I do, Dad. There's been no one else since Marcus—the man who trained me—died. Besides, you might not like what you see."

Without waiting for a reply, Gavin pivoted and left the house.

RETURNING TO THE VAN, Gavin opened all the doors and examined the scene for whatever he could observe without a full-on search. It wasn't much, but he did see what looked like a small satchel about the size of a car's first aid kit. He unzipped it, and the case folded open in his hand. One side of the case held four syringes and one open slot. The other side held alcohol swabs and a bottle designed to be used with needles.

"Huh... it looks like they injected her with Ketamine," Gavin remarked.

Kiri turned, frowning. "What's that?"

"It's an anesthetic, which means it will make a person fall unconscious, but its side effects make it popular as a 'recreational' drug. These needles don't have much capacity, so I wouldn't think she'll be unconscious too much longer. I doubt this is anything that Ovir can't handle."

"Are you sure we shouldn't have called on a few others for help?" Kiri asked. "The dracons would move heavens and earth if you asked them, and I'm sure the Sylvan Synod or the *T'Eleren* or the Sentinels of Nature or the Warpriests of Tel or even the Battle-mages of Tel would jump at the chance to aid you."

"I thought about it, Kiri; I really did. In the end, though, I want to keep as much of our world separate from this world as I can. Yes, I know; they're linked at a very fundamental level, what with Nesta sending the refugees here and now the portal back the dragons and I created. But at the end of the day, they've taken wildly disparate developmental paths, and I'd rather not intermingle the two anymore than they already are."

Kiri sighed and nodded. "I'll respect your decision, Gavin, but I don't like you facing this with only me. We don't know what we're getting into by tracking down whoever ordered the abduction."

"I think I know who ordered it," Gavin replied, "but regardless of where the search takes us, I'm confident you and I are up to the task. No one on this world understands the rules of killing wizards. Now, I need to see about creating the one thing I never thought the keep would need."

"A dungeon?"

Gavin nodded and stepped through the portal that would take him to the keep.

* * *

STEPPING INSIDE THE KEEP, Gavin walked through the ground floor, looking for a wall that would suit his purpose. He wanted it to be out of the way and somewhere that a casual observer wouldn't discover.

None of the ground floor walls were a perfect fit, but the far side of the wall that made up the back of the kitchen was close enough.

"*Rhyskaal.*"

Gavin's invocation created an archway in the stone that protruded from the wall no more than half an inch.

"*Rhyskaal.*"

Gavin's second invocation created a pocket deep enough below the surface of the Earth to impress the engineer for the presidential bunker. In effect, he disintegrated a volume of Earth's crust somewhere in the vicinity of eighteen thousand cubic feet, with an arch identical to the one in front of him on the center of one 'wall'.

"*Paedryx.*"

Gavin's third invocation created a portal connecting the two arches. He stepped through the portal to what would become his new dungeon, and it struck him how dark the space was. Of course, that was to be expected, because the only light source at the moment was whatever came through the portal... which wasn't much.

With a Word of Conjuration, "*Thyphos,*" Gavin saturated the space in light without an apparent source. Now that Gavin could see the space, he decided it would serve his purpose, once he finished it.

Over the next hour or so, Gavin created five ten-by-ten cells on opposite sides of the space. An opaque portal allowed access to these cells for anyone of the Kirloth bloodline. Inside each cell, Gavin created a metal table that stood at about a forty-five-degree angle from the floor. The final touches were a series of runes throughout the space that would continually circulate the air in the dungeon with fresh air from the forest beyond the keep. Gavin took one last slow walk through the space to make sure everything was as he wanted it, and then left to collect his prisoners.

* * *

GAVIN LEANED against the wall with the best air of nonchalance he could muster. Kiri stood nearby but far enough away to respect

Gavin's personal space. The driver of the van lay on the table; he was nude, and bands of metal molded from the table itself secured his hands and feet without causing harm. An evocation rune etched into the table to the right of the man's head kept the table at room temperature; no matter how long the man's body remained in contact with the table, his body heat would *never* warm it up.

They waited for him to wake after Gavin dispelled the sleep effect. The driver didn't show any signs of consciousness, and more than sufficient time had passed after the sleep effect ended.

A thought came to Gavin's mind, and he turned toward Kiri, standing so the driver couldn't see his face. He winked and began a slow circuit of the room, holding his hands together behind his back.

"Well, this one seems damaged beyond the point of salvage," Gavin said when he stood behind the man's head. "We have others. Cut off his head, his hands, and his feet. We'll dissolve those in acid and burn the rest of the body."

The man on the table jerked, his eyes opening wide. "Don't do that; I'm awake."

"Thought so," Gavin remarked as he continued his slow circuit and stood at the man's feet near Kiri.

"Where am I?" the man asked. "What do you want with me?"

Gavin looked the man right in his eyes. "You continue to exist— let alone live—for one purpose: to give me a name. Tell me who hired you to abduct my daughter."

The man shook his head. "You're a fool if you think I'll talk. You might as well kill me yourself."

Gavin smiled. It held no mirth. "That's odd. I don't remember promising you'd leave here alive."

"You sure are naïve in the art of interrogation," the man remarked after laughing. "If you're going to kill me anyway, what incentive is there for me to talk?"

"The method, duration, and pain level of your death is inversely proportional to your degree of cooperation," Gavin replied. "You can tell me what I want to know—the person's name—and I'll make it as quick and painless as possible. If I have to work for it, I'll make your death a Christmas present several decades in the future, long after your nervous system is far too ruined to know the difference."

"What did you mean when you said there were others?"

Gavin stepped back to resume leaning against the wall. "I do have other methods available to me to secure the information I want. Alas, none of them are pleasant, and most leave the subject as little more than a drooling idiot. Why... if you could smell what the poor sod next door just did to himself, you'd be begging to tell me already."

The silence in the room extended to the point that Gavin thought he would actually have to resort to siphoning the man's mind. He stood and took a half-step toward the table.

"Wait," the man said. "I'm the one you want. My men never communicated with any of the clients. The name you want is Jerome Toussaint. Now, can I at least have some clothes before you kill me?"

"*Klaepos*," Gavin invoked a Word of Divination. A gray aura surrounded the man on the table. "Now, repeat what you just said. If you're being truthful, the gray aura will turn white and remain so."

"Jerome Toussaint hired me to secure your daughter and transport her to his villa in the south of France."

The gray aura shifted to white as soon as the man started speaking and remained so.

Gavin nodded. "Very well. Do you have any outstanding warrants for your arrest?"

"Yes. I have warrants here in the USA and in several countries across Europe. It's the same for my team, more or less. I mean, they all have warrants, but not everyone has warrants in the same countries as everyone else." The aura remained white.

"Well, I guess I'll let Uncle Sam save me the trouble of dealing with you," Gavin replied.

"What about the four men before me?"

Gavin grinned. "You're the first one I've spoken with. I took a gamble that the driver would be the boss. This time, I won. Don't be too hard on yourself, though; if you hadn't given me the information,

I would've siphoned your mind, and you'd be voiding yourself on that table right now. We'll be back once we've arranged matters with the FBI."

Gavin turned and led Kiri through the opaque portal.

# CHAPTER 43

Jerome Toussaint's villa in the south of France looked like it dated back hundreds of years. The exterior architecture resembled a scaled-down castle, complete with several round towers medieval architects would've used in curtain walls. Ceramic tile roofs covered the main house plus all of the out-buildings, and a gravel road led up to the villa, ending in a roundabout that circled an intricate fountain.

"Are you ready for this?" Kiri asked.

Gavin shrugged. "Probably not, but that's why I've layered us with more protections than our old camp wards."

Kiri smiled. "At least I can't walk outside *these* protections."

Gavin replied to her smile with one of his own. "No... I don't think you can."

IT DIDN'T TAKE QUITE ten minutes for them to walk from their position on the graveled road to the villa's entrance. Several armed security personnel milled around the frontage, and every one of them directed bewildered expressions toward Gavin and Kiri; after all, the two 'guests' shouldn't have been able to get past the security gate a few hundred feet off the highway.

"Halt!" one of guards ordered, holding up a hand. "How are you on the property? It's surrounded by walls with only one gate, and they didn't call in that you were cleared."

Gavin smiled. "That's good, because they never cleared us. I'm here to speak with Jerome Toussaint. Tell him it's about the Recruiter."

The security personnel glanced to one another before a woman in the back lifted her left wrist closer to her mouth. She spoke in what sounded like French to Gavin. He would've been able to understand her, but the one effect he hadn't layered was the ability to understand or speak any native language. He'd have to remember that next time... if there was a next time.

"All right," the woman said. "You can go in."

Gavin nodded and offered a gracious smile. "Thank you."

He and Kiri walked past the fountain, and when the guards got a better look at Kiri, their eyes went wide.

"Halt! We're not letting you in there armed like that," the same guy said.

Gavin sighed. "Oh, for heaven's sake. If you make her disarm, we'll be here all day. Dear, I know you said you were coming with me, but do you mind waiting out here? I won't be long."

Kiri glared at the nearest guard. "Do I have to play nice while I wait?"

"Well, don't *start* anything," Gavin replied. "That would be a breach of hospitality, but if anyone lays a hand on you, feel free to settle the matter however you wish."

Kiri huffed out a breath. "Fine. I'll wait here."

As Gavin stepped into the house, the woman who'd made the call asked, "You're really okay with leaving her out there? They're kind of rough."

Gavin chuckled. "Even if she weren't protected, there's only eight of them. If she wanted a work-out, she'd wait while they called for help."

The woman froze mid-step and turned to look at Gavin. Her eyes searched his expression for several heartbeats before she resumed walking. "She's that good?"

"If you saw her in action, you'd swear she's death walking," Gavin answered, "but you'd be wrong."

"How so?"

Gavin gave her his best mirthless smile. "Because that description better applies to the guy who trained her. I wouldn't be surprised but what the Grim Reaper would step back and say, 'Damn...', if he saw the man work."

"You're... messing with me. That is how you Americans say it, yes?"

Gavin nodded. "Yes, that is the correct statement, and no, I'm not messing with you at all."

The woman fell silent at that. Her expression suggested she didn't believe him, but Gavin couldn't muster the wherewithal to care.

THE WOMAN LED him onto a veranda at the rear of the house. A pool that looked at least fifty percent beyond Olympic size dominated the view, its crystal waters reflecting the sun like polished crystal. The sole occupant of the veranda sat at a wireframe outdoor table beneath a pavilion, a newspaper written in French between his face and Gavin. He wore white pants and deck shoes.

"Here he is, sir," the woman said.

The paper came down, and Jerome Toussaint locked eyes on Gavin.

"You?" Toussaint's expression became a glare. "Do you have any *concept* of the damage you did to me with your little farce in Baltimore, and you have the *nerve* to set foot in my villa?"

Gavin approached the pavilion and helped himself to a seat across the table from Toussaint. He smiled. "The woman you called the Recruiter is my daughter. The US Government was hassling her to get to you. If we're being honest here, I couldn't care less about you or what you do in the world. Goodness knows, you aren't alone in your trade... any of them. But I do care about my daughter, more than you'll probably ever comprehend. So, I could have dismantled the government of the United States... or give them you. It was less time-consuming to give them you. And to be honest, a lot more fun."

Gavin leaned back against his seat and rested his elbows on the chair's arms, steepling his fingers.

"You paid an old friend to grab my daughter and bring her to you," he continued. "While Pierre and his crew were successful in the initial grab, I intervened, capturing them and retrieving my daughter. She's alive and well, back home. She's a little angry with you, and understandably so. I—on the other hand—am sufficiently removed from the disagreement that I can attempt reasoned discourse. I would like for you to consider the matter of your Recruiter closed. Do not seek her out. Do not attempt to return her to the fold, as it were. Walk away. She won't be testifying against you; she doesn't want to relive those years. And besides, with both Presidential and Gubernatorial pardons, neither the federal government nor the State of Maryland has any leverage to force her to testify."

"Just for the sake of conversation," Toussaint replied, "what do I get out of this deal?"

"You'll still be alive when my friend and I leave. Matter of fact, that's the *only* way you keep breathing. I promise you that right now."

Toussaint erupted in laughter. "You walk into the very center of my power, and you think you can *threaten* me? What kind of imbecile are you?"

"You're mistaken, I'm afraid. I haven't threatened you. I made a promise, and like my friend outside can attest, I *always* keep my promises."

"Only if you're alive," Toussaint spat. In a blur of motion, he pulled a subcompact pistol from his waistband and fired. Gavin didn't even flinch; his protections reduced it to smoke. Toussaint fired again, and received the same result.

After the third bullet, they had an audience, as most of the villa's guards came to see why their boss was shooting.

Gavin smiled, this time with all kinds of mirth. "You know,

Einstein once said that the definition of insanity is doing the same thing over and over again, expecting a different outcome. Are you insane, Jerome?"

Toussaint growled, shot to his feet. He stormed the short distance between them and drew back his fist. He swung, and his fist passed through Gavin's head as if he was a hologram.

"Should I take this as you responding that you won't leave my daughter alone?" Gavin asked, his tone mild and conversational.

Toussaint swung three more times to no avail. He stepped back, threw his arms down to his sides. "I will see your entire family dead and their corpses defiled! I don't care what it takes. Do you understand? I don't care if I have to impoverish whole countries; I will see it done!"

"I see," Gavin replied. "Well, that is truly unfortunate, Jerome... for you anyway. *Thraxys*."

Jerome Toussaint collapsed to the ground like a puppet whose strings had been cut. The guard force watching lifted their weapons.

"Don't be stupid," Gavin scoffed. "If the deceased idiot couldn't kill me with three bullets, three hundred from all of you won't make any difference. I have no quarrel with any of you, and for your own sakes, I strongly urge you not to give me one. *Thyphos*."

When Gavin felt his invocation take hold and knew that his voice would carry throughout and across the entire villa, he continued. "Attention, people of the villa. Jerome Toussaint is dead. I have no quarrel with any of you, unless you give me one, so I recommend you grab whatever valuables you want to take and vacate the premises at once. I will give you thirty minutes to loot to your hearts' content before I wipe this villa from the face of the world. The countdown starts... now. *Rhosed-Gozdrahk*."

Gavin's composite effect canceled the effect that broadcast his voice all over the villa and conjured count-down timers on every window. No matter whether a person looked at the inside or the outside of a window, the person saw the time that remained.

The assembled guards on the veranda looked from Gavin to the nearest window and back. Gavin made a shooing gesture with his hands.

"Well, go on," he said. "I wasn't joking about the timer. If there's anything here you want to keep, you'd better grab it while you can and run. I promise you; it won't survive the fate of this villa."

The crowd of assembled guards broke like high tide against the rocks, leaving Gavin to himself. It wasn't long before Kiri sauntered through the door leading inside. She walked over to the pavilion and sat in the chair Toussaint once occupied.

"So, what's going to happen to this place?"

"Why? Do you want to keep it?" Gavin countered.

"Not at all. I just want to know if my guess is right."

Gavin spied a small notepad and pencil by the newspaper Toussaint placed on the table. He pointed to it. "There, use that to write out your guess. Don't let me see it. When we're back at my parents' place, show it to me."

Kiri's eyes twinkled as she reached for the notepad and pencil.


By THE TIME Gavin's thirty minutes expired, he and Kiri stood a solid hundred yards down the gravel drive from the fountain. The faint wisps of dust still drifting in the air were all that remained of the servants' and guards' departure. Gavin stretched and flexed his shoulders as he formed his intent into a clear mental picture.

*"Idluhn-Rhyskaal-Sykhurhos-Uhnrys."*

The resonance of Gavin's power slammed into the ambient magic as he forced creation to reshape itself to his will. Within the space of five minutes, blue-white flames consumed the villa, boiling off the pool's water and instantly reducing anything that wasn't stone to ash. He waited until the stones of the villa were a little gooey and opened a gateway back to his parents' home.

* * *

GAVIN AND KIRI FOUND JENNIFER, Ovir, and Gavin's parents in the living room of the house. The conversation died at their entrance, though Jennifer perked up.

"Is it done?" she asked.

Gavin looked to Kiri and nodded his head toward Jennifer.

Kiri produced a folded piece of paper and walked it over to Gavin's daughter. She unfolded the paper, read it, and frowned.

"Kalinor's estate?" Jennifer asked. "Who is Kalinor, and what does his estate have to do with anything?"

"That is your answer, young lady," Ovir replied.

"Huh? I still don't understand."

"When I first met Kiri, she was a slave, owned by a rather unsavory individual by the name of Baron Kalinor," Gavin said. "My mentor went to him and attempted to arrange a peaceable resolution, wherein he ended all claim to Kiri, but Kalinor would have none of it. I don't know all of the particulars, because my mentor chose not to record them in his journal, but I saw what was left of the estate with my own eyes. He reduced that estate to molten rock and charred earth. I did the same to Jerome Toussaint's villa."

The resonance of a teleportation effect preceded the front door opening. Two men in suits entered the living room. Chelsea and Alexis Hall followed them, with three more agents behind them. Chelsea approached Gavin and stopped about five feet away from him.

"Do you have any idea what you've done?" Chelsea's voice was almost a hiss. "That villa was a *priceless* historical landmark. I've never seen the French ambassador so livid."

Gavin shrugged, utterly unconcerned. "If it was so important to them, they shouldn't have let Jerome Toussaint have it."

Chelsea's jaw clenched as her eyes hardened into a glare. She whipped her hands up, revealing a manila folder from which she drew what looked like a satellite photo of a night-shaded Earth. In the center of the photo, the Glyph of Kirloth glowed an angry red against the darker backdrop.

"We can see your handiwork *from space*, Gavin! And it's showing no signs of cooling! You are going to come with me to the White House, and you're going to take full responsibility for this. The French are screaming for blood, and they've already made noises of going to war."

"It won't ever cool. The remains of that villa will be molten rock until the end of time. And no, Chelsea, I'm *not* going back to Washington. I'm going home; I have responsibilities there."

"Don't you do this, Gavin Cross," Chelsea growled. "Don't you leave things like this."

"Or what? You'll federalize the Virginia National Guard and occupy Graham? Please... don't be absurd. Neither you nor any facet of the federal government constitutes a threat to me. I'm willing to walk away, but don't make the mistake of thinking that gives you the right to hassle my family or the town. The *first* thing I'll do is tell the press that you pardoned the member of Jerome Toussaint's organization known as the Recruiter, and I won't stop there."

All of the ire and vitriol evaporated from Chelsea's demeanor in an instant. "I did what?"

"Yep. Apparently, my daughter was the person known around the world as the Recruiter... and you pardoned her. You should probably have a conversation with your people if they never told you. Something tells me that little nugget is a whole host of chickens you don't want coming home to roost, and that's just my opening play. I have more."

"You used me," Chelsea said, her voice somewhere between a whimper and a whisper. Complete defeat.

"We both got what we wanted, Chelsea. Our daughters are safe. Don't make me an enemy. You wouldn't like that."

Chelsea turned toward her daughter. "Did you know?"

Alexis looked stunned. "No."

"Let's go," Chelsea said, heading toward the door.

Gavin waited until he felt the resonance of the teleportation effect dissipate. Then, he turned to the others. "Well, it's time for us to be going."

"You probably just cost me a good friend, Dad," Jennifer said.

Gavin shook his head. "If that piece of knowledge costs you her friendship, she wasn't your friend to begin with. *Everyone* makes mistakes. True friends accept people for who they are and who they want to be."

"I suppose so, but I still think friendships have ended over less."

"Are you sure you have to go?" Elizabeth said, standing and approaching her son. "It's been good having you home."

Gavin placed an arm around his mom and pulled her close. "Just because I'm going back doesn't mean I won't visit, Mom. Besides, they need me over there... at least until I can hand off the gold robe to someone else. But that's going to be a while. There's a lot yet for me to do."

Richard arrived at his wife's side and put his hand on Gavin's shoulder. "We understand, son. Just don't be a stranger... and invite us to the wedding."

"Count on it," Gavin replied.

Everyone walked out to the portal, and Gavin hugged each of his parents in turn as Ovir stood by the portal. Gavin came to his daughter at last. She looked at him, her expression devoid of any emotion.

"You're a ruthless so-and-so, Dad," Jennifer said after a couple heartbeats of silence. "I'm not sure Chelsea deserved how you handled her."

"It's one of those things that we'll never know how it would've turned out. But I'm not about to turn my back on the entire world that is depending on me, just to soothe some ruffled feathers across the pond. I love you, Jennifer."

Gavin turned to go, but Jennifer stopped him by enfolding him in a massive hug. She pressed herself against him like he remembered from when she was little, and his shirt muffled her words a bit.

"I love you, too, Dad."

Kiri made her goodbyes to each of Gavin's family in turn. Then, she, Gavin, and Ovir stepped through the portal.

Gavin's family stood in silence for several moments before they turned and walked back to the house.

* * *

WIND KISSED Gavin's face and tugged at his robe as he stood on a balcony overlooking Tel Mivar. The Citadel's altitude made the people in the streets below look like dots moving around a maze. Movement at Gavin's side drew his attention, and he smiled at seeing Nathrac in his humanoid form.

"Thank you for watching over everything during my absence," Gavin said.

"You're welcome, but no thanks are needed. I agreed to your modification of the Constitution that placed me in charge of Tel, and therefore, it was my duty."

Gavin turned to face Nathrac fully and leaned against the balcony's railing. "Perhaps, but I appreciate how you discharged that duty." A thought crossed Gavin's mind, and he sighed.

"May I ask what thought darkened your mind just now?"

"We have a fight coming, Nathrac, probably the biggest fight Tel has seen in recent years. It's time to remove the threat of the Necromancer once and for all."

# WHAT'S NEXT?

The story will continue in Volume V, "The Fall of Skullkeep."

* * *

Want to keep up-to-date on my projects and receive exclusive content?

Sign-up for my newsletter:
http://kfplink.com/g8i

# RATE THIS BOOK

Did you enjoy this story? If you did, please consider leaving a review.

Reviews are the lifeblood of visibility for independent authors, especially on the eBook retailers. The more reviews a book has, the more visible it will be on the retailers' sites.

I appreciate all reviews...good, bad, or indifferent.

If you would like to leave a review, visit this book's review page (https://kfplink.com/4jn).

# AUTHOR'S NOTE
## 20 SEPTEMBER 2020

First and foremost, thank you for reading...both the novel and these notes! I hope you enjoyed *Home Sweet Home*!

It has certainly been quite the year. This book is (only) two or three months behind the planned release date, but to paraphrase an old friend, no plan survives contact with life. :)

After I write Book 5 for both this series and Cole & Srexx, I'll be taking a break from them to work on a couple stories that have demanded attention with increasing urgency as the days have passed. The break will also be good for me to serve as a buffer against burn out on these two series; they're very dear friends and deserve the full ten books I feel each story requires to be complete.

But I'll share more about those stories in the months to come.

I offer my best wishes to you and yours, especially with the world as it is right now, and I hope you're able to stay as safe and healthy as possible.

If you're still reading this, thanks for the dedication...or perhaps the curiosity. :) As I said above, I hope you enjoyed reading *Home Sweet Home*. Thank you.

# TYPOS

Typos and little slips in grammar are the bane of any author. Unfortunately, they are almost impossible to eradicate completely. I can show you many traditionally published books—twenty years old and more—that have a 'whoopsie' here and there.

That being said, if you find a typo or something that seems to be an error in grammar, please do not hesitate to contact me at typos@knightsfallpress.com.

I will periodically collate any emails and produce an updated PDF and eBook files, and I'll make an announcement in my monthly newsletter when the updates have been published.

# ACKNOWLEDGMENTS

There's an old saying: it takes a village to raise a child. I don't know if that's true or not, but it certainly seems true where publishing a novel is concerned. You would not be reading this were it not for contributions from several people.

Did you like the cover? The background image was created by Jakub Skop (https://www.behance.net/JakubSkop).

No story should reach the public without passing through the scrutiny of a quality editor or editors, and Shelly and Lindsey of Acorn Author Services are two of the best. Their time, effort, and knowledge have improved this story immensely, and I thank them for it.

I also want to thank T. F. Poist for her time and expertise in making this novel the best it could possibly be.

I'm sure there are many who will see this next paragraph and think, "Goodness, he's acknowledging his parents and grandparents *again*?" My greatest regret is that I cannot hand my grandfather, Bob Miller, a paperback copy of my novels. So, yes...the Acknowledgements page of *every* book I publish will have the paragraph that follows. Consider yourselves forewarned.

Without my grandparents, Bob & Janice Miller, I honestly don't know where I'd be today; my grandfather taught me to read and love reading, and my grandmother taught me to develop and exercise my imagination. This novel (not to mention my life in general) certainly would not have happened without my parents, Vernon & Judy Kerns.

# THE NOVELS OF ROBERT M. KERNS

For a complete and accurate listing of all publications, both currently available and forthcoming, please visit Knightsfall Press.

Knightsfall Press - Books

https://knightsfall.press/books

# SO...WHO'S THE AUTHOR?

Robert M. Kerns (or Rob if you ever meet him in person) is a geek, and he claims that label proudly. Most of his geekiness revolves around Information Technology (IT), having over fifteen years in the industry; within IT, he especially prefers Servers and Networks, and he often makes the claim that his residence has a better data infrastructure than some businesses.

Beyond IT, Rob enjoys Science Fiction and Fantasy of (almost) all stripes. He is a voracious reader, with his favorite books too numerous to list.

Rob has been writing for over 20 years, and *Awakening* is his debut novel.

facebook.com/RobertMKerns

amazon.com/author/robertmkerns

bookbub.com/authors/robert-m-kerns